PRAISE FOR

Love at First Book

"Hilarious, deeply emotional, and brimming with swoon-worthy passion, this is an enemies-to-lovers tale that every romance reader should have the pleasure of enjoying at least once in their lives. . . . Dazzlingly fabulous!"

—Holly Cassidy, author of *The Christmas Wager*

"The ultimate bookish romance! . . . Amid the endlessly charming backdrop of a cozy bookshop in the idyllic Irish countryside . . . a wholly lovable supporting cast, and several heartstring-pulling subplots, and *Love at First Book* is the perfect escape for any romance fan."

—Nicolas DiDomizio, author of *Nearlywed*

"*Love at First Book* is so tender-hearted, I couldn't help but root for Kier and Red! A delight for book lovers and anyone who loves to armchair travel, I couldn't love this novel more! The setting in Ireland was an escapist dream. I read it in one sitting because I couldn't put it down!"

—Jamie Varon, author of *Main Character Energy*

PRAISE FOR
JENN McKINLAY'S ROMANCE NOVELS

"The characters are fresh and beautifully drawn, and the chemistry is magic. It's the perfect summer vacation."

—Annabel Monaghan, bestselling author of *Same Time Next Summer*

"A pure delight! Has all the elements of a perfect story: small island setting, a feisty yet vulnerable heroine, and a nerdy hero who stole my heart."

—Jennifer Probst, *New York Times* bestselling author of *The Secret Love Letters of Olivia Moretti*

"McKinlay writes sexy, funny romances!"

—Jill Shalvis, *New York Times* bestselling author of *The Sweetheart List*

"A playful breezy read that I couldn't put down!"

—Abby Jimenez, *New York Times* bestselling author of *Yours Truly*

"I devoured this clever novel in one sitting!"

—Lori Nelson Spielman, *New York Times* bestselling author of *The Star-Crossed Sisters of Tuscany*

"In turns poignant and amusing, *Summer Reading* belies its title to tackle serious issues with aplomb, exploring essential definitions of self, friendship, family, and love while maintaining a breezy wit and pleasing pace. McKinlay's writing is sure to charm."

—Shana Abé, *New York Times* bestselling author of *An American Beauty*

"McKinlay's fresh spin on a favorite trope is as frothy and pleasing as a piña colada, delivering both laughs and poignant tugs on the heart-strings. Perfect summer beach read."

—Lori Wilde, *New York Times* bestselling author of *The Wedding at Moonglow Bay*

"A delightful romance with characters I adored! Jenn McKinlay takes readers along on a fun and charming adventure in *Paris Is Always a Good Idea.*"

—Emily March, *New York Times* bestselling author of *The Summer Melt*

"McKinlay spins a funny yet poignant tale."

—Jen DeLuca, author of *Well Traveled*

"This book made me laugh and swoon and gave me some serious wanderlust!"

—PopSugar

"The must-have summer read of the year." —Fresh Fiction

"With lovable characters and swoon-worthy moments, this heart-warming tale has it all."

—*Woman's World*

"This flawless rom-com is sure to delight."

—*Publishers Weekly* (starred review)

"[An] immensely enjoyable rom-com." —Shelf Awareness

"With McKinlay's zingy prose and effervescent wit . . . she deftly pivots from moments of comic absurdity to heartfelt emotion without missing a beat."

—*Booklist* (starred review)

TITLES BY JENN McKINLAY

Paris Is Always a Good Idea
Wait For It
Summer Reading
Love at First Book

Happily Ever After Romances

The Good Ones
The Christmas Keeper

Bluff Point Romances

About a Dog
Barking Up the Wrong Tree
Every Dog Has His Day

Cupcake Bakery Mysteries

Sprinkle with Murder
Buttercream Bump Off
Death by the Dozen
Red Velvet Revenge
Going, Going, Ganache
Sugar and Iced
Dark Chocolate Demise
Vanilla Beaned
Caramel Crush
Wedding Cake Crumble
Dying for Devil's Food
Pumpkin Spice Peril
For Batter or Worse
Strawberried Alive
Sugar Plum Poisoned

Library Lover's Mysteries

Books Can Be Deceiving
Due or Die
Book, Line, and Sinker
Read It and Weep
On Borrowed Time
A Likely Story
Better Late Than Never
Death in the Stacks
Hitting the Books
Word to the Wise
One for the Books
Killer Research
The Plot and the Pendulum
Fatal First Edition

Hat Shop Mysteries

Cloche and Dagger
Death of a Mad Hatter
At the Drop of a Hat
Copy Cap Murder
Assault and Beret
Buried to the Brim

Love at First Book

JENN McKINLAY

BERKLEY ROMANCE
NEW YORK

BERKLEY ROMANCE
Published by Berkley
An imprint of Penguin Random House LLC
penguinrandomhouse.com

Library of Congress Cataloging-in-Publication Data

Names: McKinlay, Jenn, author.
Title: Love at first book / Jenn McKinlay.
Description: First edition. | New York : Berkley Romance, 2024.
Identifiers: LCCN 2023049984 (print) | LCCN 2023049985 (ebook) |
ISBN 9780593545744 (paperback) | ISBN 9780593545751 (e-book)
Subjects: LCSH: Librarians--Fiction. | Novelists--Fiction. | Booksellers and bookselling--Fiction. | LCGFT: Romance fiction. | Novels.
Classification: LCC PS3612.A948 L68 2024 (print) |
LCC PS3612.A948 (ebook) | DDC 813/.6—dc23/eng/20231106
LC record available at https://lccn.loc.gov/2023049984
LC ebook record available at https://lccn.loc.gov/2023049985

First Edition: May 2024

Printed in the United States of America
1st Printing

Book design by Kristin del Rosario
Interior art: Books © YagudinaTatyana/Shutterstock.com

PUBLISHER'S NOTE: The recipes contained in this book are to be followed exactly as written. The publisher is not responsible for your specific health or allergy needs that may require medical supervision. The publisher is not responsible for any adverse reactions to the recipes contained in this book.

This book would never have been written without
the help of my boots on the ground research crew,
Susan McKinlay, Annette Amaturo, and Alyssa Amaturo—
or as I like to think of you:
the historian, the medic, and the navigator.
Such a wonderful Irish adventure
full of wonder and laughter and rainbows.
I love you all dearly and would travel anywhere with you.

Love at First Book

One

Em, are you all right?" Samantha Gale, my very best friend, answered her phone on the fourth ring. Her voice was rough with sleep and it belatedly occurred to me that nine o'clock in the morning in Finn's Hollow, Ireland, was four o'clock in the morning in Oak Bluffs, Martha's Vineyard.

"Oh, I'm sorry. Damn it, I woke you up, didn't I?" I asked, feeling awful about it.

"No, it's fine," Sam said. "I told you when you left that I'm always here for you." There was a low grumbling in the background and she added, "And Ben says he's here for you, too."

That made me laugh. Sam and Ben had become couple goals for me. Not that I thought I'd ever find anything like the connection they'd made, but they kept the pilot light of my innermost hope aflame.

"Thank you and Ben," I said. "I'm going to hang up now. Forget I ever called."

"Emily Allen, don't you dare," Sam said. Now she sounded fully awake. *Oops.*

"No, really I—" I began but she interrupted me.

"Tell me why you're calling, otherwise I'll worry." There was more grumbling in the background. Sam laughed and said, "Ben says he's begging you to tell me so that I don't drive him crazy with speculation."

I grinned. She would, too. Then I grew serious.

Glancing around the Last Chapter, the quaint bookshop in which I was presently standing, I noted objectively that it was a booklover's dream come true. A three-story stone building chock-full of books with a small café, where the scent of fresh-brewed coffee, berry-filled scones, and cinnamon pastry permeated the air. I felt myself lean in that direction as if the delicious aromas were reeling me in.

One of the employees had unlocked the front door of the shop, and I had trailed in behind a handful of customers who'd been waiting. I'd been agog ever since.

This was it. The bookshop where I'd be working for the next year. My heart was pounding and my palms were sweaty. The black wool turtleneck sweater I was wearing, in an attempt to defeat the early November chill, felt as if it were choking me and I was quite sure the pain spearing through my head meant I was having an aneurysm.

"I'm supposed to meet my boss in a few minutes, and I think I'm having a heart attack or potentially a stroke," I said.

There was a beat of silence then Sam said, "Tell me your symptoms."

I listed them all and she noted each one with an "uh-huh," which told me nothing whatsoever as to what she thought about my condition. I was three thousand miles away and starting a new job in a bookshop, having put my career as a librarian on Martha's Vineyard on hold to chase some crazy fantasy where I traveled to a foreign destination and lived a life full of adventure.

"I think I'm going to throw up," I groaned.

"Inhale," Sam said. "You know the drill—in for eight seconds, hold for four, out for eight."

I sucked in a breath. *Ouch.* "I can't. It makes my head throb. See? Aneurysm."

"Or a lack-of-caffeine headache," she said. "Have you had coffee yet?"

Come to think of it, I had not. I'd been too nervous to make any before I left my cottage this morning so the potential for this skull splitter to be from coffee deprivation seemed likely.

"No," I said. "And I see where you're going, but I still have brutal nausea and I'm sweating. I bet I have a fever. Maybe it's food poisoning from the airplane food last night. I had the beef stroganoff."

"You ate airplane food?" Sam sounded as incredulous as if I'd confessed to eating ice cream off the bathroom floor. She was a professional chef, so not a big surprise.

"I know, I know," I said. "It's pure preservatives. I'll likely be dead within the hour."

There was a lengthy pause where I imagined Sam was practicing her last words to me, wanting to get them just right.

"Em, you know I love you like a sister, right?" she asked.

Well, that didn't sound like the beginning of a vow of friendship into the afterlife.

"I do," I said. "I also know that's how you'd start a sentence I'm not going to like."

"You're panicking, Em," Sam said. Her voice was full of empathy. "And you and I both know that bout of hypochondria you dealt with last summer was how you coped with your unhappiness."

"But I'm not unhappy," I protested. "I'm living the dream in a quaint village in County Kerry where the green is the greenest green I've ever seen and there's a sheep staring at me over the top of every stone wall. Seriously, I'm drowning in picturesque charm, which is probably why I'm about to keel over dead."

A sound came from my phone that resembled someone stepping on a duck.

"Are you laughing at me?" I asked. Rude but understandable.

"No, never," Sam said. She cleared her throat. "I just think you might be freaking out because it's your first day at your new job."

"I'm not," I protested. I was. I absolutely was. "I just think I need to come home before they discover I have some highly contagious pox or plague and I'm quarantined in a thatched stone cottage to live out my days in a fairy-infested forest, talking to the trees and hedgehogs while farming for potatoes."

"Have you ever considered that you read too much?" Sam asked.

"No!" I cried and I heard Ben, also a librarian and formerly my boss, protest as well.

Sam laughed. She enjoyed goading us.

"Just think, if I leave now, we can meet for coffee and pastries at the Grape tomorrow morning."

"While I'd love to see you, you know that, you have to stay in Ireland and see your journey through," Sam said. "If you go home now your mother will guilt you into never leaving again, not to mention clobber you with the dreaded 'I told you so.'"

"Fair point." I sighed. I glanced at the display on my phone. My mother had already called five times and texted twelve and I hadn't even been in Ireland for twenty-four hours yet. I'd let her know I'd arrived safely, but I knew that wasn't what her messages were about.

My mother had made it clear that she expected me to continue in the role of her caregiver, a position I'd assumed when my father left several years ago. Were she incapable of caring for herself, I'd understand, but there was absolutely nothing wrong with her except a scorching case of toxic narcissism. I tabled the mom problem to deal with the one at hand.

"I still think I might pass out and then I'll likely lose the job and this entire conversation becomes moot," I said.

"You won't," Sam said. "Find a place to sit down. Can you do that?"

"Okay." I was standing in the stacks—well, more accurately, hiding. The shelves were dark wood, long and tall and stuffed with books. They comforted me. Scattered randomly amid the shelving units were step stools. I found one and sat down.

"Are you sitting?" Sam asked.

"Yes."

"Good, now put your head between your knees," she ordered.

"Um." I was wearing a formfitting, gray wool pencil skirt. I tried to maneuver my head down. No luck. The skirt was too snug. The closest I could get was to look over my knees at my very cute black ankle boots. "Sorry, Sam, nothing is getting between these knees. Not even a hot Irishman."

Sam chuckled, but over that I heard a strangled noise behind me and I straightened up and turned around to see a man in jeans and an Aran sweater, holding his fist to his mouth, looking as if he was choking. He had thick, wavy black hair and blue eyes so dark they were almost the same shade as his hair. Also, if I wasn't mistaken, he was my new boss.

Two

Um, Sam, I have to go," I said.

"The breathing helped, right?" she asked.

"Totally. Call you later." I ended the call and stood up. The man cleared his throat and dropped his fist. Now that I could see his face, it was indeed my new boss, Kieran Murphy. He appeared to be trying to figure out what to say, so I jumped in and asked, "You didn't happen to hear what I just said, did you?"

My long auburn hair was pinned at the nape of my neck in a loose bun and I pushed my large wire-framed glasses up on my nose. Suddenly, I was overly warm and not in a good way. I paused to consider it. I was only twenty-nine. This could not be a hot flash . . . could it?

"Just the last little bit," he said. His voice was deep and his brogue was thick and it curled around me as if it were a magic spell being cast. He tipped his head to the side and said, "Should I take it as a warning?"

"Oh, no, it wasn't meant that way," I protested. "I'd be happy to have a hot Irishman . . . er . . ." I paused and shook my head. "That's not going to come out right either."

I wanted to smack my forehead. I didn't. Instead I stood there, feeling my face heat up with extreme self-consciousness, which no doubt would turn my pasty complexion the shade of an overripe tomato. I probably looked like I had a horrible skin condition.

Mr. Murphy's unwavering gaze had me completely rattled. Not just because he was my boss but because he *was* a hot Irishman and I was sure that penetrating stare of his could see into my very soul. What a sorry impression I was making. I felt like the human embodiment of embarrassment wrapped in mortification dipped in humiliation.

"Yes, well." He cleared his throat and said, "I think we can just leave that to be sorted another time, all right?"

"Absolutely. No need to talk about it." I pressed my lips into a tight line, determined to do just that. But being me, I couldn't. "Unless you wanted to discuss that bit of awkwardness right now, which would alleviate me from stressing about the first impressions I made, because I totally will—all day."

He looked surprised and then he laughed. It was a rich rumble that came from his chest and I felt it reverberate in my spine. It was a good laugh. When I smiled in return, he abruptly grew serious, as if he'd caught himself being amused by me and shut it right down. Huh.

"How about we just start over?" He held out his hand. "Emily Allen, I presume?"

"Yes." I clasped his hand in mine a bit too enthusiastically and he winced. I immediately let go. "Sorry."

"No need, fingers are overrated," he assured me while he wiggled the blood back into his. "I'm Kieran Murphy."

"It's nice to meet you, Mr. Murphy," I said.

"Just call me Murphy," he said. "Everyone does."

"All right, Mr. . . . uh . . . Murphy," I agreed. He didn't seem like a Murphy to me. In my mind, he was Kieran, or Kier for short, a romance-hero-worthy name for a man who certainly looked the part. I could picture him on a seaside cliff, the wind tousling his thick dark curls and lifting the ends of a red cashmere scarf he'd casually draped around his neck, while he stood with his legs braced and his broad shoulders squared, daring the wind to knock him down as he squinted out at the ocean, looking for, well, obviously his long-lost love.

He was watching me as if waiting for something. It belatedly occurred to me to invite him to use my first name.

"And please call me Emily or Em, that's what my friends call me, you know, if they're close friends, or Red, some people call me Red, well actually, no, only strangers who couldn't be bothered to learn my name have called me Red." I was babbling. I shut my mouth.

Murphy nodded. "So noted . . . Red."

Was he saying we'd remain strangers? Well, that wasn't very friendly.

He turned and we left the shelves behind us. I followed him feeling like an idiot—why the hell had I told him strangers call me Red? But was it really my fault? The man was insanely attractive. If I could have managed it, I would've taken a stealth picture of him and sent it to Sam. She would die. We'd noted he was good-looking from the picture on the bookshop's website but the live-action Kieran Murphy was next level.

I was completely unprepared for this contingency. Why couldn't he be a much older man with thinning hair, a beer gut, and a roguish twinkle in his eye?

"Why don't I show you around a bit before you meet Siobhan." He glanced over his shoulder at me. His expression was shuttered, adding one more layer to his perfection as a brooding romance hero.

No, no, no. I hadn't been on a date in forever but there was no way I was going to start crushing on my new boss. Not when I was on a mission of self-discovery. I had to keep my priorities straight. The only relationship I was having on this trip was with myself.

"That would be lovely." I sounded entirely too eager. I cleared my throat and asked, "How did you know who I was?" I didn't mean to be so blunt, but my curiosity was highly verbal and very direct.

"Deductive reasoning," he said. He gestured to the customers with whom I'd entered the building. "You're the only person I didn't recognize so I figured you must be our new hire."

"Oh." There was no faulting that logic. "Mystery fan, are you?"

He glanced at me with one eyebrow raised slightly higher than the other. It was a dead sexy look. I tried to blink it away like those spots that blur your vision when you inadvertently glance at the sun.

"Indeed I am," he said. "Mostly noir but a bit of traditional as well. And you?"

"Agatha and Dorothy are my girls," I said. He nodded in what I hoped was approval or at the very least acceptance. Mystery readers could be so judgy about the cozy subgenre.

I glanced at the signs over the shelving units. We'd moved from fiction, through books of Irish interest, and now we were standing beside the history section.

"Here's a hypothetical," Murphy said. "A lad comes in and asks for books on magic. Where do you direct him?"

"I'd tell him they all disappeared." I waved my hands in the air like a magician and grinned. His right eyebrow ticked up again. He didn't smile. I immediately grew serious. "Just kidding, you know, to break the ice with the boy." He continued to stare, clearly waiting for my answer. Okay, then. "I'd ask him what he wanted to know about magic specifically."

"Stories about magicians."

"Real or fictional?"

"Fictional."

I started to hum the theme to the Harry Potter movies and the corner of his mouth twitched, which felt like quite a victory until Murphy shook his head and said, "He's read those."

"Ah, well, then I'd show him *The Golden Compass*, *The Magicians*, *Shadow and Bone*, and the Simon Snow series."

Murphy made a *humph* sound, which I believed meant he was grudgingly impressed. He turned and continued walking through the shop. It had that delightful smell unique to bookshops and libraries that was earthy and woody with notes of vanilla and chocolate. The pragmatic librarian in me knew that the smell was caused by the organic compounds in the paper pages breaking down but the booklover in me thought it was just one more aspect of the allure of books. I was soaking it in, using it to calm my nerves, when my new boss spun around so quickly I almost slammed into him.

"An older gentleman asks you for books about Egypt. Where do you direct him?"

I paused. Another question? Was this a test? Was he quizzing me? Had the man forgotten that I was a librarian? I'd thought part of the reason I'd been hired was for my research skills. As I understood from the job offer, I'd be the assistant to the writer in residence for part of the day and a shop clerk for the rest. I was overqualified for both positions but the former was, quite frankly, the reason I'd accepted the job.

I felt a tiny prickle of unease. Was this hot Irishman looking for a reason to get rid of me? Well, I wasn't going to make it easy for him. I met Murphy's gaze, noting that he had obscenely long, thick dark eyelashes—because of course he did—and I said, "I would ask him what he wanted to know about Egypt."

"And if he said ancient Egypt?"

"I would ask him what about ancient Egypt interested him."

"Cleopatra."

"Stories or facts?"

"Facts."

"About her life?"

"Relationships."

"Marc Antony or Julius Caesar?"

"Both."

"And off to biographies we go," I said.

His dark gaze held mine and I felt my pulse pick up. Had I passed his pop quiz?

"Not bad, Red," he said. He considered me for a moment. This time I recognized the challenging glint in his eye and I was ready. I tipped my chin up.

"If a woman came into the shop and wanted to choose a book for her book club, what would you recommend?" he asked.

I blew out a breath. This was a tricky one. I'd done this sort of reference in the library, of course, but I was in a new country and maybe book clubs were done differently here. I felt my nerves ratchet up. "I would ask her what sort of books her club had enjoyed before."

"It's a brand-new club." Murphy leaned back against a gorgeous, ornately carved antique cashier's counter.

"Oh, in that case, I would ask her if they had a focus, you know, are they moms, teachers, what brought them together."

"Wine," he said. I laughed but he didn't. Feeling nervous, I adjusted my glasses and took a deep breath.

"I would check and see what books had been sitting on the

bestseller's lists for a few months and look for something like the latest Sally Rooney or Marian Keyes, because then we would have plenty of copies in stock, and I could see which of the titles appealed to her."

"Interesting approach." Murphy pushed off the counter, giving no indication of whether he approved of my answer or not. "Come on then, I'll show you the back."

Did this mean I was cleared for employment? I wanted to do a fist pump. I resisted, containing myself to a tiny hop of joy.

Murphy led the way behind the counter and opened the door that said *Employees Only*. He gestured for me to go first, so I entered the surprisingly large room. Judging by the boxes of books waiting to be unpacked, it was obviously the workroom.

There was a large man, standing at the rear of the room, holding a box cutter and wearing a green and white striped Killarney Celtics soccer jersey and khakis. He had a full gray beard and wore a black woolen flat cap.

"Oisín O'Rourke, this is Emily Allen," Murphy introduced us. He didn't sound happy about it. "Oisín is in charge of the stock."

"Hiya," Oisín greeted me.

"Hi." Unsure of my welcome after dealing with the somewhat mercurial Murphy, I gave a little wave that I was sure looked as awkward as it felt.

"Wait. You're the American?" Oisín asked. A grin peeked out from beneath his beard.

"From Massachusetts."

"That's grand. What brings you to the Last Chapter?" he asked.

"A working holiday visa," I said because it was technically true, but also, I wasn't ready to divulge what had driven me to this particular shop, in this specific village, in this foreign country.

"Accurate enough." Oisín chuckled. It was an infectious sound and I smiled in return. "Welcome, Emily. If you have questions, don't hesitate to ask. If I don't know the answer, I'll make it up."

That surprised a laugh out of me. "Thank you," I said.

Murphy pointed out three shared desks in the workroom for anyone to use at any time. Because the bookshop was small, Murphy explained that the expectation of the staff was to mind your tasks but maintain an all-hands-on-deck attitude as needed, which was very much like the public library I'd just left.

I went to slip off my jacket and put my shoulder bag away, but he shook his head. "Not now. You can settle in later . . . if it's warranted."

What did that mean? Was he thinking I wouldn't make it through the morning? Well, shit.

"Come on, Red, things to do, people to see." Murphy left, obviously expecting me to follow.

I glanced at Oisín and noticed he was staring at the doorway with an expression that could only be described as a confused-surprised mash-up. I hoped it meant Murphy wasn't usually so abrupt. Then again, if Murphy was only like this with me, that wasn't good either. Did he dislike Americans? Librarians? Women? Redheads? All of the above? I felt my stomach cramp and immediately assumed I was starting an ulcer. I shook my head. Nope. I was not doing that. Not today.

I hurried after Murphy, hoping he was just having a bad morning. Maybe he'd had a flat tire or broke his phone. Perhaps his girlfriend dumped him, or he spilled his breakfast on the floor. I hoped it was one of those things, otherwise I had to assume Murphy didn't want *me* here.

We toured each floor of the bookshop. There was a study room and a meeting room, in addition to the café. But otherwise, every spare inch was stuffed with books. Heaven.

Murphy treated me to a coffee in the small eatery, which seemed incredibly generous given his aloof demeanor. My headache was threatening to double down so the beverage was very welcome.

A pretty woman named Brigid Doyle, who appeared to be my age—thirty-ish—ran the café and welcomed me.

"How do you take your coffee?" she asked.

"Strong," I said.

She grinned. "That's the spirit. I'll fix it so you can dance on it."

I laughed. "Perfect. Thank you so much."

"No problem at all. You have to come back on your break and try my baked goods," she said. She was gently rounded and had deep dimples in her cheeks. Her light brown hair was held back from her face in a large clip. She had a maternal air and I suspected if I hugged her, she'd smell like vanilla and cinnamon.

"I'd like that," I said. "The scent of your pastries is driving me wild in the best possible way."

"Brilliant! My plan is working." Brigid smiled. "Of course, I have other items, too." She gestured to the chalkboard mounted on the wall behind her. It listed a variety of baked goods and sandwiches. Given my jet-lagged, un-caffeinated state, they all looked amazing.

"Wow, impressive," I said.

"Thank you," she said. "The kitchen is my happy place."

"My best friend is a chef and she says the same thing," I said. I felt a pang of missing Sam so intense it actually hurt. "She's always trying new recipes on me."

"You're a taste tester then?" Brigid asked. I nodded. "Would you be willing to try some new recipes I've been thinking about?"

"Of co—" I began but Murphy interrupted.

"What new recipes?" he asked. "Why do you need to change the menu, Brig? Customers like it as is. They know what's available and they can plan their day accordingly. You can't take that away from them."

Brigid and I both turned to look at him, but he was frowning at the chalkboard.

"But cooking the same thing day in and day out is dead boring," Brigid said. "I need to stretch my culinary wings, don't I?"

"I can understand that," I said. One of the reasons I'd fled home was that my life had become a blursday of one into another with no deviation. Mind-numbingly dull.

Murphy turned from the board, looking outraged. "You can't do it, Brig. What if someone came in after spending all night thinking about one of your berry scones and then when they arrived, you'd taken it off the menu? You could ruin their whole day, potentially their whole week."

"That's a lot of weight to put on a berry scone, isn't it?" Brigid asked. She crossed her arms over her ample chest.

"What if instead of taking things off the menu, you just add a tester menu?" I suggested. "It might be more work initially but you could make the test item the day's special and people could get used to it before you change the menu."

Murphy looked indignant, as if I'd just suggested a mutiny, but Brigid smiled. "That's the solution. You're a right thinker you are, Emily Allen. Prepare yourselves for tomorrow's special pastry! It's going to be amazing."

"Well hell," Murphy muttered.

"Come by later this afternoon, Em, and I'll have it ready for a taste."

"I will," I promised. I felt our mutual love of strong coffee and baked goods forming the bonds of a new friendship. I finished my restorative cup of coffee and handed the empty mug to Brigid. "Thank you."

A low grumble brought my attention back to Murphy. His brow was furrowed and his mouth turned down in the corners. I was struck by how much he resembled the Fitzwilliam Darcy of my imagination from Jane Austen's *Pride and Prejudice*, a favorite novel of mine. Oh, yes, I was a hardcore Mr. Darcy fangirl.

"If you're done meddling, our tour is finished," he said. "There's just one more person for you to meet."

He gestured across the shop to the front window. I caught my breath. The space had been unoccupied when I arrived earlier, but now there she was seated at a table. Siobhan Riordan, the author who had saved my life.

Three

I was struck by how slight she seemed. Her shoulders were narrow and she didn't take up all the real estate of her chair. Her long, curly black hair reached just past her shoulders and was held away from her face by a peacock blue and purple paisley scarf. She was wearing a sage green cardigan over a soft cream-colored top. Her head was tipped to the side, and her expression pensive, as if she was listening to a conversation only she could hear.

A stack of books and an open laptop were on the table in front of her. A notebook and pen were pushed off to the side. She was sitting perfectly still with her hands folded in her lap as if waiting for something or someone. It wouldn't have surprised me to see a portal open up beside her just like the one Tig McMorrow, the time-traveling protagonist of her young adult series, used. It would swirl into being in the shape of a round doorway lit up with sparks of color—magenta, turquoise, and gold—and then without saying a word,

Siobhan would rise and step over the threshold, disappearing into another realm where we couldn't follow.

"Are you all right?" Murphy snapped his fingers in front of my face.

I ripped my gaze from Siobhan and blinked at him. My heart was beating hard, I was covered in sweat, and I couldn't seem to catch my breath.

"Steady, Red." His eyes narrowed. "You're not a demented stalker fan are you?"

I didn't answer him. Confronted with the reality of my favorite author mere yards away, I was so overwhelmed I couldn't even form words. Murphy rolled his eyes. Normally, I would have been embarrassed by his disdain, but I was too undone to care what the handsome Irishman thought.

"I told her it was a bad play to hire a stranger because of some sycophantic gushing letter. But did she listen to me? No." He shook his head. "Come on then, let's get this over with so she can see I was right and we can ship you out on the next plane."

It took a moment for his words to penetrate the fog of emotion I was in. I hadn't known it was possible to have so much joy and trepidation coursing through me at the same time. I was actually shaking I was so nervous, but Murphy's chatter about sending me home brought me up short.

"What did you say?" I asked.

He turned to face me. That imperious eyebrow of his rose but I was not intimidated. Not one little bit.

"I said it's time to meet Siobhan and be done with this," he said. He waved a hand in my direction as if I was the "this" he found so disagreeable.

I crossed my arms over my chest and leaned back, tipping my chin up and narrowing my eyes. "You don't want me here. Admit it."

"What gave it away, Red? My utter lack of enthusiasm for your presence? The grudging tour of the shop? Or the fact that I just suggested the best outcome for all would be for you to be on the next plane out of here?" he asked. The lilt in his voice didn't soften his sarcasm one bit.

"Rude!" I said. And he was, but it did snap me out of my stupor. Now I had a nice temper going and it burned out any lingering nervousness I might have felt.

"Listen, it's not personal," Murphy said. "You simply don't belong here."

I gasped. That stung. "It might not be personal for you," I said. "But it's pretty damn personal for me. You're talking about snatching away this opportunity like it means nothing. I left my entire life to come here for this job."

He mimicked my stance, crossing his arms over his chest. "You're being very dramatic. Obviously, you would be compensated for your time and expenses."

Dramatic? I felt my lip curl. This man was the most infuriating person I'd ever met. Well, I wasn't having it. I'd made a promise to myself when I arrived in Ireland that I would no longer disregard my own feelings and put everyone else's comfort and happiness ahead of my own.

My therapist and I had been working on my need to please and this was my chance to establish a precedent for my working relationship with Murphy. I took a deep breath and said, "Let me be very clear. I am not leaving unless *I* decide it's for the best."

His dark gaze swept over me from head to foot. He looked surprised but not nearly as much as I was. Standing up for myself was new and I was so unaccustomed to it that it made me feel a bit queasy. Still, I held my ground. I was not going to be pushed around or manipulated. Not anymore.

"How familiar are you with Siobhan's work?" Murphy asked. He had clearly decided to change tactics. Fine. I could play.

"You mean do I have the entire set of Tig McMorrow books in the special edition leather covers with the gilt-edged pages, as well as the standard hardcover edition, the trade paperback edition, and the complete audio version read by the fabulous voice actor Seamus McCaffrey? That familiar?"

This did not seem to reassure Murphy. If anything, he looked alarmed. "Bollocks, you are a stalker, aren't you?"

"No!" I snapped. "I'm a devoted reader, which, given my prior occupation of librarian, should not be such a shock."

"You don't have a shrine to Siobhan back in your bedroom, do you?"

"No, and not in any other room either."

"You don't write erotic fan fiction of yourself and an adult version of Tig McMorrow, do you?"

"What if I do?" I asked. He just stared at me until I rolled my eyes and said, "Relax, I haven't . . . yet."

He glowered. "You're not looking to have her read a novel you've written, are you?"

"No."

He uncrossed his arms and shoved his hands in his pockets as he studied me. "Then why does a woman get the notion to give up her career and fly all the way across the pond to be an author's assistant and bookshop clerk in the quaint village of Finn's Hollow?"

I had to force myself not to squirm under his speculative stare. I kept my spine straight and my chin up. I was not going to be cowed by him.

"I believe I answered that question in my letter to Ms. Riordan," I said.

He waved his hand dismissively. "Yes, I know. Her books inspired you to be brave and take chances." My face must have reflected my dismay. "Yeah, I read your letter. Very touching." He pretended to dab at tears in his eyes then he scrutinized me from head to toe. "How do I know you're not a complete spoofer?"

"I'm going to assume that's not a compliment," I said. He glared. I glared right back. We were clearly at a standoff. Shockingly, my usual peace-at-all-costs persona had yet to return so I held firm.

"Kieran Murphy, are you browbeating my new assistant?" If a voice could be crafted of musical notes from the soft rain that fell upon the rolling green hills that surrounded us, this one surely was, and it lured us to its point of origin like a pied piper.

Murphy and I broke our staring contest and turned to face Siobhan. As if she knew how badly our tour had gone, Siobhan said, "Good morning, Ms. Allen. If my son is badgering you, feel free to give it back to him in equal measure."

It took a second for her words to sink in.

"Your son?" I felt my eyes widen and I glanced at Murphy out of the corner of my eye. He paid me no attention however, focusing instead on his mother—*his mother!*

"Now, Ma, when have I ever been known to browbeat or badger anyone?" Murphy asked. He strode to the alcove.

Kieran Murphy was Siobhan Riordan's son! I felt as if I'd just been let in on a deep dark secret about the notoriously private author. Despite reigning supreme as one of the most popular authors of the aughts, Siobhan had kept her private life completely locked down. All of the public information about her centered solely on her work. There was never any discussion of her personal life. In interviews, if asked about her family and relationships, she deflected the questions, and if the interviewer persisted, she ended the conversation, politely, but still she drew her line and no one crossed it, at least not that I'd been able to discover—and not to be braggy, but my research skills were top-notch.

Small surprise, I was stunned by this brand-new information. Thankfully, mother and son paid me no mind as I wrapped my head around the fact that the author I'd always pictured as living alone in a stone manor house out in the wilds of Ireland was actually someone's "mam."

"Oh, now, let me think," Siobhan said. She tapped her chin with her index finger. "There was the time your third year math teacher asked you to show your work and you refused, announcing that you did it in your head and had no need to waste your time or hers by scribbling it out."

"Yeah, and I stand by that," Murphy said. "And if anyone was a browbeater in that scenario, it was Mrs. Dooley."

"That's not the point," Siobhan said. Her gaze was equal parts amused and exasperated. "Poor Mrs. Dooley had no idea you were as stubborn as a badger." She winked and added, "Still are."

Murphy grinned at her, clearly unrepentant about his schoolboy rebellion. His full lips parted to reveal a slash of white teeth, and a deep dimple appeared in each cheek. Despite my annoyance with him, a smile like that was lethal for a terminally single woman like me. I pictured myself slowly keeling over from the impact and locked my knees as a precautionary measure to keep it from actually happening. Still, a small sigh escaped me.

Siobhan turned to me and said, "Ms. Allen, please ignore my son and have a seat."

"She prefers to be called Red," Murphy said. He turned to me, his dimples fading but still visible. So, that's how it was going to be? Fine. I walked to the alcove and sat down.

"Em, actually. I prefer to be called Em, Ms. Riordan." I was pleased that my voice was even.

"And you must call me Siobhan," she said. Her smile was warm and welcoming and her genuine pleasure at meeting me was reflected in her eyes when she met my gaze. We had spoken on the phone previously to discuss the job, but being here in Ireland with her was more amazing than I'd even imagined.

It was then that the rush of love I'd felt for her ever since reading her first Tig McMorrow book as a middle-schooler surged up inside of me, and I feared I was going to become a completely starstruck babbling moron and prove Murphy right. I kept my expression serene even though my entire body felt shivery. I lowered my hands into my lap so that no one could see them tremble.

I felt the heat of Murphy's scrutiny on the side of my face and I turned to see him watching me with a suspicious expression that I was abruptly grateful for because it forced me to check myself and stuff all of these chaotic emotions into a box and slam the lid on them or risk humiliating myself in front of him while I did fangirl all over Siobhan.

"Did you need anything else?" Siobhan asked Murphy. She gave him a pointed look, clearly dismissing him.

"I suppose not," he said. His tone was grudging. "Since introductions are sorted, I'll leave you two to get acquainted. Please don't overdo it, Ma."

"I've had writer's block for ten years," Siobhan said. "I don't think *overdoing* it is the problem."

Murphy leaned down and affectionately kissed the top of her head. As he walked away, I felt myself break out in a flop sweat of anxiety. I almost called him back to remain as a buffer between me and my idol, but I couldn't form the words.

Coming face-to-face with the woman who had crafted the stories that had carried me through my parents' turbulent marriage, my awkward teen years, the abandonment of my father, and the impossible demands of my high-strung and needy mother, I wanted to tell her how much Tig McMorrow's stories had meant to me.

Tig's magical adventures had kept me company me when I was lonely, encouraged me to be brave, taught me to be kind, lifted me up when I was depressed, sustained me when I felt everything was hopeless, and gave me the sort of love and comfort I'd needed during the darkest days of my life. But how was I supposed to express all that without sounding like a freak? "Obsessive fan" had definitely not been one of the requested qualifications on the job application Siobhan had sent me after receiving my letter. So I said nothing.

"You've made quite an impression upon Kier," Siobhan said.

This was not the opening conversational talking point I'd expected, but I was so relieved to have the silence broken, I ran with it and asked, "Good or bad?"

"I don't know yet," she said. Her smile was infectious and she leaned in and whispered, "But I'm eager to find out."

And just like that I felt as if we were two old friends sharing gossip. Siobhan was naturally charming and I felt as pulled to her genuine warmth as I was to her wordsmithing.

"He told me to call him Murphy," I said. "But it doesn't suit him."

"No, it's a terrible nickname," she agreed. "Something the lads stuck him with in school. Call him Kier. That'll put a knot in his tail."

"He's my boss," I protested with a laugh. "I'm not sure that's the best plan if I want to stay employed."

"He's only your boss when you work in the bookshop," she said. "I'm also your employer and if I call him Kier so can you."

"He did try to have you call me Red," I said.

"Exactly. That's how I knew he'd noticed you. He simply couldn't resist a bit of slagging."

"Which could be because he wants me gone," I said.

"Don't let him chase you away." Siobhan reached across the table and put her hand on my shoulder. "He likes to think he's a fierce old guard dog, but he's really just a lovable puppy at heart."

I gave her a dubious look. Murphy had not come across as particularly puppyish or lovable to me. Her smile deepened as she correctly interpreted my thoughts.

"Don't fret. Kieran is not one to suffer fools, and if he truly wanted you gone, you would be," she said.

"That's not as reassuring as you might think," I said.

She laughed and it was a delightful sound, and I was ridiculously pleased to be the cause of it.

"You're gas, Emily Allen. I think we're going to get on famously," she declared.

My heart about exploded out of my chest. My hero *liked* me. If I could have dropped dead right then and there, I might have because in that moment I doubted my life could ever get any better.

Siobhan glanced out the window. "Oh, dear, the sun has decided not to grace us with her presence today. We should go for a quick walk in the village before the storm comes. We can talk about the specifics of your position as assistant to the *writer in residence*."

She made air quotes when she said it and I gathered she was mocking herself because it had been years since she'd published a book. She rose from her chair and I noticed she took a moment to steady herself before she pulled on the jacket that had been draped across the back of her chair. She tugged a wool hat on over her paisley scarf and walked toward the door. I glanced at the table.

"Are we just leaving this here?" Her laptop and books and notes were scattered across the surface.

"They'll be fine," she said. She frowned at the blank notepad and the laptop. "Everyone in County Kerry knows there is nothing happening there."

There was a note of despair mingled with frustration in her voice and I felt a flash of panic that she expected me to be the one to help her through what was clearly a crippling case of writer's block. This was beyond my skill set and I wondered for a second, a nanosecond really, if Murphy had been right about me. I didn't belong here.

I shook it off. Siobhan led the way to the door and I followed. Honestly, I'd have followed her anywhere.

"And where do you think you're off to?" Kier appeared beside the door as if he'd been waiting.

"Out for a bit of craic," Siobhan said. I knew from reading her Tig McMorrow series that *craic* meant fun. She glanced up at Kieran, who was at least a head taller. "Don't worry, I'll have Em back in time for her shift in the shop."

She called me Em!

"That's not what I'm worried about," he said. He studied her with an expression of concern and I wondered at it. Was he afraid to let her be alone with me? How insulting. What exactly did he think I was planning to do? Abduct her? Force her at gunpoint to write the final book in the Tig McMorrow series? Who did he think I was? Annie Wilkes?

"Goodbye, Kier," Siobhan said. She glanced at me and nodded encouragingly.

"Bye, Kier." I echoed her and added a little finger wave for good measure.

His eyebrows shot up and Siobhan slipped around him and out the door, holding it open for me to follow. I scampered after her.

"The name is Murphy," he barked. "And you'd better not be late for your shift."

Siobhan blew him a kiss, so I did the same. His frown deepened and I glanced away before I laughed. Siobhan tucked her arm through mine and we walked down the narrow lane with a quickened pace, like two students ditching school. A giggle slipped out of me, and Siobhan, who was a few inches shorter than me, snorted, which made us both laugh.

"Is it too early in the day for a pint?" she asked.

"A bit," I said. There was a nip in the air and I burrowed more deeply into my coat. "Even day drinkers wait until noon, I think."

"Pity," she said. When I glanced at her in surprise, she laughed. She was teasing me.

"I can see where Kier gets his slagging skills," I said. I felt myself relax. Being with her felt like catching up with an old friend. And maybe Siobhan was. Through her books, she'd been with me through some tough stuff. She just didn't know it.

"Elevenses it is then," Siobhan declared. At my confused look, she explained. "Elevenses is a snack—tea and a biscuit—to tide you over until lunch."

I liked the sound of that.

Finn's Hollow was a proper Irish village, tucked on the edge of the Ring of Kerry, surrounded by sheep farms, castle ruins, and the Wild Atlantic Way. When I'd arrived yesterday by bus, I'd felt as if I were being driven through an actual postcard. Stone and stucco cottages with slate roofs surrounded the town, the center of which boasted quaint shops pressed together side by side and differentiated by their cheerfully colorful facades. The village was so picturesque that I almost felt as if it were a hallucination. Even now, I half suspected it was a Hollywood movie set, as it surely couldn't be real.

The streets were narrow and the sidewalks even more so, but Siobhan kept her arm looped through mine as we strolled past a paint shop, a pharmacy, a discount store, an art gallery, and a whiskey and wine shop. At the end of the street a bright red building with vibrant blue trim sported a hanging sign that declared it the Top of the Hill Pub. This seemed like a misnomer since the town was built on a slope and the pub was definitely on the lower end. I suspected there was a story there.

It was November and the sky was unsurprisingly gray, but not a single shade of grungy gray like over-washed laundry. Rather, it was turbulent and fast moving as dark gray clouds heavy with rain barreled through paler clouds as fluffy as whipped cream. It was positively cinematic and I watched the drama unfolding above us expecting to see Zeus peek out of the clouds and hurl a lightning bolt at us just for shits and grins, because according to the myths that's what gods do.

An ominous roll of thunder sounded and Siobhan leaned close and said, "The gods are in a foul mood today. We should hurry before they release the hounds."

I laughed. "I was just thinking a lightning bolt might be tossed our way."

There was a flash and we both jumped.

"You might be right. Hurry!" Siobhan cried. We dashed along the sidewalk, until Siobhan stopped in front of a narrow shop. It was short and squat and painted a vibrant shade of lemon yellow. The front windows boasted garden boxes loaded with brightly colored nasturtiums and a tangle of herbs. A small sign hanging over the door read *Hazel's Tea House.*

Siobhan pulled the front door open just as the first icy cold raindrops plopped on our heads. We tumbled inside, relieved to escape the storm.

I glanced around the dimly lit shop, inhaling the soothing scent of chamomile and a variety of other herbs. The wooden floor creaked under our feet as we stepped into the main room. There were several small tables scattered about as well as two cushy armchairs in front of a fireplace that had a crackling blaze going.

"Hiya, Siobhan," a petite woman called. She stood behind a marble counter that ran the length of the room.

"Mornin', Hazel," Siobhan replied.

"The usual for the pair of you?" Hazel asked. Her white hair was cut in a stylish bob and held back from her face by a pair of reader's glasses that sat on her head like a hairband.

"That'd be grand, thanks." Siobhan hung her coat on the rack by the door so I did the same. "Hazel, this is my new assistant, Emily."

"A pleasure." Hazel smiled at me. "Welcome to Finn's Hollow."

"Thank you."

"Shall we settle in by the fire?" Siobhan asked me and I nodded.

We relaxed into the two armchairs. The shop had other customers but they were seated at tables, one working on a laptop, another scrolling through her phone, and a third person reading the *Irish Times*. They paid no attention to us, which was extraordinary to me. Did they not realize who Siobhan was? It boggled.

"What do you think of your first day so far?" Siobhan asked.

I glanced at my watch. "Given that I've only been on the clock for a bit less than two hours, and I'm sitting in a tea shop waiting for elevenses, I'd say it's going really well."

Siobhan smiled. She leaned her elbow on her armrest and propped her chin on her hand. "All right, Em, I've been longing to ask you something, but I wasn't sure how until you arrived and I could look at you face-to-face."

That sounded ominous. My stomach twisted with nerves. What could Siobhan want to ask me? What if it was something I couldn't answer?

Get it together, Allen! You're a librarian. There's nothing you can't answer.

"All right." I hoped my voice was as calm as hers. It was hard to hear over the white noise of panic in my head.

"What made you write to me?"

I felt myself draw inward. I had expected the topic to come up but not right away. How could I explain how trapped I'd felt in my small little life on the island over the past nine years? That her series of books, which had helped guide me through my troubled youth, were one of the things in my life that felt unfinished? And that, in an odd way, I thought if she wrote the last book and resolved Tig's life then I, too, could get on with mine?

Even in my head, it sounded as bizarre as her son feared I was. There was no doubt I'd come across like a demanding fan, which I was certain she'd had her fill of over the years.

I thought about all of the series of books that had nurtured me to adulthood. What if none of them had their final volume? What if every series left the protagonist facing down a life-or-death situation with no resolution? It was the stuff of a reader's nightmares. I decided to lead with that.

"I guess I'm looking for closure?" I said. It came out like a question. She tipped her head to the side and a small frown line appeared between her brows as if my answer wasn't what she'd expected.

Four

"Here you are, my dears." Hazel arrived with our tea.

Loaded on her tray was a round pot with a brightly colored yellow and blue checked cozy keeping the tea hot while it steeped. In addition, there were two delicate china cups and two saucers, as well as cream and sugar and a plate of cookies, which I knew—again from Siobhan's books—were called biscuits here. Yum.

"Anything else, love?" Hazel asked Siobhan. She set the tray on the low table between us.

"No, thank you. This is perfect," Siobhan said.

Hazel beamed at her and I realized Siobhan had that gift, the ability to make a person feel special just because she saw them, really saw them.

"Give a shout if you need me," Hazel said. She returned to the counter where another customer waited.

Siobhan leaned forward and slipped the cozy off the pot. I could feel the heat of the fire warming the side of my face. If I had a book to read, I could have sat there all day. Siobhan poured and handed me my cup and saucer. Both were bone china but the cup was decorated with yellow roses and the saucer with a ring of colorful butterflies around the edge. Even though they weren't matching, I felt that they went together perfectly. I put a teaspoon of sugar and a dollop of milk in mine and stirred it quietly, mindful of the other customers who were working.

Siobhan prepared her tea with twice as much sugar but the same dollop of milk. Her cup was covered in purple violets and her saucer two bluebirds. She noticed my glance and said, "Hazel collects china but can't be bothered to acquire a matching set."

I glanced around the room. The windows had assorted curtains, from lace panels on the front windows to tartan plaid drapes at the rear. Random chairs sat at tables of various shapes and sizes. Even our two chairs were different, mine upholstered in a burgundy velvet and Siobhan's a brocade of gold and cream. Nothing matched and yet it all felt homey and comfortable.

"I sense a theme of sorts," I said. "And I like it."

"I do, too," Siobhan said. She leaned back with a sigh. "Whenever I'm here, I feel like I'm playing house in my grandmother's attic, using whatever I can to create my home."

I smiled and sipped my tea. Delicious. I took a deep breath, inhaling the rich scent of the peat fire mingling with the aroma of my tea and felt my spine relax just enough for me to sink back into my chair.

Yesterday, I had been nervous about—well, everything—and I'd convinced myself I had contracted bubonic plague on the flight over—my seatmate had been suffering from a headache and was sweating as though he had a fever, which are two symptoms of the plague—so after arriving late at the small guest house I was renting in the village, I had not slept at all.

Of course, my rational mind said I was being ridiculous and that my seatmate most likely had a nasty hangover instead of the plague but anxious me always won those arguments—especially when it was the middle of the night.

"Now what did you mean when you said closure?" Siobhan asked.

My spine stiffened like a string being drawn taut. I'd hoped she'd forgotten. No such luck. It looked like I was going to have to explain.

"Tig McMorrow's first adventure, *Tig McMorrow and the Ogham Stone*, came out when I was nine years old," I said. "And there was another volume of Tig McMorrow's adventures just about every year until I was eighteen. I felt as if I grew up with him."

Siobhan pursed her lips and blew on her tea. "I hear that a lot from readers."

"And you left him in a wicked cliffhanger in the last book, *Tig McMorrow and the Tree of Life*." I tried not to sound accusatory. "I need to know the end of his story. That's why I wrote the letter. At the risk of sounding overly dramatic, I feel like I can't really get on with my own life until I know what happens to Tig. There's always a part of me worrying about him like I left him behind in my teens and I need to save him if I'm going to save myself. Oh god, I do sound nutty. Please don't tell Kier. He already thinks I'm a crazy stalker fan, this will just confirm it."

Siobhan laughed. "Kier's just very protective."

Despite being on the receiving end of his suspicions, I understood. I could only imagine what Siobhan's life had been like during the height of her career and how it had impacted Kier as a teenager.

"I never intended to leave Tig stranded," Siobhan confessed. "I am sorry about that."

"It was like he disappeared into the Bermuda Triangle," I said. I wasn't trying to be unkind but it had felt like an unsolved missing person's case for most of my adulthood.

She sighed. "Believe me, I considered writing an epilogue to that effect when the writing simply wouldn't come."

"It wouldn't?" I asked. "It just stopped?"

She nodded and shrugged as if to say *What can you do?*

"At the risk of causing you to second-guess hiring me," I said, "I don't have any experience as an assistant."

"I know, but you have a deep knowledge of Tig and his story," she said. "I need your enthusiasm to motivate me to get this story written. I never signed a contract for the last book, so I have no deadline and I need something—*you*—to help me see it through to the end."

"Do you know how you want to start the story?" I asked. I assumed she must have an outline for the book. Maybe she just needed to reacquaint herself with it.

She glanced down into her cup. She was quiet for so long I thought she might be reading the tea leaves. Finally, she glanced up. "I have no idea, which has been the problem all along."

"No idea?" I repeated. My voice came out higher and squeakier than I liked. "Do you have your original outline?"

She smiled at me, crinkling her nose just the slightest bit, as if I were a cute bunny hopping across a field. I took this to mean there was no outline and I was adorable for suggesting otherwise.

"No outline then?" I asked just to be clear and extinguish any flame of hope that might be misguidedly fluttering in my chest.

She shook her head. "I've never worked from an outline."

"Never?" I asked. This was inconceivable to me. I didn't even get out of bed until I checked my itinerary for the day. I was a diehard list maker. If it wasn't on the list, it didn't get done.

"I always felt that my imagination couldn't soar if it was anchored by expectations," she said.

"Okay." It seemed bad form to challenge my idol's process within minutes of meeting her but OMG.

"You disagree?" she asked.

"Not disagree so much as can't comprehend," I said. "Being a librarian, I have a certain rage for order hardwired into my personality."

She laughed. She lifted up the plate in a silent invitation to take a cookie, as if I could comfort eat my way out of my panic that she worked without any guidelines. I took a cookie. It was a narrow rectangular shortbread dipped in chocolate. Yum.

"That's why you're perfect," she said. "I need someone who can read the map, or draw the map, or at least point me in the right direction."

"And you think that's me?" I didn't need a mirror to know that behind my glasses my eyes must be as big as the saucer beneath my cup.

"I do." She spoke with an absolute certainty that I found more unnerving than the lightning that had chased us into the shop.

"But what about your imagination?" I asked. "I don't want to stifle your creativity."

"Not to worry. There hasn't even been a bit of that over the past ten years. This attempt to write again is a long shot, as they say."

"Why do you suppose that is?" I cringed. Even before I finished asking the question, I knew I sounded just like my therapist when she pushed me to examine the whys of my hypochondria or, as she called it, Illness Anxiety Disorder.

"Life." She didn't elaborate and I got the feeling that she wasn't ready to share whatever had derailed her career.

"Do you think maybe you need someone more familiar with writing and the creative process than a well-read librarian?" I asked. I was definitely in over my head.

"I've tried taking classes, hiring writing coaches, and going on author retreats," Siobhan said. "I even had a white witch come and smudge my work area at the bookshop. Kier loved that." She smiled at the memory. "Nothing helped." She sounded perplexed.

I sipped my tea. I wondered if she expected me to offer up solutions. I had nothing. I knew nothing about writing. I was a reader, first and foremost, and a librarian second. Writing had always seemed to me to require the magical ability to put words together in a unique way. I did not have that ability. I could barely hammer out a weekly report that didn't put my boss to sleep.

"Siobhan, I'm going to be straight with you. I don't know how to help you," I said. I hated feeling as if I was failing her before we even began but I truly had no idea how I could assist her. "I mean I'd love to but I'm not a writer."

"No, but you're a reader, you know how to do research, and you know the series quite possibly better than I do," she said. "That came across in your letter."

"Reader, researcher, and Tig McMorrow fangirl," I said. I was all these things. No question. "I am skilled in the informational arts, but I don't know how that can help you."

She smiled, took a cookie, and set the plate down. "Let's just see where all of those skills take us, yeah?"

We spent the rest of our elevenses talking about our favorite books, movies, and streaming shows. When our tea and cookies were gone, I glanced at the time on my watch and said, "I need to get back if I'm going to arrive on time for my shift."

Siobhan sighed. "And I need to go rest for a bit. This is the most excitement I've had in a very long time."

Meeting me? Exciting? I smiled. Siobhan was likely being kind, but it was still flattering. We said goodbye to Hazel and pulled on our coats. The wind remained brisk and the clouds continued to churn overhead, but the storm had abated.

As we strolled in comfortable silence, I realized I liked Siobhan, genuinely liked her. It had occurred to me when I was offered the job as her assistant that she might be a diva, a writer that hit it big once and then coasted on her success, but Siobhan wasn't like that. Not at all.

Truthfully, I'd been more than a little nervous to meet her. Meeting your literary hero could go horribly wrong, like something out of a John Green novel, and I had been braced for disappointment. Instead I'd discovered a woman of warmth and kindness and I was looking forward to working with her, even if she didn't work from an outline. Yes, I was still processing that bit. It seemed as risky as taking a road trip without GPS. Who did that?

We arrived at the bookshop to find Kier waiting for us. He held the door open and Siobhan hurried inside and I followed. Kier studied Siobhan from head to foot as if checking to see if she was all in one piece. Really? What did he think I could possibly have done to her over tea and biscuits?

"You look knackered, Ma," he said with concern.

"Not at all." She smiled at him. It was a big beaming grin that practically lit up the room. He blinked. "I'm going to my house to sit and think for a bit. Do not work our Em too hard. Remember she's new."

He made a noncommittal hum in his throat. "I'll have Oisín drive you home."

"I don't want to be a bother," Siobhan protested.

"You never could be," Kier said. He gazed at her with affection. "Besides, the weather might turn and you don't want to get caught in it."

She glanced at the window and nodded. "All right, but only because I know you'll have your way whether I like it or not and it's just easier to go peacefully."

"That's the spirit of surrender I was looking for." He laughed and hugged her to his side.

I smiled as I watched them. I liked the easy affection between them. I felt a tiny spurt of envy, just a flicker, wishing I had that sort of relationship with my mother. Then I shook it off, remembering that old chestnut—you get what you get and you don't get upset.

"Your chariot awaits, Siobhan," Oisín announced as he strode toward us. He was carrying a set of keys in one hand and an umbrella in the other. "I have my brolly if the storm doubles back for another go at us."

"I'll see you bright and early tomorrow morning, Em," Siobhan said. She reached out and patted my arm. "It's going to be lovely working with you, I just know it."

A flush of pleasure warmed my face. I realized Siobhan's approval meant everything to me, so much in fact that I didn't even care that Kier's expression could only be described as deeply suspicious.

"Come on then, Red," he said. "Let's get to work."

Oisín and Siobhan stepped outside and I followed Kier to the backroom. He gestured for me to put my things away. While I hung up my coat, I saw him pacing around the room. I wondered what he was thinking, and I suspected it didn't bode well for me. I was right.

"You want me to inventory the entire shop?" I asked. Kier had said as much when he handed me an ancient laptop before we started our trek up to the third floor of the building, but I needed to confirm it.

"Yep. You can start with the top floor and work your way down." He gestured to the bookshelves. "Type every title into the search bar and see if we have it in our system. If not, you can manually add it to the collection."

"When was the last time the inventory was done?" I opened the laptop to find that it was on. Its fan was churning with a low whirring noise and it felt hot to the touch. I put it down on a nearby table. "Is there an existing inventory for me to work from?"

Kier scratched his chin with his fingers while he considered. "Um, let me think, it was . . . yeah . . . never." He sounded entirely too cheerful about this.

"Never?" I was certain I must have heard him wrong.

"I bought the shop about ten years ago." He tapped the screen of the laptop. "We're still using the same system." He said this like it was a good thing.

"You mean the same point of sale and inventory software as the previous owners from *ten years ago*?" I asked. Sheer horror was making my voice screechy.

He looked inordinately pleased to answer in the affirmative. "Yes, and they used it for more than a decade before that. You can't even buy updates for the system anymore."

I glanced at the ancient software chugging along on the pixelated screen at the pace of a sloth crossing a road and said, "Well, hello, Y2K."

"Now you're getting it."

"I've been telling him for years we need to update the software and the hardware, you know, all the ware, but Murphy hates change and won't listen." A petite woman stepped out from behind one of the bookcases. Her hair was a blunt-cut, chin-length bob and she wore a knit vest over a turtleneck sweater which caused me to suspect she was the sort of person, like me, who was always cold.

"Hi, I'm Eun-ji Park McMullen," she said. Her accent was a delightful blend of Irish and Korean. "Social media queen and avid reader." She held out the stack of books in her arms, and I smiled.

"A little light reading?" I asked. She grinned. I glanced at Kier but he was frowning at us, so I added, "I'm Emily Allen."

"The American," Eun-ji said.

"That's me."

"Failte," Eun-ji greeted me with the Gaelic word for welcome.

"Thank you," I said.

"If we're done with the niceties, I feel the need to defend myself," Kier said. "It's not that I hate change. I just don't see why you need to upgrade when the old system is sufficient."

Eun-ji rolled her eyes. Kier didn't seem to take offense, which I thought spoke well of him, considering my very presence seemed to irritate him to no end. In fact, I'd noticed the only person who seemed to annoy him was me. This was very strange. As the consummate pleaser, I'd never had a person take an instant dislike to me. It was jarring.

"Sufficient?" Eun-ji puffed out her lower lip and blew the bangs off her forehead in exasperation. "You sound just like my husband, and as I frequently say to him, sufficient and efficient are not the same thing!" She glanced at me. "You know, when I left South Korea to study in Ireland, I had no idea I would fall in love with a sheep farmer, marry him, and spend the rest of my life trying to pull him out of the dark ages." She jerked her thumb in Kier's direction. "This one is just as bad."

"Which is why I hired you to deal with all of the bookshop's social media," he said. Kier glanced at me. "She's amazing. She actually knows what algorithms and search engine optical-thingies are."

"Search engine optimizations," Eun-ji said with a sigh.

"Yeah, that," Kier agreed.

I smiled. "We'll have to talk about successful methods of organic search traffic. Coming from a library background, I imagine I have different experiences."

Eun-ji's face lit up with excitement. "Finally, someone who speaks my language."

"Oh no." Kier glanced between us with a frown. "That cyberspeak is contagious, isn't it?"

"Don't worry." Eun-ji patted his arm. "You'd have to actually live in the modern world in order to be infected."

"Phew." Kier wiped his brow with exaggerated relief.

Eun-ji did not seem at all intimidated by Kier and had no trouble telling him exactly what she thought. For his part, he didn't seem to mind. I found this encouraging, like maybe I could get him to listen to me, too, if I was persistent or patient or both.

The laptop continued to churn and I wondered if it was ever going to open the program. "I think it's about to burst into flames," I said.

Kier leaned down and pressed his ear to it. "Nah, it's fine."

I studied the screen of the ancient laptop. "Your definition of fine and mine are vastly different."

"You're in Ireland now," he said. He sounded a teeny bit defensive. "We do things differently here."

"Hmm," I hummed noncommittally. I didn't think it was Ireland that wanted to live in the technological stone age so much as it was him. Of course, I couldn't leave it. "Is it really the best use of staff time to have them do tasks that take five or ten times longer than they should because of outdated equipment?"

"No one here has complained," Kier said. I noticed he was looking out the window when he spoke, as if something fascinating was happening on Main Street. There was nothing happening on Main Street.

"Oh, I've complained," Eun-ji said. "You just don't listen."

"We all know how this system works," Kier protested.

"Yes, slowly and with the propensity to freeze mid-task," Eun-ji retorted. She glanced at me. "Truly, it's the worst. Back up frequently."

Kier looked at her as if she was a traitor.

"I can help you find new software and hardware," I said. "I was on the committee to select the online system for the library and I'm certain the features you're looking for can't be that different. You'll want to be able to add records easily, maintain your inventory, track your sales, stuff like that."

"You could do that?" Eun-ji sounded giddy. "I have so many ideas for upgrades."

"Starting with usability," I said. I glanced at the laptop half expecting to see the blue screen of death. Instead, it just kept whirring.

"Let me be very clear," Kier said. His words came out a bit garbled as his jaw was clenched tight. "We are not buying new software or hardware or anything else."

"If cost is a consideration, and of course it is, I could use that as part of the selection criteria," I said.

"You're not listening, Red, there will be no new anything. Am I clear?" he asked. His face was flushed and his eye was twitching.

"If you say so." I sent Eun-ji an *I tried* shrug and she returned it, signaling that she was also mystified by Kier's stubborn stance.

"I do say so. Now start on the far side of the room. Quitting time is at six." He made a shooing motion with his hands.

I glanced at the time in the corner of the laptop. It read 12:05. Six hours? I was going to do inventory for six straight hours? I glanced at Kier out of the corner of my eye. He seemed quite satisfied now that he'd regained control of the situation. Well, I couldn't have that, now could I?

"Thank you, Kier," I said. His eyes narrowed. I smiled at him, opening my eyes wide in what I hoped was a guileless look. It simply would not do to let him think he'd bested me on day one. "I'm really looking forward to digging through those old books. This is going to be so much fun!"

Lies, lies, lies. There was nothing fun about this. As I trudged across the room, my only solace was that he looked chagrined not to have gotten the reaction he'd been expecting, which I was certain was one of whining and complaining. Well, that was never going to happen. If I could survive my statistics class in library school, I could survive anything. Kieran Murphy would not break me.

At five o'clock in the afternoon, I was rethinking my position. If this was going to be how I spent my time every day, day after day, he might very well succeed in crushing my soul. It wasn't that I minded doing inventory. Not at all. It was just that the software was so old and slow. There were no shortcuts when entering each book's information. I had to type in every title and then if it wasn't there, I had to manually add all of the book's information, which the ancient laptop processed with the speed of grass growing. Scratch that, grass grew faster than this vintage hunk of junk and its ancient software.

I'd completed two shelving units, taking a short break afterward to visit Brigid and try out her new fig jam scones. I was back upstairs and beginning the third when the sensation of being watched caused the hair on the back of my neck to prickle. There had been no customers for over an hour and none of the ones who'd entered the shop had ventured up the stairs to the third floor. As Oisín had predicted when he took Siobhan home, the storm had turned back around and it had been raining steadily all afternoon, giving the bookshop a delightfully cozy feeling that made me long to put my head down on a nearby wooden table and nap.

This meant that whoever was up here with me was either a ghost—a delicious shiver ran over my skin. I'd always wanted to be haunted by a ghost and if not in an old bookshop in Ireland then where?—or I was suffering from some sort of delusion and imagining that I was being watched, which could be a symptom of any manner of physical or mental ailments. Honestly, I was really hoping for door number one on this.

Person or apparition, I didn't want to startle them, so I slowly put down the book I was holding and pretended to stretch the kinks out of my back, although after being hunched on the floor with stacks of books for so many hours, I didn't have to pretend very hard.

As I lifted my arms over my head, I slowly moved to the right. Just in time to see a head of dark brown hair, long and parted in the middle, disappear behind a nearby shelving unit. Not a ghost then. Disappointment!

I wondered how the person had gotten up here without me hearing them. The stairs were old and creaky and you'd have to know exactly where to step to avoid making noise. I thought about calling out a greeting but since the person was hiding, I suspected it would just scare them away.

Being an introvert myself, I tried to respect other people's unspoken leave-me-alone vibes and in this case I was a stranger and a foreigner. I decided to carry on with my work and see if the person reappeared. Maybe they just needed to get used to me.

I checked every item on the shelf in front of me, all the while extremely aware of the shelving unit where the head of dark hair had disappeared. The sense of someone watching me came and went as if the person didn't linger but kept coming back to check on me. I wondered if they were a minion sent by Kier to see if I was shirking. I found this highly probable and annoying.

Pretending not to notice, I waited until five minutes before closing time to shut down the ancient laptop after saving my work. When I tromped down the stairs, Oisín and Brigid were already there. Brigid locked the front door and Oisín shut down the computer on the cashier's counter. There was no sign of anyone else. No dark-haired person, no Kier, no Eun-ji.

"Is it just us closing up?" I asked.

"It is," Brigid said. "Kier left for home an hour ago while Eun-ji and Niamh slipped out the front door before I locked it."

"Niamh?" I asked.

"She's a student in secondary school and helps out after classes," Brigid explained. "Nice girl, very shy, though."

"Does she have dark hair that she wears parted in the middle?" I asked.

"That's her." Brigid nodded. "You met her then?"

"Not exactly," I said. "But I saw her from a distance."

"She'll be back tomorrow with Iris, another part-timer," Brigid said. "We have several people who work one or two days a week. You'll get to know them all eventually."

While I was still disappointed there wasn't a ghost in the building, I looked forward to meeting the rest of the Last Chapter's employees. It'd be nice to make some friends in Finn's Hollow, especially if Kier was trying to bore me to death with inventory.

The three of us walked into the backroom where I stored the laptop on one of the desks and we gathered our things and pulled on our jackets.

"How was your first day, Em?" Oisín asked me as he tightened a green scarf about his neck.

I pointed to the laptop. "Thrilling."

Both Oisín and Brigid laughed at the dryness of my tone.

"Don't let Murphy wear you down with the drudgery," Oisín advised.

"Oisín's got the right of it," Brigid said. "Murphy will get tired of giving you the deadly dull tasks soon enough. He's just testing you, yeah?"

"I've noticed he likes pop quizzes," I said. He'd certainly put me through my paces that morning. "Siobhan is very kind, though. I'm looking forward to working with her on her next book."

Brigid and Oisín exchanged a doubtful glance. I couldn't blame them. Siobhan hadn't written anything in ten years. It made me all the more determined to help her.

"Have any plans for tonight, Em?" Brigid asked. It was an obvious ploy to change the subject.

"None," I said. "I'll likely do some more unpacking."

"I have football practice—my partner, Gavin, and I are coaches—or I'd invite you for a pint at the Top of the Hill," Oisín said. "Another day?"

"That sounds great," I said.

"I'd like in on that," Brigid said. "But tonight I have to get home to feed my family their meat and two veg before there's a full on rebellion. Em, you'll come for supper and meet the lot of them soon?"

"Be sure to wear a helmet and shin guards if you accept that invitation," Oisín cautioned me. "She's got three pint-sized lads and one big one and they're half wild on their best days."

Brigid didn't look at all offended so I asked, "And on their worst?"

"Fully feral," Brigid said. Then she laughed. It was a good-natured cackle and it charmed me down to my socks. "But I love them just the same."

With our coats on, we shuffled out the back of the shop. Oisín switched off the lights as we went. We stepped out into the dark evening and while the day's storm had moved on, it had left behind a cold, damp wind that I felt in my bones.

"I heard you were renting the guest cottage from the Connollys," Oisín said.

"Yes." I tipped my head in the direction of my rental. "I chose it because it's within walking distance of the bookshop, the price was right, and it's ridiculously adorable."

"Maeve and Shane are good people," Brigid said. "They'll look after you."

"Talented, too," Oisín observed. I wasn't sure what he meant but took it as a positive thing.

"Thank you both for making me feel so welcome today. I appreciate it."

"Of course, you're one of us now," Brigid said. Both she and Oisín waved and began walking in the opposite direction. I turned toward home, marveling at how accepting they were of me. It certainly made up for Kieran's resistance to my presence.

The magical feeling I'd felt when the bus dropped me off in the village the night before had only grown stronger since my walk earlier in the day with Siobhan. The shops were closing but the antique-looking streetlights that lined the street cast it in a soft yellow glow and the scent of evening meals being cooked filled the air.

I turned down the side street that led to my cottage. It occurred to me that I'd arrived so late last night, I hadn't had a chance to buy any food and my stomach rumbled, informing me that this was completely unacceptable.

Yellow leaves scattered across the narrow road when the breeze gusted. A sign hanging from the local hair dresser's salon creaked as it was sent swinging. The road sloped down, causing a large puddle to form, covering the road and sidewalk. There was no way around it. Impatient, I jumped over it, but my narrow skirt was unforgiving and one of my cute ankle boots didn't clear the small pond and the water splashed up onto my skirt. Damn it.

Now I was cold and wet. I knew that I was still jet-lagged from the journey to Ireland and the long day at the bookshop. A tiny flicker of homesickness flared to life in my chest. If I was on the

Vineyard, what would I be doing? Grabbing dinner and drinks with Sam and Ben? In all honesty, no.

I'd be home, after a long day at the library, cooking dinner for my mother, Tammy Lynn, who would keep up a steady stream of island gossip until I excused myself and went to my room to read the evening away. That had been the rinse repeat of my life over the past several years. And I was over it.

With my homesickness in check, I hurried to the end of the lane where the Connollys' house sat. It was a big white stucco home with a bright blue front door and lace curtains in every window. It perched mere feet from the road like so many of the village homes. Behind the main house, they had two secondary buildings, a stone barn of some sort and the stucco cottage I was renting.

I'd arrived late last night and used the lockbox on the bright pink front door to retrieve the key and let myself in. Anxiety and exhaustion had sent me into a fitful sleep almost immediately and I'd woken up this morning moments from being late for work, so I hadn't even met the Connollys yet. I hoped that Brigid and Oisín were right that my new landlords were nice. I knew from the emails I'd exchanged with Maeve Connolly that the fully furnished cottage had been where her mother lived out her final years.

Per Maeve's instructions, access to the cottage was through the narrow alley that separated the Connolly house from their neighbors on the right. The loose gravel of the path crunched beneath my boots. I unhitched the latch of the wrought iron gate and pushed it open, stepping into the yard.

The small patch of bright green grass was thick and lush and enclosed by a border of stones that were shades of gray and covered in moss and lichen. At the end of the yard was the barn, which at the moment was all lit up, and I could hear the sound of people talking. My cottage was in the opposite corner of the yard but as I passed the barn, the big rolling door slid open, revealing what appeared to be a studio.

I stopped walking and stared into the opening. There was a small crowd of people talking and laughing and behind them was a magnificent wall of yarn in every hue imaginable. My feet moved forward before I had a chance to reconsider. The colors drew me in as if the yarn had unspooled and slipped around me, luring me in. I paused at the open door and gawked.

The barn contained what appeared to be looms of various sizes, most with projects on them. There were also several large wooden tables with measuring tapes, scissors, and a fancy sewing basket.

"Don't you worry, Sarah, you can come by and finish your rug tomorrow." A sturdy woman with silver hair swept back from her face in soft waves spoke to a younger woman who was looking at the large wooden loom in front of her while fretting her lower lip between her teeth. She looked conflicted.

"You have plenty of time to finish by Christmas," a man said. He was standing at another large loom, tightening the knobs and fussing with the threads. He wore a beautiful deep blue Aran sweater and sported a thick white beard that reached down to his collar.

"If you're sure," Sarah said. "I'll be here early in the morning before my classes."

"Bring pastries and we'll open even earlier," the man joked.

"Don't listen to Shane," the silver-haired woman said. "You can come any time. You've a real aptitude for weaving."

"Maeve says that to everyone," another woman said. She was middle-aged with dark brown hair shot through with gray. Her eyes crinkled in the corners, making it clear she was teasing. "It keeps us coming back when, if we had half a brain, we'd quit."

I glanced back at the silver-haired woman. *Maeve.* She must be Maeve Connolly. Then I studied the man with the beard and determined he must be her husband, Shane. These were my landlords and they were weavers. How cool was that?

"Ah, sure, Hannah, and now you can tell her I'm not wrong given that you've been weaving for three years now and doing very well, if I may say so," Maeve said.

Hannah laughed and said, "It's true but I'm thinking it's more that I'm obsessed than talented."

"Ha! That's the first requirement for being a weaver," Shane said.

"Well, I have that part down then," Sarah said with a smile. "I'll see you in the morning."

She and Hannah turned and left the barn. They nodded to me as they passed, and I stepped into the light, drawn to the brightly lit interior.

"Can I help you, miss?" Maeve asked.

"I just thought I'd say hello," I said. "I'm your tenant, Emily Allen, but everyone calls me Em."

"Oh, there you are," Maeve said. She turned to the man. "Shane, it's our tenant."

Shane's beard moved up in a way that I could tell he was grinning beneath it. "Pleased to meet you, Em. Sorry we didn't see you last night. Quiet as a mouse you were. Did you get in late?"

"Very," I said. "And then I had to hurry to work this morning."

"Poor lamb," Maeve clucked. "You haven't even had a chance to settle in."

Her sympathy was a balm. I had been feeling a bit harried since I'd landed in Finn's Hollow. Still, I didn't want to sound like a complainer. "I'm all right."

"We were just headed to the pub for supper," Maeve said. "I insist you join us."

"Oh, that's very kind of you but I don't want to impose."

"It's no imposition," Shane said. "We're going anyway and this will give us the chance to get to know you. It's our treat. Besides, you don't want to miss it. Tonight's special is the fish and chips and they buy their fish right off the boats in Dingle."

"Well, in that case, how can I refuse?" I asked. They beamed at me and I had the impression they were genuinely delighted that I'd accepted their invitation. I glanced around the barn and said, "I take it you're weavers?"

"Indeed we are," Maeve said. "We met in art school decades ago and discovered our passion for each other and the fiber arts. Thankfully, neither love has waned after all these years no matter how tangled the threads get."

They smiled at each other and it was such a look of pure affection and devotion that I found myself smiling as well, as if their love for each other included me just because I was there to bask in it.

"Your work is incredible," I said. I gestured to one of the largest looms, where a piece the size of a blanket was well underway. The main colors were a rich blue and a vibrant green with random threads of bright yellow and fiery red woven into it.

"Stop by tomorrow and I'll give you a proper tour," Maeve said. "But for now, let's go eat. I'm practically faint with hunger and if you don't get there early, they run out of fish and no one wants just a plate of chips."

Shane raised his hands in surrender and stepped away from his loom. "Maeve gets right surly when the hunger is upon her. Best be off."

"All right," I agreed. "If it's okay, I'm just going to change my clothes. The puddle in the middle of the road defeated me."

Maeve glanced down at the mud on my skirt and boot. "I've lost that battle myself a time or two. We'll meet you in front of the house as soon as we close up the studio."

"Excellent," I said. I turned and hurried to my cottage, leaving them to it. I changed out of my skirt and boots into a comfortable pair of jeans and a pair of all-weather lace-up boots. I checked my phone and noted it was lit up with notifications. Seven more texts and three voicemails from my mother. I scanned them quickly to be certain nothing was wrong. Each message was a variation of *I miss you* or *How could you leave me?*

I debated calling her back, but it was still afternoon on Martha's Vineyard. I could call her after dinner and not keep Maeve and Shane waiting while I tried to appease her, which could take a very long time. I left a lamp on in the cozy living room, so it wouldn't be dark when I returned.

I hurried to the main house and found Shane and Maeve stepping out the front door. The three of us set off for the pub, giving the boot-ruining puddle a wide berth. The music grew louder as we drew closer to the Top of the Hill pub. I glanced from its bright exterior up the hill to where its name would lead a person to believe it should be located. Shane and Maeve saw my glance and they laughed.

"And that there's a story to be shared over a pint," Shane said.

He pulled the door open and gestured for us to lead the way. Maeve stepped inside and I followed. The pub was packed and Maeve maneuvered us through the crowd, taking my hand and pulling me along with her.

"Ah, there's a snug opening up," she said. "I'll grab it."

She dropped my hand and hurried to a booth on the far side of the room. I made to follow her when a man stepped in front of me. I didn't have a chance to stop and slammed into his back. It didn't budge him, but I lost my balance and staggered back. Without even turning around, the man reached behind and grabbed my arm, keeping me from toppling over.

As I righted myself and straightened my glasses, the man glanced over his shoulder at me. Kieran Murphy. He turned fully around and his gaze perused me up and down, his hooded eyes revealing nothing when he said, “Evening, Red.”

My face immediately felt hot. *Why?* What was it about this man’s intense dark gaze that made me feel as self-conscious as an adolescent? Ugh.

“Sorry,” I said. I flapped my hands just to complete my signature look of awkwardness. “I didn’t mean to bump into you.”

“No problem at all. It was my fault,” he said. “Sorry I stepped in front of you.”

He seemed much more congenial than he had at the bookshop. I glanced from the pint in his hand back up to his face. “Been here a while?”

At that, he blinked in surprise and then laughed as if amused by my sass. “Not as long as you seem to think.” He started to say more when Shane joined us.

“Murphy, how are you, lad?” Shane asked from behind me.

Kieran looked past me and smiled. “Surviving.”

“That’s the best a man can do most days,” Shane said. “We’re about to grab some grub, join us?”

“No.” The word slipped out before I could catch it. Kier raised his eyebrows at me in surprise. I supposed it sounded a bit unfriendly—okay, not a bit, more like a lot. I tried to fix the damage. “I mean, I’m sure Kier is here with friends and has already eaten.”

Shane glanced between us as if trying to determine the source of the tension. I wanted to say it’s him, all him and his unreasonable suspicions about me, but I didn’t. Before I could pull it together and say anything, Kier said, “I haven’t actually so I’d be delighted to join you.”

And there went my appetite.

Five

"Your coat?" Kier asked. I clutched it to me with a questioning look and he explained, "I can hang it up for you."

He gestured to the hook at the end of the booth where Maeve and Shane had hung their jackets.

"Oh, right," I said. I shrugged out of it, feeling painfully self-conscious because he was watching me with that fierce stare of his, and handed it over. My instincts told me it wasn't wise to lose even one layer of clothing between us, as if a jacket could act as a shield to his piercing gaze, but if I sat here in my coat, I would look like an even bigger oddball than I suspected he already thought I was. I watched as he slipped it onto the hook and then sat on the bench seat beside me.

What we call booths in the States, they call snugs in Ireland and they were not kidding. Perhaps it was just the man beside me, or more accurately, my awareness of him making it seem as if he was taking up more than his share of the seat, but I found myself trying to maintain a gap between us and failing miserably as his leg pressed against mine.

The faint scents of citrus, wood smoke, and warm wool filled my senses. All smells I loved. If I didn't know better, I'd think Kieran Murphy with his swoon-worthy good looks, enticing personal scent, and intense dark gaze had been conjured by a witch just for the romance reader in me. Good witch or bad? It was hard to tell but at the moment I was leaning toward bad.

"Care for a whiskey, Em?" Shane asked. "A Teelings neat will warm you up."

"Yes, please."

"Should I make it a double?" Shane asked.

"Perfect," I agreed. I saw Kier's eyebrows lift. Was he impressed? Alarmed? I had no idea. Either way, a whiskey neat seemed like a fine idea, never mind that I'd never had one before.

"Maeve? Murphy?" Shane asked the others.

"That'd be grand," Kier replied.

"Sure." Maeve nodded.

"Are we all agreed on the fish and chips?" Shane asked. "I'll put that order in as well."

Maeve and I nodded and Kier said, "If we're having whiskey, then it's a yes from me, too."

"Excellent choice." Shane grinned and then slipped out of his side of the booth to go order the drinks and food at the bar.

Being an introvert, I was overly aware of the silence sitting like an uninvited person at the table. I wished I could think of something clever to say, a story to tell, or a question to ask, but my mind was completely blank and I was having a hard time thinking with Kier sitting in my personal space bubble.

Having lived with just my mother for most of the past decade, I wasn't used to men other than coworkers or patrons at the library. I didn't dislike men. I just wasn't accustomed to them. I glanced at the place where Kieran's hip pressed against mine. Did all men take up this much space? I tried to remember the last time I'd shared a booth with a man. I couldn't even recall the last time I'd been on a date. Not that this was a date. I pulled at the neck of my sweater feeling overheated and uncomfortable in my own skin.

"How did you find the cottage last night, Em? Satisfactory?" Maeve asked me.

I let out a sigh of relief to have the silence broken and to have something to distract me from the man beside me.

"It was perfect," I said. "After a day of flying and then the trip down from Dublin, it was wonderful to arrive at such a charming place. Thank you for stocking the kitchen. It was nice to be able to make a cup of tea when I arrived. The cottage is just lovely. I know I'm going to be very happy there."

Maeve beamed, looking pleased. "That's good to hear. My mother enjoyed it and it'll be nice to have someone living there again. If there's anything you need, you'll let me know?"

"I will," I promised. Silence fell again. Kier sipped his beer while Maeve glanced around the crowded pub, waving to the customers she knew.

After a moment, she asked, "And how was your first day at the bookshop?"

I felt Kier go still beside me and I wondered what he was thinking. Was he worried that I would complain about how he had quizzed me and set me on a task at the top of the building where it was cold and drafty and I saw no one all afternoon? I decided a little slagging was not out of order.

"Well, all I can say is that it's a good thing I've arrived." I felt Kier's entire body jerk in my direction. Ha! "Do you know that the inventory has never been done before? My holiday work visa is only for a year but I'm afraid I might have to extend it to get it all done."

I could feel his hot stare on the side of my face, but I kept my features neutral, hoping he couldn't tell that I was punking him. It took everything I had not to laugh.

"Inventory is a beast," Maeve commiserated. "We have to do it in the studio all the time. I swear I think fairies come in the night and either make off with our yarn or multiply it when I'm not looking." She glanced at where Shane stood by the bar and then leaned forward and whispered conspiratorially, "I try to make my doctor's appointments on inventory day." She laughed. "Don't tell Shane."

"He won't hear it from me," I said. "It is dreadfully dull, but so important. I already feel as if I'm making an impact on the shop."

"No argument here," Kier said. His tone was as dry as plain toast.

"More hands do lighten the load," Maeve observed and turned to Kier. "You're lucky to have her."

There was a very long pause after Maeve spoke, so naturally I felt compelled to fill the void.

"Kier has been very effusive in his gratitude," I said. "Which, of course, makes it all worth it."

I said it just as he sipped his beer, and he immediately coughed and covered his mouth with his fist. It appeared he was choking. Couldn't happen to a nicer guy.

"Kier?" Maeve frowned at me. She turned to look at him and said, "Ah! I actually forgot that Kieran is your given name. You've been Murphy for as long as I can remember, haven't you?"

"Red is having a hard time remembering that everyone calls me Murphy," he said. His voice was low and deep and I felt it thrum along my side.

I drew in a quick breath and said, "And Kier is equally struggling to recall that I go by Em, not Red."

Maeve's eyes darted between us. Judging by her smirk, she'd caught on that there was a battle of wills in play, and she was fully engaged in whatever was happening on our side of the snug.

"Now why would I call you something as bland as 'Em' when you're obviously much feistier than the name signifies?" Kier asked. "Emily is a nice girl's name. You are not nice."

I slowly turned to face him and leaned back. Again, I glanced from his pint glass to his face, trying to determine if he was sober, because I was quite certain that I, Emily Allen, the pleaser, had never been called feisty in my entire life. I squinted at him.

"What?" he asked.

"I'm not feisty," I said. "And I am very, very nice."

"Well, that's a matter of opinion, isn't it?" he argued. "And my opinion is you've been giving me what for ever since you stepped into the Last Chapter this morning."

"*I've* been giving *you* what for?" I cried. "Who accused me of being a crazy stalker, refused to learn my name, and then assigned me the most boring task in the entire world second only to watching paint dry?"

Maeve propped her elbows on the table and rested her chin on her clasped hands. She was clearly enjoying herself.

Kier shrugged. "Don't fret, Red. Not everyone is cut out to work in a bookshop."

I gasped. Was he being serious right now? I studied his face, but he was looking into his pint as he brought it to his lips and then he took a long swallow, keeping his face masked by the glass. I turned away, refusing to let my eyes be drawn to his slightly pursed lips and long throat.

"Apparently, my new boss has forgotten that I used to be a librarian, a very good one," I said to Maeve.

"Apparently," she agreed. She looked positively delighted, as if she'd stumbled upon dinner and a show.

Kier was just putting his glass on the table and looked about to protest when Shane arrived bearing four glasses of whiskey and a wooden spoon with the number three written on it.

"Fish and chips coming up," he said. He propped the spoon in an empty glass so that the server could see it, no doubt, and took his seat beside Maeve. Lifting his glass, he said, "Sláinte."

We took up our glasses and tapped them together, repeating the Gaelic word roughly pronounced "slawn-che," which meant "health." I glanced at Kier out of the corner of my eye. He leaned back in his seat looking as content as a large cat who had no remorse for the riot of emotions he was causing within me. This irked me on so many levels.

I tipped the glass to my lips. The earthy smell of the whiskey was surprisingly pleasant, so I took a healthy swallow. As soon as it hit my throat, I knew I'd made a mistake. The burn was significant and I felt a sheen of tears dampen my eyes. I hoped my face hadn't gone purple as I strangled the cough that wanted to burst out of my throat. I also hoped my nose didn't start to run as I sucked in a breath, praying the fire would ease quickly.

"Murphy and Em were just telling me about Em's first day at the bookshop," Maeve said to Shane. She did not have the same hesitation as me with her whiskey and took a healthy sip without even wincing.

"Were they now?" Shane asked. "And how is the Last Chapter?"

"Desperate for professional help," I said. All three of them turned to me. Maybe the whiskey was making me too blunt. I lifted my glass as if I could hide behind it and took a more cautious sip.

A low rumble sounded next to me, and I was pretty sure my large cat was no longer purring, in fact, I was half afraid he was going to pounce.

"I suppose you believe hiring a know-it-all from the States is professional help," Kier said.

Ha! The big cat had claws. Well, so did I. I tossed back another gulp from my glass, surprised to find it almost empty. The fire rocketing down my throat matched the fire in my belly and I turned and faced him.

"Know-it-all?" I repeated.

"I said what I said." Kier leaned toward me. We were nose to nose and I was suddenly aware of every one of the thick black eyelashes surrounding his deep blue gaze. His evening beard coated his chin with stubble and it occurred to me that he wasn't a big cat at all, nope, the man was a pirate. An argumentative, whiskey-swilling, amazing-smelling pirate. I felt something flutter deep in my belly. I shut that down immediately.

"'People generally see what they look for, and hear what they listen for,'" I said.

"Are you quoting *To Kill a Mockingbird* to me?" he asked. He looked equal parts indignant and impressed, which were emotions I shared since he'd correctly identified the quote's source.

"If the literary quote fits," I said, trying to appear casual.

"I am not *looking* for you to be a know-it-all," he said. "I have evidence. You're here one day and you have Ma believing she's going to write again, Brigid is planning to change the café menu, and Oisín and Eun-ji think we need to upgrade our entire computer system and won't stop pestering me about it."

"Siobhan is going to write her book," I insisted. "And Brigid should change the menu if it would make the job more interesting for her, and your software is ancient. Your staff deserves better than that, as do I, since at this rate I'll be doing your inventory until I'm a shriveled-up old woman."

Kier's jaw tightened and his nostrils flared. He looked as if he was hanging on to his temper by a thread. In my mind, I pulled out a sharp pair of shears and snipped that thread. I don't know what it was about this guy that made me want to goad him, but I did. We continued to stare at each other, neither of us willing to look away first.

"Come along now, Maeve, they're playing our song. Let's leave these two to sort it out." Shane slid out of the booth and held out his hand to his wife.

Maeve winked at me and said, "Hold your ground, Em. You'll never get it back if you don't." Then she took Shane's hand and they disappeared into the crowd of customers who were dancing at the far side of the bar in front of a three-piece band, cranking out trad music with a lively beat.

I collapsed against the seat back. "I think we just chased off my landlords."

Kier settled into the bench as well and said, "Nah, they just found something better to do."

I looked out across the bar. It felt as if the entire village of Finn's Hollow was packed into the joint. They were young and old, families, and groups of friends. The trio of musicians in the corner was festive and fun, and I watched Shane spin Maeve as they danced across the floor. They were smiling at each other and it made my heart swell to see their mutual joy in being together. They reminded me of Sam and Ben and my relationship goals.

Meanwhile, Kier and I sat in stony silence. Normally, I would have said nothing, stewing in my irritation, but the whiskey had oiled the hinges of the rusty cage where I kept my inner extrovert under lock and key and she pushed her way out.

"Why exactly do you dislike me so much?" I asked. I could feel my head wobble on my shoulders a bit. The whiskey was definitely kicking in.

"I don't dislike you." He didn't look at me but continued to watch the musicians while scanning the room as if looking for anyone to talk to but me.

"It feels like you do," I persisted.

He turned to face me. There was a flicker of regret in his eyes. Maybe he hadn't meant to be so harsh.

"I don't dislike you. I can't because I don't even know you," he said. "Although, given enough time around your feisty personality, I'm sure I could grow to dislike you."

"See, that right there." I slapped the tabletop with my palm and the glass with the spoon in it jumped. Kier reached out and moved it back from the edge.

"That's dislike if I've ever heard it," I said.

"No, it isn't," he argued. He gestured between us. "What I feel for you isn't personal. It's just business. The truth is, Red, you don't belong here and as soon as you figure that out, you'll hurry home to wherever it is you came from."

"Martha's Vineyard," I said. He stared at me. Why were his lips so full and with a little dip in the upper one? It was annoying. "It's an island."

"I know where and what Martha's Vineyard is," he said. He sounded peeved. Good.

"And now you know it's where I'm from," I said. "Oak Bluffs specifically. It's a lot like Finn's Hollow, actually. A small community with a heavy tourist trade."

"You sound homesick. You should go back."

"I'm not," I said. I was surprised to find that I was telling the truth. I was happy to be doing something different with my life, having an adventure in a brand-new place. It was exhilarating.

"Are you sure about that?" he asked.

I thought about my mom and how she'd refused to see me off. It had been a week of increasingly histrionic scenes leading up to my departure, which had left me wrung out and exhausted. She had done everything she could to try and get me to change my mind and stay. I'd refused. She'd become more furious and desperate with each passing day.

I knew that the hateful things she'd said to me were because she didn't get her way and there was nothing my mother loathed more than that, but it had only caused me to want to flee even farther away from her than Ireland.

"Positive," I assured him.

"So, that's how it is." He wagged a finger at me as if he'd just figured out the key to me.

I gave him a side-eye. "How what is?"

"Bad breakup?" he asked. "Is that why you wrote the letter to my mother and then accepted her ill-advised job offer? You're escaping a heartbreak?"

I laughed. It wasn't a demure giggle or an amused chortle, oh no, it was a full on guffaw. Kier looked at me in surprise but I couldn't stop.

"What?" he asked.

"I'd have to have been in love to have my heart broken," I said. "And I can state for the record that I've never suffered either of those afflictions."

"Wait." He held up his hand in a stop gesture. "You're winding me up, aren't you?"

I shook my head at him. "Nope."

Kier frowned. "But you're a grown woman. Surely, you've had breakups and heartbreak and such."

"No," I said. "I mean I've dated, but I never cared for any of the men enough to call it love. Mostly, I just felt relief when my relationships ended."

"That can't be right. Look at you, you're fit and obviously smart, how have you not been bagged and tagged by an eager fella?"

"Bagged and tagged?" I asked. "Like I'm a sheep?"

A flicker of a smile curved his lips as the server arrived, bearing four large plates of fish and chips. Her timing was impeccable, saving Kier from answering. He raised his hand and waved to Shane and Maeve on the dance floor. They stopped by the bar on their way back, bringing a pint for each of us from the local McGill's brewery.

"Murphy, the trio is in fine form tonight," Shane said. "You should take Em out for a trot on the floor."

I felt my face grow hot. Inexplicably, the thought of dancing with Kier made my hands sweat and my heart pound.

"That's never going to happen," Kier said. He picked up his fork and tucked into his batter-fried fish. I frowned at him when he glanced my way. "It's nothing personal, Red." He shrugged. "First, you're an employee and second, I don't dance."

"Oh, are you that bad at it, Kier?"

"It's Murphy, and if you value the ability to walk, you'll steer clear of me if I ever approach the dance floor," he confessed.

I laughed. I liked self-deprecating Kier. He glanced at me and this time the flicker turned into a slow smile that curved his lips, making him even more handsome. As if remembering he was supposed to be ambivalent about me, he abruptly turned away and grabbed his beer. He chugged half of it, wiping the smile from his face.

Confused, I glanced down at my plate and all thought of Kier and his smile vanished. The piece of fish nestled on top of a pile of fries, or chips as they called them, was so large it hung off the sides of the plate. There was a small pile of greens off to the side as well as several dips, one of which Maeve informed me was mayonnaise whipped with arugula and garlic. It was amazing.

My hunger overruled every other emotion and I wasn't alone as the table became silent while we devoured our suppers. The flaky fish with the seasoned batter had not been overly talked up by Maeve. It was delicious and I ate every bite.

Kier and Shane wrestled for the bill. I offered to pay and was soundly ignored. Maeve patted my hand and said, "Don't even think it. This is our way of welcoming you to Finn's Hollow."

"Thank you," I said. "I really do appreciate it."

When we turned back, the men had settled the tab and were sliding out of the snug. We followed and put on our jackets, preparing for the cold that awaited.

"Ready to go?" Shane asked. "Or do you need another nip for the walk?"

I wobbled a bit on my feet and said, "No, I'm good. Thank you."

During supper, we'd each had another whiskey and a second beer. Thankfully the fish and chips had been generous and was sopping up all of the alcohol in my system. At least, I hoped it was. The trio in the corner was still playing and I resisted the urge to tap my toes.

Maeve looped her arm through mine as we followed the men. Kier held the door open and we stepped outside with several of the locals in the bar calling out farewells as we went.

Kier and Shane walked in front while Maeve and I brought up the rear. She kept her arm in mine and I wondered if she knew I'd had too much to drink and was making certain I didn't fall on my butt. I appreciated her more than I could say—mostly because walking and talking at the same time was beyond my skill set at the moment.

"You and Kier certainly have some chemistry bubbling between you," Maeve whispered.

"Shh." I put my finger over my lips and glanced at Kier's back, hoping he didn't hear her. Judging by the way he was leaning down to listen to Shane, who was talking about the local football scores, it didn't seem likely. I moved in closer and said, "I don't think he likes me very much."

She looked surprised. "That wasn't the feeling I got. He couldn't take his eyes off you."

"Exactly. Because he doesn't like me," I said. "He's very odd about my working with Siobhan, you know, to help her write her book."

"Odd?" she asked.

"Yes," I said. "I get the feeling he doesn't want her to do it, which I think is very strange."

Maeve was silent for a bit. I glanced ahead and saw Kier say something that made Shane slap him on the shoulder and throw back his head and laugh. From the wobble in Shane's walk, I suspected he was feeling the whiskey as much as I was. Kier, however, looked as steady as a barge in a harbor.

"I imagine it does seem peculiar," Maeve said. "But I can assure you that anything Kier does in regards to Siobhan is because he's a good son who loves his mam. He protects her. He always has."

"He's protecting her from me?" I asked. "What exactly does he think I'm going to do to her?"

Maeve looked sympathetic but said, "You'd have to ask him that."

Before I could blast out the many questions I had, Shane turned around and held out his hand to Maeve. "We're coming up on the big puddle, love, take my hand and I'll guide you around it."

Maeve leaned close and whispered, "More like I'm going to keep him from a late night swim."

I laughed, feeling the lack of her warmth immediately when she let go of me to take her husband's hand.

"How about you, Red?" Kier asked. "Need a hand?"

I paused beside him. The puddle truly was a small pond and under the light of the street lamp, its surface was as smooth as glass, making it impossible to see how deep it went. I imagined stepping into it as if I were Tig McMorrow slipping into a fantastical undersea world where I could breathe through the water and harness a seahorse and live in a castle made of shells.

"Well?" he asked.

I shook the daydream off and faced him. "And give you the opportunity to drown me?" I asked. "Hard pass."

He put his hand on his chest. "You wound me, Red."

I studied him. The teasing light in his eyes belied any notion that he might be suffering hurt feelings. I also realized that the booze was hitting harder than I thought because, while I'd thought him attractive before, in this moment he was breathtakingly handsome and I had the horrifying thought that he was the sort of man a woman developed an unrequited crush on, pining for any crumb of his attention only to be ignored or dismissed because she was so far out of his league that he never reciprocated her feelings.

"Oh, hell no," I said.

He blinked and cocked his head to the side. "What's that? Are you all right?"

"I'm perfectly fine. And I fully intend to stay that way. Good night, Kier."

"It's Murphy, you infuriating woman," he growled but it lacked heat.

I ignored him and turned to navigate my way around the puddle, inching my way along the side of it until I caught up to Maeve and

Shane. They waved to Kier, who now stood on the opposite side of the small lake.

"'Night, Murphy," Shane called.

"Don't be a stranger," Maeve cried.

"Slán." Kier waved and turned to go back to the main road. I assumed he lived farther up the hill and I wondered what his house looked like. Not my business, I told myself. He was my boss, one who didn't particularly like me, and that was it.

Maeve and Shane walked me to the door of my cottage.

"Give us a shout if you need anything and welcome to Finn's Hollow," Shane said. He began to list to the side and Maeve grabbed him about the middle.

"All right, love, off you pop," Maeve said. "Good night, Em. We're so glad you're here."

"I am, too." I smiled.

I watched as they crossed the yard and entered the back door of their house. Once the interior light switched on, I stepped into the cottage and shut and locked my door. It was warm in the tiny house and I hung up my jacket and toed off my shoes, making myself at home. In my socks, I padded to the kitchen, needing a drink—not booze, definitely no more of that.

I opened several cupboards until I gathered a tin of loose leaf tea, a diffuser, and a ceramic teapot. Thankfully, being a lover of tea, I knew how to make it the traditional way. While the tea steeped, I put on my pajamas, added a warm robe, and found the novel I'd been reading on the plane when I flew over from the States. I poured myself a cup and sat on the couch, pulling a glorious ruby and cream–colored throw over my legs.

I assumed Maeve or Shane had woven it. Its deep red color was an accent all throughout the cottage. The kitchen was compact, but the living room could comfortably hold four adults on its couch and two arm chairs, cozily arranged around the fireplace. There was one bedroom and a bathroom on the opposite side of the house, both small but perfect for me.

I was short and on the slight side of medium in build. My friend Sam, the chef, was always having me taste test her recipes by saying I didn't eat enough. But I did eat. A lot. I also happened to have a very fast metabolism, probably from anxiety, which made gaining weight a challenge. In a world where the booty was the favored part of a woman's anatomy, I had a flat bottom that not even yoga pants could make cute. I wondered what part of a woman Kier found attractive. Then I shook my head. Nope. I wasn't going there.

I reached for my shoulder bag, which was on the floor by the coffee table, and retrieved my phone, opening the voicemail menu. There was a recent message from Sam, hoping my day had gone well. I glanced at the clock. It was just after ten o'clock here, which was after five on the Vineyard. I knew Sam would be prepping for her happy hour at the inn where she worked, so I decided to call her tomorrow. I generally avoided texting Sam since she was dyslexic and preferred voicemail.

Next I glanced at the other voicemail messages. Unsurprisingly, there were a lot and all from my mother. I blew out a slow breath as I felt my stress level spike. I closed the voicemail, not up to the task of listening to them, and opened my text messages. There I found what appeared to be an entire novel broken into chapters also from my mother. I scrolled through her tirade, the last three messages were the same: **CALL ME NOW** all in caps. The last one was sent a half hour ago. I needed to call her back but I knew it wasn't going to go well. As if sensing my hesitation, my phone rang and I jumped. It was Mom. Bracing myself with a sip of tea, I hit accept.

Six

"Emily Katherine Allen." My mother only used my full name when she was furious. "Do you have any idea how upset I've been? Of course you don't. You're too busy living your new glamorous life."

And there it was—the first guilt jab. I thought about the ancient laptop Kier had stuck me with and the drudgery of inventory. *Glamorous* was not the word I would have chosen.

A small sigh escaped me. "I'm sorry you were upset. There was no need to be, Mom. I called you last night to let you know I arrived safely at the cottage."

"That was last night. You didn't call me this morning or all day. For all I knew, you could have been murdered in your sleep!" she cried. "And I would never know, because you don't answer calls or texts anymore."

I felt my shoulders draw up tight. Tammy Lynn Allen was an expert at making me feel awful. No matter what I did, it was thoughtless, inconsiderate, or never enough, and it always caused her to be angry or hurt.

"I was at work all day and unable to respond." I kept my voice even. I had learned early in life not to show too much emotion around my mother or she'd weaponize it against me. "When I arrived home, my landlords took me to dinner, so I'm just getting your messages now."

"Dinner?" she asked. "You went out to dinner with new friends? How nice. I had a can of tomato soup and a grilled cheese sandwich at home. Alone."

There it was. The right hook of shame following the jab of guilt. I pictured us in a boxing ring, with me trying to outrun my mother's enormous gloved fists, but every time she hit me, painful words exploded out of her gloves, knocking me down.

"I'm sure one of your friends would love to join you for dinner," I suggested.

"No, they all have families," she argued. "Families who love them and want to be with them."

Oof! She had wound up to deliver a knockout punch of sad reproach. I was on the ropes. I closed my eyes. I took a steadying breath. Dr. Davis, the therapist I'd been seeing before I left Martha's Vineyard, had helped me understand that I wasn't responsible for my mother or her emotions. It wasn't my job to fill the void she felt after my father left. While I cared for my mother, I didn't have to sacrifice my health and happiness for her.

I'd asked my mother to come to therapy with me, so we could work on our relationship, but she refused, calling it nonsense. She felt I was just an ungrateful daughter, trying to escape my duty to her. Tammy Lynn simply could not, or more accurately would not, accept living on her own and being responsible for her own life.

My father, or as Mom called him, "the two-timing turd," had left her while I was away at college. I'd had a few glorious years of life at Smith College and then it was over. My father refused to help pay my tuition since he now had a young girlfriend to keep in the style to which she wanted to become accustomed and my mother had a complete nervous breakdown.

Unable to pay for school on my own and afraid that Mom might harm herself, I'd moved home to Oak Bluffs, switched to online school for both my undergraduate and graduate degrees, and I'd been there ever since. Almost a decade of my life spent trying to make Tammy Lynn happy and she never ever was. As far as I was concerned, I'd done my time.

During the past summer, when my hypochondria had become unmanageable, one of the things Dr. Davis helped me realize was that the unhealthy relationship I had with my mother was causing a lot of my illness anxiety disorder. Despite not really being there for me as a kid—Mom had been a full-time country-clubber with a loaded social calendar in her role as the doctor's wife—she had expected me to be there for her as an adult when her life fell apart.

As Dr. Davis explained it, I had been riding a wave of resentment for a very long time. Because of my pleasing nature, all of my suppressed anger had come out as hypochondria. When Sam and I talked about it, she theorized that I was afraid I was going to die of some horrible disease because I hadn't really had a chance to live. My entire twenties had been spent trying to appease my mother. I was done.

I still had random bouts of anxiety when I was highly stressed where I was certain I was going to die—thus my fear that I'd contracted bubonic plague on the plane—but they'd become fewer as I accepted the job in Ireland, planned my move, and drew some healthy boundaries between me and my mom, for which I was grateful.

It had been a lot of hard work, and I was not about to let Tammy

Lynn and her manipulative personality drag me back. After years of sleepwalking through my existence, I was going to live the fullest life I possibly could.

"Maybe it's time for you to expand your social circle and make some new friends," I said.

"I can't!" she wailed. "I'm old and ugly and fat and no one wants to be my friend."

"I'm sure that's not true," I said. In an instant I flashed back to a childhood of similar scenes between my parents and I felt a wave of empathy for my dad. And then, strangely, it was as if my dad's voice was suddenly coming out of my mouth. I went with it, saying exactly what I'd heard him say so many times when my mother was in one of her moods. "Listen, I have to be up early for work tomorrow so I can't talk about this right now."

"No, Emily, don't you dare hang up on me—" Tammy Lynn was revving up so I interrupted.

"Good night, Mom," I said.

"You're a horrible daughter!" she shouted.

"I love you, too," I said, surprising myself. I ended the call and muted the ringer on my phone.

I imagined there was going to be another novel of text messages on my phone in the morning. I didn't care. At least I'd have something to chat about with Dr. Davis when we did our weekly session via video conferencing.

I sat in the silence for a beat, appreciating the peace. The quiet cottage could have been scary but after years of living with a person who required a high level of chaos and drama at all times, I found it was delightfully restful and cozy. I picked up my novel and sipped my tea. My shoulders dropped, and I burrowed under my blanket and sighed with contentment.

I awoke three hours later with the book on my face. It took me a moment to remember where I was and I staggered to my feet. I picked up my mug. It wouldn't do to have my mother yell at me for leaving it on the coffee table . . . Wait. She wasn't here. She wasn't in charge. I was. I put the mug down on its coaster. It could stay on the table all night if I wanted it to. Ha!

I turned to go to the bedroom. I managed four steps until I doubled back and retrieved the mug. Damn it. I put it in the sink, but I didn't wash it. So there. Being queen of my own castle was going to take some practice, but I was eager to give it a go.

As I adjusted to my new life over the next week, it fell into a routine. I met with Siobhan in the morning and we . . . well, we wandered the village quite a bit. She introduced me to her friends, and I finally heard the tale of why the Top of the Hill pub was named so inaccurately. Michael Stewart, the owner, said the pub had started at the top of the hill but one year a horrible rainy season came upon Finn's Hollow. It rained so much that the townspeople had to use boats to get around instead of cars, the sheep began to grow gills and fins, and then one night on the heaviest rain of them all, the pub slipped from its foundation at the top of the hill and landed at the bottom.

The townspeople were happy because they didn't have to get up the hill in the rain for their usual nip, and the bar owner at the time was as well. He announced to one and all that he wasn't going to change the name because anyone who went looking for the pub on the top of the hill would surely be able to find it on the bottom.

My favorite shop was Sally's Sweet Shop. It was tucked in between Hazel's Tea House and the local wine store, and was impossible to miss because it was painted pale pink with a bubblegum pink trim and had large yellow and green flower pots in the shape of teacups adorning the ledge of its front window. In each pot was a blooming cyclamen, their pink petals an irresistibly cheering sight.

The owner, Sally, distinctive because of her short white hair with vibrant purple bangs, waved to us through the window and we entered the second most magical shop in the village, the Last Chapter being first, naturally. It was a tiny space packed from the floor to the rafters with jars of loose sweets. Siobhan and I discovered we shared a severe candy affliction, and she introduced me to an entire world of jellies. Sally held up a bag of my favorite fizzy cherry and I nodded in answer to the silent question. It felt good to be a regular, a lot like being home on the Vineyard where the servers at the Grape knew I was going to ask for a raisin Danish as soon as I walked in the door.

"Hi, Sally," I said.

"Hiya, Sally," Siobhan echoed.

"Mornin', ladies," Sally replied. Then she glanced over her shoulder at the clock on the wall. It was a cat, whose tail and eyes moved as it kept time. "Or more accurately, good afternoon."

I was due at the bookshop but didn't want to rush Siobhan. I had noticed that time had no meaning for her. She ate when she was hungry, slept when she was tired, and didn't bother much about keeping a schedule. It bent my brain but I was trying to adjust as she was my boss. Still, I was beginning to suspect that the lack of a schedule was not helping with getting the writing done. There was absolutely no accountability happening.

We left Sally's and made our way back to the Last Chapter. I was debating how to broach the subject of setting up a schedule for writing when we bumped into Father Mulligan, the local priest, who was an avid fly fisherman. We stood on the curb, munching our jellies while listening to his latest man versus fish exploit, when Kier leaned out the front door of the bookshop.

"Were you planning to work today or Thursday, Red?" His

accent gave *Thursday* a hard *T* and it was ridiculous how charming it made his chastisement of me sound. Seriously, ridiculous.

"Be right there!" I called. I turned back to Siobhan and Father Mulligan. "Sorry, I have to . . ." My voice trailed off as I jerked my thumb in the direction of the shop.

"Not at all," Father Mulligan said. "I'd talk your ears off if I wasn't checked, isn't that right, Siobhan?"

She smiled and munched on her fizzy strawberry. "Off you pop, Em. We're done for the day."

Done with what, I wanted to ask, but I didn't. Another morning had passed and Siobhan hadn't written a word. I wasn't sure what to do about that—if anything. I was just the assistant. It wasn't for me to crack the whip. If Siobhan wanted to stop at the local flower shop and browse for two hours while she chatted with Geraldine the florist, was it my place to say no? It didn't feel like it. So, I just went along. Truthfully, I enjoyed getting to know everyone, but I couldn't shake the feeling that I was failing.

"Thanks for joining us," Kier said as I stepped inside.

"My pleasure," I lied.

If my mornings were unstructured field trips about town, my afternoons were a rinse and repeat of my very first day. Each and every afternoon, I slogged my way through the books on the third floor, hoping my laptop would catch on fire and save me from being at the mercy of this antiquated equipment, but no. It just kept whirring away, moving like a snail across a sandy beach.

As I was waiting for Slo-Mo—yes, I named it—to save the latest record I had entered, I reached for the next book on the shelf. It was a slim volume entitled *The Broken Window*. The cover indicated it was a mystery in the traditional sense, which seemed promising as I always loved a good whodunit, but then I saw the author's name and I dropped the book.

The stark white background with the illustration of a hand holding a knife dripping blood as seen through a broken window was standard mystery fare, but the author's name was not. Along the bottom in a font much smaller than the title was the name Kieran Murphy.

It couldn't be. Kieran? My Kieran? No, wait, I didn't mean "my" like that, I meant it as in the Kieran I knew. Had he really written a book? Why hadn't anyone said anything? Why was it shelved way up here on the third floor in the shop's purgatory?

I picked up the book and opened the back cover. Maybe it was a coincidence. Nope. There, in a small black-and-white photo, was my brooding romance hero boss staring back at me. He looked much younger in the picture, but the same tousled dark hair, piercing eyes, and thick eyelashes were unmistakable, also he wasn't smiling, which clinched it.

"Well, I'll be damned," I muttered.

"How's it going up here, Red?" *Ack!* There he was. The devil himself coming to see if I was sufficiently miserable no doubt.

I shoved Kier's book under a pile of other books and struck a casual pose instead of just working. I don't know why, probably because I'm terrible at subterfuge. He appeared around the bookcase and leaned against it, smirking down at me. I'd noticed since Siobhan and I had done everything but write during the past week, his initial hostility toward me had waned a bit. He wasn't exactly friendly, but he seemed less suspicious.

"If by that you mean is the computer going so slow that time is actually moving backward? Then, yes, all is status quo up here," I said.

"Excellent." He nodded. "Planning to quit yet?"

No way was I quitting. I thought about his book hidden behind the others. Definitely not before I read his book at any rate.

"Sorry, no," I said.

"Pity."

"Hmm."

He glanced down at the pile of books by my feet. I felt my heart pound. Had I hidden his book sufficiently? I had no idea how he'd feel about me reading it, but I was absolutely reading it—tonight, in fact, as soon as I got home.

"What's wrong, Red?"

"Nothing." It came out too quickly and his eyes narrowed. I tried to save myself. "Other than mind-numbing boredom, ancient equipment, and a heartless boss who doesn't care about my health and well-being."

"You poor lamb." His brow furrowed and he looked genuinely distraught. "I had no idea you were suffering so. I must make amends immediately."

My surprise must have shown on my face. His smile was pure mischief when he said, "All of that gallivanting around town with Siobhan must be just brutal. I'll talk to her and see if I can convince her to assign you to the third floor for mornings as well."

My fingers itched to pick up the closest book and toss it at him. Instead, I smiled. "You miss having me around in the morning that much, do you?"

I expected him to scoff and deny it. Instead, he raised an eyebrow and held my gaze. I had no idea what he was thinking but I could feel an awareness between us spark like a live electric wire. His glance moved to my mouth and then back to my eyes. There was an unexpected heat in his gaze and I felt that same pesky fluttery feeling I'd experienced at the pub.

"Murphy!" Oisín bellowed from downstairs.

Kier hesitated for a moment but then pushed off the shelf. "Duty calls." He turned to leave, but called back over his shoulder, "Chin up, Red, it's only three more hours until we close."

I watched him walk away, waiting . . . waiting . . . waiting until he started down the stairs and disappeared from view. Then I dropped to the floor and grabbed his book. I wanted to read it right then and there but I didn't dare. Reading fiction—even not so great books—was an immersive experience for me, so much so that I completely lost track of my surroundings. It'd be a nightmare if Kier caught me, which he would because I'd never hear him coming.

The first hurdle in this covert operation was how to get the book by everyone without them noticing. Siobhan had said I could take home any book I fancied, so technically, I could just walk out with Kier's book. But I didn't want everyone to see that I was reading the boss's book. It would be awkward even if that was just my take. Without overthinking it, I shoved the book into the waistband of my pants and pulled my sweater over it. All I had to do was get it into my large shoulder bag, and I was home free. Easy peasy, right?

"What did you shove in your trousers?"

"Ah!" I yelped and jumped. I turned around and saw Niamh standing there. I put my hand over my heart, trying to calm its rapid beating. She was dressed as usual in a black wool skirt and black tights paired with a white collared shirt and a blue and gray striped tie, over which she wore a blue sweater. I had seen most of the children and teens who came into the book shop during the week wearing similar attire and realized it was the local school uniform. She wore her hair parted in the middle and hanging loose, halfway down her back.

The teen cocked her head to the side, studying me. It was the first time she'd gotten this close to me, and I felt like I was trying to befriend a wild creature. I didn't want to do anything that would scare her away. Of course, I also didn't want to admit that I had Kier's book shoved in my waistband. Dilemma.

"A book," I said.

She stared at me. I stared back. We were at a stalemate. I was on my guard, half expecting her to either put a hex on me or disappear right in front of my eyes, so I was completely unprepared for what she said next.

"You don't behave like other women around Murphy." This seemed to baffle her.

"Meaning?"

"You don't toss your hair or make big doe eyes at him." Niamh opened her eyes wide, fluttered her lashes, and threw her long dark hair over her shoulder. It was comically overdramatic, and I smiled as I'd seen more than one female customer do that when Kier entered the shop.

I nodded. "That's because other women find him attractive."

"And you don't?" She gave me a skeptical side-eye.

I felt my face get warm. Niamh had neatly backed me into a corner but there was no way I was going to admit that I had fantasized about my boss as a romance hero. I fully planned to take that information with me to the grave. "Whether I find him attractive or not doesn't signify as I'm quite positive Kier doesn't like me."

"I wouldn't be so sure of that." A small smile curved her lips, giving her an impish charm. "You should flirt with him and see."

"Ha! No." I shook my head and laughed. "Can you even imagine?" I stepped out of the shelves and clasped my hands under my chin. I batted my lashes at Niamh and in a super high, breathy voice, I said, "Oh, Murphy, are you an earthquake? Because you just rocked my world." Then I mimicked her exaggerated hair toss.

Niamh busted out laughing and said, "That's awful, truly terrible."

Encouraged by her laughter, I kept going. "Hey, Murphy, can we take a picture together? I want to show my friends what my future boyfriend looks like."

Niamh doubled over and hugged her sides. Through her guffaw, she said, "Even worse!"

I dropped my voice as low as it could go and purred, "Murphy, I hope you know CPR, because you're so handsome, you take my breath away."

With a cackle, Niamh dropped to sit on the floor. When she looked up at me, I saw tears in her eyes right before they went wide in horror. I spun around to see what she was looking at and saw Murphy leaning against a bookcase right behind me.

"I think the takeaway here is that you find me handsome, Red," he said.

My face went scorching hot. This was bad, so bad, and not just because I had his book shoved in my pants. I clasped my hands in front of me trying to hide the suspicious bulge.

"We were just . . . um . . . It was a joke." Even to my own ears, I sounded defensive.

"Right." His voice was doubtful and his eyes twinkled as he took in my complete humiliation. "In any case, I just came up to let Niamh know her mam is here."

"Oh." Niamh jumped to her feet, clearly relieved to escape the scene of the crime. "See you tomorrow, Em." With a twirl of her skirt, she disappeared down the stairs. Traitor.

"I've never heard Niamh laugh like that," Kier observed.

Drowning in embarrassment, I couldn't even appreciate the victory that Niamh had called me by name. "She's a good kid."

Kier nodded in agreement and headed back to the stairs. He was leaving without saying anything? My relief was beyond measure. I should have known better.

At the top of the steps, he paused and in a low teasing voice he said, "Take your breath away, eh? Maybe it's you who misses me in the morning, Red."

The tension pulsed between us, making my heart race. I held his stare with a steady gaze that inexplicably made him grin, triggering a tingling warmth to bloom in my belly. I held my breath until he disappeared down the stairs and thought how unfortunate it was that a meteor wasn't likely to flatten the bookstore in that moment and spare me from the humiliation of having to face him again.

With a sigh, I went back to the drudgery that was inventory, trying not to dwell on what Kier must be thinking about the scene he'd interrupted. He had to know it was a joke, right? Ugh.

After another hour of grueling data entry, I wasted no time in hustling my contraband downstairs during my break. I popped into the workroom where we kept our personal belongings and when the coast was clear, I tucked Kier's book into my shoulder bag. I desperately wanted to read it right now, but I knew the smarter play was to take it home where I could read it on the down-low.

I left the workroom and dipped into the café. I thought I could broach the subject of Kier the author with Brigid. Surely, she must know he'd written a mystery. When I arrived, she was just putting the finishing touches on her latest "tester" item. It was Irish shortbread flavored with whiskey instead of vanilla extract and she'd frosted them with an Irish whiskey–infused icing as well. I sat at the empty counter, and Brigid poured me a cup of coffee and plated several of the round biscuits.

"If I like the recipe, I'm going to get fancy and cut them into the shape of shamrocks. I think the tourists will enjoy that." Brigid watched me with a wide-eyed nervousness that I could have told her was unnecessary because she'd treated me to baked goods every afternoon and had yet to make anything that wasn't excellent.

I took a bite. It was crispy and light and buttery and I loved the smoky flavor of the whiskey. "This is fantastic," I said through a mouthful.

"What was that?" She cupped her ear with her hand. "I couldn't understand you through the biscuit." Then she laughed, letting me know she'd heard me and was pleased.

"Your best experiment to date," I said. I took a sip of coffee and another nibble of cookie. "I've had shortbread before but nothing like this."

"It's the Irish butter," Brigid said. "It has a higher percentage of butterfat so it makes the shortbread richer and prolongs the crispness." She picked up a biscuit and broke it in half. "There is no substitute."

I laughed and was about to segue the conversation to Kier's literary aspirations, when my phone chimed. I took it out of my pocket and glanced at the display. My mother.

After our disastrous call last week, I had set some boundaries as Dr. Davis had taught me. Mom wasn't to call or text me when I was at work unless it was an emergency and in return I agreed to call her every day to check in. I had suggested that I text her, but Tammy Lynn had made it clear that she wanted to hear my voice because a kidnapper could abduct me and text her using my phone and she'd never know. Fine. Whatever.

"All right, Em?" Brigid asked.

I glanced up. "Yeah, I have to take this. It's my mom."

"Of course." She nodded and moved a tactful distance away.

I hesitated. Tammy Lynn had pitched an epic fit when I had asserted my boundaries, but I was holding the line. Now I was torn. I did not want this to be an emergency call, but I really didn't want it not to be one either. I had no choice. I had to answer. I slid my thumb across the screen.

"Hi, Mom, is everything okay?" I asked. I could hear the caution in my voice and I winced. I'd wanted to sound neutral.

"No, it most certainly is not." Her voice had that particular meanness that surfaced when she was obsessing about something that was bothering her. I'd seen her do this when my father displeased her. One time, she even threw her wine glass at him when he walked in the door an hour later than expected even though he'd called to tell her he would be late. This did not bode well for me.

"What's wrong?" I asked. This time my voice was perfectly even.

"You! How could you leave me?" Tammy Lynn's voice screeched out of my phone and I jerked it away from my ear to save my eardrum. The sobbing that poured out of my phone was so loud, it sounded as if I had it on speaker.

I saw Brigid's shocked expression and I forced a smile. It actually hurt my face. I hunched my shoulders and put the phone back to my ear while lowering the volume with my thumb.

"I'm at work right now. Is there an emergency or not?"

"Of course, it's an emergency—" Tammy Lynn broke off and continued to sob. It was a gut-wrenching noise and a few months ago I would have felt compelled to stop it by any means necessary. But at the moment, I felt nothing. Maybe it was because there were thousands of miles between us or perhaps I was just worn out, either way I was numb.

When the sobbing waned, I asked, "What exactly is the problem, Mom?"

"You! You're a selfish, spoiled little bitch!" Tammy Lynn shouted. "You had no right to leave. You're my daughter. You're supposed to take care of me. It's your duty."

I sighed. Obviously, there was no emergency, which was good. It gave me the freedom to let her words drop between us, sitting there like a ball I refused to throw back.

My therapist had taught me to do this when my mother got riled up and verbally abusive. Dr. Davis said not to engage, because any defensiveness on my part would give my mother something she could throw back at me, so I said nothing.

"I need you, Emily. There. Are you satisfied?" Tammy Lynn asked. "Does that make you feel important enough?"

Still, I said nothing. Brigid was busily cleaning her kitchen counter, but I knew she could hear. My mother's voice carried like gunfire.

When I didn't answer, my mother tried a different tack, her voice sounding sad and babyish. "I miss you, Emily. Is that so wrong? To miss my baby?"

I wanted to scream. I called her every day, every single day. I knew she wanted me to say that I missed her, too, but I didn't, and I wasn't going to say it. She'd just use it against me.

"I'm glad you shared your feelings with me. I'm at work right now and this is not a good time for this conversation, so I'm going to hang up. I'll call you tomorrow," I said.

"Tomorrow?" she cried. "You have to call me tonight. You promised you'd call me every day."

"I did but now I don't need to because you called me," I said. "Goodbye, Mom."

I ended the call before she started yelling again. My phone immediately started to chirp and buzz. I put it on mute. I reached for a shortbread and shoved the whole thing in my mouth.

Brigid put down her cleaning cloth and moved to join me. She stopped short, glancing over my shoulder, and said, "I'm going to check my next batch of shortbread. Be right back."

I supposed she had no idea what to say to me. I wouldn't either, truth to be told. I took a sip of coffee, washing down the biscuit I'd swallowed practically whole. As someone slid onto the stool beside mine, I turned to give them a polite smile but it froze on my face. Kier.

Seven

Of course he was here. Because my previous embarrassment wasn't enough. I glanced away, studying the remaining coffee in my cup as if it held all the answers to the universe. I wrapped my icy fingers around the mug, letting the warmth seep in. My phone vibrated in my pocket but I ignored it. I wondered if Kier could hear it. I wondered how much he had overheard.

"How are Brig's latest tester biscuits?" he asked. He picked one up off the plate in front of us and held it up to the light like it was a rare diamond before taking a bite.

I didn't answer. My overabundance of self-consciousness made my throat tight.

"Huh. There's something subversive about these," he said.

"It's the whiskey," I replied. The words slipped out before I could check them, but I so appreciated that he didn't mention the phone call I'd just received that I would absolutely talk about a cookie and in great detail if it meant not discussing my mother.

"Whiskey?" he asked. He pulled the plate toward him and I laughed. When he smiled at me, his gaze held an understanding I wasn't prepared for. "Why don't you take the rest of the day off, Red?"

"Oh, no." I shook my head. Kier telling me to take the afternoon off clinched it. He'd definitely heard my mother on the phone.

"I insist." He raised his hand in a stop gesture. "You jumped right into work and barely got a chance to get settled. Go home and catch your breath."

Brigid was coming back from the kitchen with more shortbread. She glanced between us and appeared to be relieved by what she saw. She set the baking tray down on the granite counter. Using a spatula, she carefully placed the shortbread in the display case beside the counter.

"Tell Red I'm right," Kier said to her.

"That would depend upon what you're saying to her, wouldn't it?" Brigid asked.

"I told her to take the rest of the afternoon off," he said.

Brigid nodded. "First sensible thing you've said all day."

"He did compliment your shortbread," I said.

"Second thing then. Go on home, Em, before he changes his mind." She finished offloading the shortbread and turned to bring the baking sheet back to the kitchen.

Kier took another biscuit off the plate. "I didn't compliment the biscuits," he corrected me. "I called them subversive. I find it fascinating that you consider being called subversive praise." He leaned back in his seat and studied me with one eyebrow raised.

I felt my face grow warm with an embarrassed flush. If I didn't know better, I'd think Kier was flirting with me. But he absolutely could not be, right? Judging by all of the empirical evidence to date, he didn't even like me, never mind find me attractive.

"'Sex and creativity are often seen by dictators as subversive activities,'" I said.

Kier choked on his cookie. He reached for the cup Brigid had set down in front of him and took a sip of tea. He turned to me and asked, "Are you quoting Erica Jong to me?"

I shrugged. It was a nonchalant gesture given that I was rightly impressed that he knew the quote from Jong's piece "The Artist as Housewife." I'd only known it because I'd studied feminist theory for my literature degree. I pointed to the cookie. "Do you not like them?"

"I think they're . . ." He paused to take a bite. I watched his teeth snap the cookie. He chewed thoughtfully and I tried not to stare at the small crumbs on his lower lip. I glanced back into my cup when he swiped up the crumbs with his tongue. Mercy.

"Delicious," he announced.

"Deliciously subversive?" I asked. "Or subversively delicious."

"Precisely," he said. "'All art is subversive.'"

"And now you're bringing Pablo Picasso into the conversation." I laughed and then he grinned at me and my breath stalled in my lungs. Perhaps I hadn't been that far off when I said he needed to know CPR if he was going to smile at me like that. Without his signature scowl, he was more like a cinnamon roll hero out of a contemporary romance. Straight up swoony. Be still my heart.

"Go on, Red," he said. "We'll see you in the morning."

I thought about the novel in my bag just waiting to be read and hopped off the stool. "You know what? I'm going."

"Good?" He said it as a question and I suspected my excitement about reading his book was giving me a manic expression, which I immediately tried to tame.

"Great!" I said.

"Fantastic!" he retorted.

"Excellent!" Brigid chimed in as she joined us. We both turned to look at her. "What? Not a game then?"

I laughed and hurried from the café with a wave. In moments, I had my jacket and my things and I was out the door without a backward glance.

It felt as if the novel was burning a hole in my bag and I couldn't wait to be home. I'd done some grocery shopping at the market in the village the day before and I knew I could make a simple supper and then curl up by the fire under my wool throw and read my heart out. In other words, a perfect evening.

It was five o'clock by the time I had my situation organized. I'd changed into my pajamas and robe. Yes, it was shockingly early to be ready for bed, but I didn't care. This was my version of settling in. I had a hot bowl of potato soup and a grilled ham and cheese sandwich on the table beside me. Oh, and a glass of whiskey because why not?

I had taken the book out of my bag and now I opened it to the first page. I was surprisingly nervous to read a book written by Kier. What if it was terrible? What if it was embarrassing? What if there were explicit sex scenes? Or worse, a gory murder? Would I be getting a glimpse into his psyche? I slammed the book shut. I wasn't sure I was prepared for that.

I pushed the book away and ate my soup, dabbing my sandwich in the broth while I contemplated the cover of the book. I took a bite and flipped the book over. The back cover copy seemed straightforward enough. A traditional mystery set in an Irish village with a local garda, an Irish police officer, as the sleuth. I opened the cover again. I would simply pretend I didn't know the author. I could do that.

The opening scene was the discovery of the body as seen through the sleuth's eyes. It was descriptive but not gruesome and I pictured the village of Finn's Hollow while I read. I could hear Kier's voice in my head, and I laughed out loud when I got to the bit about the local priest who loved fly fishing. Had Kier modeled his mystery after the residents here? By the time I'd finished the first chapter, I was lost in the story.

I awoke when the sun streamed through the living room window onto my face. I blinked and reached up to rub my eyes, finding my glasses askew. Kier's book was on the floor where I'd dropped it off the couch when I fell asleep. The fire had gone out and my late night cup of tea was still on the table. I was under the red throw, burrowed into the couch for warmth.

I had read Kier's book once and then immediately started it again, passing out somewhere in the middle of my second reading. The book was . . . unexpected. The plot was a page turner, the characters were well drawn, and the mystery was clever with a wicked twist at the end. Kier could write. My only question now was why didn't he?

When I'd finished the book, I'd gotten online and searched for any other books he might have written. There was nothing.

I reached for my phone, which was on the floor by his book. I ignored the ridiculous number of messages left by my mother and checked the time. It was ten minutes until eight. *Ack!* I was supposed to be at work at eight! I threw off the throw, letting the shock of the chilly morning air jolt me awake as I ran to the bedroom.

Siobhan was waiting for me when I arrived at the bookshop. I had run all the way there in my thick-heeled boots, black trousers, and gray turtleneck tunic sweater. With my black puffy coat over my clothes, I probably looked like my own personal storm cloud. My hair was in a messy ball on top of my head and my glasses had finger smudges on the lenses from where I'd grabbed them while I ran. I was breathing heavy but trying to hide it while I wondered if I had time to grab a cup of coffee and maybe a scone from Brigid.

"Good morning, Siobhan. I'll just go put my things away and be right back."

"No don't," Siobhan said. She hopped up from her seat. "We're going on a field trip out of the village today."

"We are?"

"Yes, I had Brigid pack us coffee and scones to go." She gestured to the table where there were three large cups of coffee and a bag of scones.

"Excellent," I said. Knowing caffeine was available, I felt as if I could face anything. "Where are we going?"

"Ballymuir Castle near Tralee," she said. "I used it as the model for the castle in *Tig McMorrow and the Tower of Light* and I need to go visit it to get my head reconnected to that space."

"The fourth book in the series," I said. "I loved that one." I hoped I didn't sound too gushy but I couldn't help it. "And we're going to the castle that inspired it? A genuine castle? Let's go!"

"Not so fast, Red." Kier stepped into the alcove. He was wearing his coat, a long black wool number that gave him Heathcliff prowling the Yorkshire moors vibes.

"You're coming with us?" I asked. My tone wasn't welcoming. I didn't mean to sound unfriendly but having read his book, I was petrified I'd say something that would clue him in that I'd done so. Also, I enjoyed my mornings with Siobhan without this walking Georgian-era heartthrob distracting me with his glowers and grumbles.

"Don't fret," Kier said. "Since Ma doesn't drive, I'm essentially just your chauffer, as I've been instructed not to speak unless spoken to."

Siobhan rolled her eyes. "That's not what I said, now is it?" She turned to me. "I merely explained that you were working for me this morning and if Kier had anything to discuss with you about your work in the shop, he could wait until we returned."

"I could drive us if you have things you need to do here," I said. I wasn't sure why these ridiculous words flew out of my mouth, but I suspected it had something to do with self-preservation and maintaining healthy boundaries between me and Kier.

He looked at me in surprise. "You can drive a manual transmission?"

"Er." Technically, I could because my friend Sam had taught me, but I wasn't great at it.

"And you'd have to shift with your left hand since the driver sits on the right side of the car." He looked at me expectantly. There was no way I was going to be able to bluff my way through that.

"Might be better if you drive us," I said. He looked very satisfied at my concession, so naturally I felt compelled to add, "But I could absolutely do it."

He glanced back at me and to my surprise, he looked me up and down and said, "I don't doubt it, Red."

Was that a compliment? It felt like one, but I had a hard time imagining it coming from the man who wanted me to toil alone on the third floor for the next year like a sad girl in a fairy tale.

Siobhan clapped her hands. "Come on now. We only have half a day and it takes almost an hour to get to the castle." She handed me my coffee and grabbed the bag of scones. "We can eat in the car."

"Not in my car," Kier protested. Siobhan wasn't listening to him. Instead, she handed him a tote bag and strode past him to the door.

"Back after lunch, Eun-ji." Kier waved to her where she stood behind the cashier's counter. "Call me if there are any issues."

"Bring me back a present," Eun-ji teased, returning his wave.

We stopped by the car parked in front of the shop. It was a very sporty Range Rover. Of course Kier would drive something like this. He definitely wasn't sedan material.

Kier opened the back passenger door and Siobhan climbed in. She gestured for me to follow her. I glanced at Kier to see what he thought about this, although technically I was working for Siobhan at the moment so she was the boss.

"I'm just your driver this morning," he said. "Don't worry, I'll boss you around later."

There was no earthly reason why that should sound suggestive but it definitely did, so naturally my face got hot. I burrowed into my scarf hoping he didn't notice and slid into the car. I reached for the door handle to shut the door but the man was in the way.

When I glanced up to see why, he had the audacity to wink at me, making my face flame even hotter. This was not a great look on a redheaded woman. He stepped back and shut the door, leaving me to wallow in chagrin. Argh!

"I thought we might work while we drive," Siobhan said. "Maybe jot down some ideas for the book."

She reached into her tote bag and handed me a notebook. I flipped through it, noting all of the pages were blank. She also slid the bag of scones toward me. She already had one in hand and was nibbling contentedly while she sipped her coffee.

"No eating in the car," Kier said.

"Why not?" Siobhan shot back. "You do."

"I would never," Kier protested. I could see his expression in the rearview mirror and was certain by the glint in his eyes that he was joking.

"Oh, really?" Siobhan leaned down and picked up an empty Supermac's burger box off the floor of the car. "What's this then?"

Kier glanced at it as he backed out of his parking spot. "Circumstantial evidence."

Siobhan laughed. "Yes, the circumstance of this box in your car is evidence." She nudged me with her elbow. "Enjoy your scone, Em."

She didn't have to tell me twice. Light and fluffy and packed with berries, it paired perfectly with my hot cup of coffee. The first few bites were delicious even as I tried very hard not to drop any crumbs. I noticed Kier glancing at me in the rearview mirror every few minutes and it made me overly self-conscious. Suddenly, I was aware of every bite I took, how loudly I chewed, even how I sipped my coffee. I was relieved when I was finished. Siobhan offered me another but there was no way I wanted to put myself through that again.

I studied the passing scenery, noting that as we left the village behind, the houses became fewer across the landscape. Farms perched on the surrounding hillsides, and the lush green fields were dotted with sheep and broken up by hedgerows and stone walls and the occasional copse of trees.

My mind wandered as I thought about the history of the land and the many invaders who had tried to claim the Emerald Isle as their own. From the Vikings in the 700s through the Normans and the Dutch and several other nations right up until the French in 1760, it seemed everyone wanted to plant their flag on Irish soil. As I took in the beauty surrounding me, I could understand why. There was something magical about this place where it felt as if anything could happen.

That thought snapped me back to the present. I was here for a job. I was Siobhan's assistant and it was my job to help her finish the Tig McMorrow series. I opened the notebook she'd handed me and clicked my pen.

"Are you ready to do some plotting?" I asked.

Siobhan had taken another scone and she finished chewing and swallowed before she said, "Sure."

This wasn't the level of enthusiasm I'd expected but we were still building our caffeine reserves so I forged on.

"When we last saw Tig McMorrow—" I began but Kier interrupted me.

"You sound like a documentary filmmaker," he said.

I glanced up at the rearview mirror and his gaze flitted to mine. I couldn't tell if he was just making an observation, mocking me, or interrupting me on purpose just to be annoying. I decided to roll with it.

I did my best Keith Morrison *Dateline* impression, which admittedly wasn't very good, and continued, "When we last saw Tig McMorrow, he was trapped between worlds in a time-hopping purgatory where he couldn't slip into another realm and find his magical creature friends and he couldn't leap back into his own world either. So, how does our young hero escape?"

I turned to Siobhan, expecting her to throw out a theory or two. She sipped her coffee and pondered the remainder of her scone. "I haven't a bloody clue."

"No idea?" I asked. I was shocked. I mean she'd said she didn't work off an outline or anything, but I would have thought that when she'd decided to leave her character in a fictional no-man's-land she'd at least have devised a plan to get him out.

"The bin is empty, isn't it?" She tapped her temple with her index finger. "That's why we're going to the castle. I'm hoping that something will shake loose."

"That's as good a plan as any," I agreed. "What do we know about Ballymuir?"

"The current castle was built in 1721," Kier said. "And it's haunted."

"Over three hundred years old and haunted?" I repeated. I was thrilled, as if going to a castle for work wasn't amazing enough.

"Kier's having a bit of fun, ignore him." Siobhan sent a quelling look at the back of her son's head. If he felt it, it didn't show.

"I'm not," he protested. "There have been multiple reports of her—the ghost is a woman—wandering through the castle at night and she lingers over certain guests."

"What do you mean lingers?" I asked. "Does she harm them? Is she friendly or frightening?"

"Kieran Anthony Murphy," Siobhan said in what sounded like her stern Irish mammy voice. "Stop teasing the poor girl."

"Not a girl," I said. Being petite with the figure of a pencil, I was very sensitive to being called a girl.

"Sorry, love, of course you're not." Siobhan glanced at me and then at Kier. "Else you wouldn't have been in the pub last week downing shots of whiskey with this rapscallion, now would you?"

Kier and I exchanged a glance in the rearview mirror. I was certain my eyes were wide with panic while his glinted in amusement.

"You've hired yourself a wild one, Ma." He winked at me again and I had the sudden urge to kick the back of his seat.

"Hardly," I said. "I was invited to dinner with my landlords, the Connollys, and somehow this one drafted in on the meal."

"Drafted in?" Kier repeated. "Like I'm a race car?"

"Vroom vroom," Siobhan teased.

"Well, that's gratitude, isn't it?" he asked. His penetrating stare met mine. "As I recall, I had to wrestle Shane for the check to treat the lot of you."

"You did," I agreed. "And it was much appreciated."

"That was neighborly of you, Kier," Siobhan said. "It's a comfort to know I raised you right."

There was a sudden shift in the atmosphere, almost as if Tig McMorrow was with us and he had ripped open a portal to one of his magical realms and let in one of the Shades (these were a type of magical creature that carried around the most difficult emotions). I couldn't put my finger on it exactly but this one felt like regret.

Not wanting our outing to be dimmed by whatever undercurrent was between mother and son, I said, "It was very gracious of you, but I'm quite certain I never would have had two whiskeys and two beers if it weren't for your generosity and Shane's enthusiasm, so I hold you solely accountable for waking up with socks on my teeth the next morning."

To my relief, Kier laughed and so did Siobhan. Crisis averted. Unless, of course, I was just being oversensitive to the vibe, which was highly probable. When Siobhan put her hand on my arm and gave it a gentle squeeze, I knew I hadn't been.

"I'm so glad you're here, Em," she said.

I glanced at Kier to see what he thought of that, but if he heard, it didn't show. His gaze was focused on the road ahead. Siobhan reclined and said, "If you two don't mind, I'm going to rest my eyes for a bit."

I opened my mouth to protest that we should work on the book, but I checked myself. Siobhan was the boss and if she wanted to rest, who was I to tell her otherwise? I could write down some ideas as they came to me.

"That sounds grand, Ma," Kier said. He slowed the car to a stop. "Red, why don't you sit up here with me so Ma can stretch out?"

"Oh, of course," I agreed.

"Thanks, love. I haven't been sleeping well and I'm a bit knackered," Siobhan said. She closed her eyes and I hurried around the car and slid into the passenger seat beside Kier.

I buckled my seatbelt and he pulled the car back onto the road. We were quiet for several miles. I glanced back at Siobhan and noted she was breathing deeply and evenly, looking perfectly at peace. I had a million questions about her that I wanted to ask Kier. Why had she stopped writing, what had she been doing for the past ten years, and why was she motivated to finish the book now? What had changed in her life?

The old me would have said nothing, but the woman I wanted to be—bold like Elizabeth Bennett in *Pride and Prejudice*—wasn't letting it go. I took a steadying breath and gathered all my courage and asked, "Why did she stop writing?"

Of course, it came out like a breathy whisper, no louder than the hum of the car's engine.

"Beg pardon?" Kier leaned toward me.

Ugh. I was going to have to ask again. Apparently, my newfound boldness required practice. I cast a glance at Siobhan to see if we had disturbed her. She hadn't stirred.

"Don't worry," he said. "Once she's out, she's the deepest sleeper I've ever known. I think it was all the book tours she went on back in the day. She got really good at sleeping wherever and whenever she needed to, nothing disturbs her. Sometimes I have to bake fresh Irish soda bread so the scent will rouse her."

"Oh," I said.

Do not picture the man in an apron, I told myself. I didn't listen. The man cooked, causing his hotness meter to register even higher. I shook my head to dislodge the image. When I spoke, I kept my voice soft just in case. "So why did Siobhan quit writing?"

He considered the question, and his voice was thoughtful when he said, "Seems to me, she'd be the person to tell you."

Well, that was maddening. I studied the scenery for a bit. A sheep watched me over the lip of a stone wall. He didn't look impressed by me and I couldn't fault him. I had questions and I wanted answers. "All right, if you won't tell me why Siobhan quit writing then can you tell me why you're so opposed to her starting again?"

"I could." He nodded. "But then I'd still be talking out of turn, wouldn't I?"

"Would you?" I persisted. "Is the reason you don't want her to write related to the reason she quit?"

Kier heaved a put-upon sigh. "Persistent, aren't you?"

"I'm just trying to understand why you seem to dislike my helping her so much," I defended myself.

He was quiet for so long, I thought he wasn't going to answer, but he did. "Contrary to how it looks, it's not personal," he said.

"It feels very personal to me."

"I'm sorry for that." He drove on in silence and I thought that was that, but he surprised me. "It's not my place to tell you why she quit, but I suppose as your boss I do owe you an explanation as to why I'm not so keen to have you here."

It was a crumb of information but I'd take it. I braced myself and said, "All right."

"The truth is Ma and I have a complicated history with her writing. It took her away a lot when I was a lad and I struggled with that," he said. "And the writing takes a toll on her. She's suffered enough in life. I'd like to spare her more of that if I could."

"And you think the writing causes her suffering?" I asked.

He met my gaze and then looked pointedly at Siobhan asleep in the back seat. I couldn't argue that she did seem chronically fatigued and I supposed her efforts to write again could be the cause. No doubt, it was worrying.

Siobhan had kept her personal life so private over the years, I hadn't even known she had a son. I had no idea what her writing life was like outside of her books and it was clear Kier wasn't going to tell me, which was annoyingly loyal of him.

"Thank you for telling me your concerns." I thought about how my own father had disappeared from my life and I could sympathize with young Kier and his complicated relationship with Siobhan. It felt like a win just to have him share this much and I didn't want to push it. Instead, I tried to lighten the mood and said, "Hey, does this make us friends, Kier?"

"No, and the name is Murphy."

"What are we then? Acquaintances? Strangers?"

"I don't get drunk in pubs with acquaintances or strangers, Red," he said.

"Employer and employee?" I asked.

"That indicates a potential for a long-term association, which we will not be having as you will likely be leaving us soon," he said. He sounded very confident of that fact. I almost felt badly for how disappointed he was going to be when I refused to be budged from my mission. Because unless Siobhan let me go, I was absolutely not leaving.

"I suppose we'll see about that," I said. I stared at the winding road ahead feeling newly resolved.

"Finally, something we agree upon," he said.

"Indeed." I nodded.

"Absolutely." He spat the word with more oomph than I thought was necessary to the occasion.

I turned to study his face. The set of his chin was stubborn and it gave me a theory. Much like in the café yesterday, the man was intent upon having the last word. Not today, buddy.

"For sure," I said.

"Definitely."

"Positively."

"One hundred percent," he said.

I opened my mouth to retort but a voice piped up from the back seat.

"Jaysus, how long is this going to go on?" Siobhan muttered.

"Now I'll be having the last word and you both can shut it. Am I clear? No! Don't answer that. Let a woman have her rest now, won't you?"

Busted! I pressed my lips together to keep from laughing. A peek out of the corner of my eye and I noticed Kier was doing the same. He glanced at me and we exchanged a shared look of guilty amusement that reminded me of two kids getting chastised in class and having no remorse.

As if he abruptly remembered his indifference to me, Kier cleared his throat and stepped on the gas. The countryside became a blur as we sped through the lush green hills to the castle near Tralee.

I didn't make any notes during the ride as I wasn't struck by any brilliant ideas. Instead, I just took a moment to breathe and revel in the adventure I was having. A hot Irishman to my right, my favorite author sitting behind me, and a landscape full of magic around me. It occurred to me that in this very moment I was living my best life. I turned to the window and in my reflection on the glass I saw an enormous grin parting my lips. For the first time in a long time, I felt a burst of pure joy.

Tralee was situated on the north side of the Dingle Peninsula, it was the capital of County Kerry and a good-sized town, much larger than Finn's Hollow. Kier drove us through without stopping as we headed to Ballymuir Castle.

The trees were tall and formed an arc over the road. I recognized the golden leaves of the ash and spied thick holly bushes with their spiked, bright green leaves and red berries tucked deeper into the woods amid the black alder and birch. When the wind blew, the leaves fluttered on the breeze across our path. It felt as if they were welcoming us.

We passed through an ornate iron gate announcing Ballymuir Castle Hotel and then we broke through the woods and the castle was revealed. My jaw dropped.

I had never seen a genuine castle before, as Martha's Vineyard is not exactly known for its palaces. Sure, there were some wealthy people with extravagant mansions on the island but their flex for displaying their opulence was a joke in comparison to the sight that rose from the ground ahead of us. A castle. An actual freaking castle made of imposing gray stone, arch-shaped windows, and crenelated turrets. As the Irish say, I was gobsmacked.

Kier parked the car in the visitor's lot. I heard Siobhan clear her throat, indicating she'd woken up.

"All right, Ma?" Kier asked.

"Never better." Siobhan popped out of her side of the car and stretched, reaching up high. "How about a cuppa?"

"That'd be grand," Kier agreed.

I stepped out as well, grabbing my notebook and my shoulder bag. I was ready to jot down any brilliant ideas she shared. Kier led the way to the main entrance, while I gawked with my head tipped back staring at the towering edifice in front of us.

"How many rooms does it have?" I asked.

"One hundred and twenty-four," he said.

"Whoa." I couldn't even comprehend it.

We paused to admire the castle that loomed over us. Ivy climbed up one of the towers and in my mind I could see a fair maiden standing on the top, waving a handkerchief to her lover below. In my overblown imagination, I was the fair maiden and the lover was Kier. Of course he was. I tried to wipe the image of him from my mind, but I couldn't. The dark-haired Romeo in my daydream was definitely the man standing beside me. He would climb the ivy to get to his Juliet—i.e. me—and proclaim his undying devotion—

"All right there, Red?" Kier asked.

I blinked away the fantasy, shaking my head to dispel the image. "Yup, totally fine."

He considered me for a moment. "You do that quite often."

"What?" I asked. His scrutiny made me uncomfortable and I shifted my feet on the gravel path as if trying to ground myself in the face of what I was certain would be criticism.

"Daydream." He tipped his head to the side as he considered me. "What are you thinking about when you do that?"

Ha! I'd be burned at the stake before I admitted to fantasizing about him, so I deflected and said, "'He felt that his whole life was some kind of dream and he sometimes wondered whose it was and if they were enjoying it.'"

That one imperious eyebrow of Kier's rose and I knew he knew I was avoiding his question. He didn't call me on it. Instead, he said, "Douglas Adams's *The Hitchhiker's Guide to the Galaxy*, if I'm not mistaken."

I inclined my head. I had yet to stump him, but I would. Still, I had distracted him, so I'd take the win.

"Come along, you lot," Siobhan called from the door. "The weather is turning."

She was right. The sky had become overcast during our drive and now it was beginning to mist. My glasses accumulated a sheen of droplets as Kier and I hurried up the main steps with large marble lions on each side.

They reminded me of New York Public Library's two lions, Patience and Fortitude, and I smiled, patting one of them on the head as I passed. As we stepped inside the large double doors, I quickly cleaned my glasses with a cloth I kept in my bag for just this purpose. As soon as I put my glasses back on I gasped. Ballymuir Castle was everything a castle should be.

From the black and white marble floor tiles, the enormous sparkling chandelier overhead, and the full suit of armor standing guard in the corner, the entry screamed *castle* and I was so here for it.

I took out my phone. I had to snap some pictures. Sam would never believe this.

A man in a black suit with a narrow tie appeared in the doorway to the right. His gray hair was thin on top, but he carried himself with an air of importance even though his shoulders were stooped and he walked with the aid of a cane.

"Siobhan Riordan," he said. His lined face broke into a wide grin, revealing slightly crooked teeth and an underbite. "It's been too long since your lovely face graced these halls."

"Hugh, my dear friend, as charming as ever, I see." Siobhan stepped forward and clasped his free hand in hers. They stared at each other with matching expressions of affection before Siobhan turned back to us.

"You remember my son, Kieran Murphy, and this is my new assistant, Emily Allen," Siobhan said.

"Failte," Hugh greeted me and then turned to Kier. "You've grown up, lad. The last time I saw you, you couldn't even grow a whisker."

Kier chuckled and cupped his chin self-consciously. "And now I'm as furry as an otter. It has been a while."

"I can have tea sent up to the tower for you, if you'd like," Hugh said.

The tower! I was giddy.

"That would be lovely," Siobhan said. "If it's no trouble."

"No problem at all. Would you like an escort? I'm afraid I can't manage the stairs these days." Hugh glanced ruefully at his cane.

"That's not necessary, I still know the way." Siobhan patted his hand and they exchanged another affectionate glance.

We passed through the foyer into a large chamber with tall columns, another marble floor, and groupings of very ornate gilded furniture. A split staircase ran along each side of the room and the high walls were decorated with enormous portraits of prior castle residents, all of whom seemed to be watching our progress with mixed emotions.

Siobhan led the way up the staircase to the right. The thick crimson-and-cream carpet was soft beneath my feet. I ran my hand along the carved banister as we wound our way up several levels until we arrived at a landing with a small sitting area.

Kier moved ahead of Siobhan to hold open the door for us. We passed several rooms in the narrow hallway adorned with more family portraits until we reached the door at the end. Siobhan turned the crystal knob and we entered a small room with a tight spiral staircase. We climbed the steps to a small landing with a thick wooden door in the shape of an arch. Siobhan leaned against the wall, catching her breath while Kier turned the handle and pushed the door open. A crackling fire warmed the room and Siobhan stepped inside. She glanced at me over her shoulder and said, "Welcome to the Tower of Light, Em."

Eight

Kier slipped off his coat and held out his hand for Siobhan's. I followed suit, hanging mine on the freestanding coatrack by the door. The interior of the room was painted a restful pale blue. Three large windows on the opposite side of the entrance were curved to match the shape of the circular room and framed with cream-colored floor-length drapes that had bunches of blue hydrangea on them. Glancing outside, I could see the castle garden and the woods beyond.

It was almost an out-of-body experience to be standing there. I genuinely expected someone wearing a crown and an ermine-trimmed crimson robe to sweep into the room and declare us—okay, me—an impostor to be executed at dawn. Wow, just wow.

The furniture was elaborately carved and upholstered in a dark blue velvet. Siobhan sat in one of the armchairs by the fire. I wasn't sure which seat Kier preferred given that he was tall and broad so I stood, waiting for him to sit first. He prowled around the room, taking in the books on the bookcase, also curved, along the wall beside the desk, which sat in front of the windows.

There was a gentle knock on the door and three of the castle's staff, all wearing uniforms of black pants and white shirts with black vests, came in bearing trays that they placed on the coffee table in front of Siobhan. My eyes strayed to the three-tiered plate loaded with food. The tiny cakes looked amazing.

"Can we get you anything else, ma'am?" one of the women asked.

"Not that I can think of, thank you," Siobhan said. "Please tell Hugh he outdid himself."

"Of course." The woman smiled and they left, closing the door behind them.

"Tea?" Siobhan asked.

"Yes, please." I watched as she prepared it exactly as I liked it. It was such a small thing, but the only other person in my life who knew how I took my tea was my friend Sam. My mother probably didn't even know I drank tea.

"Thank you," I said. I glanced at the grandfather clock near the desk and asked, "Does this count as elevenses?"

She laughed. "I believe it does."

Siobhan seemed very at home here. It was a feminine room and I wondered if it had always been a woman's room, a retreat from castle life that was hers alone. This seemed like a fantastic idea to me. In my opinion, every woman should have their own turret.

I glanced at my companions. They did not appear to find the castle as extraordinary as I did. I supposed growing up in a country strewn with castles and ruins will do that to a person. According to my research there were more than three thousand castles in Ireland, if you counted ruins, and I was standing in one of them. Amazing.

"Please sit, Em," Siobhan said. "And you as well, Kier."

I sat gingerly on the edge of an armchair. No one chased me from the room when I sat down on the obvious antique so that felt like victory. Unlike me, Kier did not appear to feel out of his element at all. He sprawled on the small couch, which could barely contain his broad frame. He glanced at Siobhan and asked, "How are you feeling, Ma? This isn't too much for you, is it?"

"Not at all," she said. She poured him a cup of tea and handed it to him. I noted she didn't add sugar or milk. "I'm in one of my most favorite places, I had a nap in the car, and now there's tea. It doesn't get any better."

Kier relaxed into his seat and I remembered what Maeve had said about his protective feelings for his mother. In the car he wouldn't tell me why she'd quit writing, but he did allude to her suffering for it. I wondered how I could broach the subject with her in the cozy confines of the tower.

A buzz sounded and Kier took his phone out of his pocket and glanced at the screen. He rolled to his feet, setting his cup on the table. "Excuse me. It's a call from the shop. I have to take it."

"Of course," Siobhan said. She turned to me, and I forced my attention away from Kier, who walked to the other end of the room and stood outlined in the windows. I refused to acknowledge how the watery sunlight outlined his masculine frame. I cleared my throat and took a sip of tea.

"The battlements on top of Ballymuir are exactly as you described them in the book," I said. "I recognized it right away."

"Do you think we could start the final book here?" she asked. "Use it for the opening scene maybe?"

I stared into the fire, revisiting the series in my mind. I had read the books so many times I felt as if I knew Tig and his sidekicks, Ronan the shapeshifter and Aislinn the witch, as well as I knew myself. In the last book, Tig had been left in a purgatory that had nothing to do with the Tower of Light, or did it? Siobhan had no plot ideas, so I assumed this meant she could do whatever she wanted.

"You could," I said. "I think you have the freedom to start anywhere you like."

Siobhan put her hand on her forehead as if her thoughts were in a muddle. "That's what defeats me every day."

"Too many possibilities." I nodded in understanding. I glanced at Kier, who had his back to us, and asked, "Is that why you quit writing?"

Her eyes widened in surprise and her gaze dropped down to her cup. The Siobhan who was always smiling and eager to talk looked distinctly uncomfortable and I immediately felt terrible for trying to pry personal information out of her.

"Sorry," I said. "That's none of my business. Please forget I asked. Back to the book, can you pinpoint what exactly is causing you trouble?"

Siobhan met my gaze and I could see the relief in her eyes. She sipped her tea and said, "I just don't know how Tig's story ends. I'm . . . I'm struggling with endings right now."

"Does it have to be the end?" I asked. "Maybe you need more than one book to finish the series."

"No." She shook her head. Her hair was loose today and she tucked it behind her ears when it spilled forward and covered her face. She tipped her head to the side and I noted the faint dark circles under her eyes. She looked exhausted and I wasn't surprised she'd fallen asleep in the car. Her voice was a whisper, as if she were confessing a crime, and she said, "The truth is, Em, I don't know if Tig's story has a happy ending or not."

I blinked. It had never occurred to me that his story might not end happily. I didn't know if I could bear it if it didn't. I knew my job was to assist her with her vision, whatever that vision might be, and to keep my opinions to myself but the words burst out of me before I could stop them.

"But he has to have a happy ending!" I cried. "He's been through so much. His losses have been so great." I gasped. "You're not going to kill him off, are you?"

I thought I might faint. As a reader and longtime lover of all things Tig McMorrow—yes, I'd had the bookmarks, posters, and bedsheets and, yes, I'd even dressed up as Aislinn when I was a middle-schooler—the thought that Tig might die at the end of the series had never ever occurred to me. It felt like a betrayal on a cellular level.

"Siobhan, I have to be honest with you. If it's a choice between killing Tig off and leaving him in purgatory, I'd leave him in purgatory. I won't be a party to ending him. I'll quit and fly home to Martha's Vineyard if it comes to that."

"What's this? What did I miss?" Kier appeared beside me, making me jump.

"Do you have to sneak up on people like that?" I snapped.

"I didn't sneak." He glanced at Siobhan. "What did you say to make Red offer up her resignation?"

"Nothing that concerns you," Siobhan said. "We were merely discussing possible plot points and Em has some very strong feelings about them, which is exactly why I hired her."

"Then you're not going to . . . ?" I couldn't even say it.

Siobhan tapped her chin with her index finger, a gesture I recognized as her thinking posture. "You make a great point about what Tig deserves. Readers haven't waited ten years for me to gut them. A happy ending it is, no matter how challenging it is to write."

I sagged against the back of my chair in relief.

Kier sighed and resumed his seat. "'And so we beat on, boats against the current, borne back ceaselessly into the past.'"

Siobhan and I both glanced at him, but he was busy investigating the contents of the tiny crustless square sandwiches.

"*The Great Gatsby*," I identified the literary reference.

"Oh, egg and onion." He held up a tiny sandwich. Then he met my gaze and said, "And you're correct, Red."

Siobhan glanced between us with a curious expression but said nothing. I wasn't sure how I felt about Kier's selected quote. Did he consider me the boat or the current he was fighting against? And what past were "we" being borne back to? Their complicated relationship? Why couldn't we just be in the boat rowing together, as it were?

I watched his dark hair fall over his brow as he popped one of the sandwiches into his mouth. My fingers itched to comb the hair back. I wondered if it was as soft as it looked. I forced my gaze away and found Siobhan watching me with an appraising glance.

Oh no. Did she know? Could she tell that her assistant had the hots for her son? How did she feel about it? I felt my face grow warm, but Siobhan said nothing. She simply leaned forward and said, "Sandwiches, Em?"

I took two even though my appetite had fled the scene. Feeling the need to stay on task, I said, "Maybe we need to look at the book from a different angle."

"Meaning?" Siobhan asked.

"Instead of approaching it as Tig's last book, his story ending, maybe you could consider it a new beginning." I glanced up to find both Siobhan and Kier looking at me. "Your readers have waited for ten years to find out what happens. They've grown up, graduated school, married, started their careers. Maybe when Tig returns, he needs to be older, too."

"You're right." Siobhan nodded. She glanced at Kier. "The only constant is change."

"Whether we like it or not," he agreed.

They were having a conversation with a subtext I didn't understand. I sipped my tea and ate my sandwiches. When I swallowed the watercress, it got stuck in my throat and I had a brief moment of thinking I had a goiter, an enlarged thyroid gland, that was going to grow so huge I would— I shook my head. No, no, no. I was not doing this to myself.

"Are you all right, Em?" Siobhan asked. Her eyes were soft with concern. I nodded.

"Never better," I said.

The mist melted away as we finished our tea and Hugh arrived and took us on a quick tour of the castle. There was no sign of the ghost. We didn't discuss the book again, but Siobhan had a spring in her step that wasn't there before. Maybe she had turned a corner in the plotting.

I took a selfie with the castle behind me and sent it to Sam. I hoped it didn't wake her up but I simply couldn't resist. I mean, come on, *a castle*!

"Sharing your day with a famous author on social media?" Kier asked.

"No," I said. "I would never. I respect Siobhan's privacy."

"Be sure that you do." The brisk breeze tousled the waves of his dark curls. With his coat collar turned up, he was again the embodiment of the foreboding hero. Except now I knew something about him. He had to have the last word. Not on my watch.

"Of course."

"Good," he replied.

I smiled at him and said, "Agreed." There really was nowhere for him to go from there. Ha!

"Glad to hear it." There was a wicked twinkle in his eye, and I realized he had caught on that I knew his personality quirk.

"I'm sure you are," I said.

"Ah, sure look it." He nodded and wagged his brows at me, indicating that he thought he'd won.

But I knew that turn of phrase was essentially the Irish equivalent of the American "it is what it is" but with a more positive slant. I refused to lose.

"Whatever." I shrugged.

He narrowed his eyes at my response and I almost laughed at his chagrin.

"No, no, no," Siobhan said as she joined us. She was smiling. "There, now I've had the last word. Does this mean I win?"

Kier and I exchanged the same glance that we had in the car. The one that said we'd been busted. I smiled and turned away.

"Come on then," Siobhan said. "I need to go home and nap some more. It's where I do my best thinking."

We climbed into the car and while nothing was expressly stated, I felt as if things had shifted between Kier and me. He had actually given me a tiny peek through the window as to why he was resistant to my presence. We were getting to know each other and that changed things, whether he was willing to admit it or not.

Five hours later, I ceased feeling any such camaraderie with that impossible man. I was on the third floor with the hated Slo-Mo. It had started to rain in earnest outside and the scent of the books and the warmth of the room made me long for a nap.

I powered through the rest of the afternoon, fueled by Brigid's latest tester menu item, a black forest croissant made from a chocolate croissant filled with cherry confit, and a large cup of coffee. Amazing.

At closing, I was eager to get home and finish my reread of Kier's book. I had promised myself I would return it the next day, but I wanted to read it just one more time. It was dark and cold as I walked home, but I loved the crunch of leaves under my feet and the stiff wind pushing me toward my cottage. Shane and Maeve's lights were on and as I walked by, I could smell whatever they were cooking for supper. My stomach rumbled and I hurried inside eager to make myself dinner and read my book.

The freedom of cooking whatever I wanted for dinner was another unexpected thrill. My mother hated cooking and when my father left, she quit. When I took over in an attempt to get her to eat, the chore somehow became mine, and all of my mother's likes and dislikes and diet restrictions—many of which I was expected to adhere to as well—sucked any joy out of the task.

I once bought myself a candy bar as a treat and she snatched it out of the grocery bag, ate it, and then promptly threw it up, which according to her was all my fault because how dare I bring candy into her house? What a horribly selfish and unsupportive daughter I was. Needless to say, I didn't do that again.

Now, if I wanted cake for dinner there was literally no one stopping me. This was what adulthood was supposed to be about. Of course, I wasn't going to eat cake, but just the fact that I could made me giddy. Instead, I went with a comfort food standby of toasted open-faced sandwiches broiled with a smear of Irish butter, a thick slab of sharp cheddar, and a juicy slice of tomato seasoned with salt and pepper and garlic powder. Once the food was plated, I made myself a cup of tea and sat at the small table by the window. I had just taken a bite when my phone rang.

I grabbed my shoulder bag from its designated spot by the door and glanced at the display. It was Sam, requesting a video chat. I immediately swiped to open.

"I'm going to be eating while we talk because I'm starving," I said. Sam was in her kitchen with her hair in a ball on top of her head. She grinned and it felt like a hug.

"Excellent," she answered. "I'm baking pastries and will be taste-testing as I go."

This was the beauty of lifelong best friends. No manners required. I propped the phone up between the salt and pepper shakers and my plate. I could hear Sam cooking in the background, and it comforted me to have her with me even if it was through my phone.

"Tell me about your new job," she said. "How are you liking Siobhan Riordan? Is she everything you hoped she'd be?"

I swallowed a quick bite and said, "She's amazing." I went on to tell her about my trip to the castle with Kier and Siobhan, my night out at the pub with my landlords and Kier, and my coworkers who worked for Kier at the bookshop. I was about to tell her about Kier's mystery novel when Sam interrupted me.

"Hold up," Sam said. She put down the dish she was holding with a thump. "I thought you went there to be Siobhan's assistant?"

"I did. I am," I said.

"Really? Because your conversation seems to be all about Kieran Murphy." She stared at me with an intense gaze. "Em, do you have a thing for your new boss?"

"What?" I cried. I could feel my face get warm. I was glad the cottage was dimly lit and hoped she couldn't see me that well. "No, that would be completely unprofessional."

"Why?" she asked. "You're only there for a year. You can have a fling with your boss for a year. Who knows, maybe it will turn into something more. You're overdue for a relationship."

She looked delighted, and I knew I needed to crush any ideas she had about me and Kier.

"Nothing can ever happen between me and Kieran Murphy," I said.

"Is he married?"

"No." At least, I didn't think so.

"Girlfriend?"

"Not that I'm aware of," I said. I immediately rejected the idea of Kier with a girlfriend. He couldn't have sat with me and the Connollys at the pub if he had a girlfriend. The entire village was there. Surely, someone would have said something. I felt certain Maeve would have mentioned him having a girlfriend. Maybe she didn't know. I didn't like the twisty feeling in my gut. It wasn't jealousy. I was not jealous.

"You should find out," Sam said. She was taking something out of the oven. I wished the phone had a smell feature. Nothing smelled better than Sam's kitchen, except of course a library.

"If he has a girlfriend," she clarified. "I mean, he's all you've talked about for twenty minutes so you can deny it all you want but you like him."

"Trust me, even if I did like him that way, which I don't, it could never be anything," I said. "It's too complicated."

"What's complicated? You like him, he likes you," Sam said. "How is that a problem?"

"First of all, I don't know that he likes me. And secondly, Siobhan is his mother," I said.

"All right, I can see where that could be potentially awkward," Sam said. She took a bite of something in a round pastry and chewed while she considered my situation. "I'm working on my pastel de nata. I have to say I think I've nailed it."

Oh, she was baking my favorite egg custard with a dusting of cinnamon. Just the thought of it gave me a little twinge of homesickness. Usually, it was Ben, me, and Sam's younger brother, Tyler, taste-testing her food. I missed that.

"How's your cookbook coming?" I asked.

"No, no," she said. "I didn't mean to change the subject. The cookbook is fine. Ben is helping me write it and we only have a few recipes to go before it's finished. Back to you and your boss. So what if Siobhan is his mother? You're all adults. Surely she wouldn't care if her assistant and her son hooked up."

"That is never going to happen," I said. I pondered my sandwich, which was almost gone. "Kier has been blunt about not wanting me here, and today he finally admitted that he and Siobhan have a complicated relationship."

"Then you should definitely go after him," Sam said. "If anyone knows about complicated mother-child situations, it's you." She wasn't wrong.

"There's more to it," I said. "He also told me that writing caused Siobhan to suffer and he didn't want that for her. That's mainly why he's been so opposed to my presence."

"Suffer how?"

"I don't know, he wouldn't say."

"At least it's not personal," Sam said.

"Still feels personal."

She laughed. "Yeah, and it's an unusual stepping-off place for a relationship but it'll make a great story when you're married."

Everything went fuzzy and I steadied myself against the table. "That was a Grand Canyon–sized leap you just made."

"Maybe, but it's clear you're not indifferent to him and it sounds like he feels the same way about you."

"Doesn't matter. My loyalty is to Siobhan and helping her write the book. If he sees her suffering, he won't thank me for it."

"But that's why she hired you," Sam countered.

"I know. See? Complicated," I said. "Enough about me, tell me what's happening on the Vineyard."

There was a pause. I knew Sam well enough to know that meant there was something she had to tell me that I wouldn't like.

"What is it?" I asked. I put my fork down. There was a pit of dread in my stomach. Had something happened between Sam and Ben? I knew Ben's mother could be difficult. It was one of the things Ben and I had in common besides our profession of librarian. "Is Moira making trouble for you two?"

"No, Ben and I are annoyingly in love. I mean, I'm in this thing and even I'm annoyed by how happy we are," she said.

I laughed, feeling my heart swell. Sam was the extrovert to my introvert, the sister from a different mister, and my very best friend. Her happiness was my happiness.

"What is it then? I can tell by your tone something isn't right." I picked up my fork and stuffed a big bite of my dinner into my mouth. There was nothing better than Irish bread, butter, cheese, and fresh produce. Nothing.

"It's your mom," she said. I swallowed, feeling a prickle of dread.

"What about her?" I asked. I knew she wasn't sick because I was her emergency contact and someone would have called me.

"We kind of got into it," Sam said.

"What?"

"Listen, you know Tammy Lynn and I have had a rocky relationship over the years," Sam said.

"Oh, I know." This was an understatement. My mother loathed Sam. She called her a bad influence—she wasn't totally wrong—and a wildcard—also not wrong—but I don't think that's what bothered her. I think she resented how much Sam meant to me. Whenever I went to visit Sam in Boston, my mom and I had a fight.

Dr. Davis speculated that my mother was overly possessive of me due to my father leaving her and had a deep-seated fear of abandonment. I supposed my relocation to Ireland for a year proved to be Tammy Lynn's worst fear realized so it was small wonder that she might have lashed out at Sam, who also lived in Oak Bluffs. It wasn't a big island and during the offseason the potential for them to bump into each other was high.

"Please tell me she didn't embarrass you at work," I said.

"No, it was at the West Tisbury Farmer's Market," Sam said. "And for the record, she didn't embarrass me, just herself."

"Oh no." My voice dropped into a hushed tone. "Did she ambush you?"

"Well . . . yeah," Sam said. "But Ben was with me so it was okay."

"What did she say?" I asked. My heart was thumping hard in my chest and my brain felt as if it were on fire.

"That doesn't matter," Sam said. "What matters is I'm afraid she's going to try and manipulate you into coming back here and you should not do that under any circumstances unless it's a decision of your own making."

"What did she say?" I repeated.

Sam, who had a personality as big as the sky, was abruptly subdued. "It's not—"

"It's important to me, Sam," I said. "Please tell me so I know what I'm dealing with."

Sam sighed. It was clear she didn't want to tell me. After a beat, she said, "Tammy Lynn told me that it was my fault you went to Ireland, that I was a bad influence—not totally wrong given our wild teen years—and a dumbass and she couldn't believe that her brilliant, college-educated daughter was taking life advice from an illiterate loser like me."

I gasped. I pressed a hand to my chest. "I can't . . . I don't . . . That bitch!" The words exploded out of me leaving an echoing fury in their wake.

"Whoa," Sam said. "I didn't tell you this to make you mad at Tammy Lynn. I only told you because, well, there were a lot of people at the market that day who heard her and I didn't want it to get back to you from someone else. Also, I feel like she's going to try and force you to come back to the Vineyard and I don't think you should until you decide to come home for yourself. I'm so sorry, Em."

"You have nothing to be sorry for. I'm glad you told me," I said. I felt my throat get tight and tears pooled in my eyes. "Sam, you know nothing she said is true. You have dyslexia, you're not illiterate. You're brilliant, one of the top chefs in New England, if not the country, and Tammy Lynn is just a bitter, shriveled-up, crotchety, old mean girl, and I am so sorry she attacked you. I hate that she did that to you."

"Eh, don't feel too badly for me," Sam said. "Ben was there and when he heard what she said, he made it clear that she was never to speak to me again—as in ever. You should have seen him in action. My hero. Who knew a librarian could be so hot?"

I laughed, which I was certain was what she intended.

"Good," I said. "I'm glad Ben put her in her place. If she ever comes near you again, walk away, like speed walk super fast."

To my relief, Sam laughed. "Me running away from Tammy Lynn—that'd be a sight. Maybe I should work on my cardio."

I laughed, too, but it was tinged with sadness. My mother's toxicity had only been directed at me and my father for so long that it had never occurred to me that she'd go after someone I cared about. My leaving the island had clearly sent her into some sort of nasty tailspin. My head started to pound and I rested my forehead against my palm.

"You aren't having a stroke or an aneurysm," Sam said. "It's just some heartache. I promise."

I took several deep breaths like my therapist had taught me, and I tried to let it go. It was going to take some time and I had no idea what I was going to say to my mother the next time we spoke, which should be later today. Ugh.

I wished for the millionth time that my father had never left, but as I had come to understand over the last nine years, he'd likely run for his life because he was feeling suffocated. I no longer blamed him for leaving her, just for leaving me behind.

"Tell me something good," I said. "Otherwise, I'm going to have indigestion and convince myself I have stomach cancer."

Sam laughed. "I miss you, Em."

"I miss you, too," I said.

I finished my sandwich while Sam filled me in on all the news about our friends on the Vineyard. It was nice to hear good things about home, but as she talked I found my mind wandering to Kier. Despite my protestations to Sam, I liked Kieran Murphy . . . a lot. And I had absolutely no idea what to do about it.

Nine

"I want to visit Druid's Altar," Siobhan announced the next morning.

We were sitting at our usual table in front of the window. Brigid had supplied us with coffee and scones. The morning air on my walk to the bookshop had been frigid with a side of frosty as autumn gave way to winter and I cradled my cup in my hands to warm them.

Kier was sitting beside me, tapping away on a laptop that looked suspiciously shiny and new compared to the cinder block he had me using for inventory. Without looking up, he asked, "Drombeg, the stone circle, all right. When did you want to go?"

Siobhan stared at the top of his head. "Now."

He stopped typing and glanced up. "That's all the way over in County Cork, isn't it? We can't get there and back in a morning and I can't leave the shop for an entire day."

"I suppose you're right," Siobhan said. She sighed. "I guess you'll just have to teach Em to drive so she can take me."

She caught me on a sip and I gasped, sending hot coffee down into my lungs. I started to hack and cough. The more I tried to suppress it the worse it became. I was certain I looked like I was having a fit. Great.

"All right there, Red?" Kier asked. He reached over and thumped my back. This did not help. I was choking to death and a hot Irishman was patting me on my shoulder blades like I was a toddler. Ugh.

"I'm good." I held up my hand to ward him off and dabbed my face with a napkin, mercifully containing any leakage out of my nose.

He dropped his hand and I glanced at Siobhan. She must have been joking. Right?

"I don't know if I can handle driving on the wrong . . . er . . . the opposite side of the road from what I'm used to." I hoped it sounded more diplomatic than I felt because what I felt was a big ol' "hell no."

"Of course you can." Siobhan waved her hand as if this was the least of her concerns. "And just think, if you learn how to drive Kier's car then we can go off whenever we want."

"Are we just skipping over the part where it's my car?" Kier asked.

"You said yourself you need to be here in the afternoon," Siobhan said.

"And so does Em," he retorted. "Even if I teach her how to drive, she still needs to be back for her afternoon shift. That was our deal, remember?"

"I think our deal was brokered on shoddy information," Siobhan said. "From what I hear, all Em's doing is inventory. Surely that can't be so pressing since it's the first time it's been done in decades, now can it?"

Kier frowned. "The fact that we've never done it makes it extremely important."

"Oh really?" Siobhan asked. She met her son's gaze with a level stare. "It seems to me that with Em's skills, she'd be better served working on the main floor assisting customers instead of hidden away on the third floor with an antiquated laptop that could turn toes up at any moment."

I glanced between them. Again, I felt as if there was something happening of which I was unaware.

"It just so happens that we're getting ready to train her as a cashier," Kier said.

This was the first I'd heard of this. I studied his face, which was the picture of innocence. I sensed he was making it up as he went along.

"And when will that begin?" Siobhan asked.

"Today as a matter of fact," he said. "I was going to suggest Red follow Eun-ji around this afternoon."

"Excellent," Siobhan said. "Then you can give Em her first driving lesson this morning."

A small yip—yes, like that of a purse-sized dog—came out of my mouth. I mean, driving in Ireland? Sam had gotten me into some wild shenanigans in our youth and suddenly all of that paled in comparison to driving in a foreign country on a different side of the road. But I didn't want to disappoint Siobhan and I was going to be here for a year. Maybe I needed to know how to drive on the left side. I mean, what if there was an emergency or something?

"Ma, you can't be serious," Kier said at the same time I said, "I'll do it."

Siobhan beamed at me. "That's a brave girl . . . excuse me . . . woman."

I grinned. It had been a long time, if ever, that I'd gotten any sort of maternal praise and I soaked it up like parched earth under a summer rain.

"Excellent, that's sorted then," Siobhan said.

"Sorted?" Kier glanced at me and then at her and then back at me with his one eyebrow raised in a look of complete consternation. "You get one shot, Red, and if you bang up my car, that's it. Understood?"

It was just offensive that bossy Kier was also hot Kier. Every feminist cell in my body demanded that I not feel the flutters that were impossible to deny as he glowered at me. Fine. I lowered my glasses and peered over the top of them at him. My voice was very low when I said, "I suppose we'll find out how good of a driving instructor you are, won't we?"

I gave him a dismissive glance and turned back to Siobhan, who was watching us with her chin propped in her hand, looking pleased.

Kier closed his laptop and rose from his seat. "I see what you're doing. Spinning it back on me as if it'll be my fault if you can't handle driving here. Very clever, but I've got your number."

I rose from my seat, too, and turned to face him. "I don't think having my number is as helpful as, say, having car keys." I gave him a pointed look and wiggled my fingers. His nostrils flared just ever so slightly.

"Right. Meet me outside in ten minutes."

With that, he strode to the back of the shop. I watched him go, amused that I, Emily Allen the meek, managed to get under his skin as much as I did. It was extraordinary.

"You'd best fortify," Siobhan said. "Can't drive if the tank is empty."

"Oh, right, thanks." I sat back down and quickly ate a scone and drank my coffee.

"What will you do while I'm gone? I feel as if I'm abandoning you."

"Not at all," Siobhan assured me. "I'm going to make a list of places I want to visit that I think might help break me out of my funk. Have you ever been to the Cliffs of Moher?"

"Up until I moved here, I'd never been out of Massachusetts," I said. "Anywhere you want to go sounds great to me."

Siobhan clapped. "This is going to be grand." She glanced out the window. "Kier is waiting, off you pop."

"Wish me luck," I said.

"You won't need it." Her smile radiated confidence—*in me!* "I believe in you."

"Thank you," I said. I wasn't accustomed to receiving such unquestioning support. I feared I was going to wake up and discover that my entire Irish adventure was just a dream. I sincerely hoped not as I thought the disappointment might kill me. "I'm thinking of Tig McMorrow right now and his philosophy that the most difficult path is usually the right one to take."

"Oh, that message was a good one. Tig was so right."

I smiled. I loved how we talked about Tig as if he was an actual person and not something conjured out of Siobhan's imagination.

"See you in a bit." I tugged on my coat, hat, and gloves and grabbed my shoulder bag. I headed to the door like a soldier who'd just gotten her marching orders. I could do this. I mean how hard could it be? A car was a car. Right?

I found Kier standing outside with Oisín. They were huddled over the back of the Range Rover and I paused beside them. "What are you doing?"

They both jumped and Oisín stepped back, looking guilty. He glanced at me and said, "Hiya, Em. Just so you know, this was not my idea."

He touched his flat cap and hurried back into the warmth of the bookshop. I glanced at Kier. "What was that about?"

"This." Kier gestured to the letter *N*—a big, bold red *N* on a white background—that he'd obviously just put on the back of the car.

"What's that?" I asked.

"A warning for every other driver on the road." He walked around me to the driver's side and said, "I'll take us out of town before we start the lesson."

"All right." I shrugged. This seemed reasonable. I climbed into the passenger seat. "So, what's the *N* stand for?"

"Novice," he said. "In Ireland, when you're learning to drive, you have to have an *L* displayed on your car so that others know you're learning to drive. Once you've gotten your license, you get an *N* for novice, which is you."

If he thought I'd be offended, he was wrong. I was actually relieved. I had no problem with warning everyone around me that I was a newbie. Hopefully, they'd steer clear.

Kier started the car and pulled away from the curb, barely checking his mirrors. We drove until we were at the end of the business district. I felt my nerves ratchet up but thankfully there were only a few shops on this end of town.

"All right then." Kier shut off the engine and stepped out of the car. He gestured for me to do the same. I joined him on the curb while he scanned the area. "This looks as good as any place to start."

He handed me the key fob and we climbed back in just as a man stepped out of the barbershop holding an unlit cigarette in his hand. "Is that you, Murph?"

"Hiya, Mick," Kier greeted him. He left his door open so they could talk, which was fine except for the frigid air it let into the vehicle. "How's the shop today?"

"Up to ninety since we flipped the sign to open this morning," Mick said. He studied Kier's face. "I can fit you in if you've a mind for a cleanup."

Kier cupped his jaw with his hand and assessed his whisker situation. "Maybe later. I'm teaching Red here how to drive on the proper side of the road."

Mick laughed. He hunched over and looked past Kier at me. "You're the girl from the States, yeah?"

"I'm the woman from Massachusetts, yes," I said. I took in his crooked smile and perfectly trimmed sideburns. He had a beak of a nose, but the sideburns made it seem less so.

"Might I give you a bit of advice?" he asked.

"Absolutely," I said.

"When driving in Ireland, you always want to keep your passenger safe," he said. "To that end, you want to keep the passenger side of the car closest to the curb. That's how you'll always know which lane to be in."

I nodded. "Keep the passenger on the curb. That makes sense. Thank you."

"An easier way to remember it if you're likely to forget is 'keep the bitch in the ditch,'" Mick said.

"Oh!" I laughed in surprise. I had to give it to him, it was a catchy way to remember.

Mick glanced at Kier and added, "That makes you the bitch, Murph."

"Yeah, I got that." Kier wasn't laughing. In fact, he looked a bit annoyed.

"Oisín told me all about you." Mick leaned into the car and spoke to me. His eyes twinkled, which I was beginning to suspect was a requirement for being Irish. "He said you're sound."

"Sound?" I asked.

"That's slang for nice," Kier explained.

"Aw, I knew I liked Oisín," I said.

"I have to say he was right. Might you also be available?" Mick asked. His grin was pure mischief and I felt my face get hot. I wasn't used to being flirted with so blatantly and I had no idea what to say.

Kier frowned from Mick to me and back. "Are you on the mooch, Mick?"

"Always," he said. "And look at her. She's a ride, isn't she?"

Kier glanced back at me. His frown deepened and he turned back to his friend. "We have to go." He reached out and pulled his door shut, barely giving Mick a chance to hop out of the way. Instead of being offended, his friend laughed and spun away, putting his cigarette to his lips and cupping his hand over it while he lit it with the lighter in his other hand.

"All right, start the car," Kier said. He looked grumpy.

"Are you mad because you're the bitch in the ditch?" I asked. I coughed to cover my laugh. He glowered at me and I added, "I promise I'll keep you safe." I sent him a toothy smile.

"Start the car, Red." He closed his eyes as if praying for patience.

I did as I was told, but left it in first with my feet on the brake and the clutch and said, "I have so many questions."

"Well, the round thing is how you steer—" he said but I interrupted.

"Hilarious," I said. "What does on the mooch mean? And ride? Is that a bad thing?"

"Did it sound like it was a bad thing?" he asked.

"No, but craic is a good thing, and I have to admit, it's not very intuitive either," I said.

"That's fair." He turned in his seat and leaned over the console. "All right, just so you don't land yourself in a situation that you can't get out of, let me enlighten you. 'Ride' means sex in Ireland, so calling you a ride indicates Mick would like to have sex with you."

My jaw dropped. "No way."

"Way."

"Your mother did not cover that in the Tig McMorrow books," I said.

"Well, I should hope not," he said. "Those books were for children."

"Only the first two," I said. "After that they got more mature as Tig aged."

Kier waved a dismissive hand. "Enough. Are we driving or talking, Red?"

"We can't do both?" I asked. "Also, you didn't tell me what 'on the mooch' means."

He sighed. "It means making a play, trying to pick you up, you know, like that."

"And he was?" I asked. My eyes went wide. I glanced out the window where Mick stood on the corner, smoking. He saw me glance at him and he winked. Then he made a hand gesture like he was holding a phone to his ear and he jutted his chin in my direction, indicating that I should call him.

"What an eejit," Kier muttered under his breath. He leaned forward and shook his head no at Mick, who responded with a rude hand gesture and a laugh.

"Drive, Red, before he thinks you're interested," Kier said.

"Oh!" I turned my attention to the car. I checked my mirrors, the seat setting, and my seatbelt, then I glanced over my right shoulder, turned on the signal, and merged with nothing as there were no cars coming—hallelujah—and headed out of town.

We drove in silence as I became accustomed to the manual transmission. I thought of Sam with a surge of appreciation for teaching me to drive stick, although shifting with my left hand was awkward. When I ground the gears moving from first to second at a stop sign, I heard Kier suck a breath in through his teeth but he didn't say anything, which I was certain took considerable restraint.

The countryside was breathtaking and I soaked in the sight of the stone walls, single-story homes, and fields of sheep, marveling that I was actually here. And I was driving!

There weren't many road signs. The occasional speed limit post, in kilometers, but no billboards, even though we were on a supposed major route, although the road was pretty darn narrow to be considered a major anything. The terrain started to get hilly, and I noted a new road sign. It was just a squiggly arrow, indicating curves up ahead, I assumed.

As I drove, I realized the sign was a vast understatement as we wound back and forth along the serpentine road. My hands started to sweat as I hoped we were nearing the end. When we crested the hill, a sheep leapt onto the road right in front of us and I stomped on the clutch and the brake pedals while I swerved into the opposite lane to avoid it. I thought we were in the clear but a van appeared around the bend right as I crossed over the line and I had to punch the gas and steer back to my side of the road while shifting into a higher gear, narrowly missing the sheep and the van.

"Fecking shite!" Kier yelled. "That was close!"

"Sorry! Sorry!" I cried. I spotted a narrow pullout and parked. I did not stop gently.

We both lurched against our seatbelts and then fell back. I put the car in first gear and switched off the engine. I waited for him to yell at me. I expected it would be a diatribe along the lines of how I could have gotten him killed, that I was a fecking eejit, and that he would never let me drive his mother anywhere ever.

"Are you all right?" Kier turned in his seat to face me. I took a steadying breath and glanced at him. Shockingly, he didn't look mad as much as impressed. "That was brilliant, Red."

I put my hand on my chest to check that my heart was still beating. I was sure it must have stopped.

"Here." Kier leaned across the console and pulled me in for a hug. I found my face pressed into his shoulder as he tucked me in against his coat. One of his hands stroked up and down my back, he rested his cheek on the top of my head, while his other arm remained around me, holding me close.

The warmth from his body soothed me even as the scent of him, a combination of warm wool, coffee, and laundry detergent, made me keenly aware of him, Kieran Murphy, holding me in his arms. The man had been nothing but a hot nuisance since I'd arrived. This kindness from him should not have been sexy. It was dead sexy.

He pulled back and studied me. "All right, Red?"

"That depends. Are you going to make me walk back to town?"

He laughed. "No, you handled that perfectly." His dark blue gaze moved from my eyes to my lips and then he glanced away. "Right, let's get going then." He pointed out the windshield.

Get going? As in, I was supposed to drive?

"No thank you, I'm tapping out," I said. I lifted my hands up in the air as if to prove they were incapable of holding the steering wheel.

"You can't quit now."

"Yes, I can. I quit. See? Easy peasy."

"'There is no living thing that is not afraid when it faces danger. The true courage is in facing danger when you are afraid, and that kind of courage you have in plenty,'" Kier said. The words sounded familiar and I scanned my brain to think of where I'd heard them before.

"*The Wizard of Oz*," I said.

His lips curved up. A smile. I had nearly gotten us killed and he was smiling. "Come on, Red. I didn't take you for a coward."

"I'm not. I'm simply attempting to save us from certain death."

"Listen, what happened was my fault," Kier said. I was tempted to check him for a head injury. Maybe he'd bonked his temple on the dashboard when I was occupied with steering around the sheep.

"How do you figure?" I asked. "You weren't driving."

"No, but I'm supposed to be teaching you how to drive here, and I wasn't giving it my full attention," he admitted. "I could have warned you on the way up the hill that there might be a surprise sheep and you would have been more prepared. I promise to do better. Let's give it another go, yeah?"

I really didn't want to. I was sure I'd pulled some muscles in my butt, I'd clenched so hard. But he looked genuinely remorseful—a first!—and I didn't want to let Siobhan down. I reluctantly nodded and he clapped his hands and rubbed his palms together.

"That's the spirit, Red," he said.

I sighed and started the car. Glancing over my right shoulder, I pulled back onto the road. My fingers gripped the wheel as if I were trying to strangle it. I checked my speed. I was only going thirty-five miles per hour, or fifty-six kilometers if I looked at the speedometer like a native. The speed signs posted by the road read eighty kilometers but that seemed foolishly excessive to me.

"You're doing grand, Red," Kier said. "In half a kilometer, you're going to go through a roundabout."

"What!" I cried. "I'm not ready for that."

"You will be when you get through it," he said cheerfully. It occurred to me then that he was enjoying this. I should have known. This was clearly a brand-new way to torture me. A sound came out of my throat that sounded like a snarl.

"Now you have to yield to the cars coming from the right, so slow down and if someone is coming, stop," he said. "You're going to enter the roundabout at six and exit at twelve, all right?"

I thought I might be ill. Blue and white signs popped up, warning us about the roundabout. Fine, if this was the way my epic journey to Ireland ended so be it. I closed my eyes.

"Um . . . eyes open, Red," Kier said. "You need them to see the other cars."

"Mmm." I made a Marge Simpson growl noise in my throat.

"You've got this," he coached. "Now there is a car coming so you want to stop."

I slowed to a stop at the mouth of the roundabout. A little blue car chugged by. I glanced to the right to be certain there was no one else.

"There you go," Kier cheered me on as I pulled into the circle of death. "Steady. Stay to the outside. You're going to pass the first exit and take the second. Little blue car is going that way, follow him."

"Little blue is my friend. Got it," I said. I exited out of the roundabout behind my new buddy and the road straightened out. I sucked in a huge gulp of air. I hadn't realized I was holding my breath.

"Fair play, Red!" Kier cried. He clapped me on the shoulder. "Well done."

I turned to him and grinned. The feeling of accomplishment was heady stuff. Kier blinked at me as if he'd never seen me before, then he returned my grin full measure. Wow.

"So, you have another roundabout coming up in one kilometer," he said.

"Not funny," I said. I turned my attention back to the road.

"Not joking," he replied.

My shoulders drooped. "Oh man." It came out a little whiney but I felt like I deserved some whine since there actually was another roundabout. Who was responsible for this madness?

"All right, this one you're going to enter at six and exit at three," Kier said.

"Three?" I cried. "That's all the way around!"

"Three-quarters," he corrected me. I shot him a look and he added, "Give or take."

"Argh."

"Now, Red, you can do it," Kier said. "I believe in you."

"What is that?" I asked.

"What's what?"

"That very unlike Kieran Murphy positivity," I said. "I don't know what to do with that."

"It's Murphy," he said.

"I'll call you Murphy when you call me Em," I said.

"But you're so clearly a Red," he argued. "Stubborn, feisty, and . . ."

I waited. He didn't finish.

"A ride?" I asked. "Is that what you were going to say?"

"No," he protested. "You're my employee. That would be crossing a line, but I do agree with Oisín that you are sound."

Was that a compliment? I gave him a side-eye. I was about to ask but the signs for the roundabout popped up and I was too busy panicking to pursue the discussion.

"Easy now, remember to yield, that's right," Kier encouraged me. "No one is coming, so you're good. Keep going, all the way around, there's your exit, excellent. Good job, Red!"

I heaved a sigh and tried to unclench my body. My core was getting a hell of a workout as I navigated the twists and turns that made up the roads of Ireland.

"There's a pub up ahead," Kier said. "Why don't we pop in and give you a minute to catch your breath."

"Yes, please," I said. A few kilometers later, I pulled off the road and into a narrow parking lot. It was late morning and several cars were in the lot. I navigated around them and parked in a vacant spot away from everyone else.

We stepped out of the car and the wind whipped at my hair and coat. The sky was blue, the hills green, but dark clouds were rolling in from what I assumed was the south and I expected rain was imminent. I wasn't sure how I felt about driving in a storm. Wait, yes, I did. I didn't want to. Perhaps I should get drunk in the pub to take myself out of the equation.

"Come on then," Kier said. He led the way into the brightly colored building, yellow with a vibrant green trim. The sign over the door read *Bad Brian's Pub*, so that seemed promising.

"How about some seafood chowder? They have the best in Kerry. The son fishes in the morning and the mom cooks it up for lunch and dinner."

"Sounds amazing."

The pub was half-full and Kier led me to a snug in the corner. "I'll go order."

He went to the bar and returned with two cups of coffee. I looked at him in surprise and he said, "I noticed you drink a lot of coffee."

I wasn't sure what to make of that. Was he judging the amount of coffee I drank? No, of course not. That was just my instinctive reaction from years of living with my mother who judged everything I ate, wore, said, or did. I had to remind myself that other people weren't like her.

"Are you more of a coffee or tea guy?" I asked. This seemed like a nice neutral topic.

"I used to drink tea when I was a lad and lived with my dad," he said. "My stepmother, Meredith, didn't allow coffee in the house, because she felt it was only for the uncivilized. Naturally, once I found out about that I took to drinking it."

"Naturally," I said. I thought about my own stepmother, Jessica. As far as I knew, she only drank organic smoothies, not allowing any toxins of any kind ever into her body. Too bad they didn't make her smarter or kinder; still, she did have a heck of an ass on her.

He glanced at me. "Care to share what you're thinking, Red?"

"It's not very nice," I said. I ripped open the long sugar packet and poured it into my coffee. Kier had brought a tiny pitcher of cream with the coffees and I poured some in, stirring it with my spoon and watching it bloom in the cup.

"That's fine," he said. He pursed his lips and blew over the edge of his mug and then drank his coffee black. "I can handle it."

"Oh, it's not about you," I said. "I was thinking disparaging thoughts about my own stepmother."

"Your parents are divorced?" he asked.

I nodded. "My father left my mother when I was in college. He dumped her for the head cheerleader at my high school. Sure, he waited until she was in her mid-twenties, but still, we were in high school *at the same time*."

"That's so wrong," he said.

"I thought so," I agreed. "I also made the mistake of saying so to him. Our relationship has never recovered."

"You don't get on with them then?" he asked.

"We don't not get on," I said. "It's more that she has my father wrapped around her, well, it's probably best not to dwell on what body part she uses to keep him under her spell. Suffice to say, that since Dad's been shackled to Jessica, Dr. Allen has been MIA in my life, leaving me to clean up the mess he left, which would be my mother."

Kier nodded. His dark eyes were understanding. "Sounds like a right bastard."

"Yeah," I agreed. "I used to blame him, but I don't anymore. My mother can be . . . no, she is very difficult and I understand why he left. Still, he could have supported me more. I spent years trying to help my mother get over him leaving but she won't and I just can't anymore."

"Ah, so that's why you're here," he said. "You found an escape hatch and you jumped out."

I wanted to deny it, but I couldn't. It was true. "As far back as I can remember, all I ever wanted to do was see the world," I said. "Your mother's job offer was my first chance. I couldn't let it pass me by."

Kier looked like he was about to say something, but the server arrived at our snug with two enormous bowls of seafood chowder, a loaf of Irish soda bread with a knife wedged in it like King Arthur's sword, and a little crock of bright yellow butter. Driving had given me a hunger and all thought of conversation left me as I gazed at the steaming bowl in front of me.

"Tuck in," Kier said. He picked up the knife and cut each of us a slice of the bread.

I picked up my spoon and dipped it into the chowder. As a New Englander, I was finicky about chowder. Sam taught me that a good one had a cream-enriched broth, not that nasty flour-thickened stuff that comes out of a can. This looked promising. I sipped the broth and bit into a chunk of halibut.

"Oh. My. God." I put my hand over my mouth. It was like sipping hot herbed butter and the fish was so fresh and tender it melted on my tongue.

Kier looked at me and laughed. "You sound like that character Janice from *Friends*."

"Don't talk." I held up my hand as I took another spoonful of the chowder. "I'm having a moment with my food."

Kier watched me as I blew on the spoon, his gaze on my mouth as I pursed my lips. The intensity of his dark stare caused my pulse to quicken and I held his gaze as I slipped the spoonful into my mouth. He cleared his throat and glanced away.

"I told you, best in Kerry, if not all of Ireland." His voice was deliciously gruff.

"It's a revelation," I agreed. I took the piece of soda bread he offered and slathered it in butter. Then I dunked it into my chowder, letting it soak up the broth. It was so good.

We ate in silence, which was surprisingly comfortable. When the chowder and the soda bread were gone, our server cleared our plates and warmed our coffee. I was so relaxed; I could have sacked out on the bench seat for a nap. Instead, I decided to use Kier's relaxed state to my advantage. I wanted to understand his relationship with Siobhan and I doubted I'd ever have a better time than this.

"How old were you when your parents divorced?" I asked.

Kier looked surprised that I'd returned to our conversation, but he answered, which I took as an encouraging sign that the topic wasn't privileged information.

"Ten," he said.

"That must have been difficult," I said.

He nodded. "A family falling apart is hardest on the children, I think. My father, much like yours, wandered into a different field and my mother let him go. They weren't a good match. She was creative and he wasn't."

"That would be a challenge," I agreed. I wanted him to keep talking. I wanted to understand his life but also Siobhan's.

"Might not have been such a challenge if he hadn't jumped right into it with Meredith but he was angry, and I think he thought shacking up with a younger woman would hurt Ma," he said.

"Did it?" I asked.

Kier laughed. "She's never admitted it, but I think Ma was glad to see the back of him. He didn't support her writing. He thought she was wasting her time."

I gasped. I couldn't even imagine feeling that way about the Tig McMorrow series.

The corner of Kier's mouth tipped up in a half smile. "As I said, they weren't a good fit. Ma had the ultimate revenge, however. Da left her for Meredith and then Ma hit it big with the novels. My father was bitter about that until his dying day."

"I'm sorry for your loss," I said.

Kier shrugged. "It was seven years ago. My stepmother married their neighbor three months after Da died."

"Oh," I said.

"Exactly."

"And you lived with them?" I asked.

A shadow crossed over Kier's face. There was something unpleasant there. I didn't pry but I made a note to double back in the future if the opportunity presented itself.

"Only in the beginning when Ma was on book tours and such," he said. "It was just a few weeks at the start but then as Ma's career got bigger and bigger, I spent more and more time at my father's. My stepmother was unhappy to have me there and she made it known that I wasn't welcome unless Ma gave them a lot of money to 'support me.'"

The bitterness in his voice was unmistakable. I didn't blame him a bit. Some people were lucky and their stepparents were amazing bonus parents. This did not seem to be the case for me or Kier.

"I'm sorry you had to go through that," I said. I wanted to reach out and put my hand on his arm but the moment passed before I got the nerve.

"Who knew we'd have so much in common, Red?"

"Indeed."

We stared at each other for a moment and for just a second, I felt a connection to Kieran Murphy beyond the physical attraction that I never would have believed possible.

"Right, well, are you ready to go back?"

"Sure," I said. The food was making me overly confident. "I'm duly fortified. I've got this."

"Excellent," he said. He glanced out the window. "It's bucketing out there. Looks like you're going to get some practice driving in the rain."

I followed his gaze. The rain was hammering down in a solid sheet of wet. Shit. Little did Kier know, we were now going to be a living math problem. It would go something like this: If Emily is driving ten miles per hour while a wicked storm rages overhead, how long will it take Emily to reach home? I feared the answer was "never," as the bitch wasn't the only thing that was going to land in the ditch. I'd likely send the entire car in. Why hadn't I ordered the Irish coffee when I had the chance?

Ten

Eun-ji had me trained to use the cash register in less than an hour. The shop was quiet and we chatted about books by Irish authors that she loved and so it was that I had two short novels by Claire Keegan set aside for me. After the exhausting drive this morning, I couldn't wait to get home to my little cottage and curl up by the fire and read.

We had a busy surge in the afternoon when a tour bus came swooping into town. One of the attractions of Finn's Hollow was the Last Chapter and its exclusive collection of signed Tig McMorrow books and merchandise.

Readers young and old trooped into the shop to peruse the signed copies of the Tig McMorrow series. There were some accompanying tie-in items as well. Bobble-headed action figures, a trivia board game, backpacks, pencils, and other assorted Tig McMorrow merch. I wondered how Siobhan felt about all of this. I also wondered if she left at noon because she knew the tours came in the afternoon and she was avoiding the crowd. I couldn't blame her. Judging by the awestruck expressions on some of her readers' faces, I imagined it could get overwhelming, especially when she knew every question would be a variation on when there might be another book.

The tour left and Eun-ji and I collapsed onto the counter. Brigid brought us each a cup of tea and a scone, after which Eun-ji gathered her things and left me to work the front by myself until Oisín replaced me for the evening. The shop only stayed open late Tuesday through Thursday, and by late I mean we closed at seven—a whole hour later than the rest of the week—but still, someone had to be there.

While waiting for Oisín, I debated what to fix myself for dinner. I was considering making my own Guinness stew when Oisín appeared, looking upset. "Em, I have to go. My sister got a flat tire and she's stuck on the edge of the village."

I glanced out the window, where the weather had kicked up again. The wind was fierce, causing it to rain sideways. No one should be stuck in that. I turned back to Oisín and said, "Go! I can close up."

"You don't mind?" he asked.

"Not at all," I said. "Go help your sister. I'll see you tomorrow."

"You remember how to lock up?" he asked.

I nodded. On the nights we'd closed early, we'd all left together and Oisín had walked me through it.

"I've got it," I said. "I used to close the library all the time. How different can it be?"

"Thanks, Em, I owe you one," he said.

I smiled. "Don't worry about it."

Oisín shot out the door, and I stood in the silent shop, listening to the wind and rain. It was comforting to be safe and warm amid the books, although I was not looking forward to walking home and hoped the storm passed by quitting time.

I pressed my face against the glass window, trying to see how bad it was outside. The old-fashioned streetlamps illuminated the rain as it poured down and the bunting that had been strung across the street for the upcoming holidays snapped in the wind. Yeah, I had no problem staying here and waiting it out.

I turned away from the window when a movement caught my eye. Was someone out there in this? I couldn't see much more than a blur. I hurried to the door and pushed it open. The wind tried to rip the door out of my hands and I braced myself. The blurry movement I'd seen shot forward, ducking in between my legs, seeking refuge in the shop.

I pulled the door closed and turned around. Sitting in a puddle of its own making was the saddest looking black and white dog I'd ever seen.

"Well, who are you?" I asked. "And what were you doing out in that weather?"

The dog tipped its head to the side as if trying to make up its mind about me. I had no idea what Kier and Siobhan would say about a dog being in the shop, but there was no way I was sending the poor thing back out into the storm.

I held out my hand and the dog sniffed my fingers and gave my wrist a lick, so I figured we were good. Neither of us wanted to go out in that, so we'd huddle in here until it passed.

"Come on," I said. "Let's see what Brigid has in the café to dry you off with."

I crossed the shop and the dog fell into step beside me as if it knew where I was going. We reached the café and I grabbed a fistful of paper napkins from a holder on one of the tables and began to pat the dog down. The napkins were sodden in moments, rendering them useless. I wasn't positive but I was guessing by the black and white fur and the inquisitive face that this was a border collie, the sort the local sheep farmers used to move their flocks.

The dog sat patiently under my care and I noticed it was wearing a collar. A nametag was attached to it that read *Shackleton* but there was no phone number. Since the napkins weren't helping and the poor dog was soaked, I raided the café cupboards until I found a stash of dish towels. I told myself Brigid wouldn't mind, especially since I planned to wash and dry them and bring them back tomorrow. No one needed to know that I used them to dry off a dog.

"Where did you wander in from, Shackleton?" I asked. "You know, in weather like this you should really stay home."

The dog wagged. Agreement? It seemed a safe assumption.

"Are you hungry?" I asked. "I think Brigid has some peanut butter cookies that you could eat. Let me check."

Sure enough, there was a batch of cookies in a plastic tub under the display case. I grabbed two—yes, one for me and one for him—and sat on the floor beside him.

I broke off a piece and held it out. The dog sniffed it as if he thought I might try to poison him. "It's fine. See?" I took a bite of the cookie. The dog watched and then gingerly accepted the piece I gave him.

"Now, how are we going to find your owners?" I asked. "There's no number on your tag, and I have to close up in thirty-five minutes. I can't leave you in here, so I think you should come home with me. I can make us some dinner. You can fall asleep by the fire and tomorrow we'll find your people, does that seem like a good idea?"

I swear Shackleton understood everything I said. He barked and then gently pawed my hand, clearly indicating "more cookie, please." I obliged and he didn't hesitate to snarf up the cookie this time.

"Excellent, we have a plan," I said. I heard the front door bang open—*why would anyone be here now?*—and I glanced at the dog. He wagged again. I whispered, "I don't know who that is, so stay here until I give the all clear. Okay?"

I tossed him the rest of his cookie and rose to my feet. I glanced over the empty display case and across the bookshop, ready to assist whoever had popped in. Standing just inside the door, looking at the puddle on the floor, was Kier.

"Oh, hello," I said. I ignored how his hair was even more mussed than usual and his cheeks and nose were red from the cold, giving him a hearty handsomeness.

"Red, what are you doing here? I thought Oisín was on duty."

Kier was not exactly bowled over with happiness to see me. I tried not to take it personally. "Oisín had an emergency so I said I would stay and close."

"Really?" He was scanning the bookshop, his eyes tracking every corner. Did he not trust me?

"Yes, really. I can handle it," I said, my voice a smidge testy. I left the café and joined him by the door.

He glanced from me to the second cookie still in my hand. I felt my face get warm with embarrassment. "I can explain."

"That you're raiding the café while you're here alone?" he asked. His judgmental eyebrow rose.

"No," I protested. I forced myself not to glance over my shoulder at where I'd left the dog. If Kier was judging me for snitching a cookie for myself, I couldn't even imagine what he'd think if he knew I had a dog in the shop. "It's complicated but it doesn't concern you. Feel free to show yourself out."

"Show myself—" he began but was interrupted as forty-five pounds of exuberant canine came barreling out of the café and charged Kier at full speed. Uh-oh.

"Oh, no! Shackleton, he's a friend, don't—" I cried at the same time Kier said, "Shackleton, where have you been? I was looking for you." Kier chided the dog even while he crouched down and rubbed his ears.

"Shackleton is *your* dog?" I asked.

"As much as he belongs to anyone," Kier said. "He was named for—"

"Ernest Shackleton, the explorer," I said. Kier looked surprised that I knew where the name had come from. I pointed to myself and said, "Librarian."

He smiled. "I assume the biscuit was for the poor pup."

"Truthfully, it was more of a one for him and one for me situation," I said. I tossed the remaining cookie in the air for the pooch, who caught it and swallowed it whole. "So why Shackleton?"

"He's a wanderer. He got fired from my friend Colin's sheep farm when he showed no aptitude for herding," Kier said. "He preferred wandering into town to meet and greet people, so when Colin said he had to go, I offered to take him as a companion for Siobhan. They have quite the mutual admiration society going, but once she retires for the night, he likes to head out and explore."

I reached down to pat the dog. "You're just a free thinker, aren't you, fella?"

Shackleton leaned against my leg and gazed up at me with his tongue hanging out.

"Looks like he has a new crush," Kier observed.

"It's just cupboard love," I said.

"I think it runs deeper than that," Kier said. "You were kind to him, you gave him safety in a storm. You're a nice person, Red."

Shackleton glanced between us as if he, too, could feel the pulsing attraction that hummed between us. His bedraggled tail had begun to dry and resembled a plume and it swept across the floor.

"You say that like it's a bad thing," I said.

"It is. This whole situation would have been a lot easier if you'd been an arsehole," Kier said.

He sounded so put out that I laughed. He frowned.

"I'm sorry?" I said it like a question because really, why would I want to be an asshole? "Should I work on that? Try to be more difficult, high maintenance, a diva?"

"It's too late now," he said. "You've only been here for a few weeks and everyone adores you."

"Everyone?" I asked. As soon as the word left my lips, I wanted to snap it back like Shackleton with the cookie. Of course I couldn't, so instead I brazened it out, pretending I was a sassy romance heroine from a Christina Lauren novel.

Kier's piercing blue gaze held mine. "Yes, *every*one."

Oh my. It was a look of such pure longing that I found myself leaning forward as if compelled to touch him, to be near him, to feel his body against mine.

My phone chimed in my pocket, breaking the spell. I fumbled with it and glanced at the display. It was a weather update. The rain had stopped but there was a flood alert for all of County Kerry. I noted the time.

"It's time to close," I said. "You don't need to stay. I've got this."

"No, Shack and I will drive you home." He glanced out the window. "You have that lake to navigate and those runners are not going to get you through it."

He pointed to my sneakers and I knew he was right. Still, I opened my mouth to protest. I just wanted a moment to process what he'd said. Did he mean it when he said everyone? But Kier left me standing there and began closing the shop. I had no choice but to do the same. Shackleton stayed beside me and I reached down to pat his head.

"You've probably witnessed hundreds of women making idiots of themselves in front of him," I whispered. "Is that why you're here? To make me feel better?"

Shackleton wagged so I took that as a yes and sighed.

Once we'd locked up, I followed Kier to the car. This time I sat in the passenger seat—yes, making me the bitch in the ditch.

Shackleton hopped into the back and Kier drove the quiet streets, through my nemesis that lake of a puddle, stopping in front of the narrow path that led to my cottage.

"Thank you." I opened my door thinking this was good night, but Kier stepped out, too.

"Ma raised me to escort a lady all the way to her door." He slid out and walked around the front of the car.

Shackleton barked and I reached back and rubbed his soft head before I stepped out. "Thanks for keeping me company, buddy."

Kier and I made our way, single file, up the narrow alley to the cottage. The lights were off and it looked dark and cold. The evening air was chilly and I shivered in my coat. The hat and scarf I was wearing only covered so much. I was overly aware of Kier walking behind me.

The porch light snapped on as soon as we stepped within range. I took out my keys and unlocked the door. I reached inside and flicked on the light switch, illuminating the main room.

I turned back to Kier. He was studying the bright pink door as if he expected it to reveal something. The silence, which had been fine on the walk, now felt as uncomfortable as an itchy sweater.

"Thanks for seeing me to the door," I said. "I'd invite you in, but . . ."

"Shackleton," we said together.

"Right, I'd best be off." He stepped back.

"Did you always want to own a bookshop?" I asked. I wasn't trying to keep the conversation going. I was mostly curious to see if he'd admit that he actually wanted to be an author.

"I don't know about always," he said. He squinted into the darkness as if he were hoping someone would arrive to interrupt us.

I wanted to tell him no one was coming to spare him from this conversation. Instead, I persisted in my line of questioning. "Then what did you want to be?"

He opened his mouth and then closed it. He looked at me and said, "Guess."

"That's not fair," I said. "You already know what I wanted to do with my life."

"Cross the pond to be an author's assistant and shop clerk?" he asked.

"No, a librarian," I said.

He studied me and a small smile tipped the corners of his lips. "Honestly, I never would have guessed that you wanted to be a librarian if I didn't already know that about you."

"Really?" I asked. "Most people tease me, because I'm such a stereotypical librarian. I'm always reading, I wear glasses, and I'm quiet."

He burst out laughing and it was loud enough to scare Mr. Tom, Maeve and Shane's orange tabby who liked to sleep on the cushioned chair on my porch. He sent Kier a reproachful glance as he hopped down and strode, tail in the air, back to the main house.

"Quiet?" Kier repeated through a laugh. "In what alternate reality are you quiet?"

"I am!" I protested. "Just not around you."

He stopped laughing but his lips still tipped up in the corners and his eyes glinted with humor. "Why do you suppose that is, Red?"

My heart thumped hard in my chest and I dropped my gaze to

my shoes. Why did that annoying nickname seem like so much more when he used it?

I could have answered that I wasn't quiet with him because he irritated me like no other, which was true but that was only a part of it. There was something about Kier that made me bold. I didn't know what it was but when I was with him, I took risks I normally wouldn't, like learning to drive on a different side of the road or sticking up for myself when I felt he was being unreasonable.

I supposed I felt the need to stand my ground with Kier because I didn't want to be bowled over by his good looks and charm, both of which he had in abundance. But also, the truth was I felt safe with Kier. There was a kindness in him that I witnessed in the way he listened to me, giving me his full attention, and letting me know I mattered even when we disagreed. It was a feeling that had been missing in my life, and it made him all the more irresistible.

"Why aren't you quiet with me, Red?" he pressed. He took a step toward me and then another.

"I . . . don't . . ." I stammered. The words were just above a whisper and he had to lean down to hear me, putting him solidly in my personal space, which was a very bad thing because the urge to grab him by the lapels and kiss him was like the call of the void, that bizarre urge to jump when standing on the edge of a high place. I shoved my hands into my coat pockets, thwarting the impulse.

"You don't what?" he asked. His face was inches from mine. His dark gaze moved from my eyes to my lips, where they lingered as if studying their shape. He moved in. Was he going to kiss me?

"I don't know why I'm not quiet with you," I said. He stopped moving. I cleared my throat. He leaned back and I took a huge gulp of air.

The sweet scent of rain-soaked grass and damp earth filled my lungs, purging me of the scent of him and clearing my head. Had he really been about to kiss me? Or had I just imagined it? Probably. What was wrong with me? I needed to pivot away from this social disaster and fast.

"A pilot," I said.

"Huh?" He looked confused.

"I'm guessing that's what you wanted to be when you were a kid," I said.

"Oh, right." His expression was thoughtful when he looked at me and I wondered if he knew how much I wanted him to kiss me. Of course he didn't. How could he when I'd done everything I could to destroy the moment?

"Well?" I asked.

"No, not a pilot. Although I'm flattered that you think I wanted to pursue such a romantic occupation," he said.

"Romantic? Not at all," I said. "I assumed a pilot because you're so bossy. All that 'this is your captain speaking' stuff seemed like a good fit."

He opened his mouth to protest but I didn't give him the chance. "A chef then."

"Another take-charge profession?" he asked.

I shrugged.

"I'm not that overbearing," he protested.

"Eh." I tipped my hand back and forth as if to say it was a matter of opinion.

"Not a chef."

I glanced at the porch ceiling and decided to go for it.

"A writer," I said. I tried to appear nonchalant but his sudden laughter ruined that. "What's so funny?"

He didn't answer because he was still chuckling. This was not the reaction I'd expected. His mystery was good. He shouldn't think writing was out of his skill set. He was genuinely talented.

"'The wastepaper basket is the writer's best friend,'" Kier said.

I frowned. He had finally stumped me. "Who said that?"

"Isaac Bashevis Singer."

"Regardless, I bet you'd make a fine writer," I insisted.

"Because I'm Siobhan Riordan's son?" he asked. He stopped laughing but his eyes were still glinting with humor. It irked the booklover in me because I didn't think he should dismiss his abilities.

"No, because I read your book," I said. That sobered him up. He made a face as if he'd smelled something foul.

"How?" he asked. "Why?"

"It was on a shelf on the third floor of the bookshop. When I saw the name on the cover I thought it was an odd coincidence but then I saw the author's picture and realized it was you—younger, but still you."

"Ugh, this is how I die then?" he asked. "Of complete humiliation on the front porch of a cottage in Finn's Hollow."

"Why would you feel humiliated?" I asked. "It's a really good book."

"Yes, all three people who bought it thought so, too." His tone was dry. "Actually, I believe all three were my mam buying it under different names."

"I don't believe that," I said. "I thought it was a wonderful book. You asked me before why I'm not quiet with you. It's partly because of your book."

"Because the writing was rubbish, so it made me an imbecile in your eyes?" he asked.

"No, because the mystery was well plotted and the way you described the protagonist's grief at never having the relationship he wanted with his father resonated," I said.

"Because of your father?" he asked.

"More because of my mother," I said. "You wrote so brilliantly about Danny's longing to connect only to discover that his father wasn't capable of that type of relationship. It was very touching. That heartbreaking moment when he realizes that what he has with his father is all he'll ever have . . . I cried."

"You did not." He put his hands on his hips.

"Did." I mimicked his stance. "Twice."

He let loose a low whistle. "You are a glutton for punishment."

"Hardly," I said. "It's very good."

It was as if I'd issued a challenge. He leaned down until his face was just inches from mine. "And what do you know about good writing, Red?"

I took a deep breath to fortify myself for my counterargument that my English degree and the thousands of books I'd read to date gave me more than enough qualifications to determine what was a good book or not. I never got the chance. Before I could form the first word, Kier kissed me.

I think his intent was to keep me from arguing but instead of immediately pulling away, he cupped my face and closed the inches between us, swooping in to press his mouth more firmly to mine. It was like getting struck by lightning. Every nerve ending in my body jolted to life and I arched up, grabbing his forearms with my hands while instinctively pressing closer to him, as if my body had been waiting for his my entire life.

Kier responded by dropping one hand from my face to scoop me in even tighter. The cold night air didn't stand a chance with the heat we were generating. He tilted his head, fitting his lips to mine and plundering my mouth with his tongue as if he couldn't get enough of the taste of me. I felt dizzy and delighted and was drowning in the scent of him. I touched him wherever I could reach and his response was a low growl and a deepening of the kiss as his hands moved over my person, hampered by my puffy coat but still leaving a trail of fire in their wake. I was just about to suggest we go inside when he abruptly pulled back.

We were both breathing heavily and I slumped against the wall while I caught my breath. His hair was mussed, his scarf askew, and his eyes bright. He looked as thoroughly kissed as my favorite historical romance authors frequently described their heroines. I wondered if I looked the same.

"Well, that was delightfully unexpected." He stood in the yellow light of the porch, looking as if he wanted to say something more but couldn't find the words. I understood completely. I felt utterly witless myself.

"Good night, Red." He stepped away from the cottage and headed back down the alley.

"Good night, Kier." I felt oddly bereft when I went into my cottage. I knew he had made the right choice for both of us, yet, I was certain he'd been about to say something more . . . but what? The man was maddening!

Eleven

"And here we are," Kier announced as he turned into a very small parking area and stopped the car. As agreed, Kier had driven Siobhan and me to Drombeg. He pointed out the window. "It's a straight walk that way."

He didn't have to tell me twice. I popped out of my side, grabbing Siobhan's backpack as I went. The air was cool but the sun was warm. We were having a glorious day for this excursion.

Siobhan exited from the back seat with a large yawn. She stretched her arms over her head and then bent over at the waist as if trying to get all the kinks out. She was wearing jeans and hiking boots and a heavy Aran sweater with a colorful purple and gray scarf draped about her neck. In my puffy coat, knit hat, and sensible shoes, I felt hopelessly uncool.

"Are you ready, Em?" she asked.

"Absolutely," I said.

Siobhan led the way with Kier on one side of her and me on the other. The walk was short and flat, not strenuous at all, but when we reached the clearing where we could see the stones, I gasped.

"The circle is formed out of seventeen stones, most of which are local sandstone and three of which were discovered after excavation," Siobhan said. "The largest is the one lying down and is believed to be an altar, and across from it are the two tall portal stones, demarcating the entrance. Radiocarbon dating indicated the site was active in 1100 BC." She paused and tipped her head to the side as if she could see something we couldn't. Then she asked, "What do you suppose they worshipped here almost three thousand years ago?"

Why did that feel ominous? A shiver rippled down my spine as I thought of the people who had resided in these hills so long ago. I glanced at the earth beneath my feet. Where I stood, people had fought and loved, celebrated and mourned, and lived and died. Their lifespans were short and unless their name was carved on an Ogham stone, there was no record of them having ever been here at all.

Siobhan picked up speed and strode ahead. I would have followed her, but Kier stopped me with a hand on my arm. "I've seen that look in her eye before, Red. She's on a mission. Best leave her to it. She'll call you if she needs you."

She did not need me.

I watched as Siobhan moved along the inside of the stone ring, her dark hair and the end of her scarf gently tossed by the breeze. Her coat was unfastened and the wind tugged at it, too, as if it were a child demanding her attention. None of that deterred her.

She walked around each stone individually, letting her fingers run gently over their weathered surfaces. Her eyes were closed as if she could see and hear the ancestors who went before and they were telling her their stories and secrets.

"Come on, let's give her some space," Kier said. He led the way up the ridge, where another large stone gave us a place to sit.

I took a moment to appreciate the surrounding landscape. I could see a sliver of the brilliant blue of the Atlantic Ocean just beyond the surrounding farms. When I glanced back at the circle, Siobhan was sitting in the center of it. Her legs were crossed and her hands rested on her knees with her palms turned up.

"Looks like we're going to be here for awhile. Best get comfortable." Kier sat and I joined him.

"About last night," he said. "I owe you an apology."

My heart sank. There were a lot of things I wanted to hear about last night but an apology was not one of them. The old Em would have meekly listened as Kier said he was sorry for kissing me, that he was my boss and it was inappropriate, and I would have taken the blow to my self-esteem on the chin.

The new me, the Em who'd moved across an entire ocean to start a new life where I was no one's doormat, wasn't having it. This was my chance to be brave. To be . . . Red.

"Your apology is based on the assumption that I didn't want you to kiss me," I said. "Which is wrong." There was a beat of silence interrupted only by the chatter of the song thrushes in the nearby hedgerow.

"Red." His voice dropped to a low rumble and I wasn't sure if it was a reaction or a warning. Either way, it emboldened me.

"You know if this were a romance novel, I bet you'd take me right up against one of those stone pillars." I pointed to the circle. "I can see you dressed as a Celtic warrior—preferably shirtless—wielding the ancient weapons, a spear and oblong shield like an Irish Jamie Fraser." I glanced quickly at Kier. He was staring at me with his mouth agape. Cute! I had to squash the urge to laugh.

"You'd be a chieftain or a nobleman and your hair would be long and wild with a braid in it to keep it out of your face. Oh, and you'd have a faithful dog, like Shackleton, at your side and a woman—*me!*—in your arms," I concluded.

Kier went perfectly still. He jammed a finger in his ear and wiggled it. "I'm sorry, did you say—"

"That you'd take me—you know, like being ravished in the old bodice-ripper sense," I said. "You're a bookseller, I'm sure you've heard the term."

"Yes . . . I . . . Are you suggesting . . ." He stopped talking. I turned away so he didn't see me smile. I'd wanted to halt his apology and it looked like mission accomplished. I tried to smother the thrill I was feeling at being so forward. Not gonna lie, it was heady stuff.

"If this were a romance novel, after I took you . . . I can't believe I just said that . . ." He fanned himself. "Red, you've got me all in a fizz."

I laughed and he grinned. It was a wicked one paired with a lascivious glint in his eyes that made a seductive warmth unfurl in my belly.

"After . . . well, *after* . . . we'd have to have an enormous row and then I'd be charged to perform some ridiculous grand gesture to win your forgiveness. That third act construct is the downfall of every romance ever written."

"What?" I cried. "The grand gesture is the best part."

"Phtbth." He made a raspberry noise. "Are you telling me that if I met you on top of the Empire State Building, holding an overly large radio above my head playing 'In Your Eyes' whilst saying 'As you wish,' you'd forgive me anything?"

"I think you're mashing up several iconic grand gestures there," I said. "But, yeah, I could forgive you just about anything if you pulled off that hat trick."

"See? This is why women have unrealistic expectations in

relationships," he said. He scooted closer to me until our sides were pressed together. I tried to ignore the fluttery feeling in my chest.

"Is it that women have too high an expectation or is it more that men can't deliver?" I returned. I turned to face him fully and found we were just a breath apart.

He leaned in, his gaze on my mouth, and I knew he was thinking about kissing me again. Determined not to mess it up, I tipped my chin up. I closed my eyes, waiting.

"Everything all right, you two?" Siobhan's voice broke over us like a bucket of ice water.

My eyes snapped open and we shot away from each other with the same startled urgency as the song thrushes who burst out of the hedgerow at the sound of Siobhan's voice.

"Grand, just grand," Kier answered, swiveling to face Siobhan.

"Did you get what you needed?" I hopped up from my seat. I felt a flop sweat coat my skin.

Siobhan, seemingly oblivious to the tension between Kier and me, glanced back at the circle of stones. "Yes, I think I have."

"Excellent," Kier said. "Should we head home then?"

"Yes, please," Siobhan said. "Can you drop me off at the house after we deliver Em to the shop? I think some rest is in order."

"Of course, Ma," Kier said.

Together we walked back to the car. I wondered what would have happened if Siobhan hadn't come along when she did. In my mind, Kier in Celtic warrior form pulled me into his arms and as I had suggested, pressed me up against one of the hard stone pillars, shoved aside my clothes, and old-school ravished me in the best possible way. *Guh!*

I pulled off my hat and fanned my face with it while loosening my scarf. When I glanced up, I saw Kier watching me with a singularly steamy look in his eye. I left Drombeg feeling keenly frustrated.

. . .

There's an angry woman downstairs," Niamh said. "She's giving Oisín a right time of it."

I glanced up from Slo-Mo, relieved to have something else to do.

"Does he need help?" I asked. Since our trip to visit Drombeg last Thursday, neither Siobhan nor Kier had come to the bookstore. Oisín said Siobhan had a doctor's appointment on Friday, and of course Kier had taken her, but it was now Monday and neither she nor Kier had come in this morning. My mornings were blank on the schedule, so I assumed inventory was my task. Siobhan had sent me a message to say she would be in tomorrow, but where was Kier?

Not that it was any of my business where he went or what he did, but I couldn't help but worry that I'd been too bold at Drombeg and scared him off. It hadn't felt like it at the time, but in hindsight I wasn't so sure.

"Well, Oisín's not making any friends handling the situation on his own, is he?" Niamh asked.

I left the laptop to its whirring and hurried downstairs.

"But I want to meet her." A woman about my age was standing across the ornate counter from Oisín. His flat cap was pushed back on his head and he looked bemused.

"I'm sorry, but I already told you, she's not here today," he said.

The woman's face became a mottled shade of purple. She looked as if she was about to start yelling or smashing things.

"Can I help?" I asked as I approached. Oisín looked as if he'd wilt with relief.

"Not if you're not Siobhan Riordan, you can't," the woman spat. "I came all this way to meet her and she's bloody not here."

I tried to place the woman's accent. She wasn't American or Irish. British, perhaps? I had no idea. She did have her phone out and was filming the shop and us. I wasn't sure how I felt about that in this day and age of videos going viral and businesses getting canceled.

"Sadly, I'm not Siobhan," I said. "Did you have an appointment to meet her?"

"I don't need an appointment," the woman snapped. She held her phone up to my face. "I've bought all of her books. She owes me."

"Oh," I said. I had learned early on in the library that angry patrons usually just needed to be heard. "In what way?"

"I'm a Tig McMorrow super fan and she owes me the end of the series," she said. She looked genuinely distraught. It occurred to me that talking her down was going to be a lot like diffusing a bomb. I felt a trickle of sweat slide down the side of my neck.

"I know exactly what you mean," I said. "I have been waiting for ten years to find out what happens to Tig. She left him in purgatory, suspended between two worlds."

The woman's jaw dropped. "Exactly."

"What's your name?"

"Deirdre," she said.

"I'm Emily," I said. I held out my hand and to my relief she lowered her phone and clasped my fingers with her free hand.

"Listen, I'm Siobhan's assistant," I said. "And I'd love to treat you to a cup of tea and a scone. I can take your information and your concerns and make sure Siobhan is made aware."

"You'll do that—you promise?" Deirdre asked.

"Absolutely." I put my hand on my heart.

I took her arm and led her toward the café. Oisín mouthed the words *thank you* as we passed. I nodded. It occurred to me that a café in my library back home would have come in really handy in soothing the ire of certain patrons.

The rest of the day flew by without Siobhan or Kier ever making an appearance. I wondered at it, but working the floor kept me hopping as I rang up sales, worked with students on a research project, and fielded a variety of requests, from recommendations for thrillers to the best gluten-free cookbook.

"How exactly did we function without you?" Oisín asked when I waved another customer out the door with a sack full of mysteries.

"Not a clue," I said with a laugh. My heart swelled with a feeling of belonging.

I was beginning to get ideas for the bookshop. When I'd popped in to visit my landlords in their studio over the weekend, I thought how cool it would be to have some of their work on display and for sale at the bookshop. My unplanned meeting with Deirdre had me thinking it might be time to start a Tig McMorrow book club. We could do it online for readers all around the world.

I also thought we should cash in on the quaintness of Finn's Hollow and offer up subscription boxes with books and bits and bobs from the local area. Knowing Kier's dislike of change, I had yet to approach him with any of these suggestions, but they were bubbling in my brain along with a slew more. As we closed the shop for the day and I hurried home with the chilly wind at my back, I reminded myself that I was here for a year. I could bide my time.

Siobhan was back in her nook the next morning. Brigid had delivered our usual coffee and scones, which had become a ritual for my mornings. I wasn't sure I knew how to wake up anymore without coffee strong enough to peel back my eyelids and a fluffy berry-filled scone.

"Where are we going today?" I asked

Siobhan didn't answer me. She glanced at the screen of the open laptop in front of her and read, "Tig had no idea how long he'd been in limbo, suspended in a time loop, caught between realms. Had it been ten minutes or ten years? He couldn't say."

My jaw dropped. "Is that . . . ?" I didn't want to say it out loud and jinx it.

"The opening lines of the next Tig McMorrow book," Siobhan said. "What do you think?"

"I freaking love it," I said. "How meta to have him wonder if ten years have passed! That's brilliant!" I made a noise like a cackle and Siobhan laughed.

Her face flushed with excitement, but she bit her lip and asked, "You really think so? You're not just saying that?"

"One hundred percent I think so," I said. "And I may be your number one fan, but I would never lie to you. It's the perfect opening."

"You gave me the idea when you pointed out that my readers have aged ten years and that Tig should as well. And I thank you for it." She took a deep breath and nodded. "To work then."

As the morning progressed, I maintained her coffee level as needed and when she asked me specifics about her characters such as the witch Aislinn's origin story, I was right there with the reference from her own work.

"You really are a remarkable librarian." She complimented me when I read the passage from *Tig McMorrow and the Swamp Witch*.

"It's nothing. I—" I bit off the words as Siobhan was already back in her world, tapping ferociously at the keyboard as if it was a typing contest. She didn't look at the screen or the keys but some middle spot, as if she was staring into a world that only she could see and was reporting on the events happening there in real time.

I heard a noise behind me and I turned to see Brigid, Oisín, and Eun-ji all peeking around a tall shelving unit at us. Their eyes were wide as they took in the sight of Siobhan at work. I grinned and sent them a thumbs-up. Oisín dabbed at his eyes while Eun-ji silently clapped her hands and Brigid grinned from ear to ear. It was a great day in the Last Chapter!

There was only one person who was not thrilled to see the writer back at work. Kier. He came out of the back office looking for Oisín and found him with the others hiding behind the bookcase, watching Siobhan. He stepped into the alcove, looked at his staff and then at his mother. He frowned and then glanced at me.

"She's writing." I kept my voice low. "Isn't it wonderful?"

His face was tight when he asked, "How long has she been at it then?"

I glanced at the time on my phone. "About an hour, give or take a few minutes."

Siobhan didn't appear to hear us. She just kept typing as the story unfurled from her mind through her fingers onto the laptop.

Kier nodded. It was an abrupt jerk of his head and then he turned and strode out of the alcove. The rest of the staff followed in his wake after sending me encouraging smiles. They were clearly missing the black cloud of unhappy that was trailing after Kier like his own personal rain storm.

I watched him go, feeling disappointed. I'd had four days of not seeing him to think about our kiss and anticipate what our next meeting would be like. This was not it. While the sight of him had sent my heart rate spiking, he had appeared completely unaffected. Not only that but when he saw his mother was writing again, there was no joy on his face. In fact, he looked downright surly. He'd said he didn't want her to suffer and he feared that the writing would cause that, but as I glanced at her I had never seen her more vibrantly alive. He wasn't even giving her a chance.

I felt my temper spike. I should have let it lie. I knew I should but I felt a sudden spark of frustration. After all this time, Siobhan was finally working. Everyone else was delighted, but Kier—her own son—was not. This was unacceptable. I glanced at Siobhan and said, "I'll be right back."

She blinked and I took that to mean she'd heard me. I hurried from the alcove through the shop, past the counter, and into the workroom. Oisín smiled at me, but I must have looked like I was spoiling for a brawl because his smile vanished and his eyebrows shot up.

"Where is he?" I asked.

Oisín lifted his arm and pointed to Kier's office. The door was shut. I didn't care. I crossed the room and rapped on the door three times before I opened it and marched inside. I shut the door behind me because I didn't want everyone to hear me chew him out.

"What do you want, Red?" Kier was seated at his desk, looking at the computer in front of him. He didn't even do me the courtesy of glancing my way.

"An explanation."

"For what? Why the sky is blue? Why the dinosaurs disappeared? Help a man out, love," he teased. I was not in the mood.

"Are you broken?" I demanded.

That got his attention. He snapped his head in my direction and that one inquisitive eyebrow rose. "Excuse me?"

"No, I will not." I straightened up and crossed my arms over my chest.

He looked surprised and pushed back from his desk. His chair rolled silently and he rose from his seat. "Is something wrong?"

"You tell me."

"I would if I knew what you were talking about." He walked around the desk and sat on the corner while he took me in. I had his full attention now and, frankly, it was wreaking havoc with my purpose. He was so annoyingly attractive, I wanted to throw myself at him, but I needed to stay the course and find out what was going on with him first.

"I know you and your mother have a complicated history about her writing and that you're worried about her, but I just have to ask if you're upset about Siobhan writing again because you're jealous of her success?"

"What? No!" he cried. He looked appalled. "Red, I wrote that horrid novel while at university on a dare and it was the most miserable experience of my life."

I raised my hands in a gesture of frustration. "Okay then. You said you don't want her to suffer and that you're afraid if she starts writing it will cause her pain. Now that she is writing, you have to tell me specifically what you mean."

He said nothing. My frustration was reaching a boiling point and I closed the gap between us and poked him in the chest with my index finger. "I can only operate with the information I have. If you won't tell me what the specifics are, how am I supposed to help?"

He caught my hand in his and didn't let go. Instead, he laced our fingers together and tugged me close. We were both breathing heavily and my awareness of every inch of him—the feel of my fingers in his, the scent of him, the spot where the outside of my leg brushed against the inside of his thigh, his unruly waves of dark hair falling over his forehead, and that damn dip in his upper lip—made the longing to touch him, to have him touch me, to kiss him again, drive out every other thought.

With his free hand, he cupped my face. His thumb stroked my cheek as if it was something he'd wanted to do and was finally giving himself permission. "The truth is, Red, you can't help."

He was about to drop his hand, but I pressed my free hand to his, holding it in place. I wasn't ready to let this—him—go. I glanced up at him, committing to memory his whisker-stubbled chin, the flirty way his eyebrows arched, the noble length of his nose, and the hypnotic blue of his eyes.

"Don't look at me like that," he said. His voice was a gruff growl.

"How am I looking at you?"

"Like you want me to kiss you."

Was I? I was. Was it so obvious? Clearly.

A few weeks ago, I likely would have run screaming from the room if a man said such a thing to me, but I wasn't that Emily anymore. I was this Emily, aka Red, and she was not embarrassed about what she wanted. Okay, she was a little nervous but not enough to back down.

"And what if that's what I want?" I asked. My heart was beating so hard and fast I couldn't tell whether it approved of my boldness or was trying to flee the scene.

"Then how can I refuse?"

He leaned in and his mouth landed on mine with a surety of purpose. His lips were warm and soft and he angled his head seeking the perfect fit. I dropped my hand from his and his fingers moved from my jaw to the nape of my neck, holding me still while he kissed me with a thoroughness that left me breathless.

"More," he said.

"Yes," I sighed and parted my lips beneath his. His tongue swept into my mouth as if he'd been longing for a taste of me. I slid my hands up the front of his sweater, feeling the soft wool against my palms. I clung to his shoulders, feeling the heat between us build like a carefully stoked fire. Still his mouth stayed on mine as if he could have perched on his desk and kissed me for hours or potentially days.

I'd never been kissed with such singlemindedness before. It was all-consuming, destroying any sense of self-preservation I had. I was in over my head. I was feeling too much. I wanted him too much. I wrenched my mouth away from his, trying to steady a world that was spinning like a kaleidoscope all around me. As if he understood exactly how I was feeling, Kier pulled me into a hug. One large hand stroked my back while the other cupped my head, holding me close to his chest.

"Your heart is beating as fast as mine," I said. "I guess I'm not having a heart attack then."

Kier's voice was amused when he asked, "Did you really think you were?"

I swallowed. Yes, but I was quite certain if I told him about my illness anxiety disorder now, the man would leave skid marks. So, nope, nope, nope. Instead, I babbled, because that's so attractive.

"I . . . it . . . um . . ."

"Kissing you is . . ." His voice trailed off as if he couldn't find the proper adjective.

"Smoking hot?" I suggested.

"That and everything I suspected it would be the very first day I saw you perched on that step stool."

"You wanted to toss me out on my derrière." I leaned back to look at him.

"It was self-preservation," he countered. "I knew you were going to wreak havoc on my well-ordered world. You have confounded me at every turn, Red, bringing one change after another." He looked aggrieved.

"Is that why you tried to drive me away with the drudgery of inventory?" I asked.

"Yes, I stuck you up on the third floor because I had the foolish hope that out of sight would mean out of mind, but it didn't work." He paused and then quoted one of my favorite lines of literature, "'Each time you happen to me all over again.'"

"*The Age of Innocence*," I said. He nodded. The man just compared having me around to one of the most heart-wrenching love stories. I was shocked I didn't faint from the exquisiteness of it. Instead, I said, "You didn't think I would last."

"I didn't." He nodded. "I'm glad I was wrong."

"Even though your mom is writing again, Brigid is changing the café menu, and I saw that new laptop you were holding so Eun-ji and Oisín must be winning the equipment wars as well," I said. "Are you sure you're glad I'm still here?"

He scrunched up his brow and pursed his lips. "When you put it like that I think I need to kiss you again to be certain."

I felt my insides swoop at his words. This kiss was not the tender meet and greet of our first, or the frustration-fueled fury of the second. No. This one was an admission of want and a surrender to need. He repositioned himself on the desk so that he could pull me in between his legs, allowing our bodies to be pressed more firmly together. I could feel his arousal and it was like turning the heat on high.

Kier slid his mouth across mine, gently but insistently. My lips parted and his tongue traced the edges, encouraging me to let him in. I did. My hands slid up his arms to his shoulders. With one hand I held on to him while I played with the hair at the nape of his neck with the other. It was as soft and silky as I'd suspected.

The smell of him, wood smoke and wool with a hint of coffee, filled my senses and my mind became a blank haze where there were no thoughts, just desire. I wanted to touch more of him, taste more of him. I pulled him closer, losing myself in the kiss as I deepened it, wanting more and more and more.

"I have half a mind to swipe everything off my desk and have my way with you," he said. He was nuzzling the sensitive spot beneath my ear.

"That sounds like a fine idea to me," I gasped.

He laughed. "Ah, Red, you sorely tempt me."

I pulled back to look him in the eye. It would be so easy to let go of what had driven me to chase him into his office, but it would just rear up again. I needed to know why he was so worried about Siobhan writing again otherwise whatever this was between us didn't stand a chance.

"Kier, I still need to know . . ." My voice trailed off, hoping he'd pick up the thread. He did.

"You're right. Now that she's working again, it's best you know. The truth of it is that Ma quit writing because she was dying."

"What?" I cried. My insides went cold and I shivered. Kier ran his hands up and down along my arms, trying to soothe me.

"Sorry, I should have eased you into it," he said. "Ten years ago, Ma was diagnosed with breast cancer. She beat it, but it came back and we almost lost her four years ago. She'd been trying to write the last Tig McMorrow book when the cancer came back. When she survived the second bout, I promised myself I'd never let her work herself to death again."

"I'm so sorry," I said. "That must have been incredibly difficult."

"It was," he said. "She's been in remission for almost five years, but the doctors told us she's at high risk for it to come back again. We just need a little more time to get her to the five-year mark. That's why I don't want her to write the book. When she writes, she loses sight of everything—eating, sleeping, it's as if she's possessed. Frankly, when I was a lad, it used to scare me. I don't want her to put herself through that anymore."

And there it was. Kier was scared for his mam. How could I find fault with that?

"I wish you'd told me all of this before," I said. "I would have understood." I smoothed the sweater on his shoulders. I wasn't sure who I was trying to comfort, him or me. Siobhan had almost died. Twice. The thought of it made my heart hurt.

He shrugged. "It wasn't my story to tell. But now that I have, will you help me? There's clearly no stopping her from writing. So let's keep an eye on her and make sure she doesn't overdo it."

"Of course, if I think she's pushing herself too hard, I'll tell you immediately," I promised. "I do have an unrelated question for you."

"Oh?"

"It might be none of my business but where were you yesterday?"

"Why? Did you miss me?" he asked. His grin was wicked, clearly he was pleased.

"No . . . maybe . . . yes." I sighed.

He leaned down and kissed me, lingering long enough to almost make me forget my question.

"Well?" I whispered against his lips.

"Ma's doctor is in Dublin, so we went up on Friday and stayed at our townhouse over the weekend. Yesterday, she had a hair appointment—she likes to keep the silvers hidden—and then tea with some of her college friends, while I treated myself to a splurge at Hodges Figgis." At my blank expression, he added, "Ireland's oldest bookshop."

"Oh, so you were doing bookstore recon," I said.

"Just so." He nodded. "Also, Siobhan had a list of history books she wanted and I knew they were likely to have them."

It wasn't that I'd thought he was avoiding me after Drombeg—okay, maybe just a little—but I was relieved to hear it confirmed that I hadn't driven him away.

"Speaking of Siobhan, I told her I'd be right back. I should go."

"All right," he agreed. And yet, his hands stayed in place, holding me close, not releasing me. "But don't you think you should kiss me first? It could be hours before I get you alone again."

"Oh, did you think we were going to make this kissing thing a habit?" I asked. I tried not to grin and failed miserably.

"Well, now that we've started, I don't think we can stop, do you?" He punctuated the question with a string of kisses along my jaw. My knees went weak and I tipped my head, allowing him better access.

"No, we can't," I admitted. My hands dug into his hair and pulled his head down to mine so that I could kiss him with all of the pent-up lust in my heart. This man had driven me crazy for weeks, it was a hot rush of relief to finally be able to touch him and taste him.

I could have spent all afternoon standing in his office, kissing him, but a knock sounded on his door and we broke apart.

"Just a sec," Kier called. He reached forward and straightened my top, which was weirdly askew. Then he smoothed my hair back from my face and adjusted my glasses. He studied my face, his eyes lingering on my lips, and he said, "You look like you've been thoroughly debauched."

I took in his mussed hair, swollen lips, and bunched up sweater. "I could say the same about you."

I straightened his sweater and finger combed his hair, which may or may not have helped, but the feel of the unruly black waves was one I savored.

"All right?" Kier asked. I nodded. He turned to the door and called, "Come in."

Oisín entered with a shipping list from a box of books. "Sorry to bother you." He glanced between us as if he expected to see someone bleeding from a mortal wound. Seeing no damage on either of our persons, he visibly relaxed. "There's a discrepancy. We're short four titles that are set to be released next week."

Kier held out his hand. "I'll give the distributor a call."

"Thank you." Oisín handed him the printout. "I highlighted the four."

I headed for the door. "I'll let you two discuss."

"I'll see you later, Red," Kier said. His voice was full of wicked intent, or was that just the way I heard it? *Ack!* My face instantly went hot and I turned away, hoping that Oisín didn't notice. My romance hero boss and I were now in a thing. I had no idea what to make of it.

Twelve

Siobhan worked nonstop for three hours. My new awareness about why she had stopped writing made me watch her more closely. Was she feeling okay? Did she look overtired? Pale? Should I say something? I believed Kier was right. If she wanted me to know about her previous condition, she would have mentioned it. I decided to let it go. I didn't want to transfer my own illness anxiety onto her. That wouldn't do either of us any good.

Siobhan paused every now and again to ask me to look something up or verify a fact from the series that she couldn't remember. When she asked me the color of one of the main characters' eyes, she must have noted the surprise on my face.

"You're shocked that I can't remember, aren't you?" she asked. She paused to stretch her back and wiggle her fingers.

"No . . . well, yes, actually," I admitted. "How do you not remember the details of a character that came out of your own imagination?"

"People think I remember these stories because I created them," she said. "But the truth is that writing is more like a grand purge. The story in my head feels like a living, breathing thing. I can't take a walk or a shower or enjoy a cup of tea without thinking about my characters, what's happening to them, what it all means and why.

"They all have voices and they want to be heard and they talk to me constantly. In the quiet when I'm falling asleep and even when I'm actually sleeping, they pop up and share their struggles with me. Truth to be told, they take up a lot of space in my mind. The act of writing it down means I don't have to remember it and it frees up that part of my brain for a new story. Does that make sense?"

"Yes." I nodded. "It's as if your mind is a file cabinet that's overly full and the act of writing sorts out the files you no longer need. Like that?"

"Exactly like that, only I'd say it's less like being sorted and more like being tossed in a bin," Siobhan said. "So, what color are Menaris's eyes?"

"Bottomless black," I said. "Like onyx."

"That's right." She snapped her fingers and set back to work. After a moment, she paused and glanced up at me. "I'm so glad you're here, Em. The day I received your letter was—well, it was a difficult day—but you worked some magic and gave me my purpose back. You're like my own personal Aislinn, and having you here has far exceeded my expectations." Her eyes were damp and she blinked. I felt my own throat get tight. To be compared to my favorite female character by the creator of the character was a reader's dream come true.

"Thank you." My throat was tight, making my voice hoarse.

"No, thank you," Siobhan said. "You're such a gift to me. I really think that all this time, I was just waiting for you."

The kindness and affection in her gaze made my heart swell. It struck me that ever since I'd arrived Siobhan had shown me more maternal affection and kindness than my own mother had in my entire life. Siobhan always listened to me when I spoke, she asked questions about me and my life, and she . . . cared.

I had dutifully called Tammy Lynn every day since our last blowup. Most of the time it went fine and if or when she started to get mean, I ended the call, maintaining the boundary my therapist had helped me set. It was very liberating. For the first time in years, I felt as if I had control of my life again. The only tune I was dancing to was mine.

Siobhan was still hard at work two hours later and she showed no signs of slowing down. I didn't want to interrupt her flow but sustenance was important. I offered to bring her a sandwich and a cup of tea from the café and while she nodded, I got the feeling that she hadn't actually heard me. That was all right. Brigid's amazing chicken fillet roll with Tayto crisps on the side would get her attention.

I had almost reached the café when Kier appeared in the hallway in front of me.

"Hiya, Red, where are you headed?" he said. "Please tell me it's a quiet corner where I can kiss you." His smile was deliciously flirty and I found myself returning it in full measure.

"Sadly, no. I was just going to get Siobhan a sandwich," I said.

"Could you have Brig make it a takeaway?" he asked.

"Of course, but why?"

"I'm hoping to get Ma to go home for a bit of a lie down," he said.

"Good idea," I said. "I'll meet you in the alcove in case you need backup."

"Thank you," he said. "I appreciate the support." He cupped my face and gave me a quick kiss on the forehead as if he were comforting a child. It did not comfort. The scent of him filled my nostrils and I was mentally back in his office kissing him.

He stepped back and I could see the heat in his gaze. So, it wasn't just me. Without conscious thought, I leaned forward, wound my arms around his neck, and claimed his mouth with mine while he grasped my hips, holding me in place. As if I'd ever want to leave.

The kiss had just leveled up to scorching when the sound of two customers chatting nearby interrupted us and Kier stepped back, removing his hands from my hips. We stared at each other for a moment before I forced myself to look away and try to restart my brain.

"Sandwich," I said. I turned and walked away from him before I did something truly dumb like jump on him again.

I heard his deep chuckle behind me as I hurried away and it made me smile. I pulled my phone out of my pocket and checked the time. It was still early in Martha's Vineyard. I would have to wait and call Sam later so that we could go over every single moment of what had happened between Kier and me in great detail and scrutinize it from every angle.

There was a short queue at the café. I ordered the chicken sandwich and asked Brigid to bag it.

"No problem at all," she said. She started to turn away but then turned back. She was holding a bread knife in her hand and she pointed it at me and asked, "Who've you been kissing?"

"Kissing?" I repeated. I wanted to bluff but my face betrayed me with a hot flush.

With a yelp, Brigid clapped her free hand over her mouth and said, "I was just teasing you, wasn't I? Because your lips look as ripe as a berry. Do tell, who have you been kissing, Emily Allen?"

I glanced around the café, desperately hoping that no one overheard her. Niamh was standing nearby with a biscuit in one hand and a latte in the other. "I told you he liked you."

I covered my eyes with my hands and said, "Yes, you did."

"She knows?" Brigid asked. "You told Niamh before me?"

"More like I told her," Niamh said.

I lowered my hands and met Brigid's outraged expression with a rueful look of my own. "She did, actually."

"And who is the lucky fella?" Brigid asked. "You're winding me up leaving me in suspense like this."

Niamh looked at her and said, "He works here. There's really only one person it could be given that Oisín prefers lads."

"Murphy?" Brigid gasped. "I knew it. I knew there was something between you two."

"That's what I said," Niamh agreed. "He watches her when he thinks she's not looking."

"A dead giveaway," Brigid said.

"What's that? Who's dead?" Eun-ji asked as she joined us at the counter.

"Me from embarrassment," I said. I glanced at Brigid and Niamh and added, "This is not to be spoken of away from this counter."

"What?" Eun-ji asked. "You're not leaving me out of it, are you?"

"Em was kissing Murph," Brigid said.

"Brigid!" I cried.

"What?" she asked. "We're still at the counter."

"Sandwich!" I said and pointed at the kitchen.

"Fine," she said. She waved her knife at me again. "But I want details."

"All right, can we discuss it later?" I asked. My face still felt warm and I wanted the blush gone before I had to face Kier again.

"You and Murph? When exactly did this come about?" Eun-ji asked.

"We kissed this morning," I said. No need to tell them about the near miss at Drombeg and the kiss on my porch. "Now can we stop talking about it?"

"Sure," she said. "Was it in his office by any chance?"

I turned to look at her and found both her and Niamh staring at me, while Brigid peered over the counter, as they all awaited my answer.

"Yes, and in the hallway, too. Can we please stop talking about it?" I asked.

"Of course." Eun-ji gave a little hop of joy. "Excuse me. I have to collect my prize money from Oisín. We bet a fiver on whether Murph kissed you in his office this morning. Oisín said no, but I had a feeling." She clapped me on the shoulder, harder than I expected for such a diminutive woman, and left the café, whistling.

"I wish I'd made that bet," Niamh said.

"Here you go." Brigid held out a paper bag. "But I still want full disclosure."

"Fine, but later." I grabbed the sandwich and crisps and hurried through the bookshop. My happy, flustered bubble burst as soon as I reached the alcove. Siobhan and Kier were standing on opposite sides of the table and the tension was palpable. They were leaning toward each other and I could tell from their matching expressions of aggravation that they were extremely peeved with each other.

"I don't want to," Siobhan protested.

"This isn't really about that, is it?" Kier asked. "You have to pace yourself. You know I'm right about this."

Siobhan was holding her laptop to her chest as if she expected him to wrestle it away from her. I paused, wondering if I should back out of the room and let them finish what they started.

"Fine," Siobhan said. "But I'm only going to rest for a couple of hours, then I want to get back to work."

"I don't see any reason why you won't be able to do just that," he said. His voice was gentle, as if he was soothing a bird whose feathers were ruffled.

Siobhan turned to me and held out the laptop. "Kier won't let me take the laptop with me. Guard it with your life." She didn't look like she was exaggerating.

"Oh!" I cried. "All right."

I handed the sandwich bag to Kier and took the laptop. Siobhan pulled on her coat with quick, jerky movements that signaled her annoyance.

She turned back to Kier. "What if I take a break and the words don't come back?"

"They'll come," he said. "They've had ten years to brew, they're more than ready."

"But—" she began to protest but he shook his head.

"You won't be able to write a word if you—" He stopped talking and glanced at me. Although I knew what he was talking about, Siobhan didn't know that I knew. "You know where I'm going with that. You have to trust that the story is right there waiting for you."

Siobhan sighed. Her head drooped dejectedly. "I hope you're right."

"I am." He sounded absolutely certain and I noticed that Siobhan's shoulders lifted. It was just what she needed to hear.

"I'll be back, Em," she said. She looked very determined. Siobhan was never here in the afternoon, so if she did make it back, it would mark the beginning of a new routine. I wondered what that meant for me as her assistant but also as a bookshop employee.

"Enjoy your lunch," I said.

Siobhan started toward the door and Kier glanced at me. "Thanks for getting her something to eat."

"Of course," I said.

Kier looked as if he wanted to say something more but he glanced at Siobhan, who was already at the front door, and he shook his head. He left the bookshop, taking her arm to guide her and I noted that he seemed more like the parent and Siobhan the child. I wondered if it had been like that ever since she'd first gotten cancer. As someone who'd spent their twenties taking care of their mother, I certainly understood the role and all that went with it.

Siobhan returned three hours later. Thankfully, there were no bus tours stopping by so she worked in the relative quiet. I sat beside her. When I'd asked if I should leave her in peace, she shook her head. That was it. So, I stayed on call to refill her water, grab her a biscuit, and look up a variety of obscure facts, from the uncertainty principle in quantum mechanics to the medicinal properties of comfrey root. Meanwhile she kept her head down, her eyes vacant, and her fingers flying across the keyboard.

The muse who had been absent for so long had reappeared with a vengeance. It was early evening before she dropped her hands and stopped typing. She glanced at the document on her computer.

"Well, I'll be damned," she muttered.

"What is it?" I asked. "Is there something wrong? Can I look up something for you?"

She glanced at me and her eyes glinted with unshed tears. "Em, I've written thirty pages."

"Wow," I said. "That's incredible."

She laughed and rested her head in her hand. "I haven't written thirty pages in over a decade. I don't think I even managed a day like this during the last three Tig McMorrow books. It feels like a miracle."

"It does," I agreed. The reader in me wanted to know what she'd written so badly, it was all I could do not to take a knee and beg. I reminded myself that I was her assistant and my job was to assist, not treat myself to a sneak peek of her work. Damn it.

"Done for the day?" Kier popped into the alcove. He strode over to the table and took the seat on the other side of Siobhan. His hand slid across my shoulders as he passed behind me and I shivered in the best possible way.

"Yes," Siobhan said. "I left myself with an amazing starting place tomorrow. It's so good I'm itching to get to it."

Kier eyebrows lifted in surprise. "You haven't been this excited to write in a long time. Should we call Marcus?"

"No! Not yet at any rate," Siobhan said. "Let me see if I can keep going. Eight thousand words is not a novel. I don't want to get his hopes up."

Kier nodded. "Probably wise. Marcus is your biggest fan."

Um, no, that's me, I wanted to say but didn't.

"An agent should be, though, shouldn't they?" she asked.

"I think his admiration is for more than your work," Kier said.

I glanced between them. Siobhan swatted his arm, her cheeks turning the faintest shade of pink. "We're just good friends."

Kier shrugged. "If you say so."

Siobhan turned away from him. Her gaze when she looked at me was shy. "Em, I have a favor to ask of you."

"Anything," I said and I meant it. I'd truly do anything for this woman.

"Careful or it'll be shovels at midnight in a bog as you help me discard the body of a mean reviewer," she said.

"I have a strong back."

She laughed as I'd intended. "Hopefully, this will not be as arduous. I'd like you to read what I've written and take copious notes." She tapped one of the notepads beside the computer. "In particular, please look for any inconsistencies from the previous books in the series. Can you do that?"

"Yes!" I cried. I cleared my throat. "I mean, I'm happy to help."

She flashed me a grin and said, "That's grand. Just leave the laptop in the back office with any notes you have. I'll look it over in the morning. You are not to take it home with you. Just read what you can before you leave, all right?"

"Got it," I said. This was a big fat lie. If I couldn't finish it in the next hour, I was absolutely taking it home with me.

"I've already backed it up, so don't worry if a catastrophe happens. There's a copy saved in my highly secure cloud," she said.

"So, I don't have to throw myself out a window if I spill coffee on the keyboard," I joked.

"It's her favorite laptop, so you still might have to flee the country," Kier said. His eyes were creased in the corners and his lips turned up ever so slightly, indicating he was joking. I had kissed those lips—I shut the thought down immediately. I needed to stay on task.

"Noted," I said, returning his smile.

I waved as the door shut behind them. As soon as they were out of sight, I opened the file and started to read. In a matter of lines, I was absolutely gone, absorbed into the world of Tig McMorrow as if I'd never left.

I finished reading it once, gobbling it down like creamy chocolate. Then I went back and read it again, this time making notes as I went. It occurred to me on the second read how truly gifted Siobhan was. She set the scene of Tig's return, while describing the peril he was in and resolving it with a surprise twist. Of course, she then sent the story sideways in a completely unexpected direction. I couldn't wait for more.

I noted several inconsistencies in her world-building, which could easily be fixed, but otherwise the opening was perfect. I wrote them down on the notepad, not wanting to tamper with her original work. Then I packed it all up and stored her things in the locked cabinet in the workroom.

Oisín watched me with a guarded expression. As I turned away from the cabinet, he asked, "How is it then?" His voice was rough, as if the words had been ripped from him against his will.

I didn't know what to say. I couldn't tell him about the story. This was the long-anticipated conclusion. If word of the plot got out, it would ruin everything.

"I'm not asking for details, mind," he said. "I just want to know if her gift is back. Is she . . . Do you think . . ."

I felt a presence behind me and I turned around to find Eun-ji, Brigid, and Niamh all peeking into the room. They wore matching expressions of hopeful anxiety and I smiled. I'd felt exactly the same way when Siobhan started writing. To love these characters and this world so much and to have waited so long for a resolution, well, it was thrilling but also an anxiety-maker. "It's brilliant," I said. "Siobhan is back."

Thirteen

Something woke me while it was still the darker side of dawn. It took me a moment to pin the emotion down. It was a feeling of eagerness or excitement or both. After Kier had taken Siobhan home, he hadn't returned to the bookshop. I didn't know if my eagerness was more about seeing Kier or helping Siobhan work on her novel. Maybe both? I rushed through my morning routine and dashed out the door before the sun had even begun to lighten the sky. I wanted to read through Siobhan's first chapter one more time before she started her day.

It was cold and dark as I passed the small grocery, the post office, a hardware store, and a betting establishment. All were closed. In fact, there wasn't a soul on the street. I circled around the bookshop to the back door and used the key Oisín had given me for evenings when it was my turn to close. I pulled the door open and slipped into the backroom.

Thankfully, the shop was warm and I shrugged off my coat and unspooled my scarf, stuffing it and my gloves into the pockets before hanging it on the coatrack. I hurried to the cupboard where I'd left Siobhan's laptop and the notebook.

I unlocked the cupboard and opened the door. It was empty. I stared stupidly at it for a moment and then I felt all of the blood rush from my head to my feet. I feared I was going to pass out. I reached inside and patted down the shelf and its sides as if it could be hiding Siobhan's laptop and notebook from me. I glanced at the floor around my feet as if they'd escaped and were crawling toward the back door under their own power. The floor was bare.

I left the cupboard open and sank to my knees. My heart was thumping so hard in my chest I feared it was going to have one massive contraction and just stop. No, I was not being dramatic. I was responsible for Siobhan's laptop so it was because of me that it was missing. I must not have locked the cupboard properly. How could I have been so irresponsible? As Kier had said, I was going to have to flee the country.

The only sound I could hear was my own raspy breathing. I thought about calling Sam but it was the middle of the night. Besides, what could she possibly do other than to tell me I wasn't having a heart attack? I pushed my fist against my chest. My fingers were icy and I felt my cold knuckles through the thin knit of my sweater.

What was I going to do? What could I possibly say? I was certain I had locked the cabinet. I had checked and double-checked but somehow it was empty and her things were gone. Was that why I had woken up early? Had I known on some instinctual level?

I tried not to panic. I knew Siobhan had a secure cloud, but still, what was she supposed to write on now? The clunky old laptop I was using for inventory? I wanted to die. I'd had one job to do and—

I went very still. There was a noise, coming from the front of the bookshop. It was a tapping sound like a mouse scrabbling over the floorboards. I pushed myself up to my feet, brushing the dirt off my wool skirt, and adjusted my tights. I strode into the main room of the Last Chapter and there she was. Siobhan was in her alcove, tapping away at her laptop.

My knees went weak with relief and I bent over and took three deep breaths. Her laptop was here. She was here. Everything was okay. Yeah, sure, except for the five years this fright had just erased from my life. I wondered if I'd sprouted any white hair. I'd bet I had.

"Siobhan, good morning," I said. "Or, more accurately, good last gasp of night."

She didn't answer. Her fingers were moving over the keys with a rapid-fire speed that told me the valve for her creativity was fully open. I glanced at the table. It was just the laptop and the notebook and a stack of books. No coffee. No food. I narrowed my eyes. She was wearing her pajamas and a bathrobe. She wasn't even dressed! How long had she been here?

This was not good. I had no doubt that Siobhan had walked here and that Kier had no idea where his mother was. I glanced at her feet and noted she was wearing lace-up boots. *Phew.* Still, I did not want to be the one to call him, but I also didn't want the poor man to panic when he discovered his mother was missing. Shit.

"Siobhan, does Kier know you're here?" I asked.

She kept typing. I glanced at the café. Coffee. I needed coffee and I was betting Siobhan was going to need some as well. I decided to make a pot and then reach out to Kier. The coffee brewed entirely too quickly. I delivered Siobhan's to her but she was still in rapid-fire mode and didn't acknowledge it other than to keep typing with one hand while picking up her mug with the other and taking a sip.

"Thank you," she said, although she never looked up. I could have been a robber who served coffee and she wouldn't have known.

Her hair was tied up in a bun on her head and held in place by two pencils. Her eyes had that faraway look in them and her fingers were moving over the keys as if she were chasing the letters and trying to catch them before they slipped away.

"Siobhan," I said. I had to know how long she'd been here so that when I called Kier I could tell him what was happening. She didn't answer. I cleared my throat and tried to sound commanding. "Siobhan."

"Is not in right now. Please leave a message. Beeeeep." She never slowed in her typing.

"Siobhan!" I cried.

She snapped her head in my direction. Her expression was annoyed and her hands hovered over the keyboard as if she were guarding it. "Every time someone interrupts an author, a paragraph dies. You just wiped out an entire section of dialogue that I can never get back. Now, what do you want?"

It was the first time I'd ever heard her voice sound more like the crack of a whip than the sweet sound of a happy songbird. I shifted on my feet, feeling uneasy.

"I'm sorry," I said. "I should have stayed quiet." It was true. My first priority was to help her write her book, but as she sat here in her pajamas I was worried about her. "But . . ." I gestured to her overall unkempt appearance.

Siobhan took a deep breath and sighed. "No, *I'm* sorry. I shouldn't have snapped at you. I get grumpy when I'm in the flow and I get interrupted. You didn't deserve that." She lifted up her mug and took a long sip of coffee. "How can I help you?"

"How long have you been here?" I asked.

She glanced at the window, where the sky was just beginning to lighten from deep black to navy blue.

She shrugged. "I don't know. I woke up a little after midnight and knew I needed to be writing. So, I came here."

Midnight?!

"Did you tell anyone where you were going?"

"I didn't want to be a bother." Her gaze darted to the keyboard.

"Siobhan, you know that Kier is already worried about you working too hard," I said. "He's going to freak out if he finds out you've been here most of the night."

"Do we have to tell him?" The look she gave me was impish, like a child caught snitching sweets.

"I think it's going to be hard to hide given that you're in your pajamas," I said. "I understand that the muse is strong but is there any way you could take notes in the middle of the night to use the next day?"

Siobhan shook her head as she contemplated her laptop. "You don't understand."

"Not being a writer, probably not," I agreed. "But it seems to me that to keep the peace with your son, you need to dial back the workaholic thing."

Siobhan looked at me then. Maybe it was the dark circles beneath her eyes making them look haunted, but the intensity of her stare was mesmerizing. For a second, I imagined her hair turning into a seething mass of hissing snakes and I half expected her to turn me to stone.

"No, you don't understand what I mean," she said. "I'm out of time."

"Out of time for what?"

Siobhan turned her body toward me and held out her hands. Instinctively, I took them in mine. Her fingers were cold and delicate. I wrapped my hands around hers more securely, trying to give her my warmth. She tugged me gently until I sat on the seat beside her. I held her gaze and saw a resolve in her eyes that gave me pause.

"What is it, Siobhan? What's happening?" I asked.

"The truth is, Em, I'm dying," she said.

"What?" I cried. "What do you mean?"

"Three months ago, at my regular checkup, I was told I had six months at most," she said. "It was the same day your letter arrived."

"Your cancer is back?" I asked.

"You know?" She looked surprised.

"I'm sorry," I said. "Kier told me when I yelled at him for not being more supportive of your work."

She chuckled and squeezed my hands. "I wish I could have seen that."

"It wasn't his fault. He didn't mean to betray your confidence. I badgered it out of him."

"It's fine, Em, I'd have told you myself, except—"

"Except?"

"My pride got in the way. I didn't want you to see me as an invalid," she said. "The first time I beat the cancer soundly, but the second time around was brutal. I lost my hair and was not much more than skin and bone. I looked like one of the water creatures from *Tig McMorrow and the River of Doom*. I don't imagine I'm going to fare much better in the coming months."

"I'm so sorry," I said. "The press never reported any of that."

"No." Siobhan shook her head. "We kept it quiet. And our friends in Finn's Hollow helped. My grandparents came here from Portlaoise when they married. Despite being considered blow-ins by the locals, they had my mother and raised her here, and she married my father, who was born here. My parents lived in Finn's Hollow for the rest of their lives and it's home to me. When Kier was a lad, before I was published, we always talked about owning a bookshop here, so when I got sick we opened the Last Chapter."

I took in the information that Kier had always wanted to open a bookshop and wondered why he hadn't admitted it. It suited him. I wondered if he thought owning a bookshop wouldn't appear ambitious. I could have told him to a booklover like me, it seemed like heaven.

"I was so sure I'd beaten the cancer," Siobhan continued. "But I couldn't get my writing back. Then I was told that my hourglass was almost out of sand and your letter arrived, asking me to please finish the series. Suddenly, it felt imperative that I do just that."

She gave my hands one last fierce quick squeeze and then she let go.

"No wonder Kier wanted me gone," I said. "I'm here to help you write and he's afraid you'll work yourself to—"

"He doesn't know," Siobhan interrupted me.

I stilled. I had to be misunderstanding her. I tipped my head to the side and asked, "He doesn't know?"

"Kier thinks I'm still in remission. I haven't told him the cancer is back and that there are no more treatments available to me. I'm no longer a candidate for any of the trials and, frankly, I'm tired. I don't want to spend what little time I have left hooked up to machines if I'm just going to die anyway."

"But there has to be something." I could hardly get the words out.

"There's nothing." When she looked at me, it was with a certainty as strong as the stone circle at Drombeg. "Are you angry with me for not telling you before you came here? You'd have every right to be."

My chest hurt as I tried to process this horrific news. I couldn't seem to grasp it. "No, I'm not angry. I imagine dropping 'hey, by the way, I have stage four cancer' into a job interview could be tricky."

Siobhan laughed. "Oh, I do like you, Em."

"I like you, too," I said. "I feel as if I've just found you, I'm not ready to . . ."

The finality of her diagnosis broke me. My words jammed up on the lump in my throat and my eyes burned. Seeing my distress, Siobhan reached forward and hugged me, pressing my head to her shoulder while she made soothing sounds

"I'm not going anywhere just yet, love," she said. "Remember I've just found you, too."

She smoothed my hair back from my face and patted my back. It was this. This unconditional love and affection that my poor heart yearned for, and I sopped it up like one of Brigid's berry scones being slathered with clotted cream.

The tears spilled out of me as she rocked me gently back and forth. I couldn't accept that in a matter of months she'd be gone. I clutched her frail frame as if I could hang on to her and keep her safe. I wanted to scream and wail and curse but I couldn't do anything but cry. It wasn't right. It wasn't fair. How could this be happening?

We sat like this for a long while, taking comfort in each other. I'd never had any moments like this with my own mother. I noted the softness of Siobhan's embrace. She smelled of lavender, and a long strand of her hair had fallen out of the messy bun on her head and tickled my nose. I closed my eyes, trying to commit the moment to memory.

I tried to accept what she'd told me. Her condition certainly explained so much. I understood why finishing the book had become imperative to her.

"You have to tell him," I said.

"He would never let me work if he knew the cancer was back," Siobhan said. "He'd drag me to Dublin or London or anywhere else he thought they might have a treatment for me." She shook her head. "I don't want that. Like you, I need to have Tig's story finished. It's the most important thing to me now."

"But he's your son and he needs to know," I protested.

"You can't tell him, Em." Siobhan's expression was fierce. "Promise me you won't."

"You can't put me in this position, knowing when he doesn't," I said. She stared at me, unblinking, and I knew I would do as she asked. "All right, I'll promise not to say anything, if you promise me that you will tell him as soon as possible."

"I will—I swear—but not yet. He coddles me outrageously as it is. I just need to get more of the book written, then I'll tell him."

"I don't want to keep this secret from him," I said. "You're his mom, and he loves you so much. You two are the gold standard of the parent-child relationship."

Siobhan huffed out a laugh and shook her head. "Hardly that. I failed him in so many ways when he was a lad."

"Not telling him about this will be another failure," I said.

"Perhaps, but given that I have limited time, isn't it my choice on how I spend it?"

She had me there. But how was I supposed to pretend that I didn't know? Every time I looked at her I was going to break down and weep.

"Oh, Siobhan," I said.

"I know I'm asking a lot, love," she said. She cupped my chin and met my gaze. "But it's important to me. Can you give me just a little time, until it feels right?"

"I made a promise to Kier," I said. She dropped her hand. "He asked me to promise him that if I thought you were overdoing it, I would tell him."

She was silent for a moment, considering. "I don't see why you can't do both."

"Meaning?" I asked.

"Go ahead and call him," she said. "If I am overdoing it, tell him. But you can also keep your word to me, too."

I sighed. "Do I have a choice?"

"No." She didn't say she'd fire me if I told Kier but it was understood.

"All right," I said. "But I'm holding you to your promise."

"I will," she said. "It's just with the holidays coming and everything, I . . ." Her eyes flitted to her keyboard and it was clear she was eager to get back to it.

"Carry on then," I said. I rose from my seat. "I'll fix you something to eat since it'll be a while before Brigid is here to open the café."

Siobhan beamed at me. She reached across the space between us and squeezed my hand in hers. "What would I do without you, Em?"

I fixed Siobhan a small fry-up of some eggs and sausage with a thick slice of bread, slathered in Irish butter, naturally. If I cried while making the breakfast, that was my business. I brought her the meal and refilled her coffee, then excused myself and went to the workroom where I girded my loins for the call I was about to make.

The phone rang three times before he answered, "Yeah?"

"Hi, Kier, it's me. Em . . . er . . . Red."

"Red?" he asked. His voice was gruff with sleep. There was the distinct sound of a body shifting and bedding being tossed aside. *Don't picture him in bed. Don't picture him in bed. Too late!*

I put my hand on my forehead and closed my eyes. I tried to think of anything but Kier climbing out of his warm bed, yawning, absently rubbing his chest with one hand while he tried to wake up. I thought of burnt toast, always a bummer, a leaky toilet, equally as sad, and leaf blowers—yes, those pesky, noisy things that always sounded like an airliner about to land as they filled the air with dirt, dust, pollen, spores, and all that asthma-inducing junk. They were a crazy-maker for sure, but still not enough to dislodge the image of Kier sleepy in bed. Damn it.

"What's wrong, Red? Are you all right?"

Be still my heart, he sounded concerned. He didn't even bark at me for waking him up.

"It's not me," I said. "It's Siobhan."

"What?" He sounded fully awake and alarmed. I understood his panic and the reality that he didn't even know the half of it felt like a boulder on my chest. "What's happened?"

"She's fine," I said. "Nothing's happened except . . . she's here."

"Here?" he repeated. "Where? At your cottage?"

"No." My voice dropped. How could I explain my own need to be here so early? I couldn't, so I just went with the facts. "I'm at the bookshop."

"But it's still dark out, isn't it?" He asked this as if he thought he might have overslept. I heard a curtain being drawn.

"It is," I said.

I could hear him rustling around in the background. "Red, it's half six in the morning!"

"I'm aware," I said.

"We don't open until nine. What are you doing in the bookshop?"

"That's not really the point. I'm calling because Siobhan is here and I get the feeling she's been here for quite a while." I paused and then said, "She's in her pajamas, Kier."

"So, it's started then," he said. And he let loose a string of colorful Irish curses that would have been amusing if he wasn't clearly distraught and if I didn't know the truth of the situation. He paused for breath and said, "Don't let her leave. I'll be there in ten."

"Okay." I ended the call. I felt a nervous flutter in my belly, but I told myself I was just hungry.

I returned to the alcove to find Siobhan still at work. The food I had left her was half-eaten and her coffee was almost gone. I didn't fill it up again, not wanting to contribute to any insomnia she might be suffering. I quietly watched her work, ready to assist in any way required.

I wondered how many pages she'd written during the night and whether I would get to read them as well. She was a master at leaving every chapter at a cliffhanger and I was desperate to know what happened next.

As if she'd suddenly become aware of my presence, Siobhan turned away from the window and glanced at me over her shoulder and said, "It feels so good to create again."

She began typing. After such a dry spell, she had to be terrified that the words would evaporate before she could get them out, and of course knowing that her time was now limited had to ratchet up her need to get the story written as swiftly as possible.

"Ma!" Kier strode into the alcove. He was dressed in his wool coat, jeans, and lace-up boots. His hair was mussed as if he'd run his fingers through it and his scarf dangled, with one end hanging comically longer than the other. "What are you doing here in the middle of the night?"

"Not night. The sun is rising." She gestured to the window while still writing.

"You got here in the middle of the night," he argued. "Or have you packed it in so much that you're now just going to wear your pajamas all the time? That should make for an interesting author portrait."

Siobhan snorted. "Maybe I'll do that. Now shoo. I'm working."

"Sorry, Ma, I think it's past time to take a break," he said.

She turned to him, her expression soft with understanding. "I know this is hard for you. I know it brings back a lot of bad memories."

"That's not it," he said. "I'm worried about you."

"I know, but you can't keep me from this. It's who I am. It's what

I do. I haven't felt this alive"—Kier flinched but she ignored it—"in years. I have to do this. For me. I need this, pet, can't you understand?"

Kier glanced down at the floor. His jaw was clenched. He looked torn, as if he had to choose between two equally unpleasant options. "Find a stopping place then. I'll give you an hour."

Siobhan looked like she'd protest but instead she turned back to the laptop and started typing again, clearly motivated by the time constraints he'd put on her.

"Red, can I have a word?" Kier asked.

I wanted to say, "Sure, how about 'banana'? That's a fun word." But I didn't. I really didn't want to be alone with him because how was I not supposed to tell him about his mom? Ugh.

"I'll be right back, Siobhan," I said. She nodded, letting me know that she registered my voice if not my words. Okay then.

Kier turned and led the way back to the workroom. I followed him, finding it ominous when he shut the door behind us. "We need to talk."

Do not blab. Do not blab. Do not blab. I coached myself. It was no use. One look at his worried face and my inner voice screamed, *Tell him!*

Fourteen

I didn't know what to do. Speak the truth about Siobhan's condition and betray her? Or let him go on about his business ignorant of the clock ticking down on his mom? I was completely freaking out on the inside. My vision went gray and I started to see spots.

"Fecking shite! Red!" Kier caught me right as I began to droop. He scooped me up and deposited me onto a chair. "Are you all right?"

"I'm okay." I closed my eyes to keep the room from spinning and cupped my head in my hands. Sam's voice broke through the haze and I mumbled, "When I got woozy like this before, Sam said to put my head between my knees."

"Here, let me help you," he said. "I don't want you to fall out of the chair."

"Thanks," I said.

He crouched down in front of me, holding on to the armrests as if he was a human gate to keep me from toppling out. I slowly lowered my head until I was looking through my knees at the floor. I took several long breaths in and out.

"Sam, huh?" he asked.

"My friend back home," I explained.

"Hmm." He hummed but didn't say anything more.

For my part, I was trying to wrap my head around the fact that Siobhan had sworn me to secrecy but not telling Kier felt like a betrayal on a cellular level. My curtain of hair made it impossible to know if he could see how conflicted I was, and I wasn't ready to sit up and face him yet.

I told myself that keeping Siobhan's secret was not giving me an aneurysm, but my illness anxiety disorder kept me bowed in fear. I closed my eyes and mentally went through the list of things my therapist had taught me to do when the hypochondria kicked in.

Over the past few months when I found myself fixating on a sensation in my body and started obsessing about whether it meant imminent death, I meditated. While clearing my mind, I tensed different muscle groups in my body and then released them. It calmed me down, helped me to relax, and grounded me.

I also tried to control my ruminating thoughts. At the moment, I needed to think of something besides Siobhan and Kier and my dizzy spell. My gaze flitted around my feet, looking for something else to focus on. I saw Kier's knees, his thighs, his cro— I jerked my head up. I was not thinking about that! Still, my face burned.

"Easy there, Red." He remained crouched in front of me. His concerned gaze moved over me, assessing my well-being. "Your face is bright pink from hanging forward. You might want to move more slowly or you'll make yourself dizzy again."

"Right." I pulled my sweater away from my throat. Why was it suddenly so hot in here? "I'm okay. I'm fine. You can back up." I shooed him away with my hands. Yes, I actually shooed the hottest man I'd ever met in my life *away*. "What did you want to talk about?"

I was irrationally afraid he was going to tell me that he knew I had agreed not to tell him about Siobhan's latest diagnosis. I knew it was my guilty conscience making me imagine the worst but until he said otherwise I couldn't shake the feeling that I was in trouble.

He stayed close, ignoring my shooing. "Steady there, Red. Everything is all right. When I said we needed to talk, I meant about how we can better monitor Siobhan. She can't be trudging through the village in the middle of the night to get to her laptop."

"Oh." I nodded. "Right. Of course."

"You've had a bit of a turn, haven't you?" he asked.

"A bit," I agreed.

"Yeah, seeing Ma in her full obsessive writer mode can do that to a person. Did she yell at you?"

"Not yell so much as snap," I said.

"She gets a bit salty when she's working. You'll get used to it," he said.

Would I? Would there be enough time to? I felt my throat get tight. This sucked on so many levels.

"I'm glad you're here, Red." Kier glanced down as if too shy to hold my gaze. His long lashes rested on his sculpted cheekbones, making him devastatingly handsome. All I could think about was the heartbreak that was coming for him. It was so unfair. The whole damn situation was just so bitterly unfair.

Kier took Siobhan home before the bookshop opened so that no one would see her in her pajamas aside from Brigid, who came in early to start cooking. Once they left, I took Siobhan's laptop up to the third floor to read what she had crafted during her frenzied writing spell.

Before I locked in on the work, I called Sam in Martha's Vineyard. It was early there but this was an emergency.

"Em, are you all right?"

"Oh, Sam." I hadn't thought I'd cry but I was so overwhelmed by all that had happened I could only answer in hiccupping sobs.

"What's wrong? Did someone hurt you? I can be there in hours," Sam said. She really was my ride or die.

"No," I said. I glanced around the deserted third floor to make certain I was completely alone. Then I told her everything about Siobhan's diagnosis and how she wasn't ready to tell Kier yet. I told Sam how things were changing between Kier and me and I didn't know what to do. I couldn't betray Siobhan's trust but I couldn't stand to have Kier not know the truth.

"Oh, wow, that's a lot," Sam said. She was quiet for a bit. "There's really only one choice."

"Tell him," I said at the same time she said, "You can't tell him."

"But—" I protested but she interrupted me.

"I'm going to be really blunt," Sam said. "It's unfortunate that you know and he doesn't, but it's Siobhan's right to tell who she wants and not tell who she doesn't. You have to respect that. It's like her dying wish. You can't go against someone's dying wish even if you don't agree with it."

I sighed. Sam was right, I knew that. I simply couldn't betray Siobhan's trust and I'd just have to encourage her to tell Kier sooner rather than later.

"You're right, I know you're right," I said. "Thanks."

"Anytime," Sam said. "And I'm really so sorry about Siobhan. I know how much she means to you."

My throat was tight, but I choked out a "Yeah." It was the best I could do.

"Hey, did you tell your mom that you weren't coming back for the holidays?" Sam asked.

"Yes, how did you know?" I asked. "She didn't come after you again, did she?"

"No, one of my waitstaff at the inn lives next door to her and said there was some big drama where she threw out all of her Christmas decorations, packed up her cat, and headed for the Cape."

"Yeah, she's going to stay with her sister for Christmas or as she explained it to me, 'her real family, the ones who actually care about her,'" I said.

"Oof," Sam said. "I miss you, but I think staying in Ireland is the wise choice, especially now."

"Agreed," I said. We talked for a few more minutes and then, feeling better, I ended the call and got back to work. I opened up the document on the laptop and began to read.

Surprisingly, there was only one additional chapter. A note at the beginning of it was from Siobhan to me.

> Em—I'm sure this doesn't seem like a lot for a writer who worked through the night, does it? That's because I deleted most of it. The joy of being a writer! Please hit it with all the force of your red pen. XO Siobhan

Deleted most of it? I gulped. The idea of working on something all night and then just delete-delete-delete? My brain clenched at the mere thought.

I hunkered into a cushy chair by the window and read the chapter. I didn't know what Siobhan had written that she'd purged but this chapter was extraordinary. Again. Poignant, humorous, and a little frightening, I felt Tig's struggle to find his friends after being gone for ten years all the way down to my soul.

When I looked up from the screen, Kier was sitting in the chair opposite me. I hadn't even heard him arrive. I jumped and yelped. He laughed and then looked contrite.

"Sorry, you were so engrossed, I didn't want to disturb you," he said.

I put my hand on my chest to calm my heart and said, "'From that time on, the world was hers for the reading. She would never be lonely again, never miss the lack of intimate friends. Books became her friends and there was one for every mood.'"

Kier grinned. "*A Tree Grows in Brooklyn*. Is that how Ma's books made you feel?"

"Yes."

He glanced at the laptop and asked, "And this one, how is it?"

"Brilliant," I said. "Of course, it is. It's Siobhan Riordan." I waited a beat and then I asked, "How is she?"

"You mean after she tore into me for making her go home?" he asked.

I blinked. "I thought she was okay with it."

"She was, essentially, but she didn't like how bossy I was," he said.

"Can't really blame her for that," I said.

"No," he agreed. "She's resting now. I'm going to check on her this afternoon. You should come with me."

I went still. I widened my eyes. Was he saying what I thought he was saying?

"To her house?" I asked just to clarify.

"You're doing it again, Red, that fangirl thing."

"Sorry, but you have to understand, if nine-year-old me had

known that she would one day go to the home of the author of the Tig McMorrow series, she would have expired on the spot," I said.

"Well, that would have been tragic," Kier said. "Because then she wouldn't be here now."

My face instantly warmed. His gaze held mine and there it was. The awareness between us that had been there from the beginning was now a full-blown case of attraction that shimmered in the air around us like a carelessly thrown fistful of glitter.

"Have I kissed you yet today?" he asked.

"I don't believe so, no," I said. I was trying to keep my voice light and breezy but it dropped an entire octave, blowing my cover of feigned nonchalance.

"Terrible oversight on my part." He reached forward and grasped the arms of my chair, pulling it toward him until my legs were tangled with his. He frowned and said, "I suppose it's bad form to kiss an employee while on the clock."

"It is." I nodded. He sighed and hung his head. I smiled. "But is it bad form for an employee to kiss her boss while on her break?"

His head snapped back up and his eyes glinted with humor but also with a look of hunger that made my breath catch. It was desire. For me. I completely lost the thread of the conversation.

"Are you on your break, Red?"

"Most definitely." I moved Siobhan's laptop and my notepad to the table beside me and lunged forward. It was graceless and clumsy but Kier didn't seem to mind. He caught me by the waist and pulled me onto his lap.

I didn't wait for him to kiss me. Instead, I cupped his face and planted my lips on his. I slid my fingers into his hair and held him still while I moved my mouth over his and then traced the seam of his lips with my tongue. I had no idea what had gotten into me. I'd never been the assertive one in a physical relationship but there was something about Kier that stripped me of my pleaser nature, or rather, flipped it. Instead of constantly trying to guess what would please him I was actively doing what pleased me.

Maybe it was the way he called me "Red" and saw me as feisty or maybe it was me, choosing to be the sort of person who went after what she wanted. Either way, I liked it.

With Kier, I said what I thought. I teased. I taunted. I took no shit. Just like this kiss. He let me take the lead and judging by the low moan in his throat, he was enjoying being on the receiving end of my attention.

I could feel the stubble on his chin abrade my skin. I didn't care. His hands moved over my body, from my shoulders to my hips, gently following each curve, in a way that indicated he'd spent considerable time thinking about touching me and was now savoring it. It made my insides hum and I deepened the kiss, putting every bit of longing I felt into it and plundering his mouth with my tongue the way I'd like to be plundered myself.

"Ah, I love the way you taste, Red," Kier whispered against my mouth. I could feel him harden against my hip and felt a surge of satisfaction.

I broke away, breathing heavily, and pressed my forehead to his. "Well, that escalated quickly."

He laughed. "That's not exactly the word I would use."

"No?" I asked innocently. "You'd prefer peaked?"

He laughed again. "More accurately I'd say enlarged."

I nudged him with my hip. "I see your point."

He groaned. "You're going to give me a permanent condition, Red."

I laughed and slid off his lap and back into my own chair. I liked Kieran Murphy very much, but he was my boss and I worked for his mother, who had asked me to keep a hell of a secret. Things could get very complicated between us and I didn't want to have it all blow up in my face. I needed to convince Siobhan to tell Kier the truth.

"Sadly, my break is over," I said.

He watched me with an intensity that I felt all the way to my core. "Good thing we have a date later."

"A date?" I asked.

"After we visit Siobhan, I'm taking you to dinner," he said.

"Isn't it customary to ask a person if they want to have dinner with you first?" I was giving no quarter with this guy. I liked him too much. I'd lie down and let him run right over me if I wasn't vigilant.

"Silly me," he said. "I assumed when you kissed me that indicated you were interested in dating me."

I simply stared at him, waiting. His smile started in one corner of his mouth and slowly slid to the other side until it was a full-blown grin.

"You are something, Red," he said. Then he leaned forward, resting his elbows on his knees. His gaze was sincere and his voice serious when he asked, "Will you have dinner with me, love?"

It was the *love* that almost launched me back into his lap. I clenched my butt, refusing to let myself move. My voice when I spoke was insanely cool and collected, given how chaotic my insides were. "Why that sounds *lovely*, Kier. I'd be delighted." I didn't know who this new Emily was but I liked her. I liked her a lot.

He leaned in and kissed me quick. "I'll collect you in a few hours."

I didn't say anything. I just watched him stand, marveling that my crush had just asked me out. On. A. Date. I admired him as he walked away. It was the confident stride of man who knew his why. It was incredibly hot and I knew the next few hours were going to be the longest of my life.

. . .

Ready to go?" Kier appeared beside my desk in the workroom just before closing.

"Yes, but quick question, should I bring Siobhan's laptop?"

"No," he said. "She's having a lie-in for the rest of the day and we've agreed to discuss ways to keep her from overdoing it."

"Oh, that's a good idea," I said.

"We'll see," he said. "I think she was just humoring me so I'd leave her be."

I glanced at the carton Oisín had asked me to unbox. I'd been learning how they managed the incoming stock and I had discovered that I felt the same thrill that I had in the library when a box of books from a publisher arrived. There was simply no smell as wonderful as the ink and paper of a new book.

I unloaded the last of the volumes onto a book truck and said, "I'll just grab my coat."

Kier held it out to me. He'd already retrieved it from the coatrack. I would have felt flattered that he knew which coat was mine, but my puffy black jacket, which looked ridiculous but was very warm, was distinctive amid all of the classic thick wool coats the rest of them wore. I made a mental note to buy a new one first chance I got.

I shrugged into my coat and grabbed my shoulder bag from the bottom drawer of the desk. "I finished, Oisín. I'll be back to add the books to the inventory tomorrow."

"No problem. Give Siobhan my best," he said.

"She'll be glad to hear it," Kier said.

We left through the front of the shop. As soon as we stepped outside, Kier handed me the keys to his car. "You have to keep practicing, Red."

I sighed. "All right, if I must."

"You must," he said.

I climbed into the driver's seat while Kier took the passenger's. I adjusted the seat and the mirrors because the man had a good six inches on me. Then I started the car, shifted into first, and slowly pulled out of the parking spot. Kier directed me through town, past the side street that would bring me home and down another narrow street where the homes were set back with large front yards. He guided me to turn onto a long tree-lined drive. A gatehouse was nestled in a copse of trees on my left.

"That's where I live," Kier said.

I turned and took in the two-story stone house with the forest green door. Lace curtains were in the upper windows and Shackleton was sitting on the front stoop. I braked hard.

Kier glanced at me and I pointed. "Dog."

"Of course," he said. He stepped out and opened the back door. "Well, come on then."

The dog let out one joyous bark and raced for the car, jumping up onto the back seat as if sailing on his own happiness. I glanced at him in the rearview mirror.

"Good to see you, buddy."

He barked and I took it that he returned the sentiment. Kier climbed back in and we set off for the main house. I should have been prepared. I knew that Siobhan had been hugely successful, not as much as the famous wizard writing author, but still a pretty big deal during the aughts. Yet I was still caught off guard.

"Wow," I said. The "house" was a mansion. Two stories made of thick gray stone with a slate roof and massive windows running all along the first and second floors, it looked like something out of an Austen novel. Not Pemberley, Darcy's posh address, but not Longbourn, the Bennetts' family home, either. Rather, it appeared to land somewhere in the middle of the two, being stately and austere but with a certain whimsy about it.

"Does Siobhan live here alone?" I asked.

"Ah . . . no," he said. "She has staff."

"Well, I should hope so," I said. I wondered if I sounded like I was perfectly at ease with this sort of wealth. Probably not. There was no masking the awe in my voice.

"That's why I live in the gatehouse," Kier said. "I never really got used to having people about."

"Right? I mean when you want to walk around in your underwear, you don't want anyone to suddenly appear, vacuuming the carpets." Kier laughed and I realized what I'd said. "Not that I think you walk around in your underwear and if you do, well done, but if you don't . . . you know what? I'm going to shut up now."

"It's all right," he said. "I happen to agree completely."

I stopped the car in the circular drive in front of the house. Kier got out and let Shackleton loose and the dog bounded straight for the front door. I exited on my side and joined Kier, dropping the keys into my pocket.

"How'd I do?" I asked.

"Grand," he said. "You're really getting the way of it, Red."

"It was only a few kilometers," I said. I turned to face him. "That being said, I can't believe Siobhan walked all that way in the middle of the night to get to her laptop."

"Writers." Kier shrugged. "That was the other reason I wanted you to come with me this afternoon."

"Oh?" I asked. I didn't like the devious look in his eyes.

"Yes, I was hoping you'd help me convince Ma that if she's really going to do this, she needs to set up a schedule for her writing," he explained. "And I expect she'll take it better from you than me."

Fifteen

"Uh-huh." I looked him up and down. Then I lifted my right arm and flexed, which was ridiculous because there was nothing to see through the puffy coat. "So, what your saying is I'm your muscle."

Kier poked my bicep with his finger and said, "I think of you as more the voice of reason."

"Not as thrilling as being someone's muscle, but all right." Together we strode to the door, which was being held open by a middle-aged woman in black wool pants and a pretty ecru sweater set.

"Afternoon, Kieran," the woman said. She had warm brown eyes and a round, lightly freckled face. Her light brown hair was held back in a short ponytail at the nape of her neck. She exuded efficiency, which filled me with the unfamiliar sensation of calm. I liked it.

"Mrs. Clohessy," Kier said. "May I introduce Emily Allen."

She gave me a warm smile and stepped back so we could enter. "Very nice to meet you, Ms. Allen."

"Is Ma awake?" Kier asked.

"I just checked on her and, yes, she was starting to rouse," Mrs. Clohessy said. "And Shackleton headed straight for the kitchen."

"Looking for Mrs. Doan, no doubt," Kier said. He looked at me and explained, "Ma's cook has soft spot for him."

"May I take your coats?" Mrs. Clohessy asked.

Kier shrugged out of his and handed it to her. "If it's not a bother, we'll take tea in Ma's room. I imagine she could use the pick-me-up."

"Absolutely. I'll have Shannon bring it up straight away," Mrs. Clohessy said.

"Excellent," Kier said. "Many thanks."

"Yes, thank you, Mrs. Clohessy." I handed over my coat, as well, trying not to feel uncomfortable about it. I mean, I could hang it up myself and I hated to trouble her.

"No problem at all," Mrs. Clohessy said.

Again, it struck me how unfailingly polite the people of Finn's Hollow were. Everything was always "no problem at all."

Kier led the way to the staircase that wound up one side of the great room to the second floor.

It was reminiscent of the one in Ballymuir Castle and I admired the cream-colored wainscoting and pale gray walls. It felt very soothing. On the landing, we turned right and strode down the thickly carpeted hallway to a door at the end. It was ajar and Kier knocked twice before pushing it open.

"Make yourself decent, Ma," he said. "I've brought company."

"It had better be my laptop," Siobhan retorted.

Kier pushed open the door and strode into the room. I followed. I leaned to the side to see around him and said, "Sorry, it's just me."

"Don't be. I'm always happy to see you, dear," Siobhan said. She was reclined against a bank of pillows in an enormous canopy bed.

Her hair was loose and her complexion pale but the dark circles under her eyes had diminished.

She sat up and swung her legs to the side. She was wearing a pair of purple flannel pajamas with white piping all around the edges. She shoved her feet into a pair of fluffy white slippers and grabbed a purple and gray plaid robe off the foot of her bed. Kier stepped forward and held it behind her so she could get her arms inside and then she belted it tight.

She gestured to the sitting area beside the large marble fireplace on the opposite side of the enormous room. "Let's take a seat. I don't want to talk while lying in bed. I'll feel like an invalid."

We moved across the room and I noted that the massive windows looked out over a beautiful garden. Most of the blooms were gone as winter was coming but the evergreen hedges were trimmed so precisely I was certain that if I put a level on top, the bubble would sit right in the middle. The gravel path that led between the vacant flower beds was scrupulously maintained with nary a weed in sight and large statuary, mostly of Greek goddesses, could just be seen through the yew hedges.

Siobhan sat in one of the armchairs and I took a spot on the loveseat. To my surprise, Kier sat beside me. I glanced at him but if he recognized how out of character this was for him, it didn't show. I saw Siobhan glance between us so I gathered she sensed a change in our relationship. Did she know we'd kissed? Had Brigid or one of the others mentioned it? I wondered if she was worried that I'd confided in him. I didn't know how to signal that I hadn't.

There was a knock on the door and a pretty young woman entered. She was wearing jeans and a white collared shirt with a sweater over it. Her thick dark hair was held back from her face by a wide gray cloth headband. She looked to be in her early to mid-twenties. Her smile was wide and her brown eyes sparkled.

"Tea for you and your guests, ma'am." She carried a fully loaded tray and Kier rose to take it from her. She blushed immediately to the roots of her hair when his hands brushed hers.

"Thank you, Shannon. I'll be mother," Kier said. I smiled. From Siobhan's books, I knew the expression "be mother" meant that he'd pour the tea.

"Thank you, Mr. Murphy." Shannon's gaze when she looked at him was wide-eyed and full of worship.

"It's just Murphy," he said. His tone was gentle and her blush deepened.

"Yes, Mr. . . . uh . . . Murphy," she stammered.

Poor thing. I knew exactly how she felt. I was suddenly very grateful that Kier had been such a horse's ass when we first met or I likely would have been a stammering, blushing disaster around him, too.

"Can I get you anything else, ma'am?" Shannon asked while staring at Kier.

"No, thank you, dear," Siobhan said. Her voice was kind and her gaze amused.

"All right, then," Shannon said. She stared at Kier for a beat, who was oblivious while he fixed his mother's cup of tea, and then she audibly sighed and left the room.

Siobhan glanced at me and grinned. "Can you imagine having the power to reduce the opposite sex to incoherence?"

"No." I shook my head.

"And he's completely unaware of it." She rolled her eyes as if she couldn't comprehend being so obtuse.

"I'm right here," Kier said. He handed his mother her tea. "And that is a statement only a mother would make." He turned to me and said, "Ignore her, she's blinded by maternal affection."

He set to making me a cup of tea, bending over the pot and cups, and I found myself smiling at the top of his head. Kier's lack of awareness of his own attractiveness was definitely a point in his favor as far as I was concerned. Of course, the man must need an eye check. How could he not see how ruggedly handsome he was? I was mystified.

"All right, since you didn't bring my laptop, I assume you're here to bully me into resting some more. But you don't want to get into another row with me, so you've brought Em to do the deed," Siobhan said.

Kier handed me my tea, prepared exactly as I liked it—how did he know?—and met my gaze. His raised eyebrows seemed to say "good luck." Uh, yeah, thanks.

"Siobhan, we're here because we care about you," I said. I took a bracing sip of the hot tea. Siobhan was watching me as if waiting for the *but*, because of course there was a *but*. Except I knew that the one way to get me to do something was to tell me that I couldn't, and I suspected Siobhan was wired the same way, so I had to try and do a workaround and hope she went for it. "And because we care about you, we want to help you write the book."

In my peripheral vision, I saw Kier's head snap in my direction while Siobhan's eyes widened in surprise. My plan had been to ease her into the idea of a schedule but when I tried to form the words, I knew I needed to offer an opportunity instead of a restriction. It was the only way she'd go for it. If we helped her, perhaps we could keep her from working too hard and buy her some time.

Kier sank back onto the loveseat, his cup of tea forgotten on the table. He stared at me slack-jawed as if I'd just suggested we fornicate in front of his mom. I almost laughed at how comically aghast he was.

"I'm listening," Siobhan said.

"I know you don't outline," I said. I closed my eyes for a moment.

I couldn't even imagine not having a plan while writing. It was mayhem, like going to the market without a list when you were hungry. Nothing good could come of it. I opened my eyes to find Siobhan smiling. "How many chapters from last night did you delete this morning because you didn't work off an outline?"

Siobhan considered me for a moment. "It's my process. I always throw out hundreds of pages."

We were all quiet for a moment. I knew I had to ask my next question carefully. Siobhan needed to hear me while Kier must be protected. This was a tightrope walk. "Do you want to spend that much extra time on this book?"

Kier dropped his gaze from me to the tabletop. He reached for his tea, clearly avoiding what he expected would be his mother's fiery response in reaction to a question about her process. But Siobhan met my gaze and I saw the understanding light her eyes.

"You make a very good point, Em," Siobhan said. I heard Kier's small inhale of surprise but I didn't look at him. She continued, "I suppose the truth of it is that none of us know how much time we have and we should use it wisely."

It wasn't an admission of what was happening to her, but it was close. Maybe her plan was to ease Kier into it. I hoped so.

"I've known plenty of people who were here one day and gone the next." She glanced at Kier and added, "Like your father."

He nodded. "That's a fact, isn't it?"

Siobhan looked at me and explained, "Heart attack."

"Oh," I said.

"I don't know how long it will take me to write the book," Siobhan said. "But I do know that it's the most important thing to me."

"Why?" Kier asked. The word burst from him as if it had been ripped out against his will.

Siobhan looked at him in surprise. "Because I can't leave the story unfinished. That's what woke me up last night. A feeling of panic that Tig's story would be incomplete. I don't want to leave him stranded."

"He's not a real person!" Kier said. His voice was raised just enough to let us know he was upset without actually yelling.

"He is to me," Siobhan insisted. She stared at her son with so much love in her gaze. "His outcome is very important to me."

"It's always about the books, isn't it?" he asked. He set his cup down very precisely on the tray as if restraining himself from throwing it. He looked at his mother and shook his head. "That's all it's ever been about, hasn't it? You know what, I thought I could do this, I really did, but I can't. I can't watch you work yourself to death for a bloody book."

He pushed up from his seat and strode from the room, slamming the door behind him. It rattled on its hinges as if even the door had something to say about the situation.

"That could have gone better." Siobhan glanced at me. "You see now why I can't tell him."

"Hmm." I didn't want to agree with her even though it was clear she was right, so I hummed, hoping I sounded understanding when honestly I had no idea what the best course of action was. They were so alike in their stubbornness and they didn't even see it.

"He lost me when the first book sold." Siobhan stared at the closed door with a faraway look in her eye. "When my first Tig McMorrow novel took off, I wasn't prepared. I was so desperately grateful after so many years of rejection to finally have my book published that I accepted every invitation to book signings, conferences, guest speaker events, you name it, I lived out of my luggage for months."

"Did Kier go with you?"

"No, he was thirteen and still in school so he stayed with his father and *that* woman."

"Meredith," I said.

She turned to me, looking surprised. "He told you about her?"

"We were comparing stepmothers," I said. "I went to high school with mine."

Her mouth opened just slightly as if I'd caught her off guard. "I'm sorry. I can only imagine . . ."

"It's fine," I said. I did not want to miss anything she had to tell me about Kier. "What did *that* woman do?"

Siobhan shook her head as if to get back on topic. "In addition to lashing him with a belt when he missed a glass whilst doing the dishes or for any other transgression she could find"—Siobhan paused to take a steadying breath—"she also told him he was skinny, weak, stupid, boring, and that the reason I left him behind was because I was ashamed of him. I didn't find out about the abuse until it was almost too late."

I sucked in a breath. My father's abandonment and my mother's neglect suddenly felt so benign compared to this calculated cruelty. "That evil, twisted, vicious . . ." I was half out of my chair when I asked, "Does she live nearby because I'd love to have a chat with her."

The tears that were welling in Siobhan's eyes spilled at the same time a laugh wheezed out of her. "Oh, Em, you're a girl . . . er . . . woman after my own heart."

"How did you find out about her?" I asked.

"I got home early from a trip and went to collect Kier at his father's," Siobhan said. Her expression was grim. "I caught Meredith in the act. He was just fourteen and she was giving him a vicious thrashing. I did what any mam would do, I flattened her."

Siobhan made a fist, tightened up her face, and punched the air. "I told her if she ever came near my boy again, I'd have her charged with child abuse."

"Wow," I said. "You were a badass."

"No, I was a bad mother," she said. "How could I not have known what was going on? Kier had become sullen and moody, and I just thought he was being a teenager. He needed me, Em, and I wasn't there."

"No, but his father was." I might have been too emphatic given my feelings of resentment toward my own father but I wasn't wrong. "Fatherhood isn't a part-time job, men aren't babysitters, they're just as responsible for their children as the mothers. His father should have seen what was happening and dealt with it."

Siobhan considered my words and nodded.

"What you say is true, but Kier's father was not a happy man," Siobhan said. "He could never see past his own navel. He had no idea what was happening in his own home and Meredith told Kier that if he said a word to anyone, she'd take him away from me permanently."

"Oh, that's evil," I said.

"I only wish I'd punched her in the mouth," Siobhan said.

"I feel that," I said. "You and Kier seem close now."

"We are. Therapy helped," Siobhan said. "And I reprioritized my life. I only did book tours on school breaks so he could come with me. It took time but we found our way back together."

I glanced at the door. "Where do you suppose Kier went just now?"

"Home, I imagine," she said.

"The gatehouse?" I clarified. She nodded. "If you'll excuse me, I'm going to check on him."

"I don't want to put you in the middle any more than I already have, Em, but could you talk to him?" Siobhan asked. She looked pained, as if she hated asking but didn't know what else to do. "Could you try and explain why finishing the book is so important to me?"

"I can try," I said. "But I truly believe you need to tell him what's happening and give him a chance to support you. Otherwise all the work you did to rebuild your relationship will be for nothing."

"Maybe," she said.

I helped her back into bed and promised to call later. I stepped outside and found Shackleton waiting in the hallway. "We've had some drama," I told him. He tapped my foot with his paw and turned and walked down the hallway. I assumed this meant I should follow, so I did.

We continued down the stairs to find Mrs. Clohessy in the great room waiting with my coat. Again, just the sight of her filled me with peace.

"I believe Kieran walked home," she said.

"That would be because I have the car keys." I shrugged into my coat, pulling the keys out of my pocket to show her.

"Ah, well, that should make it easier to catch him, shouldn't it?" she asked. Her smile was encouraging and I sensed she knew there was tension between Siobhan and Kier and she wanted me to smooth it over. Sure. No problem at all.

"We'll see," I said. "Come on, Shackleton."

We left the magnificent house behind and headed for the car. I opened the passenger door for the dog and he hopped in, eager to go find his person. I was not nearly so eager. What the hell was I supposed to say? I had no idea.

I started the car and drove back down the tree-lined drive. The lights on the first floor of the gatehouse were on, confirming that Kier was there. I parked beside the house and let the dog out. He bounded up the path in between two sculpted hedges to the large wooden front door painted a deep forest green.

Without overthinking it, I raised my fist and knocked. Shackleton sat down beside me and stared at the doorknob as if willing it to turn. It didn't.

"Do you think he heard us?" I asked. "Should I knock again or just go inside? I mean I have to return his car keys, right?"

I knocked again and there was no response. Shackleton rose to his feet and nudged the doorknob with his nose.

"Just go in, huh? That's a bold maneuver, buddy."

Shackleton wagged his fluffy tail so hard his bottom wiggled. Fine. I could take a hint. I took a steadying breath and grabbed the old-fashioned brass doorknob—it was cold to the touch—and pushed the door open.

I stopped on the threshold, staring at the foyer before me. It was sparsely decorated with just a bench running along one wall. There was a jumble of shoes kicked under it. I took that as an indicator that I should leave mine there as well. I shrugged out of my coat and dropped it and my shoulder bag on the bench. Shackleton, bless his well-mannered doggy heart, waited beside me.

There was a hallway ahead of me, a staircase beside that, and a doorway to my left that led to what I assumed would be a front parlor. There was a light on in that room, so I chose that direction. I crossed the foyer and paused in the doorway.

My shoulders immediately dropped. If a room could embody the words *welcome home*, this one did. It had floor-to-ceiling windows along one wall that let in the watery light of late afternoon, and the bookshelves that lined the other walls were stuffed top to bottom with books. A large, squashy sofa and two matching armchairs, all upholstered in dark brown, faced the gray stone fireplace, where a fire crackled on the grate, filling the room with warmth.

It was there on the sofa that Kier sat, staring into the flames. A cut crystal glass half-full of a dark amber liquid, which I suspected was whiskey, dangled from his fingers.

It was too much. With his furrowed brow and dark hair curling just over his collar, he looked like he should be dressed in a blousy white shirt with a fussily tied cravat and an embroidered waistcoat, fitted breeches, and Hessian boots like one of Julia Quinn's Bridgerton heroes. In my mind, I would glide into the room in a cream-colored, empire waist muslin dress with delicate embroidery on the hem and cap sleeves, an airy cashmere shawl in a soft shade of green dangling from my elbows. I would pause beside his chair and take the glass from his hand, setting it carefully on the table. He would take my gloved hand in his, tug me into his arms, and—

"Hiya, Red. Did you manage to talk any sense into Ma?" Kier turned away from the fire to look at me. When his gaze met mine, I was filled with so many *feelings*.

With my new knowledge of his childhood, I ached for the boy who had been abused by his stepmother and ignored by his father, and I understood how he had found solace in books just like I had. I saw him more clearly now. He was a loving son, trying desperately to keep his world intact.

"Red, you're starting to worry me," he said. His frown deepened. "Are you all right?"

No, I wasn't, because it hit me right in that moment like a pie in the face that I could fall in love with my brooding romance hero.

Sixteen

"Um . . ." I stalled, taking a beat to stifle all of those *feelings* I was having. I pictured a tiny version of myself inside my chest cavity, stomping on these little flames of attachment like mini me was putting out a fire.

Thankfully, Shackleton bounded ahead of me and nudged Kier's free hand with his nose, demanding pets. I took the opportunity to shift my expression into neutral.

"I think I should be the one asking if you're all right," I said. I was relieved that my voice sounded normal. I crossed the room, taking a seat beside him.

"I wasn't the one staring off into space," he said.

"No," I agreed. "In my defense, this is a lovely room and I was just taking it all in. Both your home and Siobhan's are wonderful. It makes me wonder why Siobhan works at the coffee shop instead of her house. She must have an office there."

He nodded. "She does, but she says it's too quiet. She wrote most of her books when I was a lad, always underfoot and, according to her, quite loud."

I smiled. I could picture it easily. We were quiet for a moment and when he spoke his voice was full of regret.

"I'm sorry I stormed out like I did," he said. "I was being an eejit. I just . . ."

His voice trailed off and I let the silence settle between us. I didn't want to say anything that might keep him from speaking his truth. I didn't want to fill in the blanks and try to figure out his feelings with guesswork. It was up to him to acknowledge what he felt and express it.

I sat beside him as the minutes ticked by. Shackleton sacked out in front of the hearth and started to snore. Kier leaned forward and lifted the decanter of whiskey from the coffee table and poured a second glass, which he handed to me.

"She could do anything she wants now," he said. "She was so hampered by her cancer for so long, too weak and with a shoddy immune system, her life became very small. But now she could be fully retired and free to do anything she wants. But what does she want to do? Write."

I braced myself with a small sip. It felt like liquid fire in my mouth. I swallowed without wheezing . . . much.

"But writing *is* what she wants," I countered.

"I know. It's what she always wants."

"You sound unhappy about that. Can I ask why?"

"I told you I wrote *The Broken Window* on a dare, right?" he said.

I nodded, took a larger sip of my whiskey, and winced. His mouth tipped up in one corner.

"I was at college and one of my classmates found out who my

mother was and he dared me to write a novel, too, as if that would prove something. So I did."

"It's a good mystery."

He waved off my praise. "It was brutally hard work and that's an understatement. What I learned was that creating a novel is all-consuming, there's no room for anything else in your life. While you shave, you're thinking about your plot. You go out with the lads and you have to make notes on bar napkins because an idea struck. There's simply no peace."

It was exactly what Siobhan had described. I let his words echo in the silence.

"Ma first got published when I was thirteen. Her book was a huge success. We were so happy because her dream finally came true." He paused, drinking his whiskey. "Of course, we weren't prepared for the flipside, which was book tours and press junkets and the demands for the next book in the series. She and my dad divorced when I was in primary school and he quickly married Meredith, so when Ma had to go on tour, I was sent to live with them."

There was so much behind his words, so much pain and anger and sadness. Even if Siobhan hadn't already told me, I'd have known it was an awful situation. It was clear in the way he clenched his jaw and rubbed his knuckles over his chest as if trying to soothe an ache.

"What happened?" I asked.

"Suffice to say that Meredith and I didn't get on," he said.

"Oh?" I asked, encouraging him to tell me more because as understatements went that one was a doozy.

He turned to meet my gaze. The pain in his dark eyes was bottomless. I wanted to jump inside just to see if I could repair the damage but he didn't say any more. He didn't invite me in. He just said, "Yeah."

"Did your parents know?" I asked. I knew Siobhan had discovered it late, but I still couldn't believe that his father would have tolerated any sort of abuse of his son.

"No." Kier shook his head. "Meredith was a master manipulator and convinced me that if I said anything she would see to it that my father got sole custody of me and I'd never see my mother again."

"What a nightmare."

"Truly," he said. "Then when I was fourteen, Ma came home early from a book tour because she didn't feel well. She walked in on Meredith backhanding me because I'd accidentally made a scuff mark on the floor in the hallway with my boots."

I leaned against him, needing to be close. "I'm so very sorry that happened to you, that you had to live like that."

He rested his head on top of mine, accepting my attempt to comfort him. "Don't feel bad, I'm okay. I don't know if you're aware that Siobhan has a temper."

I thought about the fist she'd made when she talked about Meredith. "I can imagine."

"It was quite a scene, but on the upside, I never had to stay with my father and Meredith again," Kier said. He swirled the liquid in his glass. "So after Ma being away on and off for a year, I got her back and we spent some time on the therapist's couch together, sorting it all out. It was good. It helped me let go of my feelings of abandonment and understand that Ma had been pushed into the role of provider. Not just for her and me but for Da and Meredith as well. In different ways, we were both being abused. I felt like everything was finally going to level out."

"Did they?" I asked.

"The next five years were amazing. Ma and I lived in Finn's Hollow during the school year and summers were spent on book tours. Then I went off to university and Ma continued to publish.

Everything was going well until ten years ago. Right after I graduated from Trinity, Siobhan was diagnosed with breast cancer," he said.

"I'm sorry." The words had never felt more inadequate and I was sorry for so much more than he knew.

"She conquered that first round like a champ, she kept up her writing and never missed a deadline. We really thought she was in the clear but right before she hit the five-year mark, the doctors informed us that the cancer had metastasized and it came back with a vengeance."

He leaned forward, set his glass on the coffee table, and rested his elbows on his knees. "I know why you're here."

"You do?"

"Ma asked you to talk some sense into me, didn't she?" he asked.

"That's not exactly how she phrased it." I put my glass down, too. "She wants to finish the book, Kier."

"So she said."

"You said that when you wrote your novel you discovered how all-consuming it was," I said. "Is that why you don't want her to do it? Because there'd be no room for you in her life if she's spending all of her time on the book?"

"No!" he said. His refusal was swift and sharp but then he relented. "Maybe a bit, but it's more because working that much is so hard on her and she's fragile now. She's not as strong as she once was. What if she works herself right into a stroke or a heart attack?"

"That's why we'll help her," I said. My tone was fierce because I knew what he didn't. Siobhan was already running out of time.

"Yeah, about that." He turned on the couch so we were facing each other. "I brought you with me to talk her into committing to a schedule not to volunteer to help write the damn book."

"I know." I raised my hands in surrender. "But I thought that by offering to help her she'd feel less pressured to work every second of every day and we could keep her from becoming consumed with the book, which would keep her from overexerting herself."

He narrowed his eyes at me. I maintained what I hoped was a reasonable expression.

"I can't focus when you're in my orbit." He turned back to the fire. "I fancy you too much, Red. When you're this close to me, all I can think about is kissing you."

I stared at his profile. I had no idea what to say. No man had ever made me feel this desired before.

"I'm not helping write the bloody book," he said.

"But don't you want to know what happens to Tig?" I asked.

He shrugged. "Not particularly given that I've never read the books."

"What?!" I gaped at him. "How is that even possible?"

"I just never did . . ." His voice trailed off.

It was inconceivable to me, who had used the Tig McMorrow books to survive my tween and teen years, that a person could have had access to the stories while they were being written and have chosen not to read them.

"Listen, it was difficult," he said. "Meredith refused to let Ma's books in the house, even though she demanded that Ma pay her an egregious amount of child support and whatnot."

"Oh, *that* woman." My voice vibrated with hostility.

Kier looked at me in surprise and said, "You sound just like Ma." He picked up his glass and took a sip. "It wasn't entirely Meredith's fault." He cleared his throat. He looked uncomfortable. "The truth is when Ma's book took off, I felt as if I was competing with Tig McMorrow for her time and attention. When she left me with Dad and *that* woman, well, I started to hate those fecking books and most especially the fictional boy she seemed to love so much. Pathetic, right?"

And now it all made sense.

"Not at all." I reached across the space between us and took his hand in mine. Poor Kier had missed so much and it wasn't just reading the books. "So, you don't know?"

He glanced at me. "What happens to Tig? No. And I don't care."

That wasn't what I'd meant but I knew I couldn't explain it to him. He was going to have to discover it for himself but given his stubborn nature, I knew it was my job to get him there for his sake, for Siobhan's sake, and, yes, even for Tig McMorrow's sake.

"I'm sorry," I said. "Weren't you going to treat me to dinner?"

He blinked, surprised by the change of subject. "I had planned to cook for you."

"You cook?" I asked. Of course he did, because being handsome and well-read wasn't enough to make me swoon.

"I did my time working in restaurants in Dublin," he said. "I make a decent broiled salmon and mash."

"Excellent," I said. "How long will it take?"

"Thirty minutes, give or take." There it was, the *th* that became a hard *T* when he spoke. So damn sexy.

"I'll be back before it's ready," I said. I rose from my seat and headed for the door before I did something foolish like straddle him like I was a rowdy rodeo queen from Colorado instead of a demure librarian from Massachusetts.

"Where are you going?" He followed me to the foyer.

"Quick errand," I said. I jammed my feet into my boots and pulled on my coat. "Don't worry. I'll be careful with your car."

"You're taking my car?" The alarmed look on his face was comical but I didn't dare laugh.

"Why not? It still has the *N* on it so every other driver knows to steer clear," I said. He looked conflicted. Without overthinking it, I rolled up on my toes and kissed his cheek. "Bye." I hurried out the door before he could say no.

The traffic was light, making the drive back to my cottage mere minutes. I parked on the street and dashed inside. There was a small bookcase in my bedroom where I'd put the books I'd brought with me from the States. Yes, I brought books. Of course I did. I was to be here for a year. I needed my comfort books, one of which was *Tig McMorrow and the Ogham Stone.*

The dust jacket was worn and the spine loose. The many times over the years that I'd opened it and reread precious passages had aged it like a sailor who spent too many drunken weekends ashore. I didn't care. It made me love it all the more. I tucked it carefully into my shoulder bag and headed back out the door.

When I arrived back at his house, I knocked before pushing the door open. Shackleton sat just inside as if waiting for me. I ruffled his silky black and white fur, then I kicked off my boots and hung up my jacket. I left my shoulder bag on the bench. I didn't want to give away my plan just yet. I had no idea how I was going to convince Kier to read the Tig McMorrow book after twenty years of his refusing to do so, but I knew I had to try.

Shackleton led the way down the hallway through a dining room, set with two place settings, to the kitchen beyond. It was delightfully warm in here and I glanced over to see Kier standing at the center island. There was music playing in the background, some sort of jazz. He hadn't heard me come in and I took a moment just to watch him.

His shirt sleeves were rolled back and I could see the bunch of muscles in his forearm as he mashed the potatoes in the pot, pausing occasionally to add a gob or two of very yellow Irish butter. The oven beeped and he turned toward it, catching me watching him. The smile that curved his lips at the sight of me made my heart dance in my chest as if it just wanted to get to him, be held by him, make love to him.

"You're back, Red, just in time," he said. He indicated the oven. "Salmon's ready. I hope you're hungry."

"Starved," I said. I was not talking about the food but he didn't need to know that.

He plated the dishes and I carried them into the dining room. He followed with a bottle of sauvignon blanc tucked under his arm. He set down the bottle and struck a match, lighting the chubby white candle in the center of the table. Such a small gesture but to a romance-starved woman like me, it was heady stuff.

"Wine?" he asked.

"Yes, please." I knew I was going to need some liquid courage to execute my plan. I'd been running scenarios in my head about how to get him to read the book without him putting up too much of a fight, but short of hog-tying him and reading it to him, I wasn't deluged with great ideas.

Kier poured us each a glass and took the seat next to mine. His dining table was round so there was no head of the table. He'd made a tossed salad and a chopped butternut squash and apple side dish to go with the mashed potatoes and salmon. It was a perfect meal for a cold November evening and I found myself relaxing as we tucked into our food.

"Did your errand go all right?" he asked.

"Perfect."

His right eyebrow lifted as he studied me. "You have me intrigued, Red."

"No need to be," I said. "It was nothing terribly exciting. In fact, my friend Sam would have said it was dead boring." Which was not an exaggeration. My tendency to bury myself in books during our teen years had been incredibly annoying for Sam, who was much more interested in getting into trouble. Lots of trouble.

"Sam," he said. He paused to take a bit of his salmon. "You've mentioned that name quite a bit."

"Sam's been my best friend since we were toddlers."

"Best friend?" he asked. He looked cautious when he added, "Nothing more?"

"With Sam?" I asked then I smiled. "No, *Samantha* is very much in love with Ben."

"Samantha," he repeated. "I always liked that name."

"I told you before I've never been in love," I said. I reached for my wine glass as it occurred to me that if Kier kept charming me stupid this statement was in jeopardy of becoming false.

"I know but it's a damn shame," he said. "You're in the prime of life and all."

"So are you." I took a bite of mashed potatoes. Buttery, fluffy, and seasoned with a hint of garlic. I glanced at him and said, "These are so good."

"Told you I could cook."

"So you did," I agreed. I savored my meal and then said, "Have you ever been in love?'

I told myself that of course he had. I mean, look at him. He'd probably had women chasing him since he could shave. It would be normal for him to have had one, two, potentially even more very serious relationships. Just because I was a lame duck didn't mean he was, too.

He chewed his salmon thoughtfully and then said, "I thought I was once."

"Did she break your heart?" I asked. Why I wanted to know this, I had no idea.

"It felt like it at the time," he said. "We met at Trinners, dated on and off all through college with all the predictable ensuing drama of two people who don't belong together. She was a Dub and I was a culchie, so we were doomed from the start."

"I'm sorry but what's a Dub or a culchie?" I asked.

"Dub means a Dubliner and a culchie is anyone who lives out in the country," he explained. "She knew that my plan was always to come back to Finn's Hollow after commencement. She felt she was too posh for that so she went to wander around Europe with some girlfriends. She never came back."

"Never?"

"Last I heard, she'd married a Swiss banker and was very happy with her chalet in the Alps and their five children."

"Well, she clearly traded down," I said. "I mean look at you. He can't possibly be as romance book cover handsome as you."

"Romance book cover handsome? Is that how you see me, Red?" He eyes crinkled in the corners with his grin.

Oh, dear god, I'd confessed! Why didn't I just hand him my diary to read? *Ack!*

"Of course not, it must be the wine talking." *Deny, deny, deny.*

He leaned his ear close to the bottle, looked at it and then at me, and said, "No, I'm quite certain it was you."

I laughed and threw my napkin at him. "I was being nice."

He caught the napkin in midair and handed it back to me. His eyes glinted.

"Well, I thank you," he said. "Romance book cover and all."

My face grew hotter. I drank more wine because that always helped. Okay, not really, but I was flustered.

"How long did it take your heart to mend?" I asked.

"Not long," he said. "Which means I probably thought I loved her more than I actually did. I think once you discover what truly falling in love is, you realize you never really were before; don't you think?"

The directness of his gaze upon mine caused my breath to hitch. Was he saying what I thought? Were we talking in code? Were neither of us willing to admit that something was happening between us? What was happening? I couldn't form words so I simply nodded and drank more wine.

Mercifully, our conversation veered to books. We debated the difference between thriller and noir, whether Hemingway truly was a misogynist or just misunderstood, and was it necessary to have a companion volume when trying to read Joyce's *Ulysses*. I felt as if our conversation could have gone on all night. It might have if Shackleton hadn't let out a plaintive howl, clearly wanting his supper.

Kier refused to let me help with the dishes, so I perched on a stool in his kitchen while he fed the dog, who ate as if this was the highlight of his day. Once the dishwasher was loaded, we moved to the living room where Kier tended the fire, which was now just embers.

I debated my many schemes to get him to read the Tig McMorrow book. I needed to motivate him with something irresistible, but what? I had no idea.

Kier poured us each a short glass of whiskey and settled onto the couch beside me, handing me my glass. He lifted his arm and I scooted up against his side as naturally as if he'd been shaped just for me. I sipped my whiskey and thought I could sit there forever.

Unfortunately, I was on a mission. I took his glass from his hand and put it on the table beside mine. Then I did what I'd been longing to do all day. I climbed into his lap, so that I was straddling him. I'd felt desire before and I'd definitely read about it, but I had never felt anything like the hunger I felt for this man.

I shoved my fingers into his hair and tipped his head up so that I could kiss him, then I let the mad lust that had been bird-dogging me for weeks all the way out. I put my mouth on his and kissed him with an attention to detail that any librarian would be proud of. I felt him arch up toward me as his hands went right to my hips. His mouth moved beneath mine, guided by me as I slid my tongue across the seam of his lips.

I heard a low rumbling groan, but I honestly didn't know if it was me or him or both of us. He tasted of whiskey and wine and when my tongue curled around his I felt his hand slide up my back and into my hair. His fingers sifted through it as if it was something he'd longed to do and was now finally given the chance. The gentleness of the gesture against the carnality of our kiss was intoxicating.

I pulled back from him, giving us a moment to catch our breath. I studied him for a beat. There was a flush on his cheeks, his lips were swollen, and his eyes had gone even darker than usual. Satisfied that he was as deeply in the moment as I was, I took off my glasses and arched my back, reaching behind me to set them on the table.

Kier took the opportunity to pull the collar of my shirt aside and kiss the curve of my neck as I resumed my position on his lap. He nuzzled the sweet spot just beneath my ear and so intense was the shock of desire that reverberated through me that I had to close my eyes for a moment. I arched against him, wanting to feel the connection, the closeness, and, frankly, yes, the orgasm that was right there just aching to be released.

A cold wet nose—not Kier's—abruptly appeared between us and we broke apart, giving Shackleton the opportunity to lick both of our faces as if he wanted in on the kiss.

"Down, Shack," Kier said. Shackleton barked and then zoomed around the furniture three times before collapsing back onto his spot in front of the fire.

Kier looked at me and laughed and said, "I think he's acting as your chaperone, making sure we don't move too fast."

"Good boy, Shackleton," I said. The adorable dog immediately rolled onto his back with his feet in the air as if posing for a picture captioned "Cuteness Overload." I turned back to Kier and said, "It doesn't feel fast." And it didn't. In so many ways, I felt as if I had known Kier for most of my life. I just needed him to see that. "Should we slow it down by playing a game?"

His eyebrows lifted. "What did you have in mind?"

"Oh, I don't know, how about Literary Consequences?" I asked.

He laughed and asked, "Is that an American thing because I've never heard of it."

I reached for my glasses, putting them on so I could see his face more clearly. "I just made it up. But doesn't it sound fun?"

"That depends. How does it work exactly?" He narrowed his eyes suspiciously. Smart man.

"One of us says a literary quote, and the other has to identify it. If you can't, you lose and have to read a chapter from a book or lose an article of clothing," I said. "Winner's choice."

"What if you can identify it?" he asked.

"Then the person who said the quote is the loser and has to either read or lose an article of clothing—"

"The choice of which is up to the winner," he said.

"Correct," I said. I was trying to determine how this might work against me but couldn't find any obvious problems.

"So, who is the final winner?" he asked.

"The person who isn't naked or reading," I said. My voice cracked on the word *naked* and I cleared my throat as if it wasn't the thought of getting Kier in his altogether that made my throat dry. "The only condition is that I get to pick the book we read, since it's my game." I held out my hand and asked, "Are you in?"

"Oh, I'm in," he said. He shook my hand and then gestured to his library. "Go ahead and pick a book."

"All right," I said. I slid off him and stood up. Instead of browsing his bookcases, I went right to my bag in the hallway and pulled out the Tig McMorrow book. I returned to the living room to find him, sipping his whiskey.

I held the book behind my back and said, "Ready?"

"You brought a book," he said.

"I did."

"Why do I feel as if I'm about to get checkmated?"

I shrugged. "Only if you can't identify my literary references."

"Uh-huh." He waved me forward with his hand. "Let's have it then."

I pulled the book out from behind my back and handed it to him. "I brought this all the way from home. It's one of my most prized possessions."

He took the book, looked at the cover and then up at me. "You are something, Red."

Kier settled back against the couch cushions and lifted his arm. That was it? He wasn't mad? I scrambled onto the sofa and snuggled in beside him, borrowing his warmth. I could not believe my ploy had worked. He was going to read Siobhan's book.

"Well, go ahead, you can go first," he said.

I sifted through my brain for the most obscure literary quotes I could remember. Finally, one popped to mind. "'Beware; for I am fearless, and therefore powerful.'"

"*Frankenstein*. Mary Shelley," he said. It took him less than a blink. He glanced at me and said, "The shirt, definitely, the shirt."

"Shirt?" I protested. "I thought we were supposed to start with socks and work our way up."

"Winner gets to choose," he reminded me. "I'm choosing shirt."

I put up a token resistance, because the truth was he was like curling up against my own personal space heater and I was almost too hot. Besides, I was wearing two shirts.

"All right," I said. I sat up and peeled off the flannel I wore over my thermal top. "Your turn."

"'Anything worth dying for is certainly worth living for,'" he said.

"Joseph Heller. *Catch 22.*" I tapped my chin with my finger. "I choose read."

He picked up the book and opened the cover. He looked rumpled and sexy and if it wasn't so important for him to read his mother's book, I would have tossed—or rather, gently placed—the book aside and had my way with him. Instead, I prepared to listen as he read the book that I knew almost completely by heart.

"*'Chapter One. Tig McMorrow was not what one would call lucky. His parents were divorced and he lived on the edge of town in an unremarkable neighborhood where the residents minded everyone's business except their own.'*"

He had a perfect reader's voice. Low and clear and with that Irish accent, it lulled me into such a relaxed state that I was startled when he finished the chapter, nudged me, and said, "Your turn, love."

Seventeen

Clearly I hadn't thought this game through. Much to my chagrin, Kier guessed my quote from *The Life of Pi*, but instead of choosing clothing, he requested that I read. I'd thought it was because I'd gotten him hooked on the story, but instead, I discovered he had an ulterior motive.

While I read, Kier's hands seemed to be in constant motion. When his fingers found the bare skin of my lower back and he traced small lazy circles, I had a hard time focusing on the words and had to stop a few times to pull it together. But as Siobhan's words weaved the story about the young lad from Dingle with the mop of dark hair and deep blue eyes, I noticed that Kier's hands stilled.

I glanced at his face when I turned the page, and a deep frown formed two lines between his brows. He was getting it then. When I finished the chapter, he delivered a quote from *Don Quixote* and I pounced on it. Without a word, I handed him the book.

"'Chapter Three,'" he began. I relaxed back against him, letting his voice transport me to Tig's world.

Between the heat of his body and the fire and the comfort of Kier reading aloud to me, I felt more relaxed than I could remember being in years. It was delicious and I closed my eyes to savor it. If I could end every day just like this, I thought my life would be perfect.

I don't know what roused me, but I woke up with a stiff neck and the sense that hours had passed. I was lying across Kier and a throw had been pulled over the two of us, giving me the feeling of being in a cozy cocoon with him.

I lifted my head to peer at him but he was blurry. I reached up to adjust my glasses but found that they were not on my face.

"What—" I began but he interrupted.

"You fell asleep," he said. His head was on a pillow and his free arm, the one not around me, held my copy of *Tig McMorrow and the Ogham Stone*. He was still reading, and judging by the pages he only had a few chapters to go.

"What time is it?" I asked. I was groggy and disoriented.

He glanced at his watch. "About half three."

"In the morning?" I cried.

He chuckled and I felt it in his chest beneath me.

"I take it I failed at Literary Consequences," I said.

"Abysmally," he agreed. He closed the book around his finger, keeping his place, and said, "Why don't you sleep in my room. I'm going to be up for a while, finishing the book."

I was too fuzzy-headed to argue with him. I rolled off him and stood. He handed me my glasses, which were on the coffee table, and then rose from the couch. He took my hand with his free one and together we walked upstairs. It was colder up here and dark. Kier flicked a light switch and the landing was illuminated. There were four doors and he directed me through the farthest one at the back of the house. It was the main bedroom.

All I saw was the bed. It was a sea of fluffy cream-colored pillows and a pile of blankets. I dove inside like a swimmer into a choppy sea. When I popped my head up, Kier was smiling at me. He leaned down, took off my glasses, and put them on the nightstand. Then he kissed me.

It was gentle and sweet and full of affection. I wanted to twine my arms about his neck and pull him into the froth with me, but I wanted him to finish reading the book more. I yawned, already slipping back into my dreamless sleep.

"Good night, Red," he whispered. "Sweet dreams."

"Good night, Tig," I said. My eyes closed, and I heard the door close softly when he left.

I woke up in a strange bed. I was snug and warm and buried in blankets. I was also alone. It took me a moment to get my bearings and then I remembered Kier showing me to his room. I glanced at the blank space beside me and wondered if he'd ever come to bed and if not, where was he?

I pushed aside the bedcovers and found my glasses on the nightstand. I slipped them on and noted that I was fully clothed minus one of my shirts. I hurried into the bathroom. The squirrel's nest that was my hair made me yelp and I snatched the brush off the vanity and tried to tame my thick head of hair into some sort of order. It put up a fight. I debated taking a quick shower but I wanted to see Kier first.

I hurried downstairs. The lamp in the living room was still on. Was he still reading? I peered around the doorjamb feeling shy, which was ridiculous. We hadn't slept together, so there was no walk of shame to be done. A snore interrupted my thoughts and I saw a foot in a thick gray sock hanging off the end of the couch. I quietly crossed the room and looked over the back of it. Kier was dead asleep. His mouth hung slightly open as he emitted a soft snore. He should not have been attractive in his disheveled state, but he totally was with his tousled dark hair, whiskered chin, and rumpled clothing.

"Kier," I whispered his name, not wanting to startle him. He didn't move. I spoke a little louder. "Kier."

No response. If he wasn't snoring, I'd be worried he was deceased. I reached down and straightened the throw that partially covered him. It was then that I found the copy of my book. He was hugging it to his chest. He'd finished it then. I carefully removed it from his grasp and set it on the table. I suspected he'd read all night and needed to make up some sleep.

Shackleton was also dead asleep but when I went to the foyer to put on my coat and boots, he appeared, obviously looking to be let outside.

"I'm going to the main house to get coffee," I said. "Are you in?"

He tapped my foot with his and moved to the door. Well, okay then.

We stepped out into a morning that was cold, gray, and damp. I huddled into my puffy coat, pulling the hood up to keep my ears warm. I set out for Siobhan's at a brisk pace, hoping that it would warm me up. Shackleton ran ahead and then back, veered off to follow the scent of something or other, doubled back, and then trotted beside me.

I supposed I should have stayed at Kier's and waited for him to wake up but the truth was I was nervous. I had set him up. There was no denying it. And while he had been kind to me in the middle of the night when I'd been bleary with sleep, I had no idea how he was going to react today. So, I was sneaking off to Siobhan's like a coward, hoping he wasn't sore at me.

Shackleton and I climbed the stone steps to the house. It was early but not so early that the songbirds weren't already up. I saw two chaffinches dart in and out of a nearby holly bush. I wished I had that much energy—maybe after coffee.

I raised my fist to knock but the door swung open before my knuckles connected to the wood. I dropped my hand, surprised to see Mrs. Clohessy standing there.

"Good morning, Emily," she said. "Siobhan saw you from her bedroom window. She told me to tell you she has a pot of coffee and some scones up in her room if you'd care to join her."

"Oh, that would be . . . grand," I said. The Irish expression rolled off my tongue so naturally that I smiled.

Mrs. Clohessy returned it and held out her hand for my coat. Shackleton, not one for social niceties, left me and strode across the great room toward the kitchen.

"Mrs. Doan will feed him," Mrs. Clohessy said. She paused and then asked, "Will Kieran be joining you?"

"Uh." I felt my face grow warm and my brain fritzed. I had nothing but honesty to offer her. "I don't know."

She nodded, her expression giving away nothing. "Would you like me to show you the way?"

"No, thank you, I remember," I said. I hurried up the stairs, leaving my awkwardness behind me like a pair of muddy boots.

I knocked twice on Siobhan's door before entering. She was sitting on the sofa on the far side of the room, fully dressed and looking remarkably well-rested. Given that I was wearing the same clothes I had on the day before, hadn't showered or brushed my teeth, and was caffeine deficient, I didn't feel nearly as put together.

"Hi," I said.

"Good morning." Siobhan leaned forward and poured me a cup of coffee. "Here. I won't pepper you with questions until you've had at least half a cup."

I glanced at the plate of warm strawberry scones with the bowl of clotted cream beside it.

"And a scone," I bargained.

"Half," Siobhan countered.

"Fair," I said. I could chew really slowly if need be.

I sipped my coffee and felt its heat bloom from my belly all the way to my toes and the top of my head. It was strong and bitter and made life worth living. I put my cup aside and broke a scone in half. I slathered it with cream and took a healthy bite.

"You look like you've worked up quite an appetite," Siobhan observed.

I laughed. "Is that your subtle way of trying to find out what happened last night?"

"Too blunt?"

"Like a rock to the temple," I said. I took another bite and washed it down with the hot coffee. I didn't want to leave Siobhan in suspense but I wasn't sure what to tell her either. That Kier had admitted he'd always felt jealous of her fictional boy? That I'd gotten him to read her book? That I thought I might be falling in love with him? No, no, and no. I couldn't tell her any of those things.

The first two because they weren't mine to share and the third because, if I was going to tell anyone about my feelings, it would be Kier. But I was nowhere near ready to discuss *feelings* with him, especially as Siobhan had yet to tell him about her condition.

My cup was hovering at just above half and my scone was the same. Taking tiny sips and itty-bitty nibbles, I was stalling for time and I could see that Siobhan was getting ready to call me out. Mercifully, there was a knock on the door and I hoped it was Shannon with more coffee or scones or something to divert the questions I could see in Siobhan's eyes.

It wasn't Shannon. It was Kier. He stood in the doorway for a moment, taking in the sight of me with his mom. He was also in the same clothes he'd slept in last night. His wavy hair was flat on one side as if he'd just woken up and come straight away.

"You're here," he said to me.

"Coffee." I held up my cup.

He nodded. I couldn't tell what he was thinking. Was my plan about to backfire? Was he angry with his mother? With me?

I waited, holding my breath, as his gaze turned to Siobhan. When he looked at her, his expression softened. He crossed the room and kneeled down beside her. He took her frail hands in his and stared up into her face and said, "He's me."

"Yes." Siobhan spoke as if she'd been waiting for him to say this for a very long time.

"Tig is me," he said it again as if he needed to be perfectly clear.

"Yes." She smiled.

"I didn't know. All these years, Ma, and I never knew that the fictional boy who I thought was my rival for my mother's attention was actually . . . me. Why didn't you tell me?"

Siobhan stroked his hair back from his forehead. Her look was tender and I had the sense I was seeing back in time to Kier as a little boy with his mom and it warmed my heart.

"You were so angry when I went away," Siobhan said. "When I came back you swore you'd never read my books. I felt so guilty. It didn't feel right to ask you to even though you were the inspiration for the entire series. I think it's fair to say without a Kieran Murphy there would never have been a Tig McMorrow. I thought eventually I'd share that detail with you but then I got sick and it just didn't seem to matter anymore."

"It does matter, though," he whispered. "It matters quite a lot. I'm honored, Ma, and I'm sorry I was too thick to read these books when they first came out. I don't know if you know this but you're a really great writer."

Siobhan laughed through her tears and hugged him close.

I felt my throat get tight. The love between mother and son was everything it should be. When they parted, Kier grabbed a napkin from the coffee tray and dabbed her cheeks. She sniffed and smiled, taking the napkin from him and blowing her nose. Then she cleared her throat and asked, "Do you understand now why it's so important to me to finish the series?"

"Because he's me and you don't want to leave me in purgatory?"

"Exactly." Siobhan nodded.

"I can't argue against that. I'll help in any way I can."

As if remembering I was there, Siobhan turned to me and said, "Thank you."

"I didn't do anything," I demurred. "He'd have gotten there on his own eventually."

"Take the win, Red," Kier said. He rose from his kneeled position and sat beside me. "You managed the impossible and quite deviously I might add."

Siobhan's eyebrows rose. "Oh, really?"

I turned my face away from Siobhan and stared at Kier. If he told her how I had gotten him to read the book I would never forgive him. I was surprised my eyes didn't shoot lasers, so hot was my gaze. He blinked at me in a look of pure innocence.

"Red made me an offer I couldn't refuse," he said. "In fact, I think we need to renegotiate terms."

"Nope," I said. I leaned forward and topped off my coffee, keeping my attention on my cup. "It was a onetime only offer."

"Well, that disappoints," he said.

I couldn't look at him. Inexplicably, unshowered and with mussed hair and the scratchy beginnings of a full beard, he was even hotter than the first day I saw him in his Aran sweater, looking impossibly Irish and handsome and foreboding.

"How do you want to proceed, Siobhan?" I asked. I was determined to keep on task. "It's your book and you're in charge."

"Thank you." She inclined her head. "My first question is how do you propose to help me write the book? I've never worked with anyone before and I'm not clear on how it would work."

"We'll have to figure it out as we go," I said. "But I think we should start by setting up a writing schedule."

"That sounds good." Kier relaxed beside me and I knew he was relieved that I had brought us full circle back to a schedule.

"When you're ready to start, Kier and I can brainstorm with you about the day's writing before you begin. We can talk out your ideas and look at the story from all angles and then you'll have a better sense of what direction you want to take the plot and maybe spare yourself from . . ."

"Getting lost in a bog," Siobhan finished for me.

"Precisely," I said. "When you finish for the day, we'll read and edit what you've written just as I have been." I glanced at Kier. "It'll be good to have another writer on board."

He sipped his coffee. "I'm not a writer. My lone novel, if you can call it that, was also a onetime only."

"It was a good mystery," I protested. "You shouldn't be so dismissive of it."

"You've read his book?" Siobhan asked. She looked at Kier in surprise. "I thought you'd burned every copy you could find."

"Apparently my ploy to drive Red away by boring her to death with inventory bit me on the arse when she found a copy of my book up on the third floor." He met his mother's gaze with one eyebrow raised in suspicion. "I can't imagine how it got there, can you?"

"Third floor you say?" Siobhan took a hearty bite out of a scone.

"Tippy top of the bookshop," Kier confirmed.

"Imagine that," Siobhan mumbled through a mouthful.

I glanced between them. Obviously, Siobhan had put the novel up there knowing I'd find it. So devious. I was filled with mad respect for her in that moment.

"Yes, imagine," Kier said. His voice was as dry as the scone Siobhan was washing down with delicate sips of coffee. "As I said, I don't think I'll be of any use but I'm happy to try."

"Now that Tig is ten years older, you can help us figure out the male brain." I glanced at Siobhan and said, "I don't know about you but they're a mystery to me."

She laughed as I'd intended. "Agreed. Now about this schedule." She raised one eyebrow up higher than the other and looked so much like Kier when she did it, that it was clear he'd gotten this trait from her.

We spent the next fifteen minutes hashing out a tentative writing schedule, with Siobhan insisting that her muse did not work on the clock. Kier told her that her muse had no choice if she wanted help finishing the book. That seemed to decide it for Siobhan and while she still wasn't happy about it, she gave in.

Kier and I left shortly after agreeing that we would all meet at the bookshop in an hour for our first writing session. Siobhan looked the happiest I'd ever seen her and she wasn't one for being in the dumps, so that was saying something.

Kier stood up and leaned over to kiss the top of his mother's head. "I'll be back to collect you. I'm just going to give Red a lift home."

"I'll be ready," she promised.

We arrived downstairs to find Shackleton waiting by the front door. Mrs. Clohessy stood beside him, as if keeping an eye on him to make certain he didn't track in any mud when she wasn't looking.

She handed us our coats and said, "Lovely morning, isn't it?"

I glanced outside. The early morning fog had turned into a thick drizzle, the epitome of dreary, and yet, I felt hopeful.

"It is. Have a nice day, Mrs. Clohessy," I said.

"You, too," she returned.

I hurried out the door with Shackleton, leaving Kier to follow. Thankfully, his car was parked right out front and I climbed into the passenger seat while he opened the back door for Shackleton to jump in.

"Did you want to drive?" he asked.

"No, thank you, I think I've done enough of that." I wasn't sure he got my double meaning until he snorted.

"Yeah, I suppose you have." He shut the door after the dog, walked around the car, and took the driver's seat.

We shot down the driveway and through town. It was still early and most of the shops were closed. I don't know why I was relieved that most of the town would be unaware of Kier taking me home, but I was. Despite my coworkers knowing that I had kissed Kier, I wasn't prepared to publicly be a couple—not yet—not when I didn't really know where this was headed. Not when Siobhan had yet to tell Kier the truth.

"Everything all right, Red?" he asked when we stopped at an intersection.

"Yes, why do you ask?" I sounded on edge. I tried to be chill. It was an effort.

"Because you're awfully quiet," he said.

"I'm always quiet," I protested.

He looked at me in surprise. "You're never quiet, Red."

"Only with you," I countered.

"So, what you're saying is, I bring out the best in you," he teased.

"Or the worst, could go either way."

He grinned and turned onto my street, parking in front of the path. I glanced at the Connollys' but no one appeared to be up yet. I reached over the seat and patted Shackleton. "See ya, buddy."

I hopped out of the car to find Kier doing the same. He had rolled the rear window down halfway and said, "Stay here, fella." Shackleton immediately made himself comfortable on the back seat.

"You don't have to . . ." My voice trailed off as I remembered he'd said he'd been raised to walk a woman to her door.

"Yes, I do," he said.

"Right." I led the way up the narrow walkway to my bright pink door, which seemed to be singlehandedly holding off the morning gloom, at least on my front porch.

I unlocked the door and turned the knob. I stepped inside, turned on the threshold, and said, "Thanks, I'll see you—"

That was all I got out when his mouth landed on mine. He cupped my face while he kissed me into the house and kicked the door shut behind us. *Oh my.*

"I've wanted to do that all morning," he said.

In answer, I looped my arms around his neck and kissed him back with all the longing that I felt. Sleeping in his bed without him, with the scent of him surrounding me but his person nowhere in reach, had been the ultimate tease and the next time we played Literary Consequences, I wasn't going to pass out.

The need for air broke us apart. I glanced at the clock on the wall. "We have to get to the shop."

"Right," he said. He kissed me again and I forgot about everything but him. It should have worried me, but I simply didn't care.

He pulled back and pressed his forehead to mine. In a low voice, he said, "Thank you."

"No problem. Kiss me anytime."

He loosened his hold on me when he laughed and said, "Be careful, I'll take you up on that."

"I'll let you," I said. My voice was husky and his gaze dipped down to my lips. He was leaning in when I held him off and added, "Except for at work. I think we need to maintain our professionalism there."

"I suppose you're right, although I don't think Brigid could tease me about you any more than she already does," he said. He reached up and pushed a wayward lock of hair out of my face. His expression grew serious when he added, "But truly, thanks for getting me to read Ma's book. It changes things, you know?"

"I know," I said. "Were you upset when you realized Tig was you?"

"No." He shook his head. "A reader would have to know me really well to know it was me and thankfully there's only one Tig McMorrow fan out there who caught on to what Ma had done. When did you realize?"

"I suspected when she called you her son, because up until then I didn't know she had one," I said. "But then it was so obvious, the way you tilt your head when you're thinking and how your hair falls over your forehead just so, those were descriptions of Tig that I saw in you immediately. And then as I got to know you and your obstinacy and humor and kindness, well, that clinched it."

"For me, it was the runners," he said. "I had begged and begged for a brand of runners that we couldn't afford at the time and Tig longs for the same pair. That was my first clue that Ma was working out her feelings about me and being a single mother and not being able to provide for me in the way she wished."

I walked him to the door. "You'll have to let me know if the rest of the series is accurate."

"You mean . . ." He looked alarmed.

"Yes, you have to read the entire series," I said. "How else will you know what's happening?"

"But there's seven more volumes and they each get bigger," he protested.

I opened the door and gave him a gentle shove. "Best get to it then."

He looked thoroughly chagrinned when I shut the door in his face. I leaned against it and discovered I was smiling. He did that for me. He made me feel like I was someone special and desirable and valuable. It felt amazing.

For the first time in a very long time, I was excited about a relationship with a man. And now that he was fully supporting Siobhan, I felt like we were finally on the same page, pun intended. I supposed I should have been scared because even though I'd never been in love before, I knew my feelings for Kier were definitely headed in that direction.

Even just acknowledging this made my heart race and my breathing shallow. Before, I would have feared I was having a stroke or a seizure or some other medical emergency but this time, I knew it was just a flare of panic at how truly vulnerable I was. I shook my head. I pushed off the door and headed for the shower. This thing with Kier was good and right and lovely, and I was not going to freak out and ruin it. He and I were happy and there was no reason to think we wouldn't remain so.

When I was wrong, I was so very wrong.

"That doesn't even make sense!" I cried. I raised my hands in exasperation.

We were standing in the alcove of the bookshop. Siobhan was seated at the table with her laptop open and her notebook beside her.

"Yes, it does," Kier countered. His eyes sparked and it was clear he was loving every bit of our disagreement. "It's perfectly logical."

"That's not how the portal works," I argued. I glanced at Siobhan. "Tell him."

Siobhan, who had been following our back-and-forth argument as if she was watching a hurling match, shook her head.

"I'm telling you, it'll work," Kier insisted.

"Sure if you want the book to end in one chapter," I retorted. We were facing each other just mere feet apart, and I was furious that I found the man so attractive I could barely keep on topic. The broad shoulders, the square jaw, the muscled forearms, the entire package that was Kieran Murphy made me as dopey as a potato.

For a week, I hadn't seen Kier except for brief moments here and there, where he usually pulled me into a closet or tugged me behind a bookcase and kissed me until I was cross-eyed. He'd taken his assignment to heart and the rest of his time was spent reading the remaining volumes of the Tig McMorrow series. He was now up to speed on the storyline and apparently determined to ruin it.

"That would be all right with me," Kier said. "We could make it a short story. Give the readers the ending they want and not overtax Ma."

I rolled my eyes. I was just gearing up to state my case in a more strident tone, when Siobhan asked, "Does anyone care to hear what I think?"

"Of course," I said at the same time Kier said, "Absolutely."

"Excellent." Siobhan smiled. "Now go away. I know what I'm writing today and I don't need your help."

"But . . ." Kier and I said together.

"Go." She made a shooing gesture with her hands. "Go take a

walk and work out your differences so I don't waste my time listening to you. And don't come back until you're in accord."

I opened my mouth to speak but she raised her eyebrows and I shut my mouth.

"Come on, Red," Kier said. "We'd best do as she says. When she gets like this there's no reasoning with her."

If he was trying to needle Siobhan, it didn't work. She cracked her knuckles and set to typing. Together we left the alcove. Siobhan didn't even watch us go. She stared at the screen while her fingers flew over the keys.

"What do you suppose she's writing?" I asked.

"Not a clue. It seems she listens to our ideas and then writes whatever the hell she wants."

"She did use your suggestion on how to get Tig out of purgatory," I said. We stopped in the workroom. I retrieved my coat from the coatrack and he grabbed his from his office.

"And she took your advice on his reunion with Aislinn," he said. He pulled on a hat and gloves. The weather had turned cold and I wound my scarf around my neck, trying to make certain there were no gaps for the winter air to slip in.

We walked back through the Last Chapter and paused by the alcove.

"Keep going," Siobhan said without pausing in her typing. "I expect brilliant ideas for the next chapter upon your return."

"No pressure," I muttered to Kier, who grinned.

We left the shop through the front door and stood outside for a moment, surveying the village around us. December had arrived and Christmas bunting had been strung across the street from one end to the other. The red and green garlands were cheerful even in the milky daylight of a very misty morning.

"Which way?" he asked.

"Follow me," I said. "I'm not standing in the cold a moment longer than necessary."

He looked intrigued and fell into step beside me. I hurried down the street, turning onto the small side street that led to my cottage. I cut down the narrow alleyway, leaving Kier to follow. We entered the backyard of the Connollys and I could see smoke rising from the barn but the large rolling doors were shut against the frigid weather. It was just as well. I had no idea how I would explain being home at midday with my boss in tow.

I hadn't grabbed my handbag when we left but I had a key stashed under an empty flower pot for just such emergencies. I picked it up and unlocked the door. I turned the knob and a nice blast of warm air greeted me. I stepped inside and moved, giving Kier room to follow. He didn't move.

Kier stood on the front step, looking uncomfortable.

"Well, come on," I said. I waved him in. "I can make us a cuppa while we hash out our differences."

"I don't think that's a good idea, Red."

"Why not?"

He blew out a breath. "Because I want you too damn much and I don't think I'd be able to keep my hands to myself."

I blinked at him, then I reached out and grabbed him by the lapel of his coat and yanked him inside.

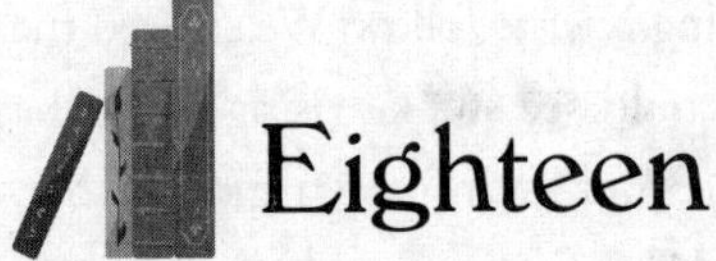

Eighteen

Oh, well, if you insist," he said.

"I do."

"All right then." His mouth landed on mine in a kiss that about set my hair on fire.

I hadn't planned for this. I knew it was likely a bad idea given what I knew about Siobhan but when he said how much he wanted me, it was like a switch flipped in my head. I went fully primal and suddenly the only thing that seemed right and true was being with him.

In moments we were shedding our coats and then our clothes, our fingers tangling as we tried to pull off each other's sweaters. In my mind, we looked like an octopus with several limp woolen arms and I would have laughed but I was too intent on my purpose.

I had never, not ever, wanted a man as much as I wanted this man. The desire was almost painful in its intensity and I felt as if it was making me a little bit deranged. When I managed to wrestle his sweater off and toss it aside, I was confronted with his thermal shirt and it frustrated me so much, a single tear spilled out of my eye. I turned my head so that he wouldn't see, but it was Kier and he always saw everything.

"Are you all right, Red?" he asked. He cupped my face and swiped the tear off my cheek with his thumb.

"I'm fine," I said. "I'm just so fuckstrated . . . wait . . . that's not what I meant . . . Wait, no, actually it is."

He laughed and pulled me into a hug. "Easy, Red. There's no race to the finish line here."

"Are you sure?" I asked.

"Positive." He sifted his hands through my hair, the tips of his fingers massaging my scalp in a blissfully soothing gesture.

"I just don't think I can take much more," I said. "It's been so long since I . . . and I'm just starved for physical affection and every time you come near me, I can't think. I just . . . *want*."

Kier cupped my face. He stared into my eyes and I saw the stark desire there, too. And it wasn't a reflection of my wanting him. It was his own need that sharpened his gaze. He wanted me just as much as I wanted him. I could hardly grasp it.

"How long do we have before we have to go back?" I asked.

He pulled me in close, until our hips pressed against each other and he said, "I believe we were told not to return until we were in accord. It's unfortunate that you're such a stubborn woman, Red."

With that, he reached down and scooped me up. I looped an arm around his neck as he carried me into the bedroom. As romantic gestures went, it was up there. He dropped me onto the bed and pounced. I found myself trapped under his solid male body and I couldn't have been happier to be so.

He reached down and gently removed my glasses. He folded them carefully and put them on the nightstand. I couldn't see him as clearly without them unless he was mere inches from my face, which thankfully, when he leaned down to kiss me, he was.

"Is this how we're working out our differences then?" he asked. He slid his mouth across mine and trailed a string of kisses along my jaw to the tender spot beneath my ear. The gentle touch lit a spark in my core and I found myself arching up against him. I knew that my dignity was in peril and I forced myself to speak.

"Unless you'd rather play Scrabble," I said. I was going for funny but it came out breathy instead.

"Would that be Scrabble consequences?" he asked. He kissed a path down my neck to settle into the curve of my shoulder.

"Not necessary," I said. "All you need to say is please."

He pulled back and glanced at me with a look that scorched. His voice was low and growly when he said, "Please."

Without breaking eye contact, I pulled my shirt over my head and sent it across the room. Next I wriggled out of my skirt and my tights. I forgot about my boots and the entire ensemble bunched up around my ankles. Normally, I would have been mortified. But at the present moment, I simply did not care.

A low chuckle was Kier's only reaction as he reached down and slipped off my boots. With his fist he grabbed my tights and my skirt and threw them onto the floor with the boots. I lay there in just my bra and underwear, thankfully both were in decent shape, but still, I immediately went into a spiral of bad body image. Years of my mother criticizing me and telling me I was too scrawny to catch a man—*like they're fish?*—flooded my head and I just wanted to hide.

Tammy Lynn wasn't wrong. I was flat-chested and had no butt, and my complexion was pasty pale and prone to flushing when I was embarrassed. And not a pretty blushing pink either; rather, it was a scorching case of chili pepper red and it bloomed across my cheeks and chest when I was feeling shy or vulnerable, which was right now as it occurred to me that I had not maintained my personal landscaping, as it were, since I'd had no idea that today was the day I going to wind up in bed with this man.

I immediately grabbed a pillow and covered my head and upper body with it. I felt a gentle tug on the pillow, but I clung to it like a barnacle on a rock, willing the red to recede from my face and chest. I could feel the heat and knew it was never going to happen. The moment was ruined. I was a freak. There was no way a man like Kier could be interested in a weirdo like me.

"You all right, Red?" Kier asked.

"No." I had a pillow over my face. It wasn't like I could lie.

"If you've changed your mind, that's absolutely all right," he said. "We're not going to do anything you don't want to do."

"That's not it," I said. "I want to . . . I just . . ."

"Just?" he asked. He draped an arm around my middle and pulled my body into his. The pillow fell away from my face and chest, but it was okay because he was behind me. He was big spooning me while still clothed whereas I was mostly naked. It was dead sexy, for sure, but I realized as his hands stayed still, he wasn't coming on to me, he was keeping me warm while I had my little freak-out.

"Just what, Red?" He pressed his lips against back of my neck, making me suck in a breath, while he splayed his hand across my middle. "Talk to me, Red."

"I'm not really prepared for this today," I said. "As in, there should have been some waxing and moisturizing and other maintenance done before we got down to the I'll-show-you-mine-if-you-show-me-yours portion of things."

Kier barked out a laugh. I felt it rumble in his chest against my back while his breath skimmed across my ear, making me squirm. I did not laugh. There was nothing funny about this situation as far as I was concerned and I started to pull away from him in a fit of pique.

"Oh, Red." He pulled me back and I flopped onto my back and reflexively crossed my arms over my chest for coverage. Kier immediately took the opportunity to settle in on top of me. "I'm going to let you in on a secret."

I stared at him. He gently reached down and took my right hand and placed it on his shoulder. He then did the same with my left. I felt completely exposed and vulnerable and, frankly, a little sick to my stomach.

"What's the secret?" I asked. Anything to divert him from noticing me.

"I don't care about maintenance or moisturizer or any of that nonsense," he said. "I want you, exactly as you are. Fiery and feisty and fierce." He leaned down and kissed my lips, my cheek, my chin, the base of my throat, and the small rise of my breasts. I glanced down at his thick head of hair and felt it softly brush against my skin. My body was immediately coated in a sheen of sweat and a steady throb of need was building between my legs.

"I'm none of those things," I protested. "I'm quiet and shy and contained."

"Yeah?" He leaned back and met my gaze. "I really noticed that about you when you were yelling at me this morning."

I huffed a laugh. "You aroused my protective instincts."

"Say that again, just the part about me arousing you," he said.

I let go of his shoulders and cupped his face. I leaned up and kissed him, just a brush of my mouth against his, and then, in the sultriest voice I could manage, I said, "You make me want to go for a ride, and not in a car."

He blew out a slow breath. "I think I can manage that, Red, if you're sure."

"I'm sure," I said. In that moment, I'd never been more certain of anything.

The smile that curved his mouth was criminally wicked. It made my entire body tingle from head to toe. He pushed up to his knees and peeled off his shirt at the same time that I reached for the button of his waistband. In a short fumble-filled minute, he was down to his underwear as well. The navy blue boxer briefs were straining a bit at the seams so I slid my hand into the waistband and tugged them free.

Kier's eyebrows rose in surprise and I asked, "Was that fiery, feisty, or fierce me?"

"I'm thinking all three," he said. He then relieved me of my bra and undies as well. We were completely naked in the middle of the morning on a weekday. It felt decadent and wild and thrilling.

It was as if we'd both been released from some polite prison. We didn't speak, but we moved, letting our hands trail over each other's bodies followed by our lips. His body was hard, hauling boxes of books around the shop had clearly been good for him over the years. His muscles were defined and I liked the way they bunched in reaction to my touch.

My self-consciousness might have returned if Kier had given me a chance to sort my feelings. He did not. He slid his hand down my body and in between my legs at the same time that he drew my breast into his mouth. He flicked my clitoris with his thumb while biting on my nipple and I was undone. The clawing need that I felt to have him inside me overrode any other thought or emotion and I was practically incoherent. I decided I needed to be a woman of action.

I reached for him, stroking him and guiding him. I had him at my entrance when he said, "Ah, Red, we need protection."

"Right," I gasped. I pointed. "Nightstand."

Kier shifted away from me and I heard him find the condom. He made quick work of sliding it on—thank goodness—and then he was back. He slid his fingers down my body as if to take up where he'd left off. I wasn't having it. I was so ready, I felt like a strong breeze would get me off.

I grabbed his hand and laced his fingers with mine. Then I spread my legs and looped them around his waist and pulled him down on top of me. "Now."

He started to grin but then as I tightened my legs and guided him inside of me, his expression turned into that of a fully aroused and focused lover, intent on bringing his partner and himself to orgasm. Wow. If he hadn't already made me half-crazy with lust, being the object of that intensity would have.

When he was fully seated inside of me, I felt my muscles spasm around him. I was so close. It had been so long. He felt so good. He made me feel so good. He started to move his hips and I let out a soft cry. I wasn't going to last. I wanted him too damn much.

"All right, Red?" he asked. His voice was the lowest I'd ever heard it and it made me shiver.

"I'm afraid it's going to be a very short ride for me," I said. I glanced at him from beneath my lashes.

Now he grinned and it was pure prideful male. I'd have told him it wasn't him but that would have been a lie. It was him. I'd never had a man make me feel this way before.

He nudged his hips forward and I felt the first ripples. He went still. He looked at me with that one impertinent eyebrow raised.

"I feel as if I'm in a position of power here, Red," he said.

"You are not—" I began to protest but he thrust his hips forward again and I felt the tremors start in my core and I couldn't speak.

"What was that?" he asked. He ran his hand down my body, pausing to pinch my nipple before sliding it down my side to my waist and around to my ass where he cupped my behind and thrust again.

"Okay, you are," I cried. I tried to move my hips against him but he was too big and I couldn't budge him.

"I think we're finally in accord, Red," he said. Then he lifted one of my legs from around his waist and held it wide, allowing him to go deeper. My heel dug into the back of his thigh as he began to slide slowly, maddeningly slowly, in and out of me. I could feel my muscles clench around him, trying to keep him inside, trying to bring him deeper.

He kissed me. It was hot and wet and his tongue plundered my mouth the way he plundered my body. When he broke the kiss, I was beyond reason.

"More," I demanded. And then because I didn't want to be denied, I added, "Please."

"If you insist, Red." He pulled back his hips and thrust deep and hard and the sweet relief when my body finally had him planted as deeply as possible caused my orgasm to rocket through me with the force of a freight train. Kier pulled me close, pressing my shivering body against his, and I felt him stiffen inside me as his own orgasm answered the call of mine. It was fucking amazing.

Neither of us moved. The quiet of the cottage was disturbed only by our heavy breathing and the occasional chirp of a bird outside the bedroom window. When our heartrates slowed and the sweat dried, Kier pushed off me. He kissed me quick and then staggered to his feet to use the bathroom.

And now the self-doubt crept in. I wasn't sure what to do with myself. Should I hop out of bed and get dressed and treat this as business as usual for me? Should I pretend to be asleep and hope he left? Yeah, that wouldn't be bizarre. I was debating my options when he reappeared with a washcloth in hand.

He didn't say a word. He just nudged my legs apart and pressed the warm wet cloth against my sensitive skin.

"You said it's been a while," he said. "This should soothe any aches."

The sweetness of the gesture about did me in. When he returned the cloth to the bathroom, I was about to hop up and get dressed, but he yanked back the covers and gestured for me to scooch over.

"Don't we need to get back to work?" I asked.

"Seriously, Red? Are you suggesting no cuddle after sex like that?" he asked. "That happens to be my favorite part—all right, second favorite part. We're not skipping the cuddle."

Well, hell, now I was definitely in love with him.

Nineteen

Kier was right. The cuddle was the second-best part, but it was a really close second, letting the orgasm win by a nose.

"What happened here?" he asked me. He was running his hand up and down my side. I looked and saw the small scar he'd found.

"Chicken pox," I said.

He frowned. "It's very deep."

"Yeah, that's my fault," I said. "I was seven and I got sick, the usual symptoms of a fever, loss of appetite, exhaustion, but my father was working late at the hospital so he couldn't diagnose me, and my mother had a function at the country club. When the babysitter canceled at the last minute, my mother tucked me in and went to her event."

Kier frowned. "She left you alone? At seven with a fever?"

I shrugged. "She was quite the socialite."

"I have a different word for it," he said.

"In any event, I woke up with this thing on my side," I said. "I completely freaked out, probably because I had a raging fever, and I thought it was—promise not to laugh?"

Kier raised his hand as if swearing an oath. "On my honor."

"I thought it was a flesh-eating alien," I said. "I was trying to cut it out with a pair of children's scissors when my dad arrived home."

To my surprise, Kier didn't laugh. Quite the opposite. His brow furrowed with concern and he pushed the hair back from my face and said, "You must have been terrified."

"I don't remember it to be honest," I said. "I do remember the fight my parents had afterward, though. I don't think I'd ever seen my father that angry before."

"I'm sorry, love," he said. He leaned back and laced my fingers with his.

"It's all right," I said. I realized this was as good a time as any to share my illness anxiety with him. If I started to spiral, at least he'd know where it came from. "Do you remember the day we met?"

"Of course. You were seated on a step stool, contemplating your boots," he said.

I laughed. Is that how he'd seen me? "I don't share this with many people, or any people, but I think you should know that I was having an anxiety attack. I was convinced it was a heart attack or a stroke or some other dire circumstance. Ever since that night with the chicken pox, I've had hypochondria or what they politely call illness anxiety disorder."

I glanced up at his face to see if his expression was one of disgust, but all I saw was gentle understanding.

"Seems to me, that makes perfect sense given what happened to you," he said. "Much like changing homes as a lad always signified something bad for me. I came to hate change. Still do."

"I still think I've contracted the plague when I get overwhelmed," I admitted.

"I've never rearranged the furniture in my house, and I've lived there for ten years."

Kier pulled me into his arms and held me close. "It seems we have more in common than I supposed. Thank you for confiding in me, Red." He paused and said, "I've never told anyone except a therapist about what happened to me as a lad. It means a lot to me that I can be vulnerable with you and I'm glad you feel the same way about me."

"I do." I kissed him, wanting him to know how I felt about him without having to say it.

"I suppose we should get back to the shop," he said.

"Right." I threw off the covers and was about to rise, when an arm hooked me around the middle and pulled me back down.

"One more kiss before we go," Kier said.

"If you insist." I repeated his earlier words back to him and he smiled as I happily complied.

It took us a bit to get sorted, meaning my tights were in a knot and Kier's idea of assisting, kissing every bare inch of me while I dressed, was no help at all. We eventually managed to leave the cottage but it was almost noon when I locked the door behind us. I didn't walk back to the shop so much as float.

The holidays passed in a blur of parties and village festivals. Siobhan hosted a Christmas party at her house, where it seemed the entirety of the village attended. The mansion was full to bursting and I couldn't remember a time when I laughed so hard and felt so much a part of things.

I played a board game with Brigid's lads, who were as feral as described but in the best possible way, danced with Oisín and his partner, Gavin, to the trad band Siobhan had hired for the party, before being passed to my landlord Shane and then Father Mulligan, who managed to tell me about his greatest fly fishing adventures while never missing a step.

I stood by the dessert table with Sally, from the sweet shop, and Hazel, from the tea house, evaluating the plethora of biscuits that everyone had brought. Naturally, Brigid's whiskey shortbread was the favorite. And I watched Kier. Mostly, I watched Kier. He looked as handsome as ever in a deep blue cable-knit sweater over a dress shirt and tie. I felt him watching me, too, and it made me dizzy to think that he potentially felt about me the same way I felt about him.

When Eun-ji and Niamh grabbed me to participate in a social media post they were creating for the shop, I didn't think to resist nor did I try to hide my innate goofiness. For so much of my life, I'd been the person on the outside looking in that to be included so completely, well, I had to take a moment to catch my breath.

I slipped out of the great room and wandered down the hall to Siobhan's private library. This was my favorite room in the house. The walls were lined with bookcases and there was a desk in front of a large window, which overlooked the now barren garden. I sat on the corner and stared out the window.

When I'd left Martha's Vineyard, I'd wanted an adventure. And now, just months after I'd arrived, everything in my world was different. I was an assistant to my favorite author, I was falling in love with her son, and I'd been embraced by the village and its residents, feeling for the first time in my life as if I was exactly where I was supposed to be. My therapist, Dr. Davis, and I had a recent video session, and she was particularly pleased that I was letting love into my life for the first time in a very long time. It was more than I had ever hoped to have.

"Here you are, Em." Siobhan entered the room. She was wearing a deep purple velvet maxi dress with long angel sleeves. She had very little makeup on, just mascara and lipstick, but she didn't need any. Writing had given her a glow she hadn't had when I'd first arrived. Her eyes sparkled and her smile came easily and often. Although she seemed to tire more easily these days, it was clear she was happy doing what she loved.

Still, when it came to Siobhan, I was on high alert. I had repeatedly asked her to tell Kier what her doctor had said but she just shook her head and said, "After the holidays. Let me have this one last joyful Christmas."

How could I refuse?

"How are you feeling?" I asked.

"I'm fine."

I tried to determine if her answer was genuine or hiding pain, exhaustion, or sadness.

"No talk about my health today," she declared. She sat on the edge of the desk beside me and said, "I have something for you."

"Oh?" I asked. We'd already exchanged gifts. I'd had Sam ship goodies from Martha's Vineyard for everyone while Siobhan had gifted me with a signed special edition collection of Tig McMorrow books and Kier had given me a beautiful, locally made sage green wool coat so that I wouldn't be embarrassed by my big puffy black one anymore. The man truly saw everything when it came to me.

"This is just a little something from me to you," she said. She reached up and pulled off the Celtic statement piece she wore. It was a torc, a rigid piece of metal crafted of silver and gold threads in an open weave, which like most Celtic designs had no beginning or end. The torc had no clasp as it fit around the neck much like a cuff bracelet around the wrist. She held it out to me. "This was the inspiration for *Tig McMorrow and the Enchanted Torc*."

"Book five," I said.

"Just so." She smiled. "It was my grandmother's, then my mother's, then mine, and now I want it to be yours."

"Oh, no, Siobhan, I couldn't," I said. I held up my hand in refusal. She ignored me and took my hand in hers, placing the torc on my palm. It was heavy and warm from being worn by her.

"You have to take it," she said. "It would be impolite to refuse."

I studied the piece. It was gorgeous. There was no way I could accept it.

"But you can't give it to me. It should stay in your family," I protested.

She cupped my chin and met my gaze. "You are my family. I couldn't love you more if you were my own daughter."

That got me and a soft sob bubbled out of me. I wanted to tell her how I felt about her, too, but the words got stuck on the knot in my throat. Siobhan seemed to understand and she leaned close and hugged me tight. Then she rose from the desk and turned toward the door. "Tell her, Kier, she has to take it."

I started and turned to see Kier, standing in the doorway watching us. His face was backlit so I couldn't see his expression. Was he furious that his mother had given me a family heirloom? I wouldn't blame him a bit.

Siobhan drifted across the floor. She paused beside her son to give him a gentle hug and then she was gone.

As Kier crossed the room, I said, "I can't accept this. Siobhan is obviously feeling the generosity of the season but this is too much." I held it out to him. "Hide it in your house and we'll just let her think I kept it."

"I have a better idea," he said. He took the torc out of my hands and very gently placed it around my neck. I was wearing a navy blue wrap dress with a fit and flare skirt. I had a lot of bare skin showing and the torc sat just below my collarbone. I felt as exotic as a Celtic chieftain's wife. As I glanced up at Kier, I saw him again as I had the day at Drombeg. He was an ancient warrior, shirtless and with his hair long and braided to stay out of his face. I sighed.

"You're doing it again, Red," he said.

"Doing what?" I asked.

"Getting that dreamy look on your face." He leaned close so that his lips were just a breath from mine. "What are you thinking about?"

"You," I said. My voice was a rough whisper and his eyes flashed with heat.

"In that case, I think you're right," he said. "We do need to take that torc to my house, but we're not going to hide it. You're going to wear it . . . it and nothing else."

"If you insist," I said in a voice so low and sultry that I barely recognized it as my own.

And that's exactly what we did.

It was mid-January during our early morning meeting in the alcove when Kier announced, "I think it's time to call Marcus."

"No!" Siobhan said. Her tone made it clear it was not open to discussion. She looked pale and I was certain she was losing weight. Her cheekbones appeared more prominent and her eyes deeper set. It was almost as if she was shrinking in on herself. I wondered why Kier, who noticed everything, hadn't noticed this and then I felt immediately guilty because I knew that all of his attention had been on me.

We were in the salad days of our relationship, when everything was fresh and new, and most of our time was spent thinking about each other, with each other, naked with each other, or planning to be naked with each other.

"But we're mere chapters from the ending," Kier protested, disregarding his mother's no. "You need to let your agent and your publisher know. You can't just spring it on them."

"I'm not ready," Siobhan insisted. "I have to write the last chapter and it's . . . I just don't . . ."

Her voice trailed off. She looked pained and it occurred to me that she was in actual physical pain and not just the mental torture of trying to write a novel, which was significant as I had come to understand over the past few months.

"About that," I said. "Do you know how you want it to end? You've really put Tig through it in this book. You're not closing on another cliffhanger, are you?"

I had thought she wanted to finish the series but with the chapters she'd been writing, it didn't feel as if there was a tidy ending coming.

"I would say that 'we' have put Tig through it," she corrected me. "Given that most of the horrible things that have happened to him were ideas from you lot."

"That's fair." Kier smiled at me. I tried to smile back but I was feeling anxious.

Something was wrong with Siobhan. I knew it in my bones, but I couldn't ask her anything in front of Kier. She still hadn't told him, and I was very much aware that we were on borrowed time.

"Yes, I know the ending," she said. She reached for her coffee cup and I noticed that her hand was trembling. Kier noticed it, too.

"Are you all right, Ma?" he asked. His gaze narrowed on her face as if really seeing her. "Have you been working too hard? Do you need to rest? We can pack it in for the day or even a week, a month if you'd like. You're not on a deadline."

Siobhan looked at me and I knew we were thinking the same thing. The word *deadline* had never been so fraught with meaning before. It made my heart hurt.

"No, I don't need to rest," she said. She pressed her hand to her chest and said, "The truth is . . ."

Ack! She was doing this now? I tried to brace myself. I glanced around the empty shop, wondering if I could scuttle off and leave them to it. I didn't want to be here. I didn't want to see Kier's face or witness his pain. Cowardly, I know, but I loved him so much. I would have given anything to spare him. From some well of courage deep inside, I reached out and took his hand in mine. Siobhan gave me a slight nod, which I took as confirmation that this was the moment.

Kier glanced from his mother to my hand holding his and back to his mother. "What's wrong?"

"I can't take any time off and I don't want to," Siobhan said. "Because I am very much on a deadline."

"You mean you spoke to your publisher?" Kier asked. "Why didn't you tell us?"

"No, not my publisher," she said. "Dr. Garrett."

"Your oncologist?" Kier slowly sank into his chair. His grip on my hand tightened. "What did she say?"

"The cancer is back," Siobhan said.

"Fecking hell." Kier banged the tabletop with his free hand. "All right, when do we leave for Dublin? We can stay in the townhouse while you undergo treatment. You've beaten it before, there's no reason to think you can't again."

"No." Siobhan shook her head.

"What do you mean no?" he asked. I could feel the anxiety and tension pouring off him. I wanted to hug him, but I didn't move.

"There is no treatment for me," Siobhan said. "The cancer has metastasized and there are tumors on several of my organs. Dr. Garrett said I have a few months at most."

Kier dropped my hand. His face went white and he was struggling to breathe. "That's not possible. You haven't even seen Dr. Garrett since November . . ." He paused and then he looked at her, understanding lighting his eyes. "How long have you known?"

His voice was a bark but Siobhan didn't flinch. She took a deep breath and said, "She told me it was going this way over the summer actually and then she confirmed it in November."

"The summer?" he cried. "And you're just telling us now? Can you believe this, Red?"

He turned to look at me, certain that I would be equally shocked. But of course I wasn't because I already knew. There was no way for me to pretend this was news, so I reached for him instead. He saw the truth on my face, however, and reared back.

"You knew?" he asked.

In the face of his outrage, I could only nod.

"And you didn't tell me?" he cried.

I shook my head. He stared at me in horror as if such a betrayal was completely beyond his comprehension.

"Em didn't tell you because I told her not to," Siobhan said. "She was respecting my wishes."

"Respecting your wishes?" Kier repeated. He shoved back from the table, his chair legs scraping against the floor with a screech of pain. "You're dying, you have just months—wait, probably just weeks—to live and you didn't think this was something you should tell me immediately?"

The hurt in his voice cut like a sharp blade. Siobhan rose from her seat to face him. "I wanted one more holiday without fecking cancer looming over us like the grim reaper it is. Is that so much to ask?"

"Don't." Kier shook his head. "This had nothing to do with the holidays. You wanted to spend your final weeks writing this bloody book. It had nothing to do with me."

"It had everything to do with you!" Siobhan yelled. "It has always been about you. You're the most important person in the world to me and I—"

"No, I'm not," he interrupted. "Or you would have told me. Jaysus, Ma, I can't believe you shut me out. Again."

He didn't give her a chance to answer. Instead he turned and left, striding away from us and out the front door. I watched through the window as he trudged down the street, without a coat, in the bitter January weather as if he couldn't put enough space between him and us fast enough.

Siobhan didn't say anything for a moment. She glanced down at the laptop on the table and resumed her seat. "Shall we get to work?"

"What if he doesn't . . ." My voice trailed off. I couldn't finish the words.

"Come back? He will," Siobhan said with a confidence I didn't feel. "He has to."

He didn't come back. He'd left behind his coat and his car keys were in the pocket, so I took Siobhan home at the end of our morning session. She looked exhausted and even though she didn't admit it, I knew she was worried about Kier. Shackleton climbed onto her bed while she napped and she seemed comforted by that.

I stopped by the gatehouse on my way back to the bookshop. No lights were on, the door was locked, and no one answered my knock. I continued back to work, wondering where Kier had gone and trying not to worry. I was just passing the Top of the Hill pub, when the door opened and out stepped Kier. Judging by the wobble in his walk, he'd spent his morning there, imbibing a liquid brekkie. Great.

I pulled over and rolled down the window. "Hey, need a lift?" I called.

He spun to face me. He blinked, seeing me behind the wheel of his car. His expression darkened into a glower. "Not from you." He turned and started walking.

I checked the road. Thankfully, it wasn't busy, and I put the car in first gear and began to follow him. "Kier, we need to talk."

"I've nothing to say to you," he snapped.

"At least let me drive you home," I said. "You don't even have a coat on."

"I'm fine." He started walking faster.

Did he really think he could outrun me? I put the car in second gear and followed. At least the exercise would keep him warm. We got to a side street and I shot ahead and pulled around the corner, stopping right in the middle of the intersection. I was done playing.

"Get in or I'll leave your car right here and take the keys with me," I said. And I meant it. Kier must have registered that I was serious through his drunken funk because he grumbled and mumbled but he got into the car.

I could smell the whiskey on him as if it were aftershave. I wished it was unpleasant but after so many evenings curled up in front of the fireplace, drinking my favorite whiskey, Writers' Tears, the scent was actually a comfort, much like that of a peat fire. These were the smells I would always associate with him.

Neither of us spoke as he buckled his seatbelt and I set out on the road to his house. We arrived at the gatehouse in silence. Kier slammed out of the car and strode to the house. I shook my head. Unless, he had a hidden key, I had his house key on his keyring and he wouldn't be able to get in. I climbed out of the car and followed him.

He stood in front of his house with his arms crossed over his chest. I held out his keys and he snatched them from my fingers and turned to unlock the door.

I wasn't sure what to do. Did I follow him in and try to talk to him now? Or should I wait until he was sober? Common sense seemed to lean toward the latter but my heart was hurting for him and I hated that we were at odds. I felt if I could just explain, he'd see why I'd respected Siobhan's wishes.

"Thanks for the ride," he said. The way he said it seemed mean, and I remembered that *ride* meant sex in Ireland. So, he was going there. Diminishing what was between us because he was angry. Well, I didn't have to sink to his level.

I tipped up my chin and said, "You're welcome." This was clearly not the time to talk so I turned on my heel and started down the path.

"That's it?" he asked. He was obviously spoiling for a fight but he wasn't going to get one.

"I'm not talking to you right now," I said. "I'll wait until you've had time to process."

"Process what? That you lied to me?" he asked.

I stopped walking. Over my shoulder, I said, "I never lied."

"Lies of omission are still lies."

"Siobhan confided in me. It wasn't my place to say anything."

"That's pure shite."

"Excuse me?"

"You heard me," he said. "I know a load a shite when I hear it."

Damn it, so much for walking away. Now I was angry, too. I spread my arms wide and asked, "What part is pure shite?" And, yes, I imitated his accent, because of course I did.

"You don't care about me," he said. He swayed on his feet. "You don't love me, you love fictional me, you love a character named Tig McMorrow."

"That's not true!" I protested.

"You've never said it."

"You've never said it either."

He waved a dismissive hand. "I'm not the one who chucked her life to come to another country just to be near her favorite author."

"What does that have to do with anything?"

"It means that Siobhan and her books will always be number one to you."

I strode forward until I was nose to throat with him and then I tipped my head back and let him see how pissed I was. "I get that today was a shock, and I'm sorry for it. I wanted Siobhan to tell you sooner, but she wasn't ready. The two of you need to work that out. But the fact is, I wouldn't betray her trust any more than I would betray yours."

It seemed so clear to me. Surely, he had to understand. He leaned forward until his face was just inches from mine and I thought maybe he was going to kiss me and all would be forgiven. Instead, he ripped my heart out and tossed it on the ground and then curb-stomped it.

"Ah, but you see, Emily, you did betray me—by not telling me." He leaned back and stepped inside, slamming the door in my face.

Twenty

I was a disaster at work for the rest of the day. Neither Kier nor Siobhan came back and I was left to assume we were not going to be having our usual dinner meeting or go over any notes. Fine. I hoped they were working things out but since I had no information to that effect, I decided a night at home would be good for me. I refused to think about how much I'd miss Kier. I had to believe we'd get through this, otherwise my heart would be smashed to bits.

"What's wrong, Em?" Eun-ji asked as we put on our coats, preparing to leave.

"Nothing. I'm just tired." I buttoned the coat Kier had bought me and felt a tear well up in my eye. I blinked it away.

"That's not it." Brigid looked me over with her critical mama's eye and said, "You and Murphy had your first row, didn't you?"

"How did you . . ." I stopped before I said too much. Kier was their boss and it would be bad form to talk about it.

"Because you look as sad as a wilted flower," Eun-Ji said.

"That bad?" I asked.

She nodded. "But to be fair, it's also because he never came back to the shop today and given that you've been riding—"

"Does everyone know?" I asked. "I thought we'd been cool about it."

"Cool?" Brigid asked. "You can't take your eyes off each other, you're always together, and you've both been annoyingly cheerful."

"Regular sex will do that for you," Eun-ji said. We all looked at her. "What? It's a scientific fact."

"I don't think even regular sex can fix what's wrong with us." I sighed.

"Don't fret, Em," Oisín said. He patted my shoulder with one of his large square hands. It was like getting comforted by a sledgehammer. "Gavin and I used to row all the time in the beginning. It'll all work out. In the meantime, let's all stop at the pub for some of the black stuff. That'll lift your spirits."

"You can have the Guinness," Brigid said. "I'm drinking Chardonnay."

"Well, aren't you posh?" Oisín opened the door and sashayed out, making us all laugh.

We arrived at the Top of the Hill pub and managed to find a snug even though the place was packed. A three-piece band was playing trad music in the corner, competing for the patrons' attention with the large-screen television showing a rugby match. Oisín was riveted by the game but turned his head to contribute whenever the conversation got interesting.

We were on our second round and in the middle of an intense discussion about whether or not eyebrows were going to be pencil thin again and what was the best way to manage them, plucking, waxing, or threading. Oisín looked horrified by the entire concept and he pushed his flat cap back on his head and stroked his eyebrows as if we'd threatened to shave them off.

"No need to worry, Oisín," Eun-ji said. "No one's trying to tame those hairy caterpillars."

"Hey!" he protested. "Don't forget caterpillars become butterflies."

"They'd sure be prettier that way," Brigid teased.

I laughed at Oisín's look of chagrin but my companions didn't. In fact, they all went still. They were staring at something behind me, and I turned to see Kier approaching us. He looked alert, so he'd clearly sobered up, but his expression was inscrutable.

"Oh, listen to that." Oisín cupped his hand to his ear. "They're playing our song, ladies." He slid out of the booth and Eun-ji, who was seated next to him, followed.

"Hiya, Murphy," they said as they passed him. Kier inclined his head.

Brigid hopped out of the snug but turned back to me before she departed and whispered, "Good luck, Em."

I watched the three of them go, wishing I could disappear into the crowd with them.

"A word, Emily?" Kier asked. Still Emily; that had to be a bad sign.

I gestured to the empty side of the snug. "Have a seat."

Kier shook his head. "I'd prefer to talk outside."

"All right." I wasn't in the mood to stay in the pub anyway.

I shrugged on my coat and grabbed my bag. I glanced across the crowd at my friends and waved goodbye. They waved back. Oisín appeared concerned while both Eun-ji and Brigid looked hopeful. I followed Kier outside, thinking Oisín had the right of it.

The night air was cold and it felt like a slap in the face after the warmth of the pub. A couple of locals greeted us as we passed through the designated smoking area, one of which was Father Mulligan. He had his hands spread wide and I suspected he was telling his latest tale of the fish that got away. He looked like he was going to loop us in, but Kier grabbed my elbow and led me in the opposite direction.

We continued down the street and I wondered how far he was going to walk to say what he had to say. I stopped. We were standing in front of the village bakery and there was no one about. He could just say it here.

"How can I help you?" I asked. I shivered in my coat but I didn't know if it was the cold or an impending sense of doom.

"I'm walking you home, we'll discuss it there," he said.

"No, we won't," I said. "We'll talk here. Now."

"Fine." He bit out the word. "I talked to Siobhan. She made it clear that she's going to finish the book with or without me so we'll resume working on it tomorrow morning just as we have been."

"That's it?" I asked. "You're not going to yell at me some more?"

"I don't see a need for it," he said. "I said what I had to say."

I could feel the wall he was building between us as surely as if I were watching him place each stone. It was infuriating but I refused to argue with him. I turned and started to walk away. "Good night then."

"One more thing, Emily," he said. It was a knife in my chest for him to use my given name in that detached tone. I paused and turned to face him. From the set of his jaw, the flare of his nostrils, and the fire in his eyes, it was easy to see he was still furious with me. "We work until the draft of the book is done and then you go."

"Excuse me?" I asked. Had I heard him right? Was I being preemptively fired?

"The agreement I made with Ma was that we finish the book together, she insists she needs both of us and she's made it her dying request." He paused to clear his throat. "I agreed under the condition that when the book is done, you leave. Go back to the States where you belong."

The air I inhaled felt like ice in my lungs, coating my insides with frost. "And if I don't agree?" I asked.

"Then I won't help with the book at all," he said.

He had me. I knew that having him work on the book meant everything to Siobhan.

"Fine, have it your way." I coughed to keep the emotion out of my voice. "I'll leave when it's done."

I turned and strode away from him as fast as I could. My throat was tight and I could feel a tsunami of tears just waiting to break free. I'd be damned before I'd cry in front of him. Instead, I focused on my rage.

I was furious. Kier hadn't wanted to talk. He'd wanted to punish me. And he'd succeeded. The heels of my half boots clacked on the narrow sidewalk with the force of each step I took. In my mind I was stomping on his thick head. Such a stubborn, complicated, eejit of a man. I turned onto the side street that led to my cottage and sensed through my angry haze that there was someone behind me.

Finn's Hollow was as safe a place as I'd ever lived but still it was late, it was dark, and I was a woman alone. I swiftly reached into my shoulder bag and grabbed the first thing I could get my hands on. It was my hairbrush. Perfect. As I neared the narrow path that led to the cottage, I whipped around and faced the person following me.

He was twenty feet away but his body, given that I was intimately familiar with it, was unmistakable. Kier.

"What the hell are you doing?" I cried. "You completely freaked me out!"

"I'm just making sure you get home safely," he said. He looked annoyed that I'd caught him. "I'd do the same for any stray . . ."

"Dog?" I supplied the word he'd held in check. Without consciously deciding to do it, I hurled the hairbrush at him as hard as I could. It hit him right in the shoulder.

"Ouch!" He rubbed his upper arm. "That's gratitude."

"Gratitude?" I cried. "First you break up with me, then you fire me, and now you're calling me a stray?" I reached into my bag and grabbed another item. It was the paperback book I carried around as an emergency read. I wound up and fired that at him, too.

"Easy there, Red, I wasn't calling you a dog." He held up his hands to ward off the book. It glanced the side of his arm. Pity. "Ow! I just meant I'd make certain any creature—"

"Creature!" I bellowed. I reached into my bag again. I was running out of ammunition, but my fingers closed around the apple I'd put in there for a snack. I threw it at him with all my might. This one hit true, right in his belly, forcing the air out of him with an *oof.*

"Don't follow me. I don't need you to look after me!" I shouted. With that, I turned and stomped to my cottage. I took my keys out of my bag with shaking hands. I supposed it was good that I hadn't thrown them at him, too.

I unlocked my door, turning to look down the narrow path as I stepped inside. He was standing there on the sidewalk, watching me. I stomped inside and slammed the door behind me loud enough that I was certain he'd heard it. It was only then that I let myself cry.

Meeting Siobhan and Kier the next morning was awkward. I had opened my door to find my hairbrush, my book, and my apple all sitting on my stoop. As I gathered them, I knew I would sprout horns and a tail before I'd thank Kier for them.

Siobhan waited until Kier left us in the alcove to go and get coffee before she addressed the situation.

"He'll change his mind," she said. "I know he will."

"About me leaving when the book is done?" I clarified. She nodded and I shook my head. "I don't think so. He was very definitive last night that I've committed an unforgivable offense."

"That's not it," she said. "He's furious with me for not telling him and probably for dying, but he can't be angry with me because I'm sick, so he's taking it out on you. He'll work through it, you'll see."

I shrugged. Seeing him, being so close to him, and knowing that he was done with me, with us, made me feel horrible. I was sick to my stomach, I had a headache, and I was exhausted from not sleeping. If I didn't know for a fact that I had a broken heart, I'd be certain it was a plague. Lucky me, broken heart, yay! For the first time ever, I was rooting for the plague. At least that was potentially treatable.

Because we'd missed reading Siobhan's work yesterday afternoon, Kier and I spent the morning reading what she'd written while she moved ahead to start the next chapter. I finished the read quickly and handed her my notes. I did not give a rip about what Kier's notes said or what he thought about mine. Working beside him was excruciating so the less time I had to spend in his presence the better.

I picked up my untouched coffee and said, "I'm going to warm this up." Instead of going to the café to reheat my coffee, I opted to walk up to the third floor and drink it cold. Was I hiding? Yup.

I sat in one of the armchairs, looking out the window down at the village. I could see the residents coming and going, doing their errands with hurried steps as they tried to outrun the cold, rainy weather.

"Did you and Murphy break up?"

I turned to see Niamh, leaning over the back of the opposite chair.

"What makes you say that?" I asked.

"Because you went from constantly looking at each other and smiling to never looking at each other and frowning," she said.

"Yeah, we broke up," I said. I hoped my tone made it clear that I didn't want to talk about it.

"Why?" she asked. Should have seen that coming.

"A difference of opinion," I said. "A big one."

"Oh." Niamh pursed her lips as she considered this. "It seems like a conversation would fix that."

"It would if both parties were willing to have a conversation," I said.

"Ah." Niamh nodded. "My mam says my dad can be a right gobshite. Do you suppose it's a man thing?"

"Gobshite?" I asked.

"Stupid person," she explained.

"It's definitely a man thing," I said.

"Do you want me to bring you some chocolate?" she asked. "Mam says chocolate makes it easier to put up with a man."

"No thank you," I said. "But your mam is a very wise woman."

"So she says," Niamh agreed. She disappeared behind a bookshelf as quickly as she'd appeared and strangely I felt a little better. *Gobshite.* Ha!

The working relationship between the three of us didn't improve over the next few weeks. Kier and I did our edits separately, rarely working in the same space at the same time. Siobhan was looking thinner and more exhausted each day. I began to fear she might not make it to the end of the book. I had no idea if Kier noticed as we weren't speaking.

We worked every day now so there was no such thing as a weekend, which was fine. The sooner we finished, the sooner I could leave and the pit in my stomach might finally ease. At the moment, I couldn't eat, I couldn't sleep, and I couldn't shake the suffocating sadness that engulfed me. Watching Siobhan become weaker each day was agony.

I stepped out of my cottage bright and early and walked down the path to find Kier parked at the curb. Despite the cold, he was standing outside his car, leaning against the passenger door with his head bowed as if he was praying. There was only one reason why he would be there. Something had happened to Siobhan.

I felt all of the blood drain from my face. I started to shiver and my hands went numb. I dropped my bag onto the sidewalk with a splat and the contents spilled everywhere.

Kier's head snapped up and he took in my expression and my fallen bag with a look of concern. "Red, what's wrong?"

"What's happened?" I asked through chattering teeth.

"Nothing," he said. He stepped toward me with his hands out and it looked as if he was going to hug me but instead he dropped into a crouch and began to pick up my things.

"Siobhan's all right?" I asked. I sank down, thinking it might be a good idea to be closer to the ground.

He glanced at me and then nodded. "As good as can be expected."

I expelled a breath. I cradled my head in my hands, still afraid I might faint.

"I'm sorry, I should have texted you," he said. "I imagine having me turn up was a bit of a surprise."

"A bit." I lifted my head to look at him. His dark hair needed a trim, his eyes had dark circles under them, and his jaw sprouted a layer of scruff. He looked as wrecked as I felt. I wanted to say something to bridge this chasm between us for real, but he was the one who'd blown up the bridge, so it really had to come from him.

With my things gathered, I grabbed the handle of my bag and stood. Kier followed me.

"What are you doing here?" I asked.

"Siobhan asked me to collect you," he said. "Her agent, Marcus Byrne, is at the house so we'll be working there while he's visiting so they can talk business."

"Oh." I nodded.

Kier opened the passenger door for me. I climbed inside and he shut the door. Alone in a car with Kier. I could do this. I was fine. A wet nose appeared in between the front seats and I yelped. A shaggy head of white and black followed the nose and I was delighted to see Shackleton.

"How are you, boy?" I rubbed his ears and kissed his head. He licked my cheek. I took that to mean he was as happy to see me as I was him.

Kier climbed into the driver's seat and glanced at the two of us. For just the tiniest moment, his expression thawed. Then he turned away. Shackleton dropped back into his seat and we drove in silence to Siobhan's house.

Ever efficient, Mrs. Clohessy met us at the door and took our coats. Kier led the way to the library and I followed, while Shackleton headed for the kitchen, his tail wagging as he went.

We stepped into the library and found Siobhan sitting on the sofa. She was bundled under a fluffy pale blue blanket. Her hair was twisted into a messy bun at the nape of her neck and she was wearing a red turtleneck under a thick gray sweatshirt. She was cradling a coffee cup in her hands and I noticed there was a fully loaded coffee tray on the table beside her. Thank goodness because I was running on fumes.

"Good morning, Siobhan," I said.

"Oh, excellent, you're here," she said. She gestured to the man seated in the chair beside her and said, "Marcus, this is the young woman I told you about, my assistant, Emily Allen."

"A pleasure to meet you, Ms. Allen." He rose from his seat and extended his hand. "I'm Marcus Byrne, Siobhan's agent." He was tall and broad, with meticulously trimmed gray hair and kind brown eyes. I clasped his hand and appreciated that his grip was warm and dry, firm but friendly. I warmed to him immediately.

"Please, call me Em," I said. "Everyone does." I didn't dare look at Kier.

"And I'm Marcus," he said.

"Have some coffee and scones, you two," Siobhan said. "I was just telling Marcus about the book."

"I'm eager to read it," he said.

As Siobhan lowered her head to sip her coffee, I saw Marcus watch her with a look of such tenderness that I caught my breath. It was clear that Marcus's feelings for her ran deep. When she straightened up, he had realigned his features into a pleasant mask. But I knew I would never forget the stark pain I had seen in his eyes.

"I think we can give you what we have so far," Kier said. "We're starting the final chapter today. If all goes well, we'll have it for you by the time you head back to Dublin."

"That'd be grand," Marcus said. "I'm here for a few days. I can read it and begin making calls to your publisher. I'll start negotiating the contract if you'd like."

Siobhan smoothed the blanket over her knees. "I think that would be best. The sooner the better."

Didn't that hit like a punch to the gut. I studied Siobhan while she and Marcus talked animatedly of his family and the business associates that they knew from years of working together. I drank two cups of coffee and devoured two scones as I listened. Kier did the same. While they talked, Siobhan slowly slid down until she was almost fully reclined.

"You all right, Ma?" Kier asked. His voice was even but I could hear the note of concern in it.

"I'm grand," she said. "It's just been a lot of excitement to hear all the news."

Marcus reached over and patted her hand. "And here I am going on and on when you have work to do. I've missed you, Siobhan."

"I've missed you, too," she said.

"I'll get out of your way," he said. "I have the draft you emailed to me and I'll go read it in my room. Please let me know if I can assist you in any way."

"Just having you here is a help," Siobhan said. She reached out and squeezed his hand.

I stared at her fingers, they looked so small and frail in his. I felt the grief I had been tamping down for weeks surge up inside of me.

"Excuse me," I said. "I'll be right back."

I put down my coffee cup with a small clatter and bolted from the room. I did not want to fall apart in front of everyone. We had work to do. I had promised to help. I couldn't collapse into my grief right now, much as I wanted to.

Once in the hallway, I didn't know where to go. I supposed I could hide in the bathroom but that seemed very middle school. I decided to step outside and let the cold February day snap me back into myself. Maybe I could freeze my tear ducts, stopping the stream of moisture that had begun despite my best efforts to hold it off. I yanked open the front door and stepped outside. It helped. I walked down the steps and followed the gravel path that led around the house to the side garden.

The rosebushes had been cut back. The flowerbeds were empty. Even the statuary looked cold. I shivered. In my mind, the statue of the Grecian lady before me holding a large basket of fruit asked me to go and get her a hat and some gloves.

"Emily!" I turned and there was Kier trudging toward me, carrying my coat. I supposed I should be grateful, but I wasn't. I didn't want him to see me like this. I lifted my glasses and swiped at my face with my sleeve. I made my expression neutral as he held out my coat to me.

"Thanks . . . Murphy," I said.

Twenty-One

Kier looked startled as if I'd slugged him. I hadn't called him Murphy since the day we'd met. He opened his mouth to say something and then closed it. I glanced at his face, but I couldn't guess what he was thinking.

"I'm just gathering my thoughts," I said. I pulled on my coat. "I'll come inside in a minute." Then I turned away from him and walked into the garden. I needed to put some distance between us because it hurt too damn much to be near him. When I looked back, he was gone.

I paused beside the freezing Grecian woman in the toga. I glanced up at her and said, "And that is why all my daydreams about him are just fantasies. If he was actually a hero, he would have pulled me into his arms and let me cry all over him. He wouldn't push me away just when we need each other the most."

She looked down at me with a sympathetic expression. It was cold comfort, but I'd take it. I took a quick loop around the garden, stuffing my *feelings* back inside like the innards of a child's well-loved stuffed animal. Then I returned to the house, the picture of librarian cool, calm, and collected.

Siobhan was asleep when I entered the library. Marcus was nowhere in sight but Kier was sitting in the chair beside his mother, watching her. The look of devastation on his face broke my heart and I felt my eyes well with tears . . . again. Damn it.

I glanced away so he wouldn't see my face and I strode to the workspace that had been set up on the table by the window. I opened up the notebook I'd been using and pretended to read my notes from the day before. There wasn't much we could do without Siobhan, so I decided to make a list of ideas for the closing chapter. There were a lot of loose ends to tie up and I had no idea which direction Siobhan wanted to go.

I flipped the pages until I found a blank one. Then I just stared at it. We'd be finished with the book in a matter of days. Once it was done, per our agreement, I would leave.

"What are you working on?" Kier asked as he took a seat at the table. His voice was low even though we both knew that nothing could wake Siobhan when she fell asleep.

"I thought I'd write out ideas for the final chapter," I said. I glanced at the couch. "Is she all right?"

He shook his head. "I think she's in more pain than she'll admit. I think she's fading faster than she expected. I'm going to have her doctor come see her."

"A house call?" I asked.

"Dr. Garrett is also a close friend," he said. He rubbed a hand over his face. "I suspect she needs to be on medication for the pain. I think the best thing we can do for her now is ease her suffering."

We sat silently absorbing the reality of the difficult days ahead. I wished so desperately that things were different between us, that I could offer him comfort, or at least just hug him for real. But that wasn't who we were anymore.

"I think we should try and write the last chapter," he said.

I stared at him. "Meaning?"

"Exactly that. We know her voice and the plot points that have to be resolved. I think we should give it a go. I don't want her to leave this world with her final novel unfinished and I just don't think she has the strength to do it herself." The sadness in his voice about broke me.

"So, you want to reverse our roles?" I asked. "We'll do the writing and she'll read it over and offer edits?"

"Yeah, that's the idea," he said. "I think it'll be less taxing for her."

I reached for the laptop. "All right, I suppose we can try it."

I opened the manuscript. It took a moment to load the one-hundred-and-ten-thousand-word document. Kier scooted his chair next to mine. It was distracting to have him so close, the familiar scent of him brought me back to the nights we'd spent together and I was filled with a bittersweet ache.

I tapped the keyboard with more force than necessary to type the chapter heading and asked, "Where do we begin?"

"We left off where Tig has to choose between his portal and his magical friends or Aislinn, the woman he loves," he said.

I hated that we had stuck our hero in this predicament. I had protested fiercely on his behalf but both Kier and Siobhan had overridden me, explaining that Tig's character arc required that he had to sacrifice for his outcome.

"He's not going to be happy if he has to choose. After all he's been through, doesn't he deserve a happy ending?" I wasn't sure if I was talking about myself or Tig at this point but it didn't matter as I knew I was going to lose the argument today just like I'd lost it yesterday.

"I've been thinking about it. There's only one way for Tig to have it all," Kier said. "His mentor has to pass on her magic to him."

"But she can only do that if she dies," I said. Morgan the sorceress had been Tig's mentor since the very first book. She appeared sporadically in the series, disappearing for long stretches of time, as sorcerers do, but she'd been his savior on so many occasions, it frightened me to think of Morgan vanishing forever.

"I think it's how Ma envisions the story ending," he said. His voice was heavy when he added, "She said something last night about leaving me like Morgan will leave Tig."

I slumped back against my chair. "That's a lot."

"Yeah." He reached over and gripped my hand in his. It was the first time he'd touched me since our breakup. He seemed to realize it, too, and quickly released me. "Let's give it a go."

"All right." I moved my hands to the keyboard. "You start."

While Kier dictated, I typed. After much back and forth, and several muttering rants under our breaths, we fashioned a final fight scene for Tig against his nemesis and a dramatic death for Morgan.

"*As he cradled her in his arms, Tig stared down at the face of the woman who had shaped him, who had given her life for his, and he knew he would grieve for her forever*," Kier said the last line of the scene and I typed it through a blurry stream of tears.

It was the most wrenching scene in the book and it wrecked me. When I dropped my hands, Kier pressed a tissue into my palm and I dabbed at my face. I glanced at him just in time to see him wipe his eyes with his sleeve.

Hours had passed and I glanced over at the couch and found Siobhan watching us. "Is it done then?" she asked. She didn't seem surprised that we had forged ahead.

"Almost," Kier said. "You'll have to read it over and give your approval and Tig still needs to find Aislinn and apologize for being such an eejit."

"Will she forgive him?" Siobhan asked me.

"Absolutely," I said. "She loves him, but we're in grand gesture territory. He's going to have to do something big."

"Bloody grand gestures," Kier muttered. "I can't believe we're forcing that on him."

Siobhan smiled. She closed her eyes and said, "I have no doubt that he'll manage it. I knew all along that they belonged together."

Kier and I exchanged a confused look. Siobhan had never plotted a page in her life. There was no way she could have known there was a happy ending for Tig and Aislinn. Or could she?

"Are you all right, Ma?" Kier asked. "Can I get you anything?"

"No, I'm fine," she said. She didn't open her eyes. "Finish the book. Finish it and give it to me later."

My heart clutched in my chest. Was this a last request? What did it mean? I could feel the panic begin to build and I started to feel lightheaded. Kier's hand settled on my back, a solid steadying weight.

"Breathe, Red," he said. "Let's not overthink it. Let's just do as she asks."

I didn't know what to make of him calling me "Red" again. Had it just been a slip? I tried not to dwell on it. We had a book to finish.

We wrote all day. We took breaks for lunch, tea, and dinner with Marcus and Siobhan. Afterward, Kier carried Siobhan up to her room where Marcus planned to sit with her until she fell asleep. I studied the faces of the household staff as they came and went about their business. Most of them looked as if they'd been crying all day.

Kier and I wrote well into the night. My back was tight from being hunched over the keyboard and my vision was getting blurry, but at two in the morning, we crafted the last sentence together and I typed *The End*. I hit save and we both collapsed back in our chairs.

"My god, I'd forgotten how hard writing is," Kier said. "Why would anyone willingly do this for a living?"

"No idea," I said. My back felt as if it was pinched in a vise and I tried to stretch out the knot between my shoulder blades.

"Let me," he said. Kier turned my chair so that my back was to him and he pushed my hair aside as he rested his hands on my shoulders and gently started to squeeze. It felt amazing. Then he dug his thumbs into the knotted muscles around my spine. *Oh my.* I was incoherent, it felt so good. When the muscles finally began to loosen, he stopped and I missed his touch immediately.

"It's too late for you to go home," he said. "Why don't you sleep in one of the guest rooms? I'm staying here, too, in case Ma needs me."

"Sure." I wondered if he knew how disappointed I was that he hadn't invited me to sleep in his room. An awkwardness fell between us. "Which room should I take?"

He stared at me for a moment, the look of hunger on his face unmistakable. But he made no move to touch me. When he spoke, his voice was completely without emotion. "The first door on the right at the top of the stairs. It's got a nice view of the woods."

"Great," I said. "I'll head up then."

He nodded. Despite all the sweat and tears we'd just shared, in the end the chasm between us remained.

Siobhan did not read over our pages the next day. Instead, she stayed burrowed in her blanket. She said she needed more time to read and edit what we'd written and we didn't push her. Frankly, I was relieved because once she was happy with the pages, I had promised Kier I would leave but I didn't want to go—not now.

Dr. Garrett came to visit and set Siobhan up with a pain management regimen that a nurse named Erin would be monitoring as she came to check on Siobhan a few times per day. Both Dr. Garrett and Erin were middle-aged women who filled the room with kindness and compassion when they entered. I appreciated their calm efficiency during a time of so much emotional upheaval more than I could say.

At Siobhan's request, Kier invited their friends and neighbors in the village to come and visit her one last time.

"Do you think you're up to it, Ma?" he asked.

"This is my home, these are my people," she said. "I'll say goodbye to them properly."

"Fair enough," Kier said. "But no one lingers. If Father Mulligan starts in on a fishing story, I get to toss him."

Siobhan burst out laughing. "Toss out a priest? You most certainly will not."

"I can distract him for you," Marcus volunteered. "One question about his favorite lure and I'll be able to usher him out the door."

"I'll be counting on that," Kier said.

I helped Siobhan tidy up by fixing her hair and applying her makeup, grateful to have her all to myself for a bit.

"I feel like a movie star getting ready for her premiere," she said. "Thank you, Em." She took my hand in hers and gave it a firm squeeze. I was relieved to feel some strength in her grasp.

"Happy to help," I said and meant it.

"How are things between you and Kier?" she asked.

"Fine." I kept my gaze on her right eyebrow, which I was gently darkening with an eyebrow pencil. I didn't want her to see the heartache I was suffering reflected on my face.

"He loves you," she said. "And he'll find his way back to you. I'm certain of it."

I lowered my hand and met her gaze. The absolute certainty in her eyes made the weight in my chest lift just a bit. "I guess we'll just have to wait and see."

"Just so." She reached up and brushed my hair from my face. "You know you're my Aislinn, don't you? You're smart and funny and kind like her, you even have her hair."

"I think a lot of women could be Aislinn," I said.

"No, you are something special," Siobhan said. "Don't ever let anyone tell you otherwise."

There it was—the maternal affection I'd been missing my entire life but that Siobhan had given me so freely. It meant everything to me.

Mrs. Clohessy knocked softly on the doorframe. "Your visitors are here, ma'am."

"Thank you, please show them in," Siobhan said.

Mrs. Clohessy nodded and Michael from the pub and Hazel from the tea shop stepped into the room. And so it began. The visits took up the next three days and somehow Siobhan never managed to edit the final chapter that Kier and I had written. In and around the visitors, Marcus negotiated the deal for the book. Siobhan insisted that Kier and I be listed as coauthors and had us sign the contract, which, given the circumstances, had been expedited as well.

I signed where Marcus indicated but I didn't read it. I could have been signing away my firstborn and I wouldn't have known. There was no thrill for me. I didn't care about any of it.

Every day, Siobhan appeared to be disappearing just a little bit more. I half expected to be talking to her one day and have her just fade away. It made me edgy and sad. I began taking long, bracing walks around the estate with Shackleton by my side.

The bookstore employees were the last of the visitors and Oisín had been so overwrought that Brigid, Eun-ji, and Niamh had to help him out to Brigid's car where his partner, Gavin, waited, letting him cry it out on his shoulder. Oisín's tears broke us all, and I escaped on my walk shortly after. I tried to tell myself that Siobhan had enjoyed a life well-lived to have so many people this sad to see her go, but I was so devastated myself that it was difficult to find any comfort in it.

I returned to the library to find Kier and Siobhan alone.

"It's time, Ma," Kier said. "You need to give us your notes on the final pages. We need to finish the book and send it to your editor."

Siobhan nodded, but it was clear she was too weak to read the pages herself. I crossed the room and said, "I can read the final chapter to you and any edits you want to make you can jot down on the pad and I'll incorporate them into it for you."

I had expected resistance, but instead, Siobhan beamed at me. Her smile was purely happy and she said, "Yes, let's give Tig the ending he deserves."

I sat down in the chair beside her. Her hand was shaking and too weak to hold the pen so Kier took the pad and pen and said, "I'll take your notes for you."

"Thank you, love," Siobhan said.

I cleared my throat and began. It was an emotional chapter to read. I had to take a break a few times to get my emotions in check. Kier watched me as I read. I had no idea what he was thinking but mercifully I could escape his gaze in the story. Siobhan settled deep into her blanket, her head resting on her pillow, and she closed her eyes as if picturing every word I read aloud.

She didn't interrupt me, not once. When I reached the final lines, I caught my breath, hoping she'd approve of how Kier and I had wrapped it up.

"'I choose you,' Tig said to Aislinn. 'Morgan sacrificed her life for mine and in doing so she charged me with finding my purpose and it's you. There is nothing in any of the realms I've been to that means more to me than you.'

Aislinn met his gaze, returning his look of love measure for measure. 'And I choose you, Tig McMorrow. In this world or any other, it will always be you.'"

The last word lingered in the quiet. I heard a snuffle come from Siobhan's nest of blankets and then she said, "It's perfect. Don't change a word."

She reached out a hand to each of us. Kier and I stepped forward, kneeling together beside the couch. "The pair of you have given me the greatest gift. You've helped me complete my life's work. It never would have happened if you hadn't written that letter, Em. And I am so glad that you did, not because of the book but because you have become so very dear to me. I love you very much."

The tears I'd been holding back flowed freely now. I pressed Siobhan's hand to my cheek and said, "You saved me, Siobhan. I was so alone in the world, but Tig and Aislinn became my friends and my family. They taught me courage and honesty and kindness when I didn't have any of that in my world. I've loved you for that since I read the very first book, but now that I know you, I love you even more."

A tear slid down Siobhan's cheek. She glanced at her son, and I knew this needed to be a private moment between them. I leaned forward and kissed Siobhan's head, taking in her soothing lavender scent and knowing I would never smell that particular fragrance again without thinking of her.

I let go of her hand and stood up. The tears were coming fast and furious now. I hurried across the room, pausing in the doorway to pull the door closed. Kier was cradling his mother's head and they had their foreheads pressed together.

"I don't want to lose you, Ma," he said. His voice was gruff and his face wet with tears.

"You'll never lose me, my boy," she said. "I will always be in here." She gently ruffled his thick hair. "And in here." She pressed her hand to his heart. "I am as much a part of you as you are of me and that connection transcends time and space and this simple mortal world."

She smiled through her tears and reached up to cup his face. "I know you hate change. I know you fight it with claws and teeth, my little badger." Kier huffed a small laugh even as his tears continued to fall. "But the one thing that will never ever change is my love for you."

I slipped from the room, closing the door to give them their privacy. I sat on a hard chair in the hallway, keeping watch so they wouldn't be interrupted, all the while feeling every crack as my heart broke into a thousand tiny shards of pain.

It was there that Marcus found me. He was carrying a bottle of champagne and four glasses. He stopped beside me.

"Has something happened?"

Before I could answer, the door opened and Kier glanced out. He looked wrecked but at the sight of Marcus, a small smile lifted the corner of his mouth. "You got her text? Come on then, let's celebrate."

"Celebrate?" I asked. Was he crazed with grief?

"Siobhan and I always drink champagne when she finishes a book," Marcus explained. "She just sent me a message saying it was done."

"Oh." I sniffed, trying to clear my head. I couldn't imagine that Siobhan was up for a celebration, but I was wrong.

She was sitting up with the blankets around her. She looked as if she'd been crying but her eyes sparkled at the sight of the three of us and she grinned at Marcus. "We did it. After ten long years, we did it."

"Indeed you did," he said. "I never doubted it. I have to be honest, and I'm not just saying this because I represent you, this is the greatest book you've ever written."

That made Siobhan beam and then laugh. It was weaker than her usual hearty chuckle but it was a laugh all the same. Marcus poured us each a glass and then held his aloft.

"To Tig McMorrow and the . . . er . . . do we have a title?"

"The Last Chapter," Kier said. "*Tig McMorrow and the Last Chapter*. We wrote the bookshop into the story."

"Oh, that's brilliant," Marcus said. "It's already the place where your readers come to pay homage to you. They'll love that."

"It felt appropriate," Siobhan said.

We clinked glasses and took a sip. It was delicious. I glanced at the bottle. It had a fancy French label and I was quite certain it was not something I could ever have afforded in my real life.

"I have a toast," Siobhan said. She looked bone weary but also content. She lifted her glass, not very high, as if it was too heavy for her. "To my coauthors. I never could have done this without you. May the publication of the book bring you your hearts' desires."

We clinked glasses again. Neither Kier nor I made a toast. I think the writing we had done had robbed us of any words we might have had left. We did finish the bottle, however. I was trying to decide how I could get a ride home when Siobhan said, "Em, please stay here tonight. It's been an emotional day, and I don't think you should be home alone."

I glanced at Kier to see what he thought but his face was impassive. Marcus gave me an encouraging nod.

"All right," I said.

Siobhan looked at Kier. "I hate to be a bother but I think the stairs might be a bit too much for me and I am knackered. Would you mind helping me to my room?"

"Not at all," Kier said. He tenderly lifted her up in his arms, blanket and all.

"Good night, Marcus, Em." Siobhan gave us a soft smile.

"Good night, love," Marcus said.

"Good night, Siobhan," I said. I watched through the open door as Kier carried his mam upstairs to her room.

I turned to Marcus and said, "I think I'm going to turn in as well. It's been quite a day."

"Of course," Marcus said. "Good night, Em."

"Good night." I returned to the guest room where I'd been staying. Maeve and Shane had brought me my things a few days ago so I slipped on my pajamas, brushed my teeth, and climbed into bed. I put my glasses on my nightstand and shut out the light. I desperately wanted to be unconscious. I wanted to escape the pain I was feeling in the serenity of sleep.

Unfortunately, sleep wouldn't come and I spent a fitful night thinking about Siobhan and Kier and the friends I'd made in Finn's Hollow because I knew that come tomorrow, I was going to have to fulfill the terms of the deal I'd made with Kier and leave. The thought of it broke me and I cried until there wasn't a single tear left inside of me.

It didn't take long to pack my things in the small carry-on Maeve had lent me. I'd return to the cottage today and start boxing my things. I had no idea where I was headed, but I didn't want to go back to Martha's Vineyard. I wanted to keep moving forward.

Sam had wanted to know all of the details about my sudden departure but I told her I couldn't talk about it yet. There were a few threats about bodily harm against Kier on her part, but when I told her about Siobhan she understood that things were complicated.

I wheeled the carry-on to the door. I glanced around the room to make certain I hadn't left anything behind. Kier still had my original copy of *Tig McMorrow and the Ogham Stone* but I didn't have the heart to ask for it back. Maybe he would send it to me one day. Ugh.

My coat was downstairs. I just needed to grab it and I could go. I hoped Marcus would be willing to drive me home. I didn't think I could bear to be alone with Kier even for a ten-minute car ride. I decided I would have coffee with Siobhan if she was up, otherwise I would simply leave, as there was no sense in prolonging the inevitable. It would just get more difficult.

There was a knock on the door just as I was reaching for the doorknob.

"Come in," I said. I assumed it was Mrs. Clohessy letting me know breakfast was ready.

The door was pushed open and Kier stood there. He looked pale and shaky. His eyes darted all around the room as if trying to latch on to something, anything, to ground him. Finally, he looked at me and I saw complete and utter devastation in his eyes.

Twenty-Two

I let go of my bag and stepped forward. "What's happened? What's wrong?"

"Ma . . . Siobhan . . ." He paused to take a breath. "She passed away in her sleep last night."

I staggered back and he reached out, catching me by the elbow to steady me. "I . . . No . . . NO!" I cried.

Kier hauled me close, his arms locking me against him as if he, too, needed someone to hold on to. I shook my head, denying his words even as I sobbed into his sweater. I wrapped my arms about his waist to anchor myself. This couldn't be true. She was tired last night but she was also happy. She couldn't be gone. She needed more time. I needed more time. It wasn't fair. It wasn't right. A wail came out of me that sounded like a wounded animal.

Kier stroked my back and whispered soothing nonsense words, trying to calm me. But I was absolutely gutted and I didn't think I would ever feel calm again.

. . .

Word of Siobhan's passing spread through the village and the world that same day. Within hours, reporters descended upon Finn's Hollow, interviewing anyone and everyone who had ever known Siobhan Riordan. Inevitably, the news was leaked that the final book in the series had been written and the world, which had largely forgotten about Tig McMorrow, went into a frenzy.

There was no thought of me leaving before the service. I knew Kier would never deny me my last goodbye and so I was swept into the preparations, trying to help as best as I could. The days became a blur of trying to navigate the endless arrival of flowers and plan the wake and the funeral, all while trying to keep it together.

Marcus, Kier, and I holed up in the library, which became a sort of command post for dealing with the press and the outpouring of condolences from the writing community. Authors I had long admired sent notes and food and gifts. It was a testament to how much Siobhan's work had influenced others.

Even in trying to honor Siobhan's request to keep it simple, there were so many decisions to be made and Kier looked like a man who was drowning every time the phone rang or someone knocked on the door. Marcus and I did our best to take on as many of the tasks as we could, but as Siobhan's only living relative, Kier carried the heaviest burden.

The wake was held at the Last Chapter, which felt most appropriate. In Siobhan's alcove, we placed a large portrait of her on the table. It was her author picture, snapped while she was in her garden. Her eyes sparkled, her lips were parted in a wide, warm smile, and her long, curly dark hair was being lifted by the breeze. Surrounded by the abundant condolence bouquets we were receiving every day, she looked as if she was in a spring meadow. It was how I always wanted to remember her.

Kier asked Marcus and I to stand with him in the receiving line, which was how I found myself in between Kier and Marcus at the entrance to the alcove. We'd made a path so that mourners could spend a moment of reflection beside Siobhan's portrait if they chose.

How are you holding up, Em?" Maeve and Shane were two of the first to arrive and Maeve gave me a quick hug before stepping back to study my face. She had tears in her eyes, which naturally made me water up as well.

"As good as can be expected," I said.

Maeve nodded. She grabbed my hand, then turned to Kier and took his hand as well. "It was a blessing to Siobhan to have you both help her finish her life's work."

"Thanks, Maeve," Kier said. "Emily gets all the credit. Without her, well, I doubt that Siobhan would be truly at peace."

I had no idea what to make of that. He was still calling me *Emily* but it sounded as if he approved of me helping his mother, which left me confused.

"No," I said. "It was you working with her that helped her the most."

Maeve glanced between us and nodded. "As I said, you were both a blessing to her."

She hugged us and moved on and the line continued.

I was hiding in the café, getting away from the crowd while nibbling on a biscuit and washing it down with a hot cup of coffee, when Marcus appeared. "There you are, Em," he said. "I'd like you to meet someone."

I hastily swallowed and put down my mug. The woman beside Marcus was dressed in an ecru cashmere sweater set and tweed trousers. Her dark brown leather half boots matched her designer handbag and she carried herself with the confidence of a longtime career woman. She was more put together than I was on my best day.

"Sloane Ryder, this is Emily Allen," he said. "Emily, this is Siobhan's editor."

"Ms. Ryder," I said. I studied her face and noted the gentle lines around her eyes and mouth. Her ash blond hair was streaked with white, so I assumed she and Siobhan had been close in age. "Thank you for coming."

"I would have been here sooner . . ." She blinked and cleared her throat. "But I was at a conference in Australia and couldn't get back in time."

"I'm sorry," I said. "If it's any comfort to you, Siobhan frequently said you were the best editor she ever worked with."

Sloane laughed even as she dabbed her eyes. "I'm the only editor she ever worked with, but I'll take it."

"Marcus!" A man across the room called Marcus away, leaving us alone.

"It's impertinent of me, having just met you, but I'm wondering now that your assistant position with Siobhan has ended, what are you planning to do next, Emily?"

"Call me Em," I said. "It's not impertinent at all. I've been asking myself the same thing for days and I have yet to come up with an answer."

"Would you consider writing?" she asked. "During the last call I had with Siobhan, just before she . . . well, she raved about your abilities as a writer."

"Siobhan was very generous," I said. "But I don't think that's where my gifts lie."

Sloane nodded. She pursed her lips and then opened her handbag and pulled out a card. She held it out to me and said, "I also read your edits on Siobhan's book, and I believe you could be a terrific editor. Would you ever consider working for me?"

I took the card and gaped at her.

"You'd have to start at the bottom and work your way up, but if your input on Siobhan's manuscript is any indicator, the climb will be very quick for you."

Me? An editor? I had never even considered this possibility. "I don't . . . I . . . Really?"

Sloane smiled. "Come to Dublin, tour the office, meet the staff, and see what you think. And if you're really settled here in Finn's Hollow, you could always work remotely and just hop on the train once or twice a week for meetings."

I didn't know what to say.

"Don't answer now," Sloane said. "I know I've caught you at the worst possible time. Think it over. The offer will remain open indefinitely. Unfortunately, I have to leg it back to Dublin right after the service tomorrow, but you can call me anytime."

With a gentle smile, she left me standing in the café, reconsidering everything I had ever thought my future might entail.

Siobhan's service was standing room only. The church, much like the bookstore the day before, was full to bursting with flowers. I sat in the front pew with Kier and the household staff while Sloane and Marcus and the bookstore employees sat in the front pew on the other side of the aisle.

Father Mulligan offered mass and then told the story of Siobhan sneaking a brand-new fishing pole into the sanctuary for him to find after his was swept down the river during a storm. He went on to tell more stories of Siobhan's generosity, the sacks of food delivered to a family down on their luck, the repairs made on an elderly couple's car when they couldn't afford them, and many, many more. Siobhan had been a force of good in the village and there wasn't a resident of Finn's Hollow who didn't love and mourn her.

I thought about the impact she'd had on my own life. She'd encouraged me and praised me and valued me. She'd mothered me when I'd never known what that felt like. In such a short time, she had left an indelible mark upon me and I was forever changed for the better.

Kier closed the service by reading a passage from the very first Tig McMorrow book. It was my copy that he held in his large, square hands, and it was a passage I had highlighted. I felt my throat get tight and my eyes pooled with tears when he read the words I had memorized so many years ago. It was a short scene but the final line was a message that reflected Siobhan's philosophy of life. "'The most difficult path is usually the right one to take.'"

He glanced up from the book and his gaze met mine. For just a moment, I felt as if we were connected in our grief and our love of Siobhan, but then he glanced away and I was left wondering if I'd imagined it.

It had been decided that there'd be a reception for Siobhan at the pub after the service. Siobhan's publisher was picking up the tab and it appeared the entire village was going to turn out. I had planned to go but as we filed out of the church, I didn't think I could bear it.

As I plodded through the empty village streets on the way to my cottage, I thought about Tig McMorrow and the line Kier had read. I knew I was being a coward, as it would be infinitely harder to sit in a pub pretending I was fine than to flee and escape the man who'd broken my heart, but I just didn't have Tig's courage today.

After meeting Sloane at Siobhan's wake, I had studied the bus and train schedules to Dublin. I'd even packed a bag. I knew there was a bus leaving in thirty minutes. If I hurried, I could just make it.

Twenty-Three

When do you start working as an editor?" Sam asked.

"In two weeks," I said. "I'm taking the opportunity to be a tourist for a bit, so I can get acclimated."

We were walking through Dublin to the Trinity College campus and I paused to look at my friends Sam and Ben.

"Can I just say for the millionth time that I can't believe you're really here," I said.

"Of course we are," Ben said. "Before Sam finished listening to your voicemail telling us you were off to Dublin for a job interview, she had the tickets booked."

I laughed. On the train ride up from Finn's Hollow, I had emailed Sloane and scheduled an interview for the next day. Of course, I had called Sam right away to tell her the news, never expecting when I booked myself into a hotel in Temple Bar that I would find Sam and Ben waiting for me in the lobby two days later.

As Sam explained it, "February is the slow season on the Vineyard so it was the perfect time to get away."

While I'd been fine with seeing the sights by myself, it was definitely more fun to have Sam and Ben with me. The Guinness Storehouse might never recover from Ben's attempts to learn how to draw a pint. They had been with me for four days and we had only scratched the surface of a city that I was falling desperately in love with.

Kier had told us at the wake that he would be closing the bookshop for a few days to the give the staff a chance to grieve. I had texted him and the rest of the crew to let them know I was in Dublin. I didn't mention the job interview but I suspected Kier was relieved to have me away so he didn't have to make a big deal out of letting me go.

It crushed me not to have Siobhan here with me. Missing her was a constant ache in my chest, as everywhere I turned I saw something I wanted to tell her about. I tried to temper my grief with gratitude that I had been lucky enough to know her as long as I had, but it was cold comfort.

My phone chimed while we crossed the Ha'penny Bridge over the River Liffey. I glanced at the display. It was a text from Oisín. It was the third text of the day. Since I'd been in Dublin, it seemed everyone who worked in the bookstore had needed to contact me for something or other. And they always asked me to send a picture of what I was doing. I didn't mind. I missed them all and the Last Chapter so much.

At the moment, it seemed Oisín couldn't locate the extra stash of packing tape in the supply room. It took me a block and a half to remember where it was. When we reached the crosswalk in front of Trinity College, I told him the tape was behind the box of mailers and sent a picture of the school.

"The bookstore again?" Sam asked.

"Yeah." I tucked my phone away as we entered through the front gate and crossed the gray stone of Parliament Square. I felt smarter just walking on the campus whose former students included Bram Stoker and Oscar Wilde.

"Have you completely ruined them from operating without you?" Sam asked.

"As Em's former boss, I can say probably," Ben said. "We still miss you at the library."

"Aw, thanks." I smiled at him. "I think everyone is just feeling a little lost right now. Time will help."

"What did Kier say when you gave him your notice?" Sam asked.

I turned and walked toward the Campanile, a marvelous bell tower, which resided in front of the Library Square.

"You did tell him, didn't you?" Sam persisted.

"I called but he didn't pick up, so I left him a voicemail that I had an appointment in Dublin but I never heard back from him, which is fine," I said. "It's only been a little over a week since he lost his mom. He's going through a lot right now. I don't want to add to it."

"Don't you think leaving without speaking to him in person might be counterproductive to his well-being?" Sam asked. She glanced at Ben and then back at me. "What is it with you librarians and your dramatic exits?"

Ben gave me a sheepish glance. "I have to agree with Samwise on that one. I have discovered through personal error that it's best to let a person know before you disappear."

"I appreciate the advice, I do," I said. "But I didn't disappear. I left a message. I'm still in Ireland and I've been in touch with the bookshop staff several times a day, every day. If Kier wanted to call me or text me, he would. And he hasn't."

Neither Sam nor Ben said anything to that. Because there was nothing to say. Kier knew I was in Dublin and he hadn't reached out.

That was all right. Particularly because I had already made the decision that I wasn't leaving Finn's Hollow.

"I'm heading back at the end of the week and Kier and I can talk when I get there. I hope we'll both be in a better headspace then."

Sam and Ben exchanged a thoughtful look. I suspected they disapproved of the way I was handling things, but they were kind enough not to say anything. I had thought long and hard about my life over the past few days. I was excited to take on the position of editor and I was looking forward to going home . . . to Finn's Hollow.

When I saw Kier again, I fully intended to make my pitch for us to give it a go. I loved him and I believed he loved me. If he could forgive me for keeping Siobhan's confidence, then I hoped we could try again. Alternatively, if he didn't forgive me, I was planning to live in my cottage in Finn's Hollow, editing books at one of the café tables in the Last Chapter, until the daily sight of me wore him down into giving us another shot. Apparently, I had a heretofore unknown stubborn streak.

"Oh, we'd better hurry," Ben said, glancing at his phone. "Our tickets are timed for the Book of Kells and we don't want to miss it. Personally, I can't decide if I'm more excited about seeing the Book of Kells or the Long Room."

"Yes, all those busts of men," Sam said. "I can't wait."

"Hey, now, they've finally added some women," Ben said. "Including Mary Wollstonecraft."

"What year were they added?" she asked.

"2023," Ben muttered. "Clearly a centuries-long oversight."

"Clearly," Sam said.

Ben was in full book nerd mode and I was right there with him. The three of us dashed around the corner to the entrance of the Old Library, where the Book of Kells exhibit was housed. It was a cold day but the sun was out and I was surprised that we were the only people in line.

We were hustled into the building, which was weirdly quiet. A staff person directed us to the Long Room and I felt a wave of excitement followed by another one of sadness. I so wished Siobhan was here and Kier, too. I sighed as I stepped into the most beautiful library I had ever seen.

It looked like something Siobhan would have created in another realm for Tig McMorrow. Two hundred thousand volumes on open shelving that was two stories tall with spiral staircases leading up to the next level while white busts of famous thinkers stood at the end of each row. My jaw dropped. I swear it hit the floor with a thud. I heard another thump and assumed it was Ben's. I turned to share the moment with him and Sam, but they weren't there.

They'd been right behind me. I frowned. Come to think of it, as I glanced around the enormous room, I discovered I was all alone. That didn't feel right. Where were the throngs of tourists?

"Hello?" I called out. It echoed in the chamber and I wondered if they'd closed and no one told us. I moved forward, pausing beside Brian Boru's harp inside its glass case. "Sam? Ben?"

Okay, I wasn't going to panic. I'd just turn around and head back the way I came.

But when I turned around, I wasn't alone. Kier was standing there looking as impossibly handsome as he had the first day I saw him. My heart leapt into my throat.

It was then that I noticed he was holding a portable speaker in one hand and as I watched, he switched it on and Peter Gabriel's "In Your Eyes" started to play. My eyes went wide and I couldn't catch my breath. Did this mean what I thought it meant?

Kier met my gaze and over the music, he said, "I couldn't figure out how to get you onto the top of the Empire State Building, but then I thought the Long Room was a better choice for two booklovers anyway."

A sob bubbled up inside of me and I covered my mouth with my hand, trying to contain it. My eyes were blurry with tears when I asked, "Is this a grand gesture then?"

He smiled at me, it was full of tenderness when he said, "As you wish."

That did it. My brain began to make a buzzing noise and my heart hammered so hard in my chest I thought I'd crack a rib. I was going to faint. I felt myself start a slow slide to the floor.

"Red!" Kier dropped his speaker and raced forward. Sam and Ben came charging out from behind a bookcase with Ben pushing a chair. I slumped into the seat just as Kier reached me.

"Em, put your head between your knees before you faint," Sam ordered.

She was crouched in front of me, and I asked, "Did you know he was here?"

"Maybe I called him before we left the Vineyard," she said. "And maybe he told me he needed my help. Come on, Em, it's not like I could say no to that accent."

"Yeah, I couldn't either," Ben confessed.

"That's fair," I said. I dropped my head again.

I heard the shuffle of feet and then it was Kier crouched in front of me. I looked up at him, got woozy at the sight of his deep blue eyes, and put my head back down.

"This feels very familiar, Red," he said.

I closed my eyes. He'd called me Red . . . twice. What did it mean? Why was he here? I wanted to have hope, but I was terrified of being wrong.

"Just to be clear." I opened my eyes and met his gaze. "A hot Irishman is not getting in between these knees just because he decided to perform a grand gesture. How did you get this room all to ourselves?"

"It helps to be Siobhan Riordan's son," he said.

"Ah." I nodded. "I think she would approve."

"I hope so." His face reflected the same grief I felt. "Although she'd likely be annoyed that it took me this long to get my feelings sorted."

"And have you gotten them sorted?" I asked.

"Yes," he said. "I don't know if you're aware of this, but I don't like change, Red."

It was my turn to laugh. "Yes, I know."

"I had my life perfectly in order, and then you showed up and changed everything," he said. "I was too thick-skulled to see it at the time, but you made everything better. You helped Ma achieve her dream and you gave her peace. And you managed to make me feel a depth of love for another person that I've never known before."

"That is a lot of change," I said. I couldn't take my eyes off him. I put my hands on his shoulders just to be sure he was real and not one of my daydreams.

"I was positive that I didn't want any of it," he said. "When you left for Dublin, I thought things would go back to the way they'd been. I thought I could make myself fall out of love with you. And that's what I wanted because I didn't want to be vulnerable. I didn't want to have my heart—that would be you, by the way—walking around unprotected."

Did he just call me his heart? Was he telling me he was in love with me? I heard Sam sigh and out of the corner of my eye, I saw Ben put his arm around her.

"It took me exactly twenty-four hours after Ma's funeral to realize what an eejit I was. I'm mad about you, Red. There is simply no getting over you for me," Kier said. "'He stepped down, trying not to look long at her, as if she were the sun, yet he saw her, like the sun, even without looking.'"

I clasped my hands over my heart and said, "Tolstoy's *Anna Karenina*. Oh my god, this really is our big moment. You, who scorned grand gestures, are giving me one."

"Well, I can't whisk you into a magical portal like Tig does Aislinn," Kier said. "So it feels a tad anticlimactic."

"What are they talking about?" Sam hissed and Ben said, "Tig McMorrow, great series. We should read them."

"Ahem." Kier raised an eyebrow at them and Sam clapped her hand over her mouth. He turned back to me. "No portal but I can tell you I'm sorry. I was angry at Siobhan and I took it out on you. You did the right thing in keeping her confidence and I wish I could have seen it that way at the time. I'm asking you to forgive me for being an eejit and come back to Finn's Hollow with me and help me . . ." He paused for a beat. "Help me upgrade the bookshop."

I propped my chin on my hand. "Do you mean you're willing to make *changes*?"

He laughed. "For you, Red, I'll change anything you want. Just come home and be with me where you belong."

I stared at the face that was so dear to me. Kier was my person, of that I had no doubt. And I'd never wanted anything as much as I wanted to return to Finn's Hollow with him.

"I love you," I said.

"I love you, too," he replied. He looked hopeful. "Does that mean you'll come home?"

I tapped my chin with my index finger. "Potentially."

"Potentially?" he repeated.

"I was thinking the bookshop would look lovely with flower boxes outside the windows," I said.

"Really, Red?"

"Uh-huh," I said.

"Fine, if you want flower boxes, you get flower boxes."

"Yay." I took a huge breath and said, "And an upgraded computer system, and we should host a monthly book club for couples that we run together, and I was thinking we could—"

His eyebrow shot up again.

"We can discuss my other ideas another time," I said.

"Another time?" He took my hands and stood, pulling me to my feet. "Does that mean yes, you'll come home?"

"Actually, I need to tell you something," I said.

He looked wary, as if rejection was coming for him and he had to brace for it.

"I've taken a position as an editor working with Sloane Ryder," I said.

"I see." He looked so disappointed I almost said I'd quit but thankfully my common sense kicked in.

"I want to keep the position," I said. "Sloane said I can work remotely and just commute in for meetings."

He stared at me. "You're going to stay on at the bookshop then?"

"I have to. Do you know how many texts I get from the staff every day? Clearly, they can't do without me. Unless . . ." I mimicked his impertinent eyebrow and said, "Unless they've been reaching out because you asked them to?"

"I have no idea what you're talking about." His voice was entirely too innocent.

"Please, I must have fielded ten messages a day from Finn's Hollow, wanting to know where things are and what I was doing," I said. "At the time, I thought they genuinely needed help and were being lovely and checking up on me, but now I suspect they were all pulled into your grand gesture scheme among others." I gave Sam and Ben a side-eye and they both immediately started studying the arched ceiling overhead.

Kier nodded and said, "To protect the innocent, I will neither confirm nor deny anything."

"That's fine," I said. "But there is one thing your spies neglected to tell you."

"What's that?"

"I was never planning to leave Finn's Hollow," I said. "I fully intended to remain in the village and win you back." I paused, holding his gaze with mine when I said, "I choose you, Kier. There is nothing that means more to me than you."

He pulled me close and kissed me. It was a long, lingering, soul-melding kiss that mended all the cracks in my broken heart, allowing it to beat again. Then he looked into my eyes and said, "And I choose you, Red. In this world or any other, it will always be you."

I twined my arms about his neck and he hugged me tight, lifting me off my feet. I never wanted him to let me go.

In my mind, I saw him in a dark suit and myself in a white dress. We were getting married. And just to his left, Siobhan stood. She was a shadow not fully formed, but she looked so happy. She was holding a bouquet of lavender sprigs tied with a yellow ribbon. I knew I was seeing something more than just a daydream, I was seeing our future and just as Siobhan had said to Kier, she was always with us.

"There it is," Kier said when he gently set me on my feet. "That dreamy look you get that I love so much."

"It's you," I said. "All of my daydreams were always about you."

I heard Sam say "Aw" from somewhere behind us.

"I feel the exact same way about you, Red." Kier leaned down and kissed me with a tenderness that revealed the depths of his feelings. I was precious to him and he wanted to be certain that I knew it. I did. I also knew that, just like Tig McMorrow, Kier and I had finally achieved the happy ending we deserved.

Epilogue

"They're here!" Oisín cried as he hauled an enormous box to the alcove where I was editing a manuscript on my laptop. Kier was seated beside me, going over the calendar of events for the bookshop.

I jumped out of my seat, grabbing him by the arm and pulling him up beside me. I always loved opening boxes of new books. The fresh smell of ink and paper, the beauty of the cover revealed in its final form, it never failed to make me giddy, but this one, this one was special.

Oisín pulled a box cutter out of his pocket and ceremoniously held it out to me, handle first, as if offering me a dagger. I laughed and he grinned. I took it and handed it to Kier.

"'It's delightful when your imaginations come true, isn't it?'" I asked.

His eyes glinted at the challenge I issued and he said, "*Anne of Green Gables*. That's lovely, Red."

I inclined my head, once again impressed that he could identify the quote. I would have thought after a year together we'd have run out of material but apparently not.

For practical reasons, I had moved into the gatehouse with him. Given that we hadn't spent a night apart since we returned from Dublin, it just made sense. Kier was still mulling over what to do with Siobhan's house. We felt it was too big for us now, but he'd hinted that it would be a nice place to raise a family and he'd kept the staff on, not wanting to displace them. The mere idea of it gave me the flutters, in the best possible way.

"You lot, the books are here!" Oisín called into the shop.

Eun-Ji, Niamh, and Brigid arrived in the alcove, as Oisín's bellow was impossible to ignore. Kier glanced at them all and then took a deep breath. When he held the box cutter to the taped seam, I noticed his fingers were trembling. I pressed myself close to his side and he immediately put his free arm around my waist, pulling me in close. He slid the knife along each edge, the tape making a popping sound as the last of it let go.

Together we folded back the flaps. Kier moved the brown packing paper aside and there they were. Fifty author copies of *Tig McMorrow and the Last Chapter* beamed out at us with their own special brand of magic. Kier stood completely still, so I took one out and handed it to him. He swallowed before he took it, his gaze lingering on the cover. A sheen of tears glistened in his eyes and I felt my own eyes grow damp.

Before I lost my vision completely, I handed out copies to the others and I heard them gasp and sigh as they took in the brilliant illustration. The publisher had hired the same artist who had illustrated the original Tig McMorrow volumes and when we described this book, he had told us he knew exactly what to do.

I picked up my own copy, felt the weight of it in my hands as I studied the artist's rendering of the front of the bookshop. He'd centered the alcove window on the cover and there she was. Seated at this very table and gazing out the window was Siobhan. Outside the bookshop were Tig and Aislinn stepping out of a magical portal as if walking out of her imagination and into her life. I felt my throat get tight as I traced Siobhan's features with the tip of my finger.

"It's perfect," I said. My voice was little more than a whisper. I glanced up and Kier wiped the tears from his eyes with the cuff of his sleeve. Oisín sobbed and the others cried, their tears coursing down their cheeks.

"Ma would think we're daft," Kier said. "And then she'd laugh."

Knowing Siobhan, I knew he was right. He turned and walked to the window and set the book on a display stand, looking out over the village of Finn's Hollow. I decided then and there that we would never sell that copy. It would stay right there for as long as the bookshop remained.

The others were composing themselves while they thumbed through the novel, examining every bit of it. Niamh had opened to the first page and wandered out of the alcove, no doubt going up to the third floor where she could read in peace. The others followed her, leaving Kier and I alone.

I moved to stand beside him, knowing he must be deluged with so many *feelings*—I certainly was—of missing Siobhan, mourning Siobhan, but also filled with a deep satisfaction that her life's work had been completed, and yet, feeling crushed that she wasn't here to see it.

But Kier surprised me. He pulled me into his arms and kissed me tenderly. It was a kiss full of unspoken promises and vows and I kissed him back with an unspoken answer in return.

With his eyes still damp, Kier pulled back, brushed a lock of hair from my face, and said, "Tig McMorrow now has his last chapter, but for you and me, Red, our story is just beginning."

And so it was.

ACKNOWLEDGMENTS

Writing this book has been quite a journey. It took me from Arizona (which is home) to Martha's Vineyard to Dublin and the Ring of Kerry. My companions, Susan McKinlay, Annette Amaturo, and Alyssa Amaturo, were fantastic. I could not ask for better traveling research buddies and I'll cherish the memories we made forever.

I am also grateful to my Irish family members who made time to visit with me and my mom—Joan Hally, Catherine Hally, Anna Lennon, and Siún Lennon, what a delight it was to spend time with you all.

Special shout-out to my Irish beta reader, Róisín Donnelly, who was gracious enough to read the manuscript in its unedited form and make certain I didn't mess it up. A thousand thank-yous!

Much love to my plot group pals, Kate Carlisle and Paige Shelton. You always help me find just that much more conflict. What would I do without you? Much gratitude to my blog pals at Jungle Red Writers—Hank Phillippi Ryan, Deborah Crombie, Lucy Burdette, Hallie Ephron, Rhys Bowen, and Julia Spencer-Fleming. I appreciate the support more than I can say. Special thanks to my assistant, Christie Conlee, for always being my magical unicorn, and to the McKinlay's Mavens FB group, who have become dear friends.

Much appreciation to my family—Chris Hansen Orf, Beckett Orf, and Wyatt Orf. You guys are my whole heart and I couldn't do what I do without you. Thanks for always listening when I am working out my plot points. Your collective patience is much appreciated.

As always, I am so very lucky to work with the best of the best—my editor, Kate Seaver, and my agent, Christina Hogrebe. Your faith in my abilities never waivers and your input and wisdom always make my work so much better. And I am just delighted to work with the stellar team at Berkley—Amanda Maurer, Kim-Salina I, Kaila Mundell-Hill, Christine Legon, Vikki Chu, Kristin del Rosario, and Alaina Christensen. When I wake up every day and get to live the dream, I know it is because of all of you and I can never thank you enough.

Lastly, I want to thank the booklovers, daydreamers, and readers who have loved the stories and the journeys we've gone on together. I can't wait to see where our next adventure takes us!

NAME PRONUNCIATIONS

Kieran—Keer-uhn

Siobhan—Shiv-awn

Niamh—Neve

Oisín—Aw-sheen

Eun-ji—Eu-n-jee

Aislinn—Ash-lin

Irish Whiskey Shortbread Recipe

A crisp buttery biscuit flavored with Irish whiskey

INGREDIENTS

1 cup Kerrygold unsalted butter, softened
½ cup light brown sugar, packed
1 Tablespoon Irish whiskey
2 cups all-purpose flour

DIRECTIONS

Line baking sheets with parchment paper. Using an electric or stand mixer, cream together the butter and sugar. Be sure to scrape the sides of the bowl. Add the whiskey. Slowly add the flour until the mixture becomes crumbly. Increase the speed until the dough blends together. Do not overmix. Using your hands, form the dough into a ball. Wrap it in plastic wrap and refrigerate for 30 minutes.

On a floured surface, roll the dough out until half-inch thick. Cut into desired shapes and place on the lined baking sheets. Place cookies in the refrigerator for one hour before baking. Preheat the oven to

350 degrees and remove cookies from the refrigerator. Bake for 15–17 minutes. Cookies should be crisp.

Store in an airtight container.

If frosted shortbread is preferred, a thick glaze can be made from 2 teaspoons of Irish whiskey and 1 cup of powdered sugar or as much as is required to reach the desired thickness. Drizzle the glaze on top of the shortbread and allow it to dry thoroughly before storing.

Love at First Book

JENN McKINLAY

READERS GUIDE

QUESTIONS FOR DISCUSSION

1. Emily Allen goes to Ireland because she's always wanted to travel the world and have adventures. Do you want to travel the world? Where would you go?

2. Kieran Murphy doesn't like change. He even admits to never rearranging his furniture. Do you like change? If you could change anything about your life right now, what would it be?

3. Siobhan Riordan has a terrible case of writer's block and hasn't written in ten years, leaving the final book in her series unfinished. Have you ever read a series that was left unfinished? How would you feel if your favorite author quit writing?

4. Em has to learn how to drive on the opposite side of the road and gamely rises to the challenge. Have you ever been challenged in such a way? How did it go?

5. Em and Kier have a mutual love of books and quiz each other with literary quotes throughout the book. Did you know most of the quotes? Did any of them surprise you?

6. Em realizes that the village of Finn's Hollow is where she belongs. She's happy there. Where is your happy place?

7. Em has a difficult relationship with her mother, but finds a satisfying maternal bond with Siobhan. Do you think the mother–daughter relationship is a difficult one? Do you have other women in your life who have stepped into the role of mom for you?

8. Em is a daydreamer, imagining extraordinary things from the ordinary. Are you a daydreamer? What do you dream about?

9. Kier is charged with making a grand gesture to show Em how much he loves her. What do you think of grand gestures in romance? What do you think of his?

10. Em and Kier do not experience love at first sight and, in fact, do not get along at all in the beginning. When do you think their feelings change? Do you think they will live happily ever after?

Keep reading for an excerpt from

Paris Is Always a Good Idea

by Jenn McKinlay.

I'm getting married."

"Huh?"

"We've already picked our colors, pink and gray."

"Um . . . pink and what?"

"Gray. What do you think, Chelsea? I want your honest opinion. Is that too retro?"

I stared at my middle-aged widowed father. We were standing in a bridal store in central Boston on the corner of Boylston and Berkeley Streets, and he was talking to me about wedding colors. *His* wedding colors.

"I'm sorry—I need a sec," I said. I held up my hand and blinked hard while trying to figure out just what the hell was happening.

I had raced here from my apartment in Cambridge after receiving a text from my dad, asking me to meet him at this address because it was an emergency. I was prepared for heart surgery, not wedding colors!

Suddenly, I couldn't breathe. I wrestled the constricting wool scarf from around my neck, yanked the beanie off my head, and stuffed them in my pockets. I scrubbed my scalp with my fingers in an attempt to make the blood flow to my brain. It didn't help. *Come on, Martin*, I coached myself. *Pull it together.* I unzipped my puffy winter jacket to let some air in, then I focused on my father.

"What did you say?" I asked.

"Pink and gray, too retro?" Glen Martin, a.k.a. Dad, asked. He pushed his wire-frame glasses up on his nose and looked at me as if he was asking a perfectly reasonable question.

"No, before that." I waved my hand in a circular motion to indicate he needed to back it all the way up.

"I'm getting married!" His voice went up when he said it, and I decided my normally staid fifty-five-year-old dad was somehow currently possessed by a twenty-something bridezilla.

"You okay, Dad?" I asked. Not for nothing, because the last time I checked, he hadn't even been dating anyone, never mind thinking about marriage. "Have you recently slipped on some ice and whacked your head? I ask because you don't seem to be yourself."

"Sorry," he said. He reached out and wrapped me in an impulsive hug, another indicator that he was not his usual buttoned-down mathematician self. "I'm just . . . I'm just so happy. What do you think about being a flower girl?"

"Um . . . I'm almost thirty." I tried not to look as bewildered as I felt. What was happening here?

"Yes, but we already have a full wedding party, and you and your sister would be really cute in matching dresses, maybe something sparkly."

"Matching dresses? Sparkly?" I repeated. I struggled to make sense of his words. I couldn't. It was clear. My father had lost his ever-lovin' mind. I should probably call my sister.

I studied his face, trying to determine just how crazy he was. The same hazel eyes I saw in my own mirror every morning held mine, but where my eyes frequently looked flat with a matte finish, his positively glowed. He really looked happy.

"You're serious," I gasped. I glanced around the bridal store, which was stuffed to the rafters with big fluffy white dresses. None of this made any sense, and yet here I was. "You're not pranking me?"

"Nope." He grinned again. "Congratulate me, peanut. I'm getting married."

I felt as if my chest were collapsing into itself. Never, not once in the past seven years, had I ever considered the possibility that my father would remarry.

"To who?" I asked. It couldn't be . . . Nah. That would be *insane*.

"Really, Chels?" Dad straightened up. The smile slid from his face, and he cocked his head to the side—his go-to disappointed-parent look.

I had not been on the receiving end of this look very often in life. Not like my younger sister, Annabelle, who seemed to thrive on "the look." Usually, it made me fall right in line but not today.

"Sheri? You're marrying Sheri?" I tried to keep my voice neutral. Major failure, as I stepped backward, tripped on the trailing end of my scarf, and gracelessly sprawled onto one of the cream-colored velvet chairs that were scattered around the ultrafeminine store. I thought it was a good thing I was sitting, because if he answered in the affirmative, I might faint.

"Yes, I asked her to marry me, and to my delight she accepted," he said. Another happy, silly grin spread across his lips as if he just couldn't help it.

"But . . . but . . . she won you in a bachelor auction two weeks ago!" I cried. I closed my mouth before I said more, like pointing out that this was hasty in the extreme.

The store seamstress, who was assisting a bride up on the dais in front of a huge trifold mirror, turned to look at us. Her dark hair was scraped up into a knot on top of her head, and her face was contoured to perfection. She made me feel like a frump in my Sunday no-makeup face. Which, in my defense, was not my fault, because when I'd left the house to meet Dad, I'd had no idea the address he'd sent was for Brianna's Bridal. I'd been expecting an urgent care; in fact, I wasn't sure yet that we didn't need one.

Glen Martin, Harvard mathematician and all-around nerd dad, had been coerced into participating in a silver-fox bachelor auction for prominent Bostonians by my sister, Annabelle, to help raise funds for Boston Children's Hospital. I had gone, of course, to support my sister and my dad, and it had mostly been a total snooze fest.

The highlight of the event was when two socialites got into a bidding war over a surgeon, and the loser slapped the winner across the face with her cardboard paddle. Good thing the guy was a cosmetic surgeon, because there was most definitely some repair work needed on that paper cut.

But my father had not been anywhere near that popular with the ladies. No one wanted a mathematician. No one. After several minutes of excruciating silence, following the MC trying to sell the lonely gals on my dad's attempts to solve the Riemann hypothesis, I had been about to bid on him myself, when Sheri, a petite brunette, had raised her paddle with an initial offer. The smile of gratitude Dad had sent Sheri had been blinding, and the next thing we knew, a flurry of numbered paddles popped up in the air, but Sheri stuck in there and landed the win for $435.50.

"Two weeks is all it took," Dad said. He shrugged and held out his hands like a blackjack dealer showing he had no hidden cards, chips, or cash.

I stared at him with a look that I'm sure was equal parts shock and horror.

"I know it's a surprise, Chels, but when—" he began, but I interrupted him.

"Dad, I don't think a bachelor auction is the basis for a stable, long-lasting relationship."

"You have to admit it makes a great story," he said.

"Um . . . no." I tried to sound reasonable, as if this were a math problem about fitting sixty watermelons into a small car. I spread my hands wide and asked, "What do you even know about Sheri? What's her favorite color?"

"Pink, duh." He looked at me with a know-it-all expression more commonly seen on a teenager than a grown-ass man. Hmm.

"All right, who are you, and what have you done with my father?" I wanted to check him for a fever; maybe he had the flu and he was hallucinating.

"I'm still me, Chels," he said. He gazed at me gently. "I'm just a happy me, for a change."

Was that it? Was that what was so different about him? He was happy? How could he be happy with a woman he hardly knew? Maybe . . . oh dear. My dad hadn't circulated much after my mom's death. Maybe he was finally getting a little something-something, and he had it confused with love. Oh god, how was I supposed to talk about this with him?

I closed my eyes. I took a deep breath. Parents did this all the time. Surely I could manage it. Heck, it would be great practice if I ever popped out a kid. I opened my eyes. Three women were standing in the far corner in the ugliest chartreuse dresses I had ever seen. Clearly, they were the attendants of a bride who hated them. And that might be me in sparkly pink or gray if I didn't put a stop to this madness.

"Sit down, Dad," I said. "I think we need to have a talk."

He took the seat beside mine and looked at me with the same patience he had when he'd taught me to tie my shoes. I looked away. Ugh, this was more awkward than when my gynecologist told me to scoot down, repeatedly. It's like they don't know a woman's ass needs some purchase during an annual. *Focus, Martin!*

"I know that you've been living alone for several years." I cleared my throat. "And I imagine you've had some needs that have gone unmet."

"Chels, no—" he said. "It isn't about that."

I ignored him, forging on while not making eye contact, because, lordy, if I had to have this conversation with him, I absolutely could not look at him.

"And I understand that after such a long dry spell, you might be confused about what you feel, and that's okay," I said. Jeebus, this sounded like a sex talk by Mr. Rogers. "The thing is, you don't have to marry the first person you sleep with after Mom."

There, I said it. And my wise advice and counsel were met with complete silence. I waited for him to express relief that he didn't have to get married. And I waited. Finally, I glanced up at my father, who was staring at me in the same way he had when I discovered *he* was actually the tooth fairy. Chagrin.

"Sheri is not the first," he said.

"She's not?" I was shocked. Shocked, I tell you.

"No."

"But you never told me about anyone before," I said.

"You didn't need to know," he replied. "They were companions, not relationships."

"They?!" I shouted. I didn't mean to. The seamstress sent me another critical look, and I coughed, trying to get it together.

Dad shifted in his seat, sending me a small smile of understanding.

"Maybe meeting here wasn't the best idea. I thought you'd be excited to help plan the wedding, but perhaps you're not ready."

"Of course I'm not ready," I said. "But you're not either."

"Yes, I am."

"Oh, really? Answer me this: Does Sheri prefer dogs or cats?"

"I don't—" He blinked.

"Yes, because it's only been two weeks," I said. "You remember that lump on your forehead? It took longer than two weeks to get that biopsied, but you're prepared to marry a woman you haven't even known long enough for a biopsy."

My voice was getting higher, and Dad put his hands out in an *inside voice, please* gesture. I would have tried, but I felt as if I was hitting my stride in making my point. I went for the crushing blow.

"Dad, do you even know whether she's a pie or cake sort of person?"

"I . . . um . . ."

"Do you realize you're contemplating spending the rest of your life with a person who might celebrate birthdays with pie?"

"Chels, I know this is coming at you pretty fast," he said. "I do, but I don't think Sheri liking pie or cake is really that big of a deal. Who knows, she might be an ice cream person, and ice cream goes with everything."

"Mom was a cake person," I said. There. I'd done it. I'd brought in the biggest argument against this whole rushed matrimonial insanity. Mom.

My father's smile vanished as if I'd snuffed it out between my fingers like a match flame. I felt lousy about it, but not quite as lousy as I did at the thought of Sheri—oh, but no—becoming my stepmother.

"Your mother's been gone for seven years, Chels," he said. "That's a long time for a person to be alone."

"But you haven't been alone . . . apparently," I protested. "Besides, you have me and Annabelle."

"I do."

"So why do you need to get married?" I pressed.

Dad sighed. "Because I love Sheri and I want to make her my wife."

I gasped. I felt as if he'd slapped me across the face. Yes, I knew I was reacting badly, but this was my father. The man who had sworn to love my mother until death do them part. But that was the problem, wasn't it? Mom had passed away, and Dad had been alone ever since, right up until he met Sheri Armstrong two weeks ago when she just kept raising her auction paddle for the marginally hot mathematician.

I got it. Really, I did. I'd been known to have bidding fever when a mint pair of Jimmy Choos showed up on eBay. It was hard to let go of something when it was in your grasp, especially when another bidder kept raising the stakes. But this was my dad, not shoes.

One of the bridal-salon employees came by with a tray of mimosas. I grabbed two, double fisting the sparkling beverage. Sweet baby Jesus, I hoped there was more fizz than pulp in them. The bubbles hit the roof of my mouth, and I wished they could wash away the taste of my father's startling news, but they didn't.

"Listen, I know that being the object of desire by a crowd of single, horny women is heady stuff—"

"Really, you know this?" Dad propped his chin in his hand as he studied me with his eyebrows raised and a twinkle in his eye.

"Okay, not exactly, but my point—and I have one—is that you and Sheri aren't operating in the real world here," I said. "I understand that Sheri is feeling quite victorious, having won you, but that doesn't mean she should wed you. I mean, why do you have to marry her? Why can't you just live in sin like other old people?"

"Because we love each other and we want to be married."

"You can't know this so soon," I argued. "It's not possible. Her representative hasn't even left yet."

My dad frowned, clearly not understanding.

"The first six months to a year, you're not really dating a person," I explained. "You're dating their representative. The real person, the one who leaves the seat up and can't find the ketchup in the fridge even when it's right in front of him, doesn't show up until months into the relationship. Trust me."

"What are you talking about? Of course I'm dating a person. I can assure you, Sheri is very much a woman," he said. "Boy howdy, is she." The tips of his ears turned red, and I felt my own face get hot with embarrassment. I forged on.

"Dad, first, *ew*," I said. "And second, a person's representative is their best self. After two weeks, you haven't seen the real Sheri yet. The real Sheri is hiding behind the twenty-four-seven perfect hair and makeup, the placid temper, the woman who thinks your dad jokes are funny. They're not."

"No, no, no." He shook his head. "I've seen her without makeup. She's still beautiful. And she does have a temper—just drive with her sometime. I've learned some new words. Very educational. And my dad jokes are too funny."

I rolled my eyes. I was going to have to do some tough love here. I was going to have to be blunt.

"Dad, I hate to be rude, but you're giving me no choice. She's probably only marrying you for your money," I said. Ugh, I felt like a horrible person for pointing it out, but he needed protection from gold diggers. It was a kindness, really.

To my surprise, he actually laughed. "Sheri is more well off than I am by quite a lot. I'm the charity case in this relationship."

"Then why on earth does she want to marry *you*?" I asked.

The words flew out before I had the brains to stifle them. It was a nasty thing to say. I knew that, but I was freaked out and frantic and not processing very well.

"I didn't mean that the way it sounded," I began, but he cut me off.

"Despite what you think, I'm quite a catch in middle-aged circles."

He stood, retrieving his coat from a nearby coatrack. As he shrugged into it, a flash of hurt crossed his face that made my stomach ache. I loved my father. I wouldn't inflict pain upon him for anything, and yet I had. I'd hurt him very much. I felt lower than sludge.

"I'm sorry, Dad. Really, I didn't mean—" But again he cut me off.

"You did mean it, and, sadly, I'm not even surprised," he said. "Listen, I have mourned the loss of your mother every day since she passed, and I will mourn her every day for the rest of my life, but I have found someone who makes me happy, and I want to spend my life with her. That doesn't take away what I had with your mother."

"Doesn't it?" I argued. This. This was what had been bothering me since his announcement. How could he not see that by replacing my mother, he was absolutely diminishing what they'd had? "Sheri's going to take your name, isn't she? And she's going to move into our house, right? So everything that was once Mom's—the title of Mrs. Glen Martin and the house where she loved and raised her family—you're just giving to another woman. The next thing I know, you'll tell me I have to call her Mom."

A guilty expression flitted across his face.

"No." I shook my head. "Absolutely not."

"I'm not saying you have to call her that. It's just Sheri's never had a family of her own, and she mentioned in passing how much she was looking forward to having daughters. It would be nice if you could think about how good it would be to have a mother figure in your life again."

"I am not her daughter, and I never will be," I said. My chest heaved with indignation. "How can you pretend that all of that isn't erasing Mom?"

Dad stared down at me with his head to the side and his right eyebrow arched, a double whammy of parental disappointment. He wrapped his scarf about his neck and pulled on his gloves.

"You know what? I don't know if Sheri will take my name. We haven't talked about it," he said. "As for the house, I am planning to sell it so we can start our life together somewhere new."

I sucked in a breath. My childhood home. Gone? Sold? To strangers? I thought I might throw up. Instead, I polished off one of the mimosas.

"Sheri and I are getting married in three months," he said. "We're planning a nice June wedding, and we very much want you to be a part of it."

"As a flower girl?" I scoffed. "Whose crazy idea was that?"

"It was Sheri's," he said. His mouth tightened. "She's never been married before, and she's a little excited. It's actually quite lovely to see."

"A thirty-year-old flower girl," I replied, as tenacious as a tailgater in traffic. I just couldn't let it go.

"All right, I get it. Come as anything you want, then," he said. "You can give me away, be my best man, be a bridesmaid, or officiate the damn thing. I don't care. I just want you there. It would mean everything to Sheri and me to have your blessing."

I stared at him. The mild-mannered Harvard math professor who had taught me to throw a curveball, ride a bike, and knee a boy in the junk if he got too fresh had never looked so determined. He meant it. He was going to marry Sheri Armstrong, and there wasn't a damn thing I could do about it.

"I . . . I." My words stalled out. I wanted to say that it was okay, that he deserved to be happy, and that I'd be there in any capacity he wanted, but I choked. I sat there with my mouth opening and closing like a fish on dry land, trying to figure out how to mouth breathe.

My father turned up his collar, bracing for the cold March air. He looked equal parts disappointed and frustrated. "Don't strain yourself."

He turned away as I sat frozen. I hated this. I didn't want us to part company like this, but I was so shocked by this sudden turn of events, I was practically catatonic. I waited, feeling miserable, for him to walk away, but instead he turned back toward me. Rather than being furious with me, which might have caused me to dig in my heels and push back, he looked sad.

"What happened to you, peanut?" he asked. "You used to be the girl with the big heart who was going to save the world."

I didn't say anything. His disappointment and confusion washed over me like a bath of sour milk.

"I grew up," I said. But even to my own ears I sounded defensive.

He shook his head. "No, you didn't. Quite the opposite. You stopped growing at all."

"Are you kidding me? In the past seven years, I've raised millions to help the fight against cancer. How can you say I haven't grown?" I asked. I was working up a nice froth of indignation. "I'm trying to make a difference in the world."

"That's your career," he said. "Being great at your profession doesn't mean you've grown personally. Chels, look at your life. You work seven days a week. You never take time off. You don't date. You have no friends. Heck, if we didn't have a standing brunch date, I doubt I'd ever see you except on holidays. Since your mother passed, you've barricaded yourself emotionally from all of us. What kind of life is that?"

I turned my head to stare out the window at Boylston Street. I couldn't believe my father was dismissing how hard I worked for the American Cancer Coalition. I had busted my butt to become the top corporate fundraiser in the organization, and with the exception of one annoying coworker, my status was unquestioned.

He sighed. I couldn't look at him. "Chels, I'm not saying what you've accomplished isn't important. It's just that you've changed over the past few years. I can't remember the last time you brought someone special home for me to meet. It's as if you've sealed yourself off since your mother—"

I whipped my head in his direction, daring him to talk about my mother in the same conversation in which he'd announced he was remarrying.

"Chels, you're here!" a voice cried from the fitting room entrance on the opposite side of the store. I glanced away from my dad to see my younger sister, Annabelle, standing there in an explosion of hot-pink satin and tulle trimmed with a wide swath of glittering crystals.

"*What. Is. That?*" I looked from Annabelle to our father and back. The crystals reflected the fluorescent light overhead, making me see spots, or perhaps I was having a stroke. Hard to say.

"It's our dress!" Annabelle squealed. Then she twirled toward us. The long tulle skirt fanned out from the formfitting satin bodice, and Annabelle's long dark curls streamed out around her. She looked like a demented fairy princess. "Do you love it or do you love it?"

"No, I don't love it. It's too pink, too poofy, and too much!" I cried. The seamstress glared at me, looking as if she were going to take some of the pins out of the pin cushion strapped to her wrist and come stab me a few hundred times. I lowered my voice a little. "Have you both gone insane? Seriously, what the hell is happening?"

Annabelle staggered to a stop. The spinning caused her to wobble a bit as she walked toward us, looking more like a drunk princess than a fey one.

"How can you be happy about this?" I snapped at her. I gestured to the dress. "Have you not known me for all of your twenty-seven years? How could you possibly think I would be okay with this?"

Annabelle grabbed the back of a chair to steady herself. "By 'this' do you mean the dress or the whole wedding thing?"

"Of course I mean the whole wedding thing," I growled. "Dad is clearly having some midlife crisis, and there's you just going along with it. Honestly, Annabelle, can't you recognize an emergency when we're having one?"

Annabelle blinked at me, looking perplexed. "What emergency? Dad's getting married. It's awesome. Besides, I feel like I have a vested interest given that it was my auction that brought Dad and Sheri together."

"Because you, like Dad, have gone completely nuts!" I declared. "Two weeks is not long enough to determine whether you should marry someone or not. My god, it takes longer to get a passport. What are you thinking supporting this craziness?"

"Chels, that's not fair and you know it," Dad said.

My expression must have been full-on angry bear, because he changed tack immediately, his expression softening.

"When did you stop letting love into your heart?" he asked. His voice was gentler, full of parental concern that pinched like shoes that were too small, but I ignored the hurt. He didn't get to judge me when he was marrying a person he barely knew. "Is this really how you want to live your life, Chels, with no one special to share it with? Because I don't."

I turned back to the window, refusing to answer. With a sigh weighty with disappointment, he left. I watched his reflection in the glass grow smaller and smaller as he departed. I couldn't remember the last time we had argued, leaving harsh words between us festering like a canker sore. Ever since Mom had died, the awareness of how precious life was had remained ever present, and we always, always, said *I love you* at the end of a conversation, even when we weren't getting along.

I thought about running after him and saying I was sorry, that I was happy for him and Sheri, but it would be a lie, and I knew I wasn't a good enough actress to pull it off. I just couldn't make myself do it. Instead, I tossed back my second mimosa, because mimosas, unlike family, were always reliable.

Photo © Jacqueline Hanna Photography

JENN McKINLAY is the award-winning *New York Times*, *USA Today*, and *Publishers Weekly* bestselling author of several mystery and romance series. Her work has been translated into multiple languages in countries all over the world. She lives in sunny Arizona in a house that is overrun with kids, pets, and her husband's guitars.

VISIT JENN McKINLAY ONLINE

JennMcKinlay.com
JennMcKinlayAuthor
McKinlayJenn